**Edwina Currie** is a former government minister and for fourteen years was the well-known Member of Parliament for Derbyshire South. She is now a successful broadcaster and bestselling novelist.

*Also by Edwina Currie*

# This Honourable House

## EDWINA CURRIE

timewarner
paperbacks

A *Time Warner* Paperback

First published in Great Britain in 2001
by Little, Brown and Company
This edition published in 2003 by Time Warner Paperbacks

Copyright © 2001, Edwina Currie

The moral right of the author has been asserted.

Every effort has been made to trace the copyright holder and to clear
reprint permission for 'Simply the Best'. If notified, the publisher
will be pleased to rectify any omission in future editions.

A CIP catalogue record for this book
is available from the British Library.

ISBN 0 7515 3218 5

Typeset in Ehrhardt by M Rules
Printed and bound in Great Britain
by Clays Ltd, St Ives plc

Time Warner Paperbacks
An imprint of
Time Warner Books UK
Brettenham House
Lancaster Place
London WC2E 7EN

www.TimeWarnerBooks.co.uk

# AUTHOR'S NOTE

This is a novel about modern British political life. I have tried to make it as authentic as possible, to convey some insight into how MPs live and work, but my plot and my central characters are completely imaginary and no reference is intended to the real people holding these offices at the time in question, or to any other person.

Edwina Currie, London, 2001

# This
# Honourable
# House

# CHAPTER ONE

'I wish,' said Frank Bridges venomously, 'that somebody would sort out the bloody cow once and for all.'

He picked up the chunky pint glass and downed the remains of his beer in a gulp. There were clucks of sympathy around him. To many of the thick-set, grizzled men seated at his table and nearby, Frank was the local hero. His successes were theirs, his worries grafted seamlessly on to their own. If Frank was upset, so were they.

The Right Honourable Frank Bridges, fifty years old, overweight, red-faced, crumple-suited and aggressive, should not have been upset. Indeed, he had considerable reason to be hugely pleased with his own situation, and with life in general. Newly elevated to the seat in the Cabinet he could once only have dreamed of, he was trusted by the public, envied by colleagues, and regarded with ragged affection by his constituents, who included the scruffy occupants of the Admiral Benbow, a run-down pub in a Bootle side-street near the now derelict docks.

Vic, Scouser, Bill the Fixer, Mad Max and others had truanted with him from the inner-city school where expectations were destroyed with the cane and sarcasm. As boys, they had scattered down alleys behind his stocky form, their pockets stuffed with illicit loot. But Frank had kept running, beyond the despair and hopelessness. None of the others had followed where he led. He had not gone to the dogs like them but had made something of himself. He had risen to the top, or close to it. Of Frank Bridges they were inordinately proud.

For Frank was a salt-of-the-earth type, the press generally agreed. A police sergeant had once challenged him to make a man of himself. Shamed, he had applied, with the sergeant's gruff help, to join Liverpool police cadets; to his surprise and the ribbing of his mates he had been accepted. He had worked his way up through the byzantine networks of the force to national prominence, particularly during the bitter dock strike of 1982. In that prolonged struggle, he had contrived to become a solidly admired figure. While speaking in the same strong Merseyside accent as the militant strikers and displaying an understated, dignified disdain for the government of Margaret Thatcher, he had contrived to prevent conflict and bloodshed even as the nation's trade was brought to a standstill. His erstwhile comrade Arthur Scargill had asked him how he had managed such a feat. Frank had begun to confess that he did not know, that chance had played its part. Then he had thought better of it and suggested vaguely that working with the system was better than trying to destroy it, that politics might achieve more than the picket line. Scargill's derision convinced him. Soon afterwards Frank offered himself as a parliamentary candidate. He had represented the Dockside division of the seaport ever since.

'It's a bummer, it is,' came a voice, as more pints were splashed down on the sticky table top. The air hung thick and acrid with smoke. 'Salt and vinegar okay?'

Frank nodded glumly and ripped open the packet of crisps, eating them two or three at a time. He brushed crumbs from his midriff, tugged impatiently at his tie and unfastened the top two buttons of his shirt. He was sweating, a damp line visible on the inside of his collar. 'Mustn't eat too many of these,' he mumbled, indicating the crisps. He waved away a cigarette. 'Look gross on the telly. Gotta keep a new young wife happy. An' that's another story.'

'She's a peach, your new lady,' said Scouser respectfully. His accent was so strong that even Frank sometimes asked him to repeat himself. 'Hazel, innit? You're a lucky dog, you.' An elbow was dug into Frank's ribs.

'I know, I know.' Frank sighed. 'But I could murder Gail. Really murder her. And that slob Melvyn. Spin doctor. The sanitation squad, he's called. I'd like to sanitise *him*. Did you hear what happened? I could slaughter them both. Maybe I should arrange with some of me old mates to tie the pair of 'em together with a lump of concrete and chuck 'em in the Mersey one dark and stormy night. They deserve it.'

'You should've told Melvyn where to go,' said Vic. He wiped a roughened fist across his mouth and flexed his biceps. Vic had tried his hand at boxing in his youth; his convictions were all for GBH. Not a man to argue with.

'Nah, couldn't do that.' Frank brooded. His listeners settled happily in anticipation. They were not to be disappointed.

'There we were,' Frank started, 'all packed and ready to go on holiday, in the VIP lounge at Heathrow. The luggage was checked in. Gail was excited, kept prancing around and ordering more coffee just for the sake of it. God, does she love being important! I thought to myself even then, If you'd taken more interest on the way – not moaned so much about "Where are you going, Frank, you off out again, Frank, another meeting is it, Frank?" – then I wouldn't have minded. But she never used to lift a finger. Now she's Lady Muck and adores every minute.'

He took a prolonged swallow of his beer. His audience sat quietly. Once Frank was embarked on a tale, he needed no prompting.

'So the phone goes. The mobile. I'd forgotten to switch it off – you know how keen the Boss is that we keep in touch. "Oh, Frank," she says,' he mimicked a woman's high-pitched voice, ' "oh, Frank, not again. Surely not.

We're going on holiday. To the *Seychelles*." ' He raised his voice to show that Gail was determined everyone in earshot should hear. ' "First class. Couldn't you have left it at home for once?" Only what she didn't know was that it was that bastard Melvyn. An' he's on the line to say the *News of the World*'s gotta story on me and Hazel. Pictures of her coming out of my flat in Westminster. And what do I want to do?'

'How did they get them pictures? Was it a set-up?' Vic asked.

'Nah. Not really. She comes to my place regularly in her car, see, and parks it on a meter. So I go out in the morning when my driver comes, and I feed the meter. And there's a journalist hanging about, and instead of pushing off when I leave, he's curious. He knows Gail's in Cheshire. So why'm I feeding a meter? Who's there? And when Hazel shows and jumps in her car, his nose tells him he's gotta scoop. After that he hovers with a photographer till it happens again, and out they pop and confront her. Bob's your uncle.'

Heads were shaken at the brazen callousness of the gutter press. 'They don't care,' said Mad Max, and cracked his knuckles.

'Bastards,' added Vic, with menace.

'So then we have Mr Melvyn O'Connor, spin doctor number two – number one, Mr Alistair McDonald, being on duty elsewhere – Mr Melvyn O'Connor, who's never done a proper day's grafting ever, calling me to say the

Boss is asking which way I'll jump. Who's going to be on the guest list in future? Is it the wife, or the girlfriend? He'll back my decision either way and doesn't want to push me, but they need an answer so they can put out a statement. Would I mind deciding? Honest, right in the middle of the VIP departure lounge, with me cursing like a trooper and Gail telling me to mind my language. God.'

Frank was breathing heavily. The events he was describing had taken place barely three months before. 'So I looked at my lovely wife, and all I could see was this mouth with big teeth in it opening and closing, and it was like no sound was coming out. And I thought, I've put up with enough. I don't want to spend another minute with you. At least Hazel's kind, and takes an interest in politics, and gives me a kiss in bed.'

Conscious perhaps that he had gone a bit far, Frank cradled his glass. His audience shifted restlessly.

'She's young enough to be your daughter, you old dog, you,' came an anonymous voice from the back of the group. Laughter floated in the air, and Frank chuckled.

'There is that,' he agreed. 'But the big difference with this younger generation, compared to, say, the girls we grew up with, is they're keen on it. Sex, I mean. Take it for granted. You don't have to negotiate, just perform. With Gail at times, getting a fuck was like taking on the entire TUC in a triple composite motion. Between the two of them there was no contest.'

The middle-aged drinkers contemplated in mute

wonder the prospect of readily available sex. Stifled sniggers came from two younger men and were quickly hushed. 'But now,' Vic snorted, 'now she's getting her own back, isn't she? Or trying to.'

For answer Frank put his head in his hands. A groan came from the depths of his unshaven jowls. 'She's been on every telly programme, on all channels and cable. BBC Radio Two, Four and Five Live, twice. LBC and TalkSport. They had a field day. She's been to see that Clifford Maxwell. He must reckon there's mileage in it. Plus something for him. He got her out of those purple suits and costume jewellery and into a soft little cream knitted number. Taught her to keep her mouth shut in answer to questions and just look pained. She must have been practising for bleedin' hours. I don't remember Gail ever shutting up long enough for anyone else to get a word in edgeways. On radio she gulps as if she's going to cry. Christ!'

'The wronged wife,' murmured Scouser.

'Trying to fix you up,' agreed Bill the Fixer.

'A woman scorned,' added Max, the intellectual of the group.

'And now, to top everything, she's going to write a book. Says she'll lay bare the secrets of our unhappy marriage. About my drinking. My womanising, so-called. My tyrannical behaviour. How I put ambition and politics before everything else. How I made her days and nights a misery. I shouldn't be surprised if we get the screwed-up secrets of the bedchamber, with her as the willing partner and me incapable. Huh!'

'You're not incapable, are you, Frank?' Scouser asked anxiously. 'As you get older . . .'

'No, of course not,' Frank answered brusquely. 'Don't talk crap. If I was, Hazel wouldn't have stuck by me, would she? No sweat in that quarter.'

'So your Gail's going to say you were chasing other women but couldn't get it up with *her*?' A note of incredulity had entered Bill's voice. Frank grunted.

'You was too young, you and her. She wasn't twenty-one when you got married.' Vic had sat behind both Gail and Frank at Toxteth secondary modern school on those few occasions he had attended.

'Yeah, well, she'd announced she was in the family way, hadn't she? I couldn't leave her in the lurch. An' I wanted to be married, to be truthful. Them days, you wanted sex, it was tarts or the register office. I fancied the idea of having it off every night on demand, and my shirts ironed and a hot dinner on the table to boot.' Frank grinned wryly. 'Maybe I was always respectable at heart. Then: no baby. Said she'd lost it. Turned out no babies were possible, ever.'

'Maybe she'd have been less of a shrew if she'd had some.'

'Now, now. She's not a bad woman. We were together over a quarter of a century – remember our silver wedding at the Adelphi? And we did have great times. But if she carries on like this, if she publishes this damned fantasy book she's threatening, and doing what that sod Clifford Maxwell tells her, she'll turn me into a laughing stock.'

'It won't affect your career, though, will it?' Scouser pinched Frank's arm, then collected the empty glasses. 'I'll get them in – it's my round.'

'Of course it bloody will,' Frank called loudly after him. 'Bloody squeaky clean new government, promising Nirvana on earth, got itself elected with the biggest majority for a century and plans to stay there. No more "one term and you're out". The Boss intends to settle in at Number Ten. The Great Project means we're in for a generation. And that means *no mistakes*.'

The bartender slouched across, sodden cloth in hand, and made a show of wiping spills. Frank raised his head. 'You know what else? They're giving her a column in a women's magazine. She's going to offer advice to readers who write in with their problems. Her! She couldn't sort out her own stupid problems, let alone anybody else's. But she'll be the credible one in future, and I'll be a standing joke.'

His supporters were aware of that already. In nightclubs and comedy routines up and down the country Frank's amorous antics were the subject of much ribald comment.

'You could do with her shutting up, then, Frank,' came from the edge of the crowd. Others clucked again and whispered.

'I could do with her being scared shitless,' Frank growled. His speech was becoming slurred. 'Never mind bloody woman scorned. I could do with somebody telling her that hell hath no bloody fury like a Cabinet minister driven to distraction. I've only been in the job five minutes, for heaven's sake. Never thought I'd get this far. In the Cabinet! Hundred grand a year, chauffeur-driven Jag, first-class travel, all found. Everybody grovelling, yes, sir, no, sir, three bags full, sir. Worked fucking hard for it, mind you. But bloody Gail's doing her best to spoil it. And bloody Gail's got to go.'

'Understood, Frank. Now don't you upset yourself any further,' Bill the Fixer soothed. A fistful of filled glasses was deposited on the table. 'Drink up. Would you like a chaser?'

# CHAPTER TWO

Mrs Maddie Ashworth adjusted her son's grey silk tie, lifting it out from his neck in an exaggerated arc. The shoulders of his black tail coat had acquired bits of fluff, which she swept off with gloved fingers and an expression of distaste. She stood back. 'That's better,' she announced, and allowed herself a satisfied nod.

Benedict flattened the tie to its original position. His nose wrinkled discreetly against his mother's perfume: too much, and too girlish a scent, for a mature woman. Avoiding her fluttering hands, he pinned the carnation to his lapel without mishap, then brushed his thinning hair and turned his slim frame to and fro in front of the mirror.

'So, will I do, Mother?'

'Oh, yes, m'dear. You'll do,' said his mother. As usual she made no attempt to hide the north Devon accent. For years her son had squirmed at his speech and tried to eradicate it, but more recently its lilt had marked him out as distinctive without being outlandish, and he had allowed it to emerge once again.

Her bosom swelled beneath the orange tulle, and the cartwheel hat dipped in pride. She had also, Benedict noticed, applied far too much lipstick; soon it would be transferred to glasses, cups and whatever cheeks she could reach. He resolved to avoid it on his own, though that would require as much tact as he could muster. Smudges of facial apricot in the press photos would never do.

A knock on the door heralded his cousin Lawrence who had volunteered to be best man. Lawrence avoided the lipstick with an adroit air kiss, and grinned over his aunt's head.

'Got everything?' Benedict whispered. 'The ring? Your speech?'

Lawrence patted his morning suit breast pocket. 'Everything's in order.' He turned to Mrs Ashworth. 'You must be immensely proud of your son today. What a summer it's been for him! First the election, then becoming leader of the party, and now—'

'Trust you to think of politics first,' Mrs Ashworth chided. 'Today of all days. With that adorable girl waiting for him too. Shame on you.'

'It hasn't been quite so brilliant. True success would have meant we ended up holding the balance of power. Then I might have had a seat in the Cabinet.' Benedict was distractedly collecting wallet and keys as he spoke, but his tone was mild.

'You doubled the number of seats. You made the party a force to be reckoned with.' Lawrence was firm. Maddie Ashworth snorted her impatience but was ignored. 'The government has to take you seriously now, and the media. That's more than can be said for your predecessor.'

'But *I* didn't win those seats. I can't take the credit. We did best where the turnout was low, where the voters hated the old government but didn't trust the new lot. So we New Democrats benefited from a "plague on both your houses" mentality. If we're to get to the stage where Cabinet office is automatically mine, we have a mountain to climb. Not least since the official Leader of Her Majesty's Opposition is after it too.'

'I wouldn't want to be in his shoes,' Lawrence remarked, a tad smugly. 'You're leading success, he's leading failure. Sleaze, incompetence, indecision – they lost the plot, didn't they? And they're still fighting like cats over who to blame. The old Prime Minister's been airbrushed from history, while his predecessor thinks she's still in the driving seat. Poor Johnson has a helluva job on, if he's to knock that rabble into shape by next time.'

'No chance. Not unless the Prime Minister comes a complete cropper. And I don't think he will – only a few weeks into the job, but he's been very sure-footed so far.'

'The Grand Project! He plans to be there till his dotage.' Lawrence looked rueful. Then, realising that perhaps this was not the most encouraging comment to make to the leader of one of Westminster's minority parties, he added hastily, 'By which date he'll be relying heavily on you, and us, to hang on. We'll be calling the shots.'

'I do hope so,' said Benedict graciously, but his eyes were amused.

'You'll be Prime Minister some day, I've often said so,' said his mother stoutly. 'You could've joined either party. You could've been Prime Minister yourself already.'

Benedict exchanged wry glances with his cousin. 'I'd rather you didn't go round suggesting that my commitment to the New Democrats is less than sincere, Mother,' he said smoothly. 'I joined them at college because I believed in what they stood for.'

'But you've met the Queen. Kissed hands! What was it? Some council?' His mother's nervous energy, which Benedict had inherited and regularly obliged himself to quell, surfaced in her hectoring tone.

'The Privy Council. All that means, Mother, is that I'm a Right Honourable. And that the Prime Minister can tell me state secrets, if he should so choose. Not that he will, naturally. It's an honour, no more. Power does not reside in anything so simple.'

At a warning glance from Lawrence, who tapped his watch, Mrs Ashworth's mouth snapped shut. Benedict found her bag and gave it to her. 'Meanwhile, Mother, we have other matters to attend to today.'

He opened the door and ushered her through. She

began to march down the hall. As soon as she was out of earshot, Lawrence put an urgent hand on his cousin's arm. 'You absolutely sure you're doing the wise thing, Benedict?'

Benedict glanced away, his face sombre. 'Of course I am. Christine is a wonderful person. She understands. We have talked about it. I'm not a complete idiot, nor would I mislead her. What do you take me for?'

Lawrence stepped back, squared his shoulders, hesitated, then smiled. 'A happily married man, in a few minutes,' he offered. 'Let's go.'

The wedding of a second-rank politician would not normally have caused a stir. But, as Jim Betts of the *Globe* had to admit, there was something so fresh and charming about Benedict Ashworth that his doings attracted more than their fair share of interest. He was the type of public figure who restored the faith of a jaded electorate. Every man's neighbour, every mother's son, the journalist reflected, as the cable television cameras caught Benedict emerging from his flat near Trafalgar Square into the sunshine.

With Lawrence on one side and his outlandishly dressed mother coquettish on his arm, Benedict started to walk along Whitehall towards St Margaret's. The New Democracy Party leader was quite tall, though on television that often did not register. He had risen to prominence not by brilliance in the Commons chamber (though his quips were earning a place in anthologies), but because he pursued the bywaters of popular communication: daytime television, live radio, the satellite channels, whose audiences adored him. Like many others in the trade he was handy with a soundbite, but his remarks were distinguished by their pointed humour and intelligence. Benedict did not *claim* to talk common sense, like 'poor Johnson', the struggling opposition chief. Benedict simply went ahead and did it. In the studio he had rapidly mastered the techniques of the small gesture, the slight shrug of self-deprecation that made him the darling of matrons like his mother and the target of the affections both of younger women and of some men.

Jim Betts paced restlessly about the *Globe*'s newsroom. The monitor on the wall showed Benedict's progress past the statues of Montgomery and Allenbrooke outside the Ministry of Defence, past Whitehall Palace and Richmond House. Police officers kept well-wishers and the curious at bay. At the Department of Health a gaggle of protestors on abortion waved banners at him but he acknowledged them without breaking his stride. Already the Democrats' new leader was widely recognised, with hands held out to him to be shaken. A teenage girl detached herself from a family cluster, darted forward and gave him a hug, leaving the recipient obviously startled; but the cameras caught his half-smile even as he side-stepped out of harm's way.

Betts stroked his upper lip pensively, then remembered

that the moustache had gone. He had taken a razor to it the day he had achieved his own ambition, promotion to political editor. It wouldn't do: hair round the mouth looked louche and a senior post-holder needed gravitas. The lips had to be seen to move cleanly, as if this guaranteed the probity of the words spoken. Ken Livingstone and Peter Mandelson had gone the same route; indeed, in the months leading up to the election, many of the new Prime Minister's acolytes had done exactly the same thing. Beards and facial hair, once the badge of left-wing defiance, had vanished. Out, too, went denim jackets and T-shirts. If the future Prime Minister chose to be photographed in a white shirt and neatly anonymous tie, as if he'd trained at McKinsey's, then that was the official style. His troops, apart from a few Neanderthals, had adopted it with alacrity.

That left a problem for the women. But after some confusion and a spate of unflattering grey and beige, Betts had been intrigued to observe their increased adherence to the sartorial styles of a previous incumbent of Number Ten, whom the new Prime Minister was known to admire. The lady Members turned to power dressing in bold colours with big shoulders. It was no accident that many of them began to resemble the first woman Prime Minister.

The performance was all. Betts had to guess what was genuine and what wasn't. On his off-days, of which this was one, his task was reduced to reporting what the politicians wanted him to report. For once his editor Pansy

Illingworth, the chain-smoking, scatty-haired, husky-voiced survivor of feminist writing and life, who was usually a straightforward cynic, wouldn't have it any other way. A warm human story about the Ashworths was what she had demanded at the morning conference, and she had instructed him to tell it straight. 'We congratulate the happy couple, wish them every happiness, their perfect day' – sentiments of that sort. The notion made Betts feel quite ill.

A commotion behind him and the reek of a Gauloise announced Pansy's arrival in the newsroom. Only she dared defy the no-smoking notices throughout the building. Mostly she kept moving fast enough to outwit the smoke detectors, but security staff were aware that, should a fire alarm sound, they should check her location first. It was believed that Pansy had had a smoking clause written into her contract; the newspaper's proprietors, keen to stem falling circulation and frantic to secure her services, had not quibbled.

'Hi, Jim!' Pansy pinched his arm. 'How's it going? How are the lovebirds?'

Betts controlled a grimace. He preferred to be called James, or even the more manly Betts, and he did not like being patronised by his superiors. For answer he pointed at the screen. The camera outside Christine's Chelsea home showed her resplendent in white, being helped into a Rolls-Royce by her father. The future Mrs Ashworth was thirty, curvaceous, brainy and ambitious. Quite a catch.

It was generally assumed that this was a political

marriage with shared ideals and objectives. They had been seen out together for a year or two, and had reportedly met at party conferences where she had been head of communications while Benedict was in charge of research. It was rumoured, however, that pressure from his formidable mother plus hints from the constituency had led to his proposal. A man of thirty-five should be married, especially if he wished to preserve his wholesome image. Of course, in the new century such considerations shouldn't matter, but they did, especially outside the metropolis. Christine, it was said, had needed no persuading.

'She needs watching, Jim. It doesn't feel real to me.' Pansy sniffed. 'Why should a smart young woman like that be willing to throw up her own career to follow her husband? If economic policy and the constitution fascinate her so much, why doesn't she stand for Parliament herself?'

'She's not throwing up a career,' Betts pointed out. 'She's simply taking on a new one, that of the official Mrs Ashworth. She's set up her own PR company. She intends to give her clients excellent service.'

'So naturally, Jim, you'll keep an eye on which clients. Conflicts of interest, for sure.'

Betts nodded. This assumption of the amorality of anyone who might merit a headline suited him fine.

'It's more independent than slaving in her husband's office, I guess,' Pansy conceded. She flicked cigarette ash on the floor. 'But there's something rotten in that woodwork, I can feel it. She's got class. She could be a leading light of the piddling little New Democrats herself. Why the hell would she want to ride around on her husband's coat-tails?'

'Love, maybe?' Betts said, but the suggestion made them both guffaw. He became bolder. 'Look, Pansy, it may be hard for you rabid feminists to accept that some women prefer to float around in somebody else's jet-stream, but it makes for an easy life. Used to be standard practice for all Tory wives, for instance. Till their husbands' infidelity exposed it for the sham it was.'

Pansy snickered. 'And you were in the forefront of the exposers, Jim.'

Betts preened himself. The Press Gallery Award for Journalist of the Year was framed above his workspace. 'Mrs Christine Ashworth, as she's about to become, is no fool. She's figured out what's in it for her. She's not in competition with her hubby. But if she, or those like her, get to play hostess at Chequers or Number Ten, then it'll be as a spouse, not as an office-holder in her own name. They play dumb but they ain't. They can avoid responsibility for what's dodgy but bask in reflected light when things go well. That'll keep her very happy.'

'Mmm. I bow to your judgement. Our readers might agree, the older ones, but remember our target audience is much younger, Jim. So, Ashworth himself, what do you make of him? What makes our Benedict everybody's darling?'

'He comes across as nice. Genuine, if you like. A polite boy, sweet to that ghastly ma who'd try the patience of a saint. Basically decent.' Betts shrugged.

'God save us from decent politicians. They'd put us out of business in no time – we'd have nothing to write about. Only the mad, the bad and the stupid want to go into Parliament. Isn't that the view you peddle at every morning conference?'

'Correct. I can't figure out why anybody normal would sincerely *want* to be an MP.' Betts waved away the offer of a Gauloise. 'The money's terrible, the hours anti-social, the rewards dismal. They're blamed for everything that goes wrong and get no credit for any success – certainly not from us. The daily thrust of the job's a chore, answering all those whingeing letters from constituents and pressure groups. Waiting to catch the Speaker's eye for five seconds of prime time. When light dawns on the brighter ones, it's too late. Outside politics, most are unemployable.'

'With a few exceptions who write for the *Guardian* or get jobs on talk radio,' Pansy joined in, laughing.

'How many ex-MPs did we discover had ended up on the dole? About forty, wasn't it? And those are the guys who were running the country last year,' Betts agreed.

'It's a funny old world,' Pansy drawled, in a passable imitation of Margaret Thatcher.

She pinched his arm again and scurried away. The discussion had served to focus Betts's own doubts about the

fairytale pictures unfolding on the screen. He watched
Benedict's arrival at the church. Like so many others of
his ilk the man had read politics at university, been active
in the student union, got a job, probably unpaid, in some
MP's office, done a stretch in the party's research department and been hooked for life. It was a sickness, an
infection. Whether they were born with oversized egos or
acquired them along the way was a moot point. There
should be a government warning issued with every college
politics course that the condition was catching, dangerous
and incurable, and would leave sufferers the object of
ridicule for as long as they were remembered. Their opiate
was public adulation. Being forgotten, of course, was the
ultimate humiliation.

Nobody sane would see Parliament as a respectable
occupation, Betts reasoned, not if he or she could earn a
living doing anything else. They should be out running a
business or tossing money around in the City, or in the
wig and gown of a lawyer. Betts shuddered. He hated
lawyers. In a just world, newspapermen would be free to
comment and criticise as they thought fit. A call from the
office of a new female Secretary of State had already been
taken: she was furious with some anodyne remarks he had
made in a leader column. Why anybody should object to
being dubbed 'vile' was beyond him, but she had taken
umbrage. Betts had a nasty feeling that that was not the
last he would hear of it.

He peered more closely at the monitor. The Ashworth

betrothal had been greeted with pleasure on every side. The guest list included frontbenchers from other parties. The most important, for whom Betts was now searching, was Andrew Marquand, Chancellor of the Exchequer. He had been Ashworth's tutor at St Andrew's. It was there, apparently, that the bridegroom's passion for politics had been kindled. So Marquand had more than a double hike in petrol tax to answer for: he had been responsible for corrupting the attitudes of a whole cohort of youngsters, convincing them that the political world was full of sweet opportunity. Several, including Benedict, had accompanied their guru into the mire of Westminster.

As if on cue, the Chancellor appeared at the entrance to the church. St Margaret's was the old parliamentary place of worship, situated opposite the Palace of Westminster under the shadow of Westminster Abbey. The twelfth-century crypt chapel under the Palace could have been used but would not hold enough guests. Cameras were allowed inside St Margaret's but would have been barred from the Palace. Benedict had chosen wisely.

Crashing rolls of organ music announced the arrival of the bride. Above her head, bells rang out joyously. The crowd were giving faint cheers, as if it were expected of them, though many were foreign tourists and somewhat bewildered. Christine was radiant in cream silk, a slight furrow on her brow as she switched the bouquet of lilies and roses from one hand to the other and adjusted her veil. The diamond tiara, it was reported, had been lent by a friendly peeress. Two tiny bridesmaids and an older girl fussed over the dress and train. Then, calmly, she stood proudly on the arm of her father and began to move inside at a regal pace.

So who was that with Andrew Marquand? Betts peered closer. The face was familiar: she was dark-haired, trim, pretty, in a smart navy suit. Betts picked up the phone and murmured a question. He did not have to wait long. 'Fiona Sutton,' came the answer. 'Works in the PR agency that handled the election for the government.'

'A PR girl, then?' Betts murmured. As Christine's face hove into view on the screen, he added, 'Another PR girl. Place is lousy with them.'

He reached for his black notebook and recorded the information. He would find out more. Some day, it might turn out useful.

One person watching television at home felt an uncomfortable mix of wistfulness and despair. It would have been too easy to cry. A box of Kleenex was at her side, an open packet of chocolate digestives in her lap.

Gail Bridges, Frank's estranged wife, had been married in a hasty register office ceremony in Leece Street within odoriferous distance of the Mersey, near the main police station to which her fiancé had been transferred. He had been in uniform, at her insistence: she adored a man in uniform. It made him so respectable. The silver buttons had shone and you could see your face in his boots. He'd still had a hangover from the stag night, and so had his mates: he had leaned on her when they signed the register.

Gail had worn a big cartwheel hat, rather like Benedict's mother's; a defiant gesture. The photographs, taken with a box camera by her brother, a mite out of focus, had recorded that same concentrated furrow of the brow that Christine had. No doubt for a similar reason, for the thoughts of every bride are the same: Do I look okay? Will I make a fool of myself? Did I make a mistake in saying yes? Did I have any choice, when it came down to it? Will he make a good husband, or will I live to regret this moment for the rest of my life?

A lump came to Gail's throat. She was sprawled on the floor of their Cheshire home, though it would not be hers for much longer. She had dressed in leggings and an ancient sweater and sat surrounded by the soft toys of which she had made a collection, much to Frank's annoyance. He used to speculate that they were a substitute for children, which might have been true but was still hurtful. Gail had retorted that he should be thankful she hadn't taken to breeding chihuahuas or poodles. He had snorted, and that had been an end of it. Till the next time the subject of her barrenness came up.

It was not her fault. The doctors had said there was no obvious reason why she should not have children, and suggested that Frank should have a test. He had rejected that idea out of hand. Gail suspected that he did not want the results of any such tests. If a woman was infertile, that was her responsibility. If it was the man, especially a man so full of macho sensitivity as Frank, his self-esteem was irreparably damaged. And that would never do. A modern couple might have pursued the issue via IVF, with donor sperm. Another man's children? That was unthinkable, for them both. The conversation had never taken place, but Gail could have repeated it word for word, exactly as it might have occurred.

In any case, his days were full without children. Had he been a father, he would have been a neglectful one, Gail was sure. He was a fine man as he was, with political intrigue as his baby. Perhaps it had been better for them both that the pregnancy had proved false.

This house had been sold. Her belongings were already half in, half out of packing cases. Of course, it was too big for her, with five bedrooms and an acre of garden. Gail could not recall now why such a mansion had ever seemed desirable; perhaps they had been showing off to each other when he was first elected, back in the days when housing was cheap. The bathrooms had impressed her relatives, while the neighbours were much more refined than she was used to. They, in turn, basked in the reflected glory of an MP in their midst and had been cordial. But even with the promised fees from the magazine column and the proposed book, she would have been hard pressed to keep it up, and in fact she didn't want to. It reminded her too much of weekends when Frank had been pleased to come home to her, and had talked long into the night about his ambitions for the future, until the drone had sent her to sleep.

She had humoured him, never thinking that a person from such a limited background could have got nearly as far. This was a man who was hard-pressed to write a letter for himself and whose tortured syntax on the public platform still drew sneering comment. A man who had to rely on other people, such as herself, to fill in forms and to ensure that the television licence and the car tax were paid on time. Her post-school education, it was true, ran only to the college of commerce, but it was more than his. Without secretaries his obvious lacunae would have tripped him up long ago. Secretaries including That Woman.

But give him an issue – especially a row where attitudes had become entrenched – and Frank was the master. He could grasp what each faction needed, their fears and bottom lines, better than anyone. He could negotiate a deal in which everyone came out on top – or, at least, felt they did. Even as a police officer that had been his forte. And Frank, dear Frank, would be shaking hands all round, the centre of an admiring band of former enemies. Frank was always surrounded by friends. He didn't need kids, or family. He was never alone. But she was.

And now . . . *now* didn't bear thinking about. Gail cuddled a doll and blinked away tears as Benedict and his new wife, confident and smiling, stepped out of the church under a hail of rice. Confetti was banned in Parliament

Square, but pigeons and seagulls were free cleansing agents. What a handsome pair, she could not stop herself admitting. It would be churlish to wish them anything other than a full and happy married life.

Frank had probably considered getting married in the same fashion, this time. Deprived of a white wedding on the first occasion because of the rush and expense, he would have discussed with That Woman how they might flaunt their relationship. Some churches would do it, despite the divorce. An ecclesiastical blessing, perhaps, some time after the register office. She would not have put it past the Usurper to lead Frank by the nose to the nearest altar in a flurry of Brussels lace and posh headgear. Frank in a topper would cut quite a dash.

Gail's chin came up. She needed to consult her adviser. If he said she should attend and wait outside the church, then that was what she would do, however horrible the experience. If he told her to stay at home and arranged for a sympathetic woman journalist and photographer or TV crew to record her anguish, then she would grit her teeth and do that, too. Mr Clifford Maxwell was a godsend. Nobody else had been as considerate. No one else had come up with so many smart wheezes that had enabled her to put across her point of view. No longer the sad silent little wife – ex-wife, soon, when the decree absolute came through – she was now a person in her own right. Frank had treated her badly, dropped her like a hot potato in two minutes flat after decades of loyal marriage. Expected

her to take it meekly, as ever. Brayed at her in the VIP
lounge to belt up, then shouted into the mobile that he was
ditching his wife for his mistress. Humiliated her in the
most dreadful manner. And now dear Mr Maxwell and his
skills had ensured that everyone knew about it.

That was her sole consolation. Gail pulled a fresh tissue
out of the box and waved it at the screen as the young
couple climbed into the flower-bedecked Rolls. The
Ashworth reception was to be at the Savoy, the honeymoon destination was a secret. Her reception had been in
her mother's front room with the smell of mothballs on
her aunties' dresses, and the honeymoon had been three
days in New Brighton. They had lived for years on a
police constable's wage of seven pounds a week. She had
supported him steadfastly. And this was all the gratitude
she got.

The screen returned to a commentator. The phone was
ringing. If that was another request for an interview about
why marriages failed, she would accept, and tell her side of
the story to anyone who would listen.

# CHAPTER THREE

Diane Clark sat up in bed and pressed the switch of the remote control. 'That damned wedding,' she said. 'Isn't there anything else on?'

'You wanted to watch the news, Diane. That *is* the news, today,' came a muffled response from the depths of the bedclothes.

It was early evening. From between drawn curtains, hanging motionless in the still air, a narrow shaft of sunlight spread itself over the carpet. The flat was warm and stuffy; the remains of a bouquet of white roses drooped in a vase. The silvered presentation pieces on the mantelpiece gleamed dully. The framed photographs on the living room wall were in shadow: President Mandela with Diane, a young Diane in a delegation with Israeli Prime Minister Golda Meir, Diane with spiky hair and anorak

under a banner on an Aldermaston march, Diane with a
stud through her nose with the women of Greenham
Common. The only other picture in the flat, showing
Diane as a pigtailed child being hugged by Aneurin Bevan,
was hung in the bathroom.

In deference to the wedding, the parliamentary sched-
ule had been light. Those who yearned to debate pest
control in zoos had had the entire afternoon and an empty
chamber to themselves. Diane, whose department did not
deal with such matters, had a different agenda for spare
moments. She had excused herself from the office, said
she was going to catch up with some reading and cleared
off. Calls were to be held or diverted. She was not free
indefinitely, however: a dinner with the Polish ambassador
loomed. In an hour the official car, a Rover Sterling, would
arrive. As a middle-ranking Cabinet minister she was not
entitled to a Jaguar – yet.

Diane switched off the television and tossed the remote
control on to the bedside table. She glanced coolly at herself in the mirrored doors of the wardrobe. A faint mauve
vein showed on her neck and the jaw had a slight slackness
that was absent from the Aldermaston picture, but otherwise time had treated her well, far better than many of her
male colleagues. She rubbed her hands over her big
breasts and cupped them, peering down at their firm full-
ness. 'See, I'm all flushed. Pink as a baby,' she said, and
played her fingers over her breastbone.

'Naturally,' came the sleepy voice from the bed. A

tousled dark head surfaced, with damp fronds and a shadow over the jowls, then fell back again on the pillows. 'You've been making love. With your usual fire and passion. God, what a woman! I'm knackered, Diane, and I'm twenty years younger than you.'

The young man struggled to sit upright and pushed back the sheets. He had the thinness of youth, with pale skin, narrow shoulders and sinewy arms. A trickle of sweat led from his throat to his navel following the line of black hairs. Together they peered at his groin where a limp, shrunken penis flopped on his thigh. He tapped it with a finger. 'Finished,' he said, with a giggle. 'You've done it again.'

'Well, why not? What else is there for a man and a woman to do? But, Mark, sweetheart, don't remind me about the age gap. I thought it didn't matter to you. It certainly didn't last year.' Diane returned to examining herself frankly in the mirror. What she saw appeared to give her satisfaction, for she flopped down beside the young man, wrapped a leg around his and laid her head on his shoulder, a hand on his damp, flat belly.

Mark stroked her arm. 'No, it's not important. I don't worry about it. You're fabulous. And you've been very kind to me.'

'Kind? Hah!' Diane snorted. 'Nothing *kind* about it. You walked into my office offering yourself in any capacity you were needed. It didn't take you long to twig where you'd be more use than most. Your help with the paperwork's much appreciated, natch, but it's *here* you've been outstanding.' She patted the bed.

'Yeah, it's been fun.' The young man fell silent. He was staring at the ceiling, his eyes unblinking.

Diane pulled on a towelling robe and disappeared into the tiny kitchen. She reappeared with two tumblers full of ice and fizzy liquid. 'Rum and Coke okay? Mostly Coke. I have to make a speech tonight.'

'Yeah, thanks.'

She sat beside him. 'Hey, Mark, what's going on? You said it's *been* fun, as if it's over. You've mentioned the age gap, which normally is taboo. It's tough, you being married and that, but I don't gossip and neither do you. So what's up?'

'Nothing,' he murmured, and indicated the detumescent member again. 'Nothing's up, as you can see.' Neither of them laughed. He took the tumbler with both hands. 'Maybe that's it, Diane. You're fabulous, but it can be hard keeping two women content. And if I fail with Susie, she starts to cry.'

'Oh, I get it. The wife comes first, is that it?' Diane could not stop herself sounding peevish.

'But of course,' he answered slowly. 'This is a fling, as you've often made clear. I accepted that. Susie isn't a fling, and she needs me more than you do.' He shifted awkwardly and avoided her gaze. 'When I started researching for you, you were a member of the opposition. We could have a lot of *fun*, out of the public eye. Now it's changed.'

'No, it isn't. I'm the same, you're the same.' Fear curdled her voice.

'You're in government. That alters everything. Even if your staff and officials don't chatter – and I wouldn't put it past them – you're under far closer scrutiny than ever before. You have to consider your own position. A Secretary of State with a boyfriend who's a brand-new fellow Member of Parliament, married and twenty years younger – the press'd have a field day. Wouldn't they?'

Diane jumped up from the bed, seeking distraction. 'The press don't need facts. They make them up. At least, Jim Betts and the *Globe* do. Did you see that horrible piece he wrote the day I was appointed? Said I'd exploited my sexuality to advance myself. Implied that I'd slept my way to prominence. Here it is.'

Mark was familiar with the article in question, but it would have been impolite to stem Diane in full flow. He read:

Diane Clark. Women's rights champion. She who has set herself up as the voice of womanhood throughout the kingdom. Yet who is she? What gave her the right to campaign on behalf of other women? She has never had a successful relationship in her entire life. She was married for only two years, and ditched the chap in favour of a string of lovers. She tub-thumps on behalf of

mothers with children, yet she's never been a
mother herself. How can we trust her?

'It's awful, Diane,' her lover said. 'He's a complete
turd, that Jim Betts. Doesn't care who he craps on. You
shouldn't get upset.'

'He called me the "vilest lady" in the country. Me!
And what for? What did I ever do to him? Not content
with implying that I've slept my way to power, when
nothing could be further from the truth, he suggests
that I have no grounds to campaign as I do. What balls
that is.' She sat down heavily on the bed, her mouth
puckered.

'But can't you see,' Mark ventured carefully, 'how
much worse it would be if he *did* have some material? Me,
for instance.' He wiped his fingers, wet from the conden-
sation of the glass, over her hot cheek. The airless room
smelt headily of sex.

Diane shook her head. 'Campaigners like me are
needed. You don't have to have suffered the aggression of
a drunken husband to know that it's not the best environment to bring up children. Sods like Betts, who isn't
partnered either so far as I'm aware and who tends to fall
over dead drunk at press bashes, have absolutely no right
to criticise or to try and silence me. That's why this rubbish is so unfair.'

Mark rolled away from her, preparing his body and
hers for the moment at which they must part. He said, 'I

saw your mother at the count. She seemed a bit out of it. How's she coping with your new status?'

Diane shrugged. 'It gives her a new reason to moan. It's a pain, being an only child. My mother would like me to be in daily attendance on her, and she's the sort who believes the only role for women is a caring one. She still doesn't think I've got a proper job. This politics lark will wear off, she says, and I'll see sense. I'll go home to Manchester and wait on her hand and foot. Except I won't.'

'But there's nothing much wrong with her, you told me.'

'No, but she's ailing – she's always ailing, and there's nothing anyone can do about it, except make appropriate noises. At such moments, God help me, I can begin to believe the victim theory of violence. Some people seem to invite it. My father was a weak man and a creep, but she must have driven him crazy with her whining. I suspect he died of despair, not a heart attack. As soon as I could, I got out. Up the ladder and over the wall. And here I am.'

Not for the first time, the young MP reflected that Diane Clark found it much easier to offer the milk of human kindness to strangers *en masse* than to members of her own family. It was a common enough trait in the political world. Not unexpectedly, it led to allegations of hypocrisy; such a charge, had the *Globe* made it in that form, would have been far closer to the truth than Betts's tirade. Yet Diane's efforts on behalf of battered wives and damaged children had been a lifelong commitment, impossible to deride as a pose. The tabloids, however, were not interested in the thoughtful investigation of a complex personality. They were seeking scandal, and in Diane's case would not have far to go to find it.

'So what are you intending to do?' Mark slid out of bed and gathered up his clothes. He pointed cautiously at the newspaper clipping.

'God, I've no choice. I singed ears with a couple of quick phone calls, then made an appointment to see Lord Godman, the QC. We've had an exchange of letters so far, with no apology. He agrees that the sentiments are clearly defamatory, and if I decide to issue a writ for libel, he'll act for me.'

'You might be better to forget it. It was weeks ago already. You've more significant fish to fry than Mr Jim Betts or his editor. Plus, this side of the election we need all the allies we can get. Not enemies. Before, the media accepted our version of events when we attacked the government. Now that we're in charge, their guns have swivelled about and are pointed in our direction. We're the targets now.'

He pulled on shorts and trousers and busied himself fastening his belt.

Diane stood up and, as if suddenly ashamed of her nakedness, pulled a sheet around her. She kissed her lover's damp forehead. 'One of the things I like about you, Mark, is you talk such sense. Unfortunately, this particular article is so nasty that it could do me real harm. The comments resurface every time I give an interview. I want to talk about helping the Third World or benefits for the disabled, and the interviewer asks sweetly how I react to being dubbed the vilest lady in the country. I'm promoting a greater role for women in society and the questions are lifted straight from the *Globe*: why did my marriage break up, am I against marriage, do I intend to curb my wild ways now I'm in the Cabinet? So I'm listening to advice, but without a withdrawal and a grovelling apology soon, I'll probably go ahead and sue.'

Mark's glum expression was more eloquent than words. Diane loosened the sheet around her hips. She reached out for the young man's hand and guided it to her crotch, but he pulled away. With a brusque movement she sat down on the bed. 'Out with it. What's eating you?'

'Not the article, though I don't think the Boss'd be too pleased at your pursuing Pansy Illingworth and her crowd. We want them with us, not against us. But, Diane, this has got to stop. Our – our affair. I wanted to tell you before but it's come to a head.'

'Go on.' Diane's face had darkened. The empty glass was cradled in her hand. She sat holding herself quite still.

'Oh, Lord, there's no easy way to put this.' Mark struggled into his shirt, began to do up the buttons then realised he had mismatched them, undid the lot and started again, fingers trembling. 'I can't, I really can't, keep you happy, and my wife, whom I love, plus do my work as an MP. That job is more gruelling than I anticipated. I'm a new backbencher, so I have to be in the House till ten night after night. That's taking its toll, as you can imagine. It's a four-hour journey up to the constituency at weekends, *and* we hope to start a family. Kids will come first, Diane.'

'Yeah, understood,' she answered, a trifle impatiently. 'I was half expecting this.'

'But, Diane, there's more. Better coming from me than anyone else. I have so enjoyed being with you. How many times do I have to say that? You're a fabulous woman, enticing, exciting, and magic in bed. But you should be more careful. You took a hell of a chance with me, though I would never let you down. I won't talk – you can count on it. The very fact that I'm married, and ambitious, means I have as strong an incentive as you to keep my name out of the papers. And I reckon you like the thrill of the illicit, don't you? Me too. But the more you select younger men as lovers, the more risks you run. You'll get set up one of these days. Then you could come a cropper.'

'What makes you think younger men are any less trustworthy?'

'They're not. Look, if you were having it off with, say, a chap in his fifties who is free and adores you, a companion like that might produce plaudits, not criticism. But there's something – ah – indecent about an older woman with, well, boys. Especially when she's in a position of seniority, as you are.'

'What I do with my personal life is my business, and nobody else's,' Diane said stiffly. 'The way we fulfil our office is what matters. Not who we sleep with, or where, or what particular tastes we like to indulge. That's nobody's business.'

'But it is,' Mark insisted. 'The punters are fascinated by our private lives. We live in goldfish bowls. And we actively invite such attention. We offer ourselves up, in our election manifestos and addresses, as having special virtues. We promise honesty, and truth, and altruism of the highest order. The moment one of us is discovered engaging in behaviour that doesn't match those high ideals we can go swing for our credibility.'

'And how,' said Diane, with a sharp edge to her voice, 'could having younger boyfriends be regarded as damaging my credibility?'

Mark turned away slowly as he fastened his tie, and addressed his next remarks to the wall. 'It's exploitation. You don't intend it like that, but it is. A youngster comes into your circle, and catches your eye. You've made it clear you don't believe in celibacy, you won't go more than a few weeks without a man, but they must be cute. There's quite a lot of rivalry among certain types to come and work for you. To make it as far as here,' he indicated the rumpled bed behind him, 'is quite a coup. But in the end you're their employer. If you were to make a pass and got turned down, or worse, laughed at, they could get the boot.'

'No. I wouldn't do that.'

'Please. Get wise. There's the anxiety that if they refused you, then wanted to leave, you wouldn't write a reference. Or you could make it tough to move elsewhere. Again, loving you as I do, I'm certain the idea of such vindictiveness wouldn't occur to you. But outside it looks too bloody likely.'

'That's bullshit.' Diane leaned against the bedside table, frowning. 'Tell me, did you feel exploited? Do you now?'

'A little,' Mark admitted. 'And, to be honest, I calculated that if you were pleased with *all* my efforts, you'd help me get on. That's why I didn't let myself think twice about deceiving Susie, so perhaps I'm as much to blame as you. You did help, loads, and I'm terribly grateful. But you'll have to find somebody else. I'm out of here.'

'And if I've got any sense my next lover'll be a fat-arsed fifty-five-year-old with a heart condition and a pension? Oh, come on.'

The young man bent down and retrieved his shoes from under the bed. He did not reply.

Diane softened. 'I don't see,' she said slowly, 'how my extending the hand of friendship to remarkable blokes like you could in any way be called exploitation. You're accusing me of manipulating you, of having put you in an impossible bind. That is such an offensive suggestion.'

'Is it? Tell me, Diane, when President Clinton got caught with a twenty-one-year-old intern, Monica Lewinsky, who did you blame?'

'Him, of course. I'm on record on that. He was the guilty party. He seduced her. Silly cow that she was, she was in no position to run away.'

'Exactly. I rest my case.'

After Mark had left, Diane stood irresolute, bath towel in hand. She pulled the bed-sheets untidily into place, opened the curtains and unlatched a window. The light air that blew in dispelled the lingering odours of love-making and brought with it the piny smell of leaves that had spent the day in the sun. Down in St James's Park a military band was playing. Starlings rose in squawking flurries as the shadows lengthened. She had a bare half-hour to get ready.

After a shower, as she dressed swiftly, dabbing on perfume and makeup, Diane's mind fluttered and protested over Mark's comments and would not settle, much like the fractious birds in the eaves. Did he truly mean it, that the affair was finished? Next time she touched his shoulder, or rang his private line and proposed going over a briefing paper together, would he refuse, however politely? Was he about to become part of the past, along with every other handsome, virile youth whose performance in bed had thrilled her? And did that mean she would have to cast her roving eye about, and find somebody new?

But, as he had pointed out, dalliance was far more dangerous now than it had been. If Mark was correct that her tastes were widely discussed, he had done well to keep his name out of the press. Perhaps they'd simply been lucky. But luck could vanish in an instant. Mark was right: chasing men, and especially junior staffers, had become a risky enterprise.

It meant, paradoxically, that the case for suing the *Globe* was strengthened. The article was such a mishmash of snide invention, so devoid of fact, that an apology would serve as an example to other papers. She was vulnerable and had to make herself less so. A solidly backed threat to Betts and his ilk might keep the trash-peddlers at bay for some years. To let them get away with such a scurrilous piece would imply either that she didn't care or, worse, that she didn't dare challenge their innuendo. To protect herself, she had little option but to start proceedings, and fight to win.

'Damn,' she muttered, as the lipstick smudged. She wiped it off and tried again, as the image consultants, whose ministrations she had so resisted, had shown her. 'I'm going to be late, as usual. If the press alleged that Diane Clark was well-meaning, scatty and found adjustment to the top flights of public life tricky, I couldn't sue. They'd be spot on.'

The bell rang. The driver announced that he had ministerial boxes for her; could he bring them up? Hastily Diane flew round the living room, trying to conceal the evidence of the afternoon's dalliance, then pressed the intercom button to admit him. A thick-set man in his forties entered, averted his eyes from the bedroom and set the heavy boxes on the floor by her desk.

She locked up and followed him down, hoping that the blue silk outfit was suitable for the event and rehearsing in her mind the remarks due after the dinner. She nodded 'good evening' on the stairs to the elderly couple who lived above her; they were returning home laden with shopping. At the front entrance she paused. 'Dave, can I ask you something?'

'Certainly, madam.' He drew back his shoulders in the plain grey suit. He had been a driver in the Royal Corps of Signals; the government car service was an obvious step to take into Civvy Street.

'Do you think I should be more discreet with my private life, now that I'm a Cabinet minister?'

The man's eyes popped. 'I – I couldn't begin to say, madam,' he stammered.

'Am I being watched the whole time? That's what I mean.'

'Well, madam,' the ex-soldier recovered his composure, 'if I were you, I should act as if I was.'

'Hmm. That's difficult.' Diane hesitated. 'Dave, you married?'

'I am, madam. Three kids, and a missus that'd cut my balls off if I strayed.'

'Ah, I see.' Diane caught the man's eye, and they both

half smiled. 'Oh, Lord, Dave. If I'd realised what was entailed, maybe I'd never have started out on this path. I could have been a college lecturer and worked a twenty-hour week and had long holidays and screwed my best students. Instead I'm an Aunt Sally for every frigging journalist, and I have to *behave*.'

'Yes, madam,' the driver said, and chuckled softly. 'Front seat or back, madam?'

It was not till much later in the evening that, flushed with wine, Diane returned to the flat, made a pot of coffee and settled at her desk with the red boxes. Inside the top one was a first draft of the social-security review. It gave her a headache just to flick through the pages. The new government had promised to abide by the budgetary restrictions of the previous incumbents for at least two years. With such a pledge no extra spending was possible; but without it the punters would have taken fright. The election would have been lost, as voters' fears of the spendthrift tendency would have outpaced an increasing liking for the man who was now Prime Minister.

'We are stuck,' Diane scribbled crossly in the margin, 'with the budget we inherited.' She saw, with a wry smile, that she was already using 'we' to mean the government, as if it were a seamless continuum. 'Any action requiring largesse will have to wait. The legislative programme is also tight, with House of Lords reform taking precedence. So please fillet out those possibilities that *don't* require either new money or new laws, and I will consider them. One page of A4 only, please.'

That was how the big issues got deferred. Given the broad sweep of the review, there must be enough minor proposals to keep junior ministers occupied. Diane marked up one or two, more as illustrations than as instructions. She was determined not to become demoralised: *force majeur* meant they could not do everything at once, and would jeopardise the whole Project if they tried. 'And if I protested,' Diane muttered to the photo of Mandela, 'I'd get the sack, pronto. But if I stay, we have some chance of keeping our consciences intact.'

Midnight came and went, the coffee pot emptied. In the bottom of the third box was a stack of buff folders from her constituency secretary, mostly letters prepared for her signature. The same old complainants. Mrs Cartwright was still worried about her dripping tap: a letter to the council should suffice. Mr Heathway had kids throwing stones at his window. He would not accept that if he ignored his tormentors they might pester someone else. Did he need a sympathetic social worker? Was that the answer? Would anyone in the local office take any notice of him? He was lonely. Maybe the British Legion could help. Diane rubbed her eyes, tired.

One last folder. This time, she brightened. It contained the applications to replace Mark on her personal staff. The advertisements had been placed promptly, for his resignation was inevitable, now that he was an MP himself.

Perhaps she should have anticipated his departure as lover also, but it was still a painful blow. To be honest, his success at the hustings had been unexpected, a wonderful surprise on the crest of the electoral wave that had swept away so many of the previous government's supporters. Several of the new arrivals had cherished only the faintest hope. Now Mark had left not only a gap in her workforce but also, if he stuck to his word, in her bed. The rejection hurt.

On the other hand, replacements were available. Diane began to read.

She could not take them in. So many excellent candidates. Twenty in total, including five females. A single post was in the offing. Normally she would have glanced at the girls' CVs and tossed them aside with a twinge of guilt, maybe sent a scribbled note of encouragement. She would have scrutinised the men's with more care, starting with the photographs. She would try to imagine them in the flesh, wonder whether any would be amenable and how they might respond. But the savour of the chase had gone.

She picked up her diary and earmarked a spare morning. Her secretary could do the preliminaries. On a Post-it note she wrote, 'Pick the best half-dozen and ask them to come in for interview Tuesday next. I'm sure they're all marvellous. Thanks.'

Then she shoved the papers back into the folder, closed and locked the last red box, and went to bed.

# CHAPTER FOUR

Christine lay still. The sheets felt clammy against her hot skin. The air-conditioning hummed an invitation to roll over and close her eyes again, but she was not sleepy. Beside her lay the prone body of her husband. He moved frequently in bed but would not wake, if previous experience were any guide, for another two hours.

Outside it was getting light. Parakeets chattered in the palm trees. A faint clatter down the corridor in the service alcove heralded room-service breakfast. Christine tried to remember what time they had ordered theirs for, and wondered whether pancakes with blueberries and sour cream had been a sensible request. Fresh pineapple and mango would have been better for them both. If he continued eating too much Benedict would need a crash diet the moment they got home. On the other hand, maybe a little solidity would not go amiss: it would help confirm the picture of a contentedly uxorious man.

Christine shifted restlessly. The room felt too warm. She longed to throw off the bedclothes and spread her naked limbs out over the bed, but any sudden movement would disturb Benedict. Let him sleep. The desired image, the one that mattered, would not be aided by black circles under the eyes on their return.

The image. Why did it keep floating through her mind? Why did she have such a precise idea, down to the last visual detail, of how they would appear to photographers in the arrivals hall at Heathrow? The matching 'his and hers' luggage in brown leather. The linen suits, stylishly crumpled after the long flight. Benedict would have to be reminded to shave before the plane landed. The light tan, the result of doggedly nagging her husband to strip off. His fair skin, he protested mildly, disliked strong sun. A honeymoon on the Scottish moorlands might have been more in his line, but that would have left him even paler than usual and would have marked him permanently as lacking trendiness. One Prince Charles was enough. It would have marred the overall package, and that would never do.

She leaned on one elbow and gazed down at her sleeping spouse. He shifted position again, and snatches of unintelligible words escaped his lips. That was what had disturbed her sleep.

Her efforts to spruce him up were mostly greeted with

mild objections, but after a short while, when she quietly explained the changes she proposed – only small matters, the sort of trivia that weighed with other people but not with them – he acquiesced, normally with good grace. He was not accustomed to so much attention being paid to the impression he made. He had spent far too much time in the company of other young Turks engrossed in politics. Intellectual, eager and committed they might be, anxious to put across the issues, but their notions of what was convincing dress and behaviour in public left much to be desired.

For modern politics was about more than issues, as Benedict was ruefully willing to accept. A substantial part of what the electorate liked was *image*, pure and simple, but its creation required skills as complex as any astronaut's. In the ten-second burst he might get on the evening TV news, as big an impact as possible had to be made. The eye registered before the ear, and often only a garbled half-sentence emerged after the editing. Sometimes they did not broadcast his words at all, merely a voiceover from the presenter as Benedict mouthed silently, helpless. Never mind the issues; the audience would notice his tie, the colour of his shirt, his manner, the lift of an eyebrow, and make snap judgments on that.

The new Prime Minister had grasped that essential fact before many others in his party. His hair had been cut shorter and kept that way. The suits had become *de rigueur*, but standard, non-threatening. He was never seen without a plain shirt and sober tie – no pinstripes or loud colours – except in the company of his young children, when instead he sported a knitted sweater. *Always*. The message that he was a loving and responsible father for his own kids and thus to be trusted by the whole nation was communicated subliminally by Fair Isle patterns, corduroy trousers and a shy, embarrassed smile. Even cynics were full of admiration.

To everyone's astonishment he had even managed to bolster his support for family values by putting his own wife in the family way. For the fifth time, which did seem a mite excessive. Downing Street, which had harboured Ted Heath's grand piano and the tinkle of Margaret Thatcher's Sèvres porcelain, would thrill to the sound of a gurgling baby. The nation's grandmothers sighed with pleasure and the poll ratings jumped accordingly.

Previous opposition leaders had turned up their noses at image-makers, to their and their party's detriment. One had appeared at the Cenotaph on Remembrance Day in a scruffy, unfastened Duffel coat and no hat. A noted pacifist, he had meant no disrespect to the dead, but television viewers were appalled. Such a man could never be put in charge of the nation's security. He was a loser.

The Welshman who followed him had ginger hair, a high colour and freckles. In themselves they were not a gross handicap, but he was vain, and tried to hide his baldness by combing long strands of hair from one ear across to the other. Caught in an unkind breeze at the seaside, his Brylcreemed locks took flight. The resulting photos emphasised, as nothing else could, that he sought to hide what he lacked. When subsequently he was caught on film falling over on the beach as the tide came in, his lack of sure-footedness became his bane. He, too, led his party to disaster.

The icon for all parties was Margaret Thatcher. Christine, to her delight, had been compared to her more than once. But when she had arrived at the House Margaret had been a brunette, not a blonde. The peroxide had come later. So had the deepened voice, and the sexy little twist to the mouth. Christine had seen early footage when she was first elected to the leadership. Then, her nerves showed in a constant clearing of the throat at the end of each high-pitched sentence and a frightened-rabbit flicker in the eyes. But once the Right Honourable Member for Finchley had made it to Number Ten, she took advice. Out went the fussily patterned frocks with their complicated necklines. Off came a stone in weight, though nobody ever mentioned it. Down floated the voice. Up went the skirt length; in came navy suits that showed off her slim legs. The Iron Lady, product both of a steely character and a chunk of splendid PR, was born.

Christine slid out of the hot bed and padded into the bathroom. She stood for several minutes gazing into the mirror. No wrinkles yet; the hint of a smile line exactly where she wanted it. An alarm clock announced that it was six-thirty. Still not time to get up.

She brushed her teeth. She was not averse to using her mouth and tongue in sex, as they had tried again last night. It seemed rude to rise and clean her teeth immediately afterwards. She had noticed that Benedict's body language, when he kissed her down *there*, indicated that he would like to wash his mouth at once, but she did not let him; she held him to her, and murmured gentle words, and he relaxed a bit, until it was time to try something else.

So much of this was new to him – that was plainly obvious. Christine was loath to admit to her husband that she was an experienced player: to do so might have entailed too many explanations, none appropriate on a honeymoon. She had no wish to talk about old lovers and their styles, so anything she introduced had to be paraded as her own spontaneous idea, or something any healthily adventurous female would do with a man she fancied. That was pretty close to the truth, anyway. The veil was to be drawn over Benedict's innocence, or it was to be portrayed between them as an attractive trait. He had been so engrossed in politics that sexual activity had not featured much in his life. He had never been in love before, he had told her, and she believed him. He was thrilled and amazed that she had accepted his proposal to be his wife. She believed that, too. Wherever she led in bed, he would follow. He was determined to satisfy her.

His determination was not in question, Christine reflected, as she rinsed and replaced the toothbrush. Whatever Benedict set his mind to he would achieve, whatever it took. It was his ability that gave rise to the niggle of concern.

Her bed had been made by nobody but herself. And she would lie on it. Nobody as sweet, as dear, as *interesting* as Benedict had ever crossed her path before. So many other men, and most women, had flitted past who were so boring that their presence in the same room was a trial. But her and Benedict's tastes and views were miraculously well matched, and they hugely enjoyed each other's company. She was impressed that he intended to get himself into the front rank, and was keen to encourage him in every step. If they were compared with the Clintons, or with other political marriages where the curious asked, 'What *does* she see in him?' or 'Why on earth does she stand by him?', Christine Ashworth took it as a compliment.

This way, of course, she could enjoy the fruits of success without having to go through the motions herself, but her support of Benedict was unselfish. They had become friends, close and affectionate, before anyone in the media had noticed. Then the question of marriage had been mooted, and both had found it beguiling. By then they were seldom away from each other for more than a few days, and each would admit with increasing warmth to missing the other greatly during those absences. It was not quite clear who had wooed whom, and it didn't matter. They loved each other, they had the same outlook and objectives, and that was all that counted. This was what made her tick.

Christine slipped back into bed. Benedict was still whispering to himself, his eyes tight shut. She let her mind roam again to when they would be going home. They were to live in his flat. It was large enough, and convenient for the Commons and for her company, whose headquarters were in Whitehall Place, an address that would impress clients, though naturally she would avoid anything too high profile.

The flat's décor needed attention: it was much too masculine. While Benedict was tied up at the House, Christine would give it some thought and devise colour schemes. Nothing too elaborate, just something brighter, less drab, and more suited to the private entertaining that would be required for his career and hers.

They must get some decent paintings, or at least prints. Benedict's taste in wall decoration ran, like that of many busy MPs, to posed snaps of himself with various dignitaries. He had installed framed photos of college days, where he was surrounded by other students in gowns, on graduation day and the like. Even when the other participants included well-known faces such as Andrew Marquand's that one might discreetly point out to guests, Christine found them too dull for words. They would have to go.

Beside her, Benedict stirred and opened one eye. 'What time is it?' he murmured.

She told him, and touched his hand. He let her fingers rest on his wrist for a moment, then slowly withdrew and rolled over, away from her. But not before, half-asleep, he spoke again. 'I'm sorry,' he mumbled. She nodded without reply, and let him return to his troubled sleep.

Tuesday at ten was not the most convenient timing. He would have to ask for the morning off work, without saying why. It was risky to let it be known that he was chasing another post, not with a rival company but outside the City. That might jeopardise everything, if he was not successful.

Edward Porter reread the cream letter with the embossed green portcullis. 'Thank you for your application for the post advertised in the *Guardian*,' it read. 'We should be grateful if you could attend for interview . . . Please bring copies of university certificates, testimonials, etc. For your information the post will be in the parliamentary office of the Rt Hon. Diane Clark.'

The sentences made him catch his breath even though he had them by heart. The original advert had stated baldly that a vacancy had arisen on the private staff of a leading member of the government. For security reasons and to deter time-wasters the name had not been published, though when he telephoned a secretary had been happy to hint that it was a woman. In fact he was delighted that it was Ms Clark. Diane, as everyone called her. A more controversial, outspoken and vigorous employer could not be imagined. The very thought made his pulse race with excitement.

Edward smoothed down his dark hair. A glance in the mirror showed a slim man of above average height with pale clear skin, a square jaw and a nose turning aquiline. He was smooth-shaven, had short neat hair and wore rimless spectacles to read. He favoured grey or navy blue suits, single-breasted without pinstripes, and a silk tie in his school colours. It was a uniform suitable for a man in his position, but flamboyance was not his style.

He began to plan the days ahead meticulously. He would have a hair trim on Monday: that would have to be booked. He would tell his supervisor that he had a dental appointment on Tuesday, and stay late the evening before to leave no cause for complaint. He would even return to the office holding the side of his mouth and talking oddly. His chances of getting this post must be slim: there would be hundreds of keen applicants, many better qualified than he was. Best to treat it as a rehearsal for the next opportunity that came up. Edward was suddenly determined to move from his City desk, and as soon as possible.

On any objective assessment his lack of confidence was well founded. He had not read history or politics or sociology or any related subject at college, but law. At that time, a career at the bar had seemed glamorous and held out the prospects of both intellectual stimulus and financial reward. But somehow he had drifted into the commercial side and found himself appearing in civil cases in which one large corporation was suing another for an exorbitant sum. His days had revolved around the small print of contracts that nobody else ever read. Success meant a million-pound invoice presented to the losers, or perhaps to both. Increasingly he had to manufacture an interest in his clients' doings and the outcome of cases. It did not help that, with only half his mind engaged, he was exceptional at it. Regular clients (and some were frequent litigants) demanded his services. The bonuses were handsome. The senior partner slapped him on the back at the Christmas party. His team was responsible for a significant chunk of the firm's billing. His salary reflected his usefulness: he had more money than a single man with few outside interests could easily spend. But the work was boring beyond endurance

Then, one idle morning, as he had flicked through the *Guardian* adverts without knowing quite why, he found himself envying those who would apply. The problem with his current post, he had concluded slowly, was that he was doing nothing worthwhile, and it wasn't as if his day-to-day satisfaction could be improved upon by shifting to another practice, or trying to teach. He hated being in the legal profession: it was little more than a conspiracy to make money out of fools. He ached inside.

Black Dog loomed briefly. How well Winston Churchill had named it, that trough of depression that lurched like a slavering canine ready to bite and bounded up on him unawares. Edward had realised ages ago that he didn't need to be in a mess to feel unhappy. At certain times, like Churchill, he could feel pain even when pain was absent. But whenever he was stressed, even though the outcome might be much desired, Black Dog would pad silently behind him. Like now. 'I am your closest friend,' Black Dog would pant, its dank flanks heaving. 'I am here to help you. When you want to feel sorry for yourself, come walk beside me. I am always here. I will not hurt you. I am better than being alone with your fears.'

But the creature came from depths that could only be visited by abandoning any vestige of normality or balance. Given too much leeway it would seize him in its jaws and drag him down. Edward Porter knew exactly how that could happen and how horrible it felt. Black Dog had bitten him several times already in his thirty years. The temptation to court the creature had to be kept at arm's length. It was too easy to give in and lose one's sense of reality.

Edward sighed, and tried again to make neat notes, to keep his mind on the essentials that might just help him win this new job. What questions might be asked, and how might he respond? The first, obvious one was: what relevant experience had he? None at all, but this might be turned to advantage, surely. He had never served in opposition; he had no baggage. His experience was entirely practical, in the business world, which arguably would be

useful to an administration most of whose minions had
never handled a balance sheet. He wanted to work, not in
politics as such, but with someone in power. He had no
dogma to offer, and would rely on the best outcomes available. If that meant he would be accused of pragmatism, he
had a feeling that this new untried government would not
take it amiss. The answers to practical problems were
seldom written on tablets of stone brought down a mountain by some bearded Moses. He would say so, firmly, but
with a pleasant twinkle in his eyes.

He might be quizzed, with a hostile edge, as to what he
could offer when so many volunteers had slaved away,
brought the party into Whitehall, and now needed
employment? Wasn't he a carpetbagger? If politics hadn't
grabbed him before when the party was suffering in opposition, why should it now? The answer was obvious, and
true. He wanted to do something useful, and be of benefit to his fellow man. The possibility that a speech in
Parliament, or a neatly crafted piece of legislation, could
be of direct service to millions of citizens fascinated him.
Nothing like that could be said of his appearances for this
or that plc before a judge. Black Dog could be kept more
easily at bay, Edward told himself, if he could justify his
own existence. To do it in the shadow of a splendid woman
like Diane Clark would add enormously to the savour.

Edward rummaged in a drawer for the necessary papers.
The references would follow. He wondered whether his
birth certificate and other personal documents would be

required, then decided against. There were – gaps. Some elements might need explanation, though it would be a harsh employer who refused him on those thin grounds. One aspect of Diane Clark that particularly appealed was that she seemed free of prejudice. Indeed, her reputation had been made fighting for equality for the downtrodden. She was exactly the sort of person who might sympathise.

Edward warmed to the idea. He had never spoken about Black Dog to anyone, but perhaps Diane would understand. It wasn't as if he had asthma, or epilepsy, or any other condition that in fairness he had to communicate to a potential boss. If the new post became his and met his expectations, his depression might be permanently put to flight. That alone was a strong reason to seek pastures new.

And he would take this suit to the cleaner's today, so that he would make the best impression. And buy a new tie. Diane was a single woman, feisty and energetic. His appearance, as a modest, passably handsome young man, might make the difference.

'You really expect me to say all this?' Frank Bridges got himself ready to explode. It was bad enough that he was to give the keynote speech at the Institute of Directors Annual Dinner. The audience would be well-heeled businessmen, and a few women, resolutely opposed to the new government and its philosophy. They had fought many of the most advanced ideas of the manifesto including the minimum wage, the windfall tax on utilities, the New Deal for the unemployed and membership of the euro. Getting the nation's so-called entrepreneurs to embrace new thinking was God's own job. Worse, the damn thing would be black tie, which he loathed. He was beginning to feel like a bloody penguin.

'I wouldn't mind quite so much,' he prodded the page, 'if it wasn't such goddamn obscure twaddle. If I don't understand it, I bet they won't. It doesn't say *anything*.'

The private secretary twisted his hands together. He was a thin grey man, in a charcoal grey suit, silvery grey tie, with greying hair and, Frank noticed grimly, pale grey eyes with a slight tic. It was as if all colour had been drained out of him along with his blood supply years ago, as a precondition of seniority in Whitehall. He writhed under Frank's glare. 'But, Secretary of State, that's the whole idea.'

Frank was bewildered. 'You've just lost me entirely.'

'It's supposed to be obscure.'

'Oh, is it? Why, in God's name?'

'Because it isn't *supposed* to say anything.'

Frank held his head in his hands. The open ministerial box was mute in its sympathy. His interlocutor pressed home his advantage. 'Instructions. We can't have you making any more promises, Number Ten won't allow it.'

'That I'm well aware of. We got our knickers in a twist before the election by making far more pledges than we'd bargained for. The bills don't add up. Mouths are to be sealed shut from here onwards. At least, till the next election, and that's way off.'

The private secretary visibly relaxed. 'Any initiatives have to be cleared first. The pecking order, as you know, is Number Ten press secretary, then Number Eleven, and if there's any chance of a vote on it in the House, Number Twelve.'

'The spin doctor, the Chancellor, and the Chief Whip. Yeah, I know,' Frank growled.

The civil servant looked pleased, as if a recalcitrant pupil had at last grasped an important lesson. 'So obscurity is the order of the day, Secretary of State.'

Frank shuffled testily through the papers, crossing out the clarifications he had hoped to make. 'I don't suppose there's much chance of you dropping that "Secretary of State" lark, at least while we're in private? Makes me sound like a bird-of-paradise or something. Can't you call me Frank?'

The anxious tic returned. 'I'd rather not, Secretary of State, if you don't mind. It's not form. But you can call me William.'

Frank checked to see if the public-school educated official was having him on, but decided that 'William' was sincere. 'And what about the press on the evening, and questions?'

'No problem. You'll speak at the end of the meal, replying to the toast to the government, and that'll be that. The media will not be present in force. They'll get this press release and guidance from the press office as to what it means, and they'll be quite satisfied. The Institute of Directors are very reliable on security, Secretary of State. That's why we thought this would be a useful opportunity for you.'

'You mean they're safe, there won't be any trouble, and I'll be hard-pushed not to behave myself?'

'Something like that, sir.'

'Even if I say nothing at all?'

William bowed slightly.

'And I suppose,' Frank persisted glumly, 'that if I add any remarks off the cuff, crack a few jokes or try to be a human being there'll be hell to pay? Then I'll be wading in deep doo-doo for days?'

'Not only you, Secretary of State. If there's any kind of fuss, we will have to answer as well.'

'You especially, I suppose, William?'

'I am responsible for the content of that script, yes. And for persuading you to stick to it. If I can. *Sir*.'

'Frigging hell,' said Frank, under his breath, but further resistance was futile. He sighed, threw the hated speech back into the red box and closed the lid with a furious bang.

Gail awoke with a headache. Her eyelids were stuck together. A shoulder ached where she had lain on it awkwardly. Her mouth tasted foul. London: the atmosphere was so polluted. Not like the fresh country air of

Cheshire. But Cheshire was gone, and she would have to adjust.

The bottle was on its side, a single drip still on its lip. Ring stains marked the bedside table. The smeared glass was still half full. Head down, Gail trudged into the small kitchen, threw the bottle into the bin, washed out the glass and up-ended it on the draining-board. The latest television interview yesterday afternoon had gone well, but the line of questioning had upset her. Getting drunk on neat gin afterwards had not healed anything, but it had been worth a try.

The flat was still crammed with cardboard cartons full of her stuff. She had not had the heart to sort it out, to send what was no longer needed to a charity shop, to hang up her clothes and put away the rest. Some of the prettier outfits would still serve for her media appearances. Mr Maxwell had advised her not to overdress but she had been unclear exactly what he meant: downbeat or scruffy was not in her repertoire. A formal suit required costume jewellery and red lipstick, though the ring finger was left painfully bare.

Only the dolls had been lovingly unpacked, and arranged over the living room, their glass eyes twinkling brown or blue under the electric light. The computer still sat in its box; it presented a challenge and a reproof, for Gail had never felt confident using it. But her skills would improve with time, Mr Maxwell had assured her, and he urged her to take a course, to master the damn thing, to become a thoroughly modern single woman. Like thousands of others in London, this God-forsaken hole.

It was horrible being alone. Not the same as waiting for Frank on the tedious evenings when he was at a meeting. Then, there was the certainty that he would soon breeze in, bang the door, fling his briefcase on the stairs, forget to hang up his coat, and give her a kiss. After his election as an MP, if she got fed up during weekdays when he was at Westminster, she could take the train to London and potter round, go to an exhibition or to an afternoon matinée. She had never been one for socialising and did not have a coterie of friends to gossip or have lunch with. The wife of a busy political man had to be circumspect in what she said, but that had suited Gail's shy nature – she had found the noisier public affairs rather a trial.

This was different. The room was empty except for herself, and it would remain empty. The flat had been chosen for its convenience and price, not for its proximity to any acquaintances or family. Without a supreme effort, she would stay alone.

The letter-box rattled. The sound inside her head was of jailers' keys, metallic and threatening. The post would be smaller now, no longer the dozens of fat brown envelopes addressed to Frank that would absorb his entire attention over breakfast and had so irritated her. Some post was still being sent on; these days, the main items were junk mail, from companies that never bothered to update their mailing list. They followed the bottle into the overflowing bin.

Two white envelopes were addressed to her, both with printed addresses. One was from the bank. A reminder, courteous for the moment, to pay an overdue credit card bill. She would have to concede defeat on that one soon, cut the card across, put it in the envelope and mail it back to them. The money dear Mr Maxwell was arranging for her would be needed for expenses, or a rainy day. Frank, she felt bleakly, could not be relied upon to keep up his payments, not with That Woman guarding the cheque book. The other was from the council, asking coolly whether she would confirm that she lived alone since it would entitle her to a discount on her council-tax payments. Gail stared at it, biting her lip. Its thoughtless cruelty took her breath away. She hid it under the wizened apples in the fruit basket.

She filled the coffee machine with water, listlessly folded a filter paper, measured stale ground coffee into the container. To distract herself she flicked once more through the pile of newspapers that lay in a disorganised heap next to it. The headlines – 'Cabinet Minister's Ex-Wife in Desperate Straits' and 'The Public Should Know What A Creep My Husband Is' – should have pleased her, but instead intensified her sense of loss.

Perhaps this furious tirade against her husband and his new wife was a mistake. The old Gail would not have indulged in such petty attempts at revenge. She should

never have sunk so low. Maybe those who said she should
have borne her humiliation in mute dignity had had a point.
But the campaign had its own momentum and was virtually
unstoppable. It gave her grim satisfaction when interview-
ers expressed their sympathy. Besides, it filled her days.

A brown envelope and a small package remained. The
first contained a note from the library in Cheshire about
an overdue book. That went under the apples also. The
package was a battered Jiffy-bag, re-used, the old lettering
covered in obliterating stickers, her own name and address
handwritten in crude capitals. The postcode had been
added in pencil at the sorting office. There was no sender's
name or identification mark. It puzzled her. She let it sit
on the kitchen table for a few minutes as she fetched cereal
and milk from the fridge. After a few spoonfuls she felt
slightly better. She found a pair of scissors, cut across the
end of the package and tipped it up.

What fell out made her recoil in horror.

Two blue razor blades, the old-fashioned kind with
both naked edges sharp and glittering, narrowly missed
her thumb. She yelped and put her fingers into her mouth
as if to protect them, like an infant. Two sheets of paper
followed. A crude sketch of a woman's face, the hair her
own colour and style, primitively drawn, the mouth exag-
geratedly lipsticked and the eyes mere slits. Both cheeks
were slashed crosswise in red ink. And there was a note,
created from bits of newspaper crudely stuck on – one of
the letters fluttered to the floor:

BITCH! KEEP YOUR MOUTH SHUT ABOUT
OUR FRANK. OR IT'LL BE THE WORSE
FOR YOU. NEXT TIME THE SLASHES
WILL BE FOR REAL.

# CHAPTER FIVE

Inspector Stevens had had a bad day, although it was only ten o'clock in the morning. His fountain pen had leaked in his breast pocket and stained his shirt. The cleaners had knocked the model Porsche 911 off his desk and broken its spoiler. Two of his team had phoned in sick, which left him badly undermanned. He suspected their illnesses had much to do with the international boxing televised in the early hours: both men were keen fans and had probably spent the dawn hours watching together. Chapman was most likely still on Jones's sofa, empty six-packs at his side. It would serve them right if he assigned the pair of them to permanent nights.

Michael Stevens had been a police officer for twenty-six years. On days like this he wondered why he had stayed, then reminded himself that in four years' time he could retire on full pension, on his fifty-fifth birthday. He would be young enough still to enjoy it, unlike men in other professions who had to stick it out another decade, and old enough to be satisfied with a working life spent in uniform in the service of others. Old enough, in fact, to be close to heartily sick of it. With police morale in such a poor state and the Met, in particular, frantic to fill vacancies – it was virtually a force in terminal decline – nobody would blame him for going at the earliest opportunity. Nor could he condemn, in all honesty, those of his officers who preferred a morning lie-in.

Stevens was a tall, rangy man with the thick moustache that had been the hallmark, in his day, of the Metropolitan Police officer. The sideboards were greying at the edges, the jowls sometimes sagged after a late call, but he would be fit and capable for some years yet. The deep-set eyes shadowed by shaggy brows imposed a headmasterly air, belied by a mild manner and a passion for fast cars that he could not afford. Cars! Speed! That was why he had been tempted to join the police in the first place, and why he cultivated the friendships of car dealers, ignoring their sometimes shady operations in the faint hope that some day they might put a cheap second-hand roadster in his path. It hadn't happened yet and probably never would. But a man could dream.

Outside his window came a commotion. Somebody was shouting. 'Sarge! Sarge!'

Stevens hauled up the window and stuck out his head. Around him and in the opposite building other faces appeared. 'What's up?' he called down.

'Bloody thieves!' came back a yell from a young PC below. 'Look!'

Stevens craned to see. Cars and vans were parked neatly in rows, ready to be booked out on duty. The lack of staff meant more were there than usual. For a moment he could see nothing amiss.

The constable, dancing with rage, pointed under one of the fast response vehicles, a nearly new black Subaru Impreza Turbo WRX, a performance motor that Stevens himself had recommended. Two others were parked in a far corner. The inspector saw, with a nasty lurch in his stomach, that all three cars were resting tidily on their axles.

'Fucking nicked the wheels, haven't they?' The constable waved his arms in impotent fury. 'Cheeky buggers!'

Stevens withdrew his head and pulled down the window. 'Fulda High Performance – two hundred quid apiece for the rubber alone,' he muttered gruffly to himself. 'No wonder the budget's gone through the roof.'

A knock came on the door. The desk sergeant peered tentatively round. 'Sorry to bother you. Don't worry about that racket outside. We'll sort it. They haven't touched your vehicle, sir. This is something else. There's a lady here, insists on seeing the most senior officer. Won't deal with me or anybody else.'

Stevens sighed. 'Bloody 'ell. You sure? Try your charm on her, Ron. I've got reports to do. I can't spend my time listening to moans about the neighbour's cat.'

'We've tried. It isn't a neighbour complaint. At least, I don't think so. She's a name.'

'A name?'

'Yeah.' The sergeant grinned. 'A VIP, you could say. Anyway, I've other members of our esteemed public queuing downstairs at my desk. Plus some wheels to order. Shall I show her in?'

Gail twitched her skirt about her knees and tried to sit up straight. She was familiar with police stations. Years ago, newly wed, she had hung around in the canteen of more than one, waiting for Frank to go off duty. If she stayed at home he would disappear with his mates or informants for a quick pint that would turn into three hours' drinking. The dinner would be burned and her pride with it. Eventually, however, Frank had pointed out testily that she was in danger of making a fool of him. Nobody else's missus played wallflower like that. It was undignified. With a few tears she had accepted her fate and stayed in, becoming an expert at speedy meals. The sense of isolation that had resulted was similar to her feelings now.

'I've come to report an offence,' she blurted out. The envelope was in her hands, wrapped crudely in a plastic carrier-bag. 'Careful. There could be fingerprints on it.'

Stevens glanced at her, surprised. He withdrew his hands, then pressed a bell under the desk. 'Then we'd better have *it* examined properly, Mrs Bridges. Whatever *it* is.'

The sergeant entered, listened to Stevens' whisper, disappeared and returned with a packet of surgical gloves. The inspector sat back as the sergeant donned the gloves and gingerly shook the bag's contents out on to the desk.

'See!' exclaimed Gail. She felt herself go white and bit her lip to get a grip on herself.

'What have we here?' Stevens whistled under his breath. He used a pencil to poke at the razor blades, turning over the drawing and the letter. He studied the items for a long moment, then put down the pencil and pressed his fingertips together. 'Now, Mrs Bridges, weren't you on television a few days ago? Our civilian clerk said she'd seen you. And I caught a few clips on the news. You've been having problems, haven't you?'

'Oh, yes,' said Gail eagerly. 'I've been having a terrible time. I don't think anyone appreciates it. You can't know how it feels, to be publicly humiliated like that. Told in public that I'm to be discarded, like an old coat. Replaced by a newer model. As if he could keep up with *her* – thinks he's a new man himself, I dare say. She'll find out, she will. Won't take long. After everything I've done for him, all those years when he left me alone in the evenings . . .'

The two men sat impassive. Her voice trailed away and

she fidgeted with her handbag. 'Sorry. It gets me. You only want to know about the package.'

Stevens nodded. Gail described its delivery and her horrified reaction. 'I didn't hesitate. I knew you'd need to see it at once. Then you can arrest Frank.'

'We can what?' The sergeant's eyes rounded.

'Arrest my husband. It's from him. It must be.'

'And how do you figure that out?' The inspector kept his voice mild.

'Well, it's obvious, isn't it? I've thought and thought about it. He doesn't like me talking about him. He wants me to stop. Mr Clifford Maxwell says I should reveal the truth and not be intimidated, but my Frank is aware that I'm bad news for his precious career. And for that marriage. Though it's so rocky, it won't take months before falling apart. She'll find out. He's all piss and wind, isn't he?' Gail paused, panting slightly, startled at her own fierceness.

She had not meant to sound such a harridan. In the back of her mind doubt niggled. It was not possible that Frank, or anybody she had rubbed shoulders with, could perpetrate such an atrocity, was it? But someone had done it, someone who meant her harm. Who else could it be, if not him? Who else had anything to gain by her enforced reticence?

'Is this the politician Frank Bridges we are referring to, madam?' the sergeant asked officiously. His eyes were hostile.

'Certainly. There is only one. Mr High and Mighty. Yes.'

'The former police officer?'

'The same. I only wish he'd stayed in the force. At least then he was doing something worthwhile. Now he rides around in a limousine with a posh new wife and I'm not good enough for him.' There was a pricking at the back of her eyes. *Oh, God, don't let me cry*, she thought desperately.

'Can I fetch you a cup of tea?' The sergeant had switched tack. 'I'll see if there's a fingerprint bod about. I think the detectives are out. We could get this, ah, evi-dence checked now.'

'Yes, thank you.' Gail's tears subsided as the sergeant went out, the carrier-bag in his gloved hands. She glanced down at her own, noticed dully that her nails were dirty and cracked, the cuticles ragged.

'Mrs Bridges.' The inspector's voice was measured and calm. Gail looked up hopefully. 'I'm sorry you've had such an upset. It's a horrible experience to receive hate mail like this, especially when you're not used to it.'

'We did have it once or twice in the past, when Frank was first involved in politics – funnily enough when he was sorting out that dreadful strike. Then we had nasty stuff pushed through the letter-box. And threats.'

'Like that?' The inspector jerked his head towards the door.

'Yes,' Gail agreed, encouraged by the tone of the

questioning. 'Very similar. The product of a warped mind, I suppose. Or somebody under enormous pressure. Frank used to say we shouldn't judge. I'm trying not to.'

'They're usually very stupid people who indulge themselves with such rubbish.'

'Oh, yes, that's right.'

'Not quite what you'd expect from a man of your husband's eminence, though?'

Gail felt cold. If not Frank then a stranger, and that was far more frightening. But surely it was no coincidence that this material should arrive hot on the heels of the adverse publicity she had given him. And at her correct new address. It stood to reason, unpalatable though it might be. 'I can see your point, Inspector. But of course he wouldn't write it himself, would he? I'd spot his handwriting at once. That's why he's used newspaper letter cut-outs.' She paused. 'If it isn't him, then it's somebody he's persuaded to do it. Or paid.'

'Quite the detective, aren't we?' The inspector's eyes strayed to a photograph of himself on the wall, receiving the Queen's Police Medal from the Duke of Gloucester. His glory days were behind him. Outside came more raised voices; he heard the phrase 'missing engine' and closed his ears. 'You should leave those sort of deductions to us. In fairness to your husband, Mrs Bridges, it could have been anyone.'

'It's Frank. I'm sure of it. He wants my silence. He can't buy it, so he's putting the frighteners on me.'

Stevens grunted. 'Do you really believe he's capable of this, Mrs Bridges?'

Gail hesitated under the gaze of the shadowy, intelligent eyes. She was silent for a moment, then held herself rigid. 'Yes,' she said slowly. 'If you'd seen the way he dumped me, in public, without shame, you'd agree he was capable of anything.'

The sergeant returned. 'Nobody about who can help for the present, I'm afraid. But we can take a statement, and your fingerprints.'

'Mine? Why do you have to do that?' Gail clasped her hands.

'In order to eliminate them from our inquiries,' came the sergeant's reply. 'Then we'll be in touch, Mrs Bridges.' He held open the door for her.

The inspector stayed seated as Gail rose jerkily to her feet, but he shook hands with her amiably enough. 'Goodbye, Mrs Bridges. Oh, one more point.'

'Yes?'

'We don't want to encourage this type of nastiness. Don't give anyone ideas. So my advice to you is not to mention it in your interviews. We do get copycat crimes.'

'I see,' Gail said uncertainly.

'And, naturally,' Stevens continued smoothly, 'if it was your husband, or anybody else, we have to avoid pre-trial publicity. So it's best not to say a word.'

'You'll catch him quicker?'

'We're more likely to put him away.'

Gail nodded. 'I'll do my best. But if I'm asked if I've had any comeback from him, it'll be impossible to lie. I have to be able to speak out about these matters. I have to.' She gathered up her bag and followed the sergeant out.

It was some hours later, towards the end of the shift, that the sergeant returned with a closely typed piece of paper. He put it wordlessly on Stevens' blotter and pointed.

'I guessed that might be the case,' the inspector said. 'Only her prints on it, eh?'

'That's it. And loads of them.'

'We could take a DNA sample and check the saliva.'

'The letters are stuck on with Pritt stick. The envelope's done with Sellotape. Somebody with savvy, I'd say, sir.'

'Hmm. Should we get CID to look at it, if only for form's sake?'

The sergeant shrugged. It was common knowledge in the office that Stevens had spent five years on the detective side and had returned to uniform willingly, his opinions of his investigating colleagues somewhat soured. The inspector toyed with a pencil. Then: 'Perhaps not today. She was upset. Got a powerful sense of grievance.'

'If you ask me, she was lucky he stayed that long. She's a bit of a shrew. My sympathies lie elsewhere.'

'I wasn't asking you, Ron. She may have been badly treated, as she claims. The question is, has an offence been committed here?'

'My considered opinion is, no.'

'She did it herself?'

'Makes sense, sir. Though we must keep an open mind.'

'Indeed. Poor woman. But it figures. He *was* one of us, wasn't he?'

# CHAPTER SIX

'I loathe Brighton. I detest the Grand Hotel. I hate the conference season.'

Pansy Illingworth, editor in chief of the *Globe*, was holding forth. Jim Betts sniffed in mournful solidarity and offered her another cigarette. They were slouched on stools in the Grand's grandest bar. It was early yet and the bar was not busy. Pansy accepted without thanks, lit it from a flaring lighter and blew out a stream of smoke, tossing back frizzy brown hair in a gesture Betts found irritating. She fidgeted, rubbing her open palm fretfully over skinny thighs in designer suede jeans. The painted nails threatened to tear the soft calfskin.

'Bloody politicians! You'd guess they'd see quite enough of each other while Parliament's sitting without devoting their precious recess to glad-handing the faithful. And in a third-rate seaside resort in the off-season,' she continued. 'Or maybe they agree with our poncy travel editor's opinion that Brighton's *sooo* trendy now. Why can't they meet up in Marbella or Kos?'

'Because they'd have to pay for it themselves,' Betts answered. 'Their fact-finding trips abroad are at taxpay-ers' expense. The more exotic the better. They'll check out satellite installations over Mauritius and the Indian Ocean on our behalf. Or the quality of British aid in the nicer parts of the Amazon basin, followed by a colloquium in Florida. The average backbencher takes four trips a year covering eight thousand miles. Brighton must seem com-fortingly homely after that.'

'It's the grottiest place on earth,' Pansy moaned, as she picked at the edge of a red-tipped nail. 'Cold, dirty and frigging expensive. Marbella would be sunnier *and* cheaper. The booze, especially. Or Amsterdam. Then we could get stoned, legally.'

'We'd lose 'em in the red-light district,' Betts said, with an air of experience. 'They'd vanish into the arms of some voluptuous East European lovely and that'd be that.' He indicated the terrace. 'Some action soon. The Ashworths are expected at six.'

'Tanned and handsome after their honeymoon.' Pansy snickered. 'The golden couple. It'll be interesting to see whether he's a changed man.'

'Now, now, Madam Feminist Editor. Bit of rogering never did anybody any harm.'

Pansy poked him firmly in the chest. 'Don't you get any fancy ideas, Mr Betts. My favourite sleeping partner may not be arriving till Wednesday, but that doesn't mean I'm free tonight. Gotta couple of editorials to write in advance of tomorrow's editions. We have to warn the nation of the full dire implications of the conference speeches.'

'Before they're delivered?'

'Sure. The spin doctors have already informed us what they hope their bosses mean. We'll manufacture a flaming row out of it. Shock! Horror! The delegates will get mighty uppity and demand a vigorous response. By the end of the week we'll be riding high, our every prediction of splits and backstabbing borne out. And if not, we'll keep stirring. That's the game, Jim.'

'Yeah.' Betts dipped a hand into a bowl of peanuts and stuffed them into his mouth. His eyes darted about as delegates began to drift into the bar.

The bartender, a swarthy man with sideburns, sidled over, his eyes drifting to Pansy's crotch. 'Here for the con-ference?'

'Yep. We're with the *Globe*,' Betts announced proudly, and flashed his press badge.

'On the tab, then, is it?'

Pansy smiled sweetly.

The barman began to wipe the bar. 'Conference season – ain't what it was. The Conservatives' gatherings used to be the best.' His eyes went misty. 'Champagne, and put it on the slate, and I say, by Jove, let's have your best whisky! They didn't always pay up, mind, but they had style. Not these days. Tory supporters are mostly doddery old dears who'd like a small sherry. The fellahs that come with 'em are either gay and drink spritzers, or fat and forbidden alcohol by their doctors.'

Betts made a mental note. The conference gossip column was his responsibility. 'What about Labour? They've also seen fashion shifts, haven't they?'

'Not as many as you'd imagine,' the bartender said. 'See, years ago it was in to drink Newcastle Brown with a chaser, or Guinness to demonstrate solidarity with Sinn Fein. That was in the Thatcher era when Ken Livingstone was their hero. Hasn't he done well for himself? In the nineties it was a chilled chardonnay, *dahling*, and guacamole instead of mushy peas, not that they knew the difference. And Bombay mix not peanuts. Now it's back the other way. I have to lay in Tetley's bitter specially. And natter in a Yorkshire accent. Heartlands! That's all you hear from them now, even if they've never been north of Camden.'

Betts choked on his nuts. 'What's it like when the conferences have gone home?'

'Dead. The only money round here is pink.'

'Huh?'

'Gays. Around twenty per cent of Brighton male residents are gay, according to the mayor. Even the local Tory candidate's that way inclined, official. I do a couple of shifts weekends in the Pink Elephant club down Ship Street. Gotta complete set of black rubber gear for it.' He put a hand on his hip and wiggled suggestively.

'Interesting. You that way inclined yourself?' Betts could not help asking. In a bondage get-up the bartender, a fleshy man, would be a sight for sore eyes. Then he realised that this might be mistranslated as a pass, and flushed scarlet.

The man smirked down at Pansy's suede thighs. 'Me? Nah. I keep my backside pressed well up against the bar, believe me. It's all in a day's work, isn't it?'

He was called away to the other beer pumps. Betts's and Pansy's eyes met, and they both giggled. 'A fresh twist on a dirty weekend in Brighton,' he said *sotto voce*, and reached once more for the bowl.

'I shouldn't, Jim,' she chided. 'You don't know who's been handling those nuts. Especially given the conversation we've just had.'

'Come again?' he said, fist halfway to his mouth.

Pansy slid elegantly off the bar-stool and collected her bag. 'You don't read your own newspaper. Didn't you see the research,' she said coolly, 'in our *Modern Life* section, which showed that the first thing many chaps do after they've been for a leak is plunge their smelly paws into the peanuts?'

Christine passed the clothes brush briskly over his jacket and tweaked the shoulder seams to vertical. 'This is a very important dinner,' she reminded her husband, who waited impassively. Not to resist had been best with his mother; it was becoming a useful tactic for dealing with his wife. He patted the folded silk handkerchief in his breast pocket.

She stood back. 'You know, I'm not sure this double-breasted suit is quite you,' she murmured, as if the observation slipped naturally into her briefing on the dinner. 'Are you absolutely certain the tailor is a supporter?'

'He claimed to be, yes,' Benedict answered, and set her aside gently so that he could check in the mirror. 'It's okay, isn't it?'

'I'm not sure. I wonder if he's played a trick on us,' she said. 'The two extra buttons. They're positioned over your nipples. Stick your chest out and you'll see.'

Benedict twisted this way and that, then chuckled. 'You're right, but is it so obvious? Does it make me look a prat?'

Christine considered. 'We'll give it to Madame Tussaud's for your waxwork. Their visitors are mostly foreigners and don't care who you are, so it won't matter. You're into single-breasted suits from here on.'

'Thank you, darling.' Benedict bent to kiss her, a half-smile on his lips. 'I'm so glad to have you with me. I would never have noticed anything like that.'

'These little touches are significant,' she ploughed on, peeved that he lacked the appropriate indignation. 'When the public see you striding into the room in a jacket that's a mite too fitting, with buttons flashing over your bosoms, your dignity is diminished. They don't quite know *why* they infer you're a bit lightweight, but they do. A dodgy impression like that is hard to eradicate once established.'

'And that's what you do so brilliantly. For me, and for your profession. Spot the little touches. You're so clever.'

Christine cast him a sharp glance. There were times when Benedict's dry levity was not appreciated. 'Anyway, this dinner,' she continued. 'Three big donors are on the guest list. One's from a dot com company who sold out at the peak and now feels guilty about it so he's pledged the party a quarter of a million. Only he hasn't written the cheque yet. One's the grandson of Jo Grimond, doesn't like what happened to that lot, and has switched to us. The third provided us with transport at election time. His company's going down the pan and he's convinced we're anti-European, so don't disabuse him of that notion, will you?'

'Why exactly did he help us, then?' Benedict undid his tie and started to refix it, with a looser knot, as a louche antidote to the offending buttons.

'The last government stopped building motorways, this lot are trying to tax the internal combustion engine out of existence, the Greens want everything ferried about by push-bike. How they'd pay for the NHS, then, God knows. You might explore the inherent contradiction of an Exchequer so dependent for revenue on what they're trying to diminish, though I'm not sure your host is intellectually up to it. We're not anti anything on wheels, though we favour an integrated transport system.'

'Which means what?'

Christine frowned, as if she were being set a test question. 'There's a policy paper in the folder somewhere. The buzz words are about buses and trains connecting with each other, getting the trains moving again. Nobody could object, anyway.'

'But it's hardly earth-shattering,' Benedict remarked, almost to himself. 'It sounds sensible, and that's about it. Between John Major's cones hotline and New Labour's New Deal, nobody has big ideas any more, do they?'

'The nitty-gritty of everyday life is what wins votes.'

'Is that so? I wonder.' Benedict broke away from her, tossed his notes on to the bed and began to pace about. 'Bus and train timetables are not what I came into politics for. And I bet they bore the pants off the electorate: that's why the turnout's so low.'

'But what else are governments at Westminster to do?' Christine allowed herself to sound exasperated. 'Think about it. Most business is global and run from Seattle or Singapore. The currency, even the poor old pound, is subject to the whim of international bankers who never go near a ballot box. The economy runs itself, more or less. That's fine by most people. The profession they don't trust is politicians.'

'Maybe that's because we persist in debating the number of angels who can dance on a pinhead. We seem to lack confidence to attempt anything big. The great issues of life and death, where are they? How come they always get pushed to the back of the agenda and we never reach them? Why is everything we have to deal with *so trivial*?'

Christine stood stock still and opened her mouth, but Benedict persisted, not letting her interrupt. 'Last century, the creation of the National Health Service was a huge upheaval in politics. So is war: that's why prime ministers can't resist bombing other countries, whether Iraq or Kosovo. But the big deal today? Slagging off the other parties at Prime Minister's Question Time for a bit of point-scoring. No wonder our continental cousins are bewildered. What happened to the great-leap-forward mentality we used to have?'

Christine stared. 'For heaven's sake, don't start wittering on at this dinner about the need to join the euro.' Benedict flinched. Her voice softened. 'It's our job to inject the glamour. Real politics *is* boring, if that's what you're implying. But personalities are exciting, and voters can relate to them. That's why we did so well in the election.'

'Because we said very little of substance, but we said it beautifully?' Benedict's face was flushed. 'Didn't that spin doctor Melvyn O'Connor protest that debating with us was like trying to nail jelly to the ceiling?'

'You could do worse,' Christine said tartly. 'You could be on the receiving end, instead of dishing it out. Imagine trying to pin the Prime Minister down on anything.

Except maybe on how to enlarge one's family. Now remember, be nice to the sponsors, and for heaven's sake don't tell them what you truly believe about Europe or they'll take fright.'

The bar was filling up. A group of five men and a woman walked in, found a table and sat down. The tallest, a giant of six foot four in a cut-down T-shirt, was deputed to buy the round. Five and a half pints of lager fitted easily into his massive fists. Soon the group was huddled deep in conversation, attracting no interest from fellow drinkers.

'You brought your uniforms?' The leader was a solid, clean-shaven man the others addressed as Steve.

Nods came from everyone present, except the woman. She had straight blue-black hair cut in a bob across her forehead and was heavily made-up with green eye-shadow and glutinous black mascara. The crimson lipstick matched the close-fitting wool dress that curved over a substantial bosom and hefty hips. She crossed black-stockinged legs defiantly. 'Not marching as a Rifle Regiment lance-corporal, am I?' she answered, in a gruff voice.

'Honestly, Letitia, that's the whole idea,' Steve reasoned with her. 'We're none of us supposed to be in uniform, not now we've been drummed out of the forces. That's what the protest is about, isn't it? Our demand for reinstatement.'

'I'm with you all the way, Steve,' Letitia shot back. 'I'm

as entitled to compensation as you are. But I've been living as a woman for eighteen months now and I love it. I'm not going back into trousers.'

'Nobody wants you to, love.' The gentle giant who had fetched the drinks put a hand on her arm. His voice was as deep as hers, but with a softer burr. 'It's to make a stand. You were mentioned in despatches. You've got your medals from Northern Ireland and Bosnia. You should be out there, flashing them.'

'I'd rather be flashing these.' Letitia uncrossed and recrossed her well-muscled legs.

'They do have females in that regiment now,' Steve pointed out.

'Yes, but I don't have a female uniform,' she retorted, swift as a cat.

The committee was sunk in gloom for a few moments and drank their beer quietly. Giant broke in. 'How's your ma?' he asked Steve.

The leader brightened. 'She's great. So proud of me you'd think I was still firing off ground-to-air missiles instead of earning my keep as a part-time computer programmer,' he answered. 'She keeps yelling, "Don't take the ten thousand! You're entitled to a lot more."'

'She's dead right,' another member of the group joined in. He was nattily dressed in a suit, a briefcase by his side. 'We should never have been sacked. Not for our orientation alone. That violated our human rights. We're entitled to reinstatement with full restoration of privileges and rank, or failing that, compensation. *And* interest.' The man, evidently a lawyer, smiled smugly.

'Ten grand would be nice, though,' Letitia said wistfully. 'My operation's going to cost a packet.'

'Can't you get it on the NHS in your area?' Giant asked sympathetically.

'Oh, they're *butchers*,' came the answer with a shudder. 'You don't know what it's like. You lot want to keep your dangly bits. I can't *wait* to get rid of mine. But I want a tidy job, and something functional instead. *And* beautiful.' She crossed her legs again, this time defensively.

More drinks were fetched. The group continued to talk in low voices. 'How many are we expecting, then?' Giant inquired.

'Couple of hundred, we hope,' Steve answered briskly. 'It'll make a good show. Coaches are coming from Aldershot, Stafford and even Catterick. The girls are laying on about fifty, mainly Quarancs and Wrens, Stonewall are sending the rugby team and there'll be backup from local Gay Pride – they've promised a marching band, though God knows what they can play. A selection from Gilbert and Sullivan, most like.'

'"*Three little maids from school . . .*"' the lawyer warbled mischievously. Giant dug a warning elbow into his ribs.

'Nobody from Scotland, more's the pity,' Steve continued.

'Yeah, well, up there they still assume every jock in a

skirt is a raving hetero,' came a gloomy comment in a Dumfries accent.

'You told your mum, yet, Duncan?' Giant asked.

The Scotsman shook his head. 'Nah. Probably never will. It's not her that's the problem. It's me dad. It'd kill him. And then he'd kill me. When I'm home I have to pretend I'm away chasing the lassies and simply haven't been caught by one yet. I talk to him about tits and bums like an old pro. You'd be impressed.'

The conversation drew to a fitful close. Letitia mollified the rest of the committee by offering to carry the heaviest banner provided she could do it as a woman. Loath to practise against any of their number the discrimination each had suffered too often, it was agreed. Letitia rose and picked up her coat. 'I need a gentleman to escort me to my hotel,' she announced loftily. 'Any volunteers?'

Giant glanced longingly at the bar, then uncoiled himself to his full height, immediately dominating the room. Heads turned, took in the bull neck, the rippling triceps and biceps bulging from the T-shirt, whispered and turned away.

The crowd parted and he began to move, arms swinging naturally as he had been trained years before as a boy soldier, legs striding smooth from the pelvis, the paratrooper's classical testosterone-laden swagger. Behind him teetered the lady on high-heeled shoes, wig slightly askew, her nose up. Flakes of face-powder fluttered in the air as she passed. Astonished eyes followed them through the lobby, out into the foyer and seafront. Then the bartender made a brief obscene remark, the watchers dissolved into laughter and the bar became noisy once more.

Betts punched the *answer* button on his phone. 'Yeah?'

'Jim?'

'Yeah. Who's this?' Betts was too far gone to interpret the caller's number on the mobile's face, even if it had been light enough to do so.

'Melvyn. Melvyn O'Connor. Your old mate.'

'Yeah, Melvyn. Whatcha got for me?' Betts snapped his eyes open and reached for a Biro. It wasn't late, but triple brandy and Benedictines were guaranteed to send him to bed in a stupor.

'Andrew. Andrew Marquand. You're aware of the rumours about him?'

'I can reel off a few. Mostly to do with his supposed celibate state, and having loads of young male students when he was a university lecturer. You gonna confirm they're true?'

'Nah, Jim.' Melvyn's reply held a note of triumph. 'The opposite. Can you arrange for your chaps to be at the Mirabelle Thursday at around nine?'

'The Mirabelle, eh? Candlelight and sweet music, gypsy violinist, the lot? Have you set up a seduction scene?'

Melvyn's voice became suspicious. 'Who told you? It's supposed to be my secret. I've been working on it for weeks.'

'Have you, by Jove. You'll get the credit, I'll make sure of that. So who's the lucky girl? Are we entitled to advance info?'

Melvyn became coy. 'That's for me to know, and you to find out, Jim. But I can confirm that they're very close, and have been seeing a lot of each other. I understand — obviously I can't confirm this — that she was spotted examining engagement rings in Hatton Garden last week. Maybe this is the big night.'

Betts spluttered. 'You aren't hinting that Andrew, who has never in over forty years of his life so far shown the least interest in a woman, is about to get hitched? Pull the other one, Melvyn. It's hard enough to swallow Benedict bloody Ashworth getting his leg over that statuesque Christine. Why can't they simply admit they're homos and get on with it?'

'Because you'd make mincemeat of them, that's why,' Melvyn answered huffily. 'In Andrew's case it doesn't apply. I can assure you of that, definitely. It's simply that he's been too busy to have a social life. When you're running the country, romance has to take second place.'

'Now tell me,' said Betts, writing furiously and hoping he would be able to decipher the scribble in the morning, 'what kind of job does this young lady do? She is young, I take it? Or are we stalking a second Camilla here?'

'Oh, yes, she's young,' Melvyn agreed hastily. 'She has her own company.'

'She wouldn't be in PR, by any chance?'

'She might. How did you guess?' Melvyn allowed himself a snicker. 'But you'll fix it, Jim, it's too hot to miss. Terrific pictures for your daily editions, more for the Sundays. And a soft-centred human image for my master. Who could ask for more?'

There were moments, Alistair McDonald fumed, when he wondered whether those who opted to work in the media had to pass an examination in stupidity.

'The Prime Minister,' he said icily, to the BBC girl radio reporter, 'is about to make a speech to the Foreign Press Association over lunch. Yes, it is set to coincide with the speech of the social security spokesman for the New Democrats at their conference in Brighton, but no, we don't believe that's a nuisance as nobody will be listening to the bugger anyway. Theirs, I mean, not ours.'

The young woman blinked away tears. She was employed by *Countryfile*, not the lunchtime news. 'But I haven't got a copy of the speech,' she wailed.

'That's because you weren't here for the lobby briefing this morning,' he grated.

'But I'm not lobby—'

'I can't help that. You should have asked your lobby people.'

'Oh, I couldn't. I'm so lowly they wouldn't notice if they tripped over me. I've only got a pass for Pebble Mill. Though they are brilliant,' she added hastily. Then,

'Maybe you could give me the gist of what the Prime Minister's going to say?'

'Actually,' said McDonald frostily, 'if you turn on digital TV right now they are covering the whole speech. You can listen, and find out for yourself.'

'Oh, gimme a break,' the girl pleaded. 'I've got to file in ten minutes. What's he saying, and what does it mean?'

McDonald gazed down stonily. 'Do you want me to write it for you, word for word?'

She gasped in delight. 'Oh, would you? Yes, please . . .'

Benedict stood pensively at the hotel window. It had been a successful conference, so far, if adulation from the delegates was any guide. The worry he had felt when mounting the platform on the first occasion as their new Leader had turned out quite unnecessary, as Christine had assured him it would be. The former Leader had been welcomed with a bear-hug and many expressions of honour, but then had been gently set aside. The silvery-haired man had brought them closer to victory; now it was time to move on, to face the future eagerly with Benedict and his charming bride. Indeed, the cheers for Christine had been louder than for anybody else on the platform.

His wife had adored it. She had basked in the warmth of that moment, had smiled shyly then blown the assembly a brief kiss. The delegates, mostly much older, adored her back. They loved her youth and beauty, they drank in the hope of vigour and new life she seemed to offer them. How fortunate he was to have her by him. How utterly competent she was, in everything that mattered.

The offending suit was back in the suitcase, the tailor's name crossed off the Christmas-card list. Brighton's Austin Reed shop had been delighted to furnish the visiting politician with two mid-range suits made in England and had been pleased that he was photographed buying them by the local, and national, press.

On one matter Benedict had resisted Christine's advice. She had urged him to have a different haircut, to remove the wispy locks that covered his ears. A Bruce Willis close shave, she said, might appear more manly. At this Benedict had jibbed, saying, with the full force of reason, that since he was not Action Man by nature nor a character from *Die Hard*, to pretend would promptly be exposed as hypocritical. Since the whole point of image-making was to reinforce and advertise strong qualities, preferably those the subject actually possessed, an aggressive masculinity on his part would be both inappropriate and unsustainable. *No*, in other words. And on that, he had won, though he suspected only temporarily.

Christine was out, trailing round a maternity hospital, an invitation he had been glad to pass on to her. She would return in an hour, saying little but with a wistful glint in her eye. When the Prime Minister's wife was so blatantly fecund, the lack of babies *chez* Ashworth had to be explained away. Benedict swallowed hard. Tonight, there would be no excuses. The setpiece speeches had been well received. The sponsors' dinner had passed without incident. She would have spent hours gazing in wonder at maternal lumps and scans of pulsing foetuses. Tonight he would *have* to perform.

It was close to dusk. From outside the open window came snatches of music, the remains of some march or demonstration that was breaking up for the evening. He could hear a jazz-style trumpet being blown with energy – 'When The Saints Come Marching In' –a trombone following with less skill, a cornet bringing up the rear, a bass drum booming. It was always unwise to stick one's head out to stare. *Paparazzi* were on the alert, aware of which room was his. But he could peek from behind the curtains.

The straggling march was coming to a halt. The banner that read 'Rank Outsiders' had been pelted with eggs and tomatoes, but was still held aloft, though out of the vertical, by a bizarre figure in a red dress, tights and high heels, but with a shorn head and grossly exaggerated makeup, as if it had started out done up to the nines as a female. A stubborn rictus distorted the individual's face as he, or she, struggled to keep the weighty banner upright. At a signal from someone behind, however, the banner was at last allowed to droop and rested in a tangled heap on the pavement. The standard-bearer rubbed a beringed hand over stiff shoulders and over the naked pate.

Behind him stood ranks of men and women in military uniform. Benedict noted the khaki, brown and blue of the army and air force, and three young men in sailors' whites. They were attracting more than their share of wolf whistles from a small crowd. In front marched two naval officers, braid gleaming in the dying sun. The girls were mainly short and butch, except for the androgynous banner-holder.

As Benedict peeped cautiously, keeping himself hidden, a youth emerged from the crowd clutching what looked like a black cat; but it was lifeless, and Benedict realised it was a scalp of silky hair. Tentatively, the boy held it out to the shorn man who took it, turned it over, shook it out then set it on his head and straightened it with a defiant tug. Instantly he was transformed into a female, admittedly one who might have been dragged through a hedge backwards, but with vestiges of verve and femininity. The gaggle behind broke into a ragged cheer. The youth, emboldened, stepped forward and kissed the banner-holder's cheek. The supporters laughed, relaxed, and applauded. The youth took his place quietly beside them. Then the marchers began to break away into groups and disappeared towards the seafront pubs.

Upstairs in his hotel room, Benedict was also clapping his hands together but softly, making no noise. His face was ashen, and his eyes were half closed as if in pain.

'Is this the restaurant?'

Betts consulted his notes. 'The Mirabelle. Yeah.'

The photographer shifted the bag from one shoulder to

another, reached inside, took out a camera and screwed on a zoom lens. 'Spending freely, isn't he? You can't get away with a dinner for two here light of a hundred and fifty quid.'

'Well, it's the new government, innit? Paying themselves a hundred grand a year. He can afford it.'

'Didn't you say it was a set-up? He's probably putting the bill on the promotion budget of his department.'

'We can check it out later. But not even he'd be that dumb.'

'Don't be so sure,' the photographer mumbled, his mouth busy tearing the foil from a fresh film. 'Can't you imagine the conversation? Him, stiffly, "I'll do it if you absolutely insist. But I'm not paying for it."'

'You're a cynic, Jack. Not all politicians are like that,' Betts chided. He shivered and pulled up his jacket collar.

The photographer snapped the back of his camera shut, pressed a button and heard the film whir into place. 'None of them hold a candle to Lady Thatcher,' he answered doggedly. 'She wouldn't have gone in for a lark like this. We ought to have her back, pronto. The country's gone to the dogs without her.'

'She's history,' said Betts testily. 'Silly old bag. Mad as a hatter. If she were dining here tonight with some decrepit old paramour, it wouldn't even be news. You ready?'

The two men pushed open the door and began to saunter towards the far corner where Betts had been warned to expect his quarry. The restaurant was dimly lit and almost full. Suddenly their way was barred by a portly man in a striped waistcoat. 'Good evening, gentlemen. Do you have a reservation?'

'Reservation? Nah, we're not here to dine,' said Betts stuffily. The wondrous odours of garlic, olive oil and shallots made his nose wrinkle none the less. With some difficulty he could make out the Marquand table thirty feet away complete with lit candles, a half-empty bottle of French wine and a soup-plate filled with a cascade of rare beef and pimento. Plus the apparently embarrassed girlfriend. Fiona, that was her name. From this distance she was quite impressive; he might make contact with her himself. Perhaps she'd prefer an award-winning journalist with a fund of hilarious stories to some useless government twat who hadn't the least intention of a night in the hay. At a nearby table *sans* candles or wine sat Melvyn with the bodyguard, the latter stiff and uncomfortable, a glass of beer untouched before him.

'Then I'm sorry, gentlemen. I'll have to show you out.' The portly man called loftily over his shoulder. 'Luigi? Some help required here.' From an alcove emerged another, bulkier individual with the air of a bruiser. The two barred their way.

The photographer lifted his camera to his face and began to focus. Betts could see Melvyn half rise.

'No! I'm sorry, you'll have to leave!' The *maître d'* made a grab at the camera while Luigi took a menacing step.

'But we're here by arrangement—' Betts protested.

'Not with us, you're not,' the *maître d'* concluded grimly and seized Betts by the arm. 'Now, be off or I'm calling the police.'

With yelps and protests the gentlemen of the press were bundled outside and the door slammed firmly shut against them. Other diners craned their necks to see through the smoked-glass panes, then sniffed, patted their jewellery and returned to their seared lobster and pan-fried barracuda. As he picked himself up Betts could see two fingers being lifted in his direction by the grimacing Luigi.

'Bloody 'ell,' the photographer muttered, examining his camera for signs of damage. 'Frigging maniacs. A wasted evening. I could've been watching Chelsea on the telly. I tell you, it'd never have happened in Mrs T's day.'

They started to trudge disconsolately down the road. They had gone barely fifty yards when the restaurant door was flung open and Melvyn could be seen, yelling and waving his arms. 'Come back! Come back! It's all a mistake. You're welcome, honest . . .'

# CHAPTER SEVEN

Inspector Stevens sucked his teeth and cursed that he had allowed his better nature to prevail. He had been feeling guilty until he came into the flat. Guilty, because of the nagging worry at the back of his mind that perhaps he should have treated this complaint with far more seriousness, should have called in Special Branch or CID.

If the lady concerned had still been the wife of a VIP there would have been no question. Had she been the wife of a known villain he would have handed the case over, pronto, conscious of the aggravation such individuals could cause. But with vacancies at the current level, car thieves cocking a snook at them in their own back yard and the pressure on to compile the force statistics by the end of the month, other priorities had necessarily prevailed. His gut instinct, like the sergeant's, was that no offence had been committed. Police officers of long experience could tell. To devote a ton of scarce resources to proving the obvious was a negation of his duty. But he had, none the less, felt obliged to pay the visit himself.

He should have sent his sergeant, whose bluff manner concealed no great brain but whose compassion for the victims of crime was limitless and delicately expressed. Stevens himself could be sympathetic, but knew his limits. Boredom and exasperation would inevitably intervene.

Gail Bridges was seated in an old armchair, a crumpled heap of tissue screwed up in her hand, her face doleful. From the kitchen came the unmistakable smell of a blocked drain; through the door he could see unwashed crockery piled high in the sink. As he politely removed his leather gloves and cap, Stevens could not help reflecting that if this woman stopped feeling sorry for herself long enough to clean up her flat and apply some makeup, her whole outlook on life might improve – she must once have been quite attractive. It would certainly make his own task easier. There came unbidden the unworthy reflection that he could almost see why her husband had left her for someone else. 'I'm sorry,' he could hear himself saying.

'No action?' she repeated. 'But a crime's been committed. A very serious crime.'

'Ah, yes. The trouble is, Mrs Bridges, there isn't much for us to go on. No fingerprints or DNA, for example. We have tried.'

'But you've got a motive,' Gail wailed. 'He wants to scare me! Why don't you arrest him?'

'Mrs Bridges.' Stevens could feel his temper rising and fought to control it. 'A motive is not sufficient. Before we can put a case to the Crown Prosecution Service, we need to have a reasonable chance of obtaining a conviction. Otherwise we can be accused of harassment. Your husband has rights too, you know.'

Gail blinked. She held herself rigid, but her hands fluttered as if escaping from her control. 'It seems to me, Inspector, that he's the only one who does. Nobody seems to consider *my* needs. When I was his wife, people like you couldn't do enough for me. Now I feel like a non-person.'

The inspector pressed together the leather gloves, stroking them as if for comfort. The odour from the kitchen made him want to blow his nose. 'I could get Victim Support to talk to you, if you like,' he offered lamely.

'At least that would recognise that I am a victim,' Gail said. 'But no, thanks. What I'd like to hear is how I'm to get justice. *Why* won't you bring a case?'

'Because, as I've explained, we have to be sure we won't make fools of ourselves, or of you. The prosecution like to be fairly certain that they can prove their argument. If your husband, or anybody else, were to bring a claim for wrongful arrest it can cost a packet in compensation.'

'Not to speak of your prospects of promotion, I suppose.' But Gail's faint attempt at sarcasm fell on deaf ears.

Stevens was unlikely to rise more than one rung up the ladder before retirement, which, on days like this, could not come too soon.

She was silent for a moment, picking at the ball of tissue until bits began to detach themselves like confetti and litter the floor at her feet. 'I can't just leave it. Tell me honestly, Inspector, what would be my chances if I brought a private prosecution?'

'You could try,' he answered cautiously, 'but I really wouldn't recommend it. Not least because if we haven't any evidence neither have you. And, most importantly, you have to establish that a crime has been committed in the first place.'

She stared at him, blinking, for a whole minute. He could hear the tick of an unseen clock, but otherwise the flat was quiet. Then, slowly, 'You all believe I did it myself, don't you? That I'm off my rocker or something?'

'No, no, not at all,' he started to say, but she had jumped out of the chair and lunged at him, as if to strike at his face. He tried not to flinch. She was muttering, 'You think I'm some sort of nutter! Christ, you're as bad as my husband. You're all the same. All in this together!'

Then she fell back into the armchair, hugging herself, her mouth working emptily. It seemed to Stevens that this unhappy woman was suffering from too little sleep, that her vision of events was distorted by her misery and isolation. She needed, as his mother might have said, to get out more. But he was a police officer, not a social worker.

He stood in front of her, trying to produce some soothing remark, and failing. When she refused to meet his eye again he shrugged, gave up and let himself out, though his step down the staircase was heavier than it had been when he arrived.

It was not a good day for the decorator. Christine sighed. It was not the best week, to put it mildly, not when tomorrow was the State Opening of Parliament.

Benedict was closeted in his study with Lawrence, preparing his speech in answer to the Gracious Address. That required second-guessing what the Queen would say, and how the Prime Minister would open the debate. For days the media had been filled with tantalising snippets. The efforts of Number Ten to massage the news, to dampen down expectations or keep secrets for the big day, had been frustrated by the eagerness of certain Cabinet members to be seen as having faced an impossible battle and winning against the odds. So the nation was aware that the Environment Secretary had fought a fierce rearguard action against the Treasury and by his own account (filtered through his press office) had emerged triumphant. That meant Frank Bridges would be piloting a lengthy bill this session to privatise the London Underground, much against the wishes of the travelling public and his own party stalwarts. The Treasury should have been delighted at the prospect, since the Tube ate money; but sweeteners agreed at late night meetings to induce private investors to take on the ramshackle system would gobble up the whole of the reserve for the next two years, so the Chancellor was gloomy.

It was relatively easy for an opposition leader to poke fun in such circumstances, especially since Benedict was not required to come up with an alternative. He could claim sincerely to be speaking for the people. The *Globe* editorial had already launched into a tirade against the proposals. If he could discomfort the government front bench, he would score. Christine could hear bursts of laughter from the study as Benedict and Lawrence dreamed up another clever quip. The two cousins, politicians to their fingertips and closer than brothers, were in their element. By the sound of it, the process was going famously. She must not be jealous.

But it left her at a loose end on a day when she had to be in the flat. He could have opted to do the writing in his office at the Commons and kept out of her way. The division bell and light were installed over the flat's living room door, but since the House was not sitting, it would not ring. An aide or a secretary might still require his presence for urgent papers or inquiries. She found herself grumbling that, if one of them had to stay at home, he might have offered more firmly to do it. On the other hand, Benedict would have no idea about the bloody decorator, and might have sent the poor woman away confused or upset.

Christine paced around the room, touching items here

and there, picking up books and idly examining dedications to Benedict on the fly-leaves. Several were first editions of publications by friends from college days, mostly politics or history. On her husband's desk, neglected for the moment, was a tentative bid to write his biography. It seemed too soon: yet it took time to get such a volume researched and published. In a year or so it might be handy, as minds started to focus on the election to come.

Christine wondered languidly how politicians managed to stay fresh and engaged, speech after speech, year after year. Of course she was completely committed to Benedict, to his career and to his future. That meant having no doubts about the party he had joined as a student, though it was hard to see why he had chosen this insignificant bunch when Andrew Marquand, the tutor who had been such a mighty influence on him, had wisely entered politics for what had soon become the government party. Marquand had risen rapidly by force of character and intellect, and by backing the current Prime Minister for the leadership against staider names. Marquand was by nature, Christine accepted, a big fish who would always want to swim in the ocean, and who sensed accurately where the tide flowed.

Did that suggest that Benedict preferred to paddle in a smaller pond? Her husband insisted that he had chosen the New Democrats out of conviction, but such considerations seldom entered true political minds. The shrewdest would plan ahead, extrapolate which party was likely to be on the wane, which improving in the polls at about the date that they themselves might be ready to emerge. Andrew Marquand had finessed it beautifully, had spent a useful stretch on the losing side, building experience and a high profile. By this reasoning an ambitious youngster in the late 1970s when Labour was in power was bound to emerge a Tory. Conversely, but by the same process, an emerging tyro in the mid-nineties wouldn't have touched the Tories with a bargepole: New Labour was the coming thing. But Benedict was not like that. He did not calculate to his own advantage. He honestly believed what he said, or appeared to. This was what she loved about him.

It was important to cling to that. Nobody was perfect, human beings least of all. As a guffaw came from behind the study door, Christine moved away discreetly. Benedict's fretfulness about the dearth of big issues seemed to have abated. In there, applying his brain to the delivery of a speech, he was on home territory. With the punters, on television, with his constituents, with party workers he was at ease, warm, friendly, natural. Apparently natural: Christine was aware how much effort it could take to march up to strangers, look them in the eye and shake them engagingly by the hand.

John Major was famous for doing it beautifully, for giving each contact the feeling that, for those few seconds, he or she had the Prime Minister's total attention. There would be a squeeze of the fingers, sometimes repeated.

For the favoured few, the free hand would be pressed on top, a double handshake, the grip firm and convincing. The individual would be left with an indelible impression of the remarkable Major sincerity and niceness, even as exactly the same manoeuvre, with the identical effect, would be on offer further down the line.

The decorator was late. The woman had been recommended for her design skills, not for her punctuality. Perhaps it would help if a few of these dreadful old photographs were taken down – then everyone could see more clearly what she intended. They were so unsuitable for a sophisticated home where guests of quality would be entertained. Benedict was no longer the earnest schoolboy or the university undergraduate; it was inappropriate that so many pictures were from that era. They hinted, possibly, that he was reluctant to grow up. Only the wedding photos, in glorious colour, were new, resplendent in their chased-silver frames.

Chased? Chaste, more like. It was ages since the wedding. In that time, *nothing*. Or nothing much. Christine ran her fingertip over the silvery scrolls and frozen flowers of the showiest frame, the one showing them bending over the register. It was Benedict's favourite. With a stab of pique Christine wondered whether for her husband signing the contract had been the most significant element in the ceremony. If that were so, it was a pity he did not keep his side of the bargain.

It wasn't that he didn't try. For the first few weeks,

during and after the honeymoon, he was naïve in bed but keen. He would strip off willingly enough, and seemed to have no shame in standing naked before her though with a towel in one hand like an infant's security blanket. And he would examine her curiously, eyes roaming over her breasts and belly, and tell her how lovely she was, and what a lucky man he knew himself to be. He would grasp her shoulders and kiss her on the mouth with every sign of pleasure. It was what happened after that. Or, rather, what didn't happen.

If he got an erection, it was only by letting her hold his penis and rub it gently, then with more rhythm, until the lazy thing sluggishly came to life. He would wince if she touched his scrotum, or tried to slip her fingers between his legs. During this interlude his eyes were tight shut. More than once Christine had had the impression that the image Benedict was conjuring up behind those blue-lined lids was not hers. He seemed much happier when it came to her own needs, massaging her with some enthusiasm, and holding her close when the climax came. In fact that activity was carried out with a gritty professionalism, as if, whatever else, he was determined that she should enjoy herself to the full.

But everything failed, night after night, when he tried to insert the modestly erect penis into her vagina, however much they panted and shoved. Within seconds it died, became about as capable of action as a piece of damp flannel. The failure upset him, of that there was no doubt. He would twist away, muttering angrily to himself, and try with his own hand to get it restarted. Once when she had lain on her stomach in despair, he had rolled on to her back and she could feel its hardness; but when he attempted to enter her from behind, it had collapsed.

'It's nerves,' he groaned, and she had accepted the explanation. Or, 'I'm shy – I didn't think I would be with you, but I am.' Or, 'We must have had too much to drink,' usually after only a glass or two of wine. One night he had said, tetchily, 'Not everybody does it brilliantly, you know,' before marching off to the bathroom and locking the door, leaving her aghast.

There had been evenings when they had curled up together in their nightclothes, not bothering to try. Benedict slept better like that than after a session of sexual struggle, when he would moan in restless slumber and wake drenched in sweat. They had learned to cuddle like children: she would lie away from him on her side, her knees tucked into her abdomen, hugging herself, and he would be curled prone behind her, his hands over hers, his shins pressed neatly against her legs, their private parts not touching.

He had not lied to her. He had never had full sex with a woman. He had told her that frankly, and she had found the knowledge intriguing, that she would be the only one. He was not entirely a beginner either, he had led her to believe, but those early experiences had been mere fumblings and had brought no understanding or joy. Indeed, he had been so young they had amounted to abuse, though he did not retain any lasting ill memories or bitterness. Only a yearning for true, unselfish love. When asked who it had been, the answer was a shrug and 'Someone older.'

When she reran the fractured conversations through her mind, she realised with a start that she had assumed that this older person was female. It stood to reason: Benedict was an attractive man, which must have been manifest throughout his youth. She had wondered, but without asking him, whether it might have been one of his mother's friends. Ultra-respectable though Maddie Ashworth herself might be, Christine could imagine no end of fevered matrons scheming to lay their middle-aged paws on the youngster. It was said that nice Mr Major had sown his wild oats with a thirty-three-year-old divorcée, a neighbour, much to the chagrin of his family. The plot of *The Graduate* was not entirely fanciful.

But if that were the case – if Benedict's initiation, however limited, had been with an older woman – that still left a mystery. He could manage everything except penetration, it seemed, but *that* was the object of the exercise. Without it they were, as a married couple, going nowhere. Had Christine been a virgin on her wedding day, she would still be a virgin now.

She shook her head as if to escape these dismal reflections. Determined to get a grip, she removed two of the pictures from the wall and examined them. Both were of college days, ranks of men and a few girls in formal dress posing for an official record. The frame was simple, black and gold, the lettering ornate and filigreed: the name of the university, a coat-of-arms, the faculty and the year. In the middle of the front row, smug in his billowing gown, mortar-board in his lap, sat Andrew Marquand, the youngest head of department that the ancient seat of learning had appointed for a century. When he resigned to stand for Parliament his colleagues had been scandalised. 'You could be Provost one day,' they had told him.

'That's why I'm leaving,' was the reply, which none of them understood.

The back of one picture was loose. Christine poked at it curiously. Something moved beneath her fingers. A piece of paper or thin card had been inserted between the picture and the backing. Using her nails Christine managed to catch hold of it, and pulled it out.

It was another photo, in black and white, far less formal than those that had graced the wall a minute ago. This one showed three men, their chests bared, on a sunny beach. Their arms were flung intimately about each other's shoulders, their hair was ruffled by the breeze. The man to the left of the picture was gawky and unfamiliar; Christine ignored him. In the trio's centre was Marquand, his dark hair wet and tousled and an extraordinary grin on his face. He was being kissed on the cheek by the third young man, clearly for the benefit of the camera.

That third man was Benedict, who looked fresh and

innocent, yet knowing at the same time. And, it had to be confessed, utterly relaxed and very happy.

With a small cry Christine dropped the frame and its contents. It fell awkwardly on to the rug and broke apart at the corners, the black and gold edges flying away from each other. The photographs fluttered and lay still, picture side up. The kiss and the leer on Marquand's lips were there for anyone to see.

'What's the matter, darling?' Benedict emerged from the study, stretching stiffly, Lawrence behind him.

His eyes went at once to the broken frame, then to the empty space on the wall, then to his wife's shocked face. He strode across and picked up the pictures without a word. He made as if to calm her, then seemed to think better of it as she shrank away.

'We'll be another half-hour,' he said, in a low voice, as he ushered Lawrence back into the smaller room. 'Why don't you go over to the House and get something to eat?'

But Christine had already grabbed her coat, and was gone.

# CHAPTER EIGHT

Frank Bridges gazed at his wife's new hat and sighed. 'You'll definitely get noticed in that,' he said, and tried to make his tone complimentary.

Hazel removed the pink silk topper with its oversized silk roses and veil. Balancing it on one finger she twirled it around. 'That's the whole idea,' she announced, with spirit. 'It's rather fetching, don't you think? It'll be in all the papers tomorrow.'

'Yes, but what is *supposed* to be on the front pages, next to the Queen radiant in the Crown Jewels as she emerges from her sodding gold coach, is the PM and his wife. Wreathed in smiles. Her with her enormous pregnant bump. If his luck holds she'll deliver the blinkin' baby right there, in front of everybody. They're the ones who are supposed to look fetching, not us.'

'Oh, come on.' Hazel fitted the hat roguishly on her head and began to pirouette. 'You're taking loyalty a bit far. It'll be a big plus for the government if other members of it beside the Boss and his sprouting spouse are in the height of fashion. What would you prefer – a cloth cap?'

'It might be cheaper,' Frank muttered. He was unsure how much the milliner had charged and did not dare ask.

'Darling Frank.' She sidled up to him and laid a hand on his shoulder, the blue eyes wide. 'This little titfer will do you no harm, I promise you. It'll draw attention to your wonderful Transport Bill and how vitally important you are to the party. I'll be up in the gallery and I'll be so proud of you.'

'That's something.' Frank was mollified. His former wife had never wanted to attend the great occasions and had had to be bullied to make any kind of public appearance. In contrast Hazel practised the wifely duties with gusto. If sometimes she went over the top – and he feared the hat was one such example – he was torn. At least it meant, as she had implied, that the Bridges would be in the papers, when colleagues as worthy were forgotten.

He wished, however, that she was not quite so demanding. It was only the start of the parliamentary season and he was already exhausted. Hazel seemed to have no understanding that a man of his age needed his sleep. The frolics the night before had not been the finest preparation for a day in the spotlight. And he had felt such a fool.

'Heavens, you're so old-fashioned.' Hazel had hitched

up the yellow and black silk basque and patted the creamy bosom that billowed out over the top. Her curvaceous thighs seemed to form a heart shape, the knees deliciously rounded. 'You fancy me in this get-up, don't you?'

Frank had seized the opportunity to sit up on the edge of the bed. Not for the first time he had blenched at the shaggy grey of his chest hair. He could barely see his thighs for his podgy belly. The naked legs were spindlier than he would have liked. A varicose vein bulged on his calf. He had gazed at Hazel out of slightly bloodshot eyes. 'Darling, you know I adore it,' he said weakly. 'Agent Provocateur has done you proud. How much did you say it cost?'

'Never you worry.' Hazel had giggled. 'A bob or two. Wait, I need to adjust the suspender. It's got twisted.' She rolled over on her back on the vast expanse of white linen.

Frank told himself for the umpteenth time that he ought to be counting his blessings, not feeling ungrateful. It was fortunate that the Secretary of State's official London residence was large enough to take the king-size bed Hazel had requested as a wedding present, the better, she said, to please him in. He was happy with the bed, he was thrilled with the outrageous outfit, he was sated with pleasure. Mostly.

He gritted his teeth. He did not want to risk losing Hazel's affections; any further adverse publicity about his love-life was taboo. What he was unhappy about was being asked to do too much. And, worse, being ordered to do what he regarded as utterly unnatural. Not any strange acts, Hazel's tastes did not run that far – or, at least not at present. It was what she wanted him to shout out loud that seared him.

His gorgeous spouse flexed a shapely leg in the air and began to unfasten the sliver of black velvet that passed for a suspender from the lacy top of the seamed stocking. It was a precursor, he knew, to the moment when he could unhook the basque and get his hands on the majestic untrammelled flesh. She wriggled her toes. 'Oooh, that's better,' she crooned. Then she sat up and prodded her husband's back. 'Come on, darling, for your baby,' she wheedled. 'It's not much to ask. But when you say it, it really turns me on. Makes me go wild with desire. Please? Pretty please?'

There would be no rest till he gave in. A heavy day on the morrow notwithstanding, Frank had neither inclination nor energy to fight his wife. He had, after all, married her with precisely such nights of passion in mind. It was not fair to feel resentful that the pressures of his post and the ravages of middle age threatened to defeat him in mid-exercise. Had he wanted an easy life he could have stayed with Gail. With Hazel he had obligations.

He got down on the floor with a world-weary sigh. 'Okay, sweetheart, whatever you want.'

Hazel knelt at the end of the bed, clutching the edge and leaning forward so that her fabulous bosom almost leaped out of its corset. Frank swallowed: such a sight usually brought on a powerful erection immediately. With Hazel, potency was no problem. It was what she urged him to do next that went against the grain. A man, a real man, should not have to grovel. A man was meant to be in charge.

He was on all fours, the broad back swaying, white buttocks prominent. '*Darling*,' he hissed between his teeth, 'Darling, I am your servant. Your complete and abject slave. You are my master. Please, master, you are in charge. You are the boss. I am but the dirt beneath your fingernails. Humiliate me, do what you want with me . . .'

Frank groaned at the memory and shuddered. Hazel was giving him strange glances, as if she guessed what was running through his head. She was entwining herself around his arm and threatening to deposit beige Pan Stik on his lapel. Her perfume – Oscar de la Renta, wasn't it? – would cling to his jacket if he wasn't careful. Colleagues would sniff at him and tease. Quickly he kissed her mouth. 'You'll be terrific, sweetheart, and everyone will envy me. But don't chatter when the PM's on his feet, will you? And wherever you are, even in the loo, keep smiling. Ears and eyes everywhere. This'll be a great day for us, and don't you forget it.'

'Sure,' said Hazel, and danced lightly away from him, the shimmering pink hat in hand.

The Serjeant-at-Arms peered over the top of his half-moon spectacles. In a previous incarnation Major-General

Sellers had commanded troops in Northern Ireland, in the South Atlantic, in Bosnia and Belize. This was supposed to be a retirement job, but at times he wished the distinguished appointment board had preferred one of the other candidates. Facing the Argies on a windswept hill or flushing out Serbs from Muslim villages was kinder to the blood pressure than coping with the myriad fatuous demands made on him at the State Opening of Parliament.

Her Majesty, thank heavens, had come and gone without mishap. That had been the main priority. She had managed to stay sufficiently ahead of her son and his partner to outwit every cameraman who had tried to capture the Queen and Camilla together. Not that it mattered: their picture desks would create a photo-montage anyway.

Her Majesty had indeed remained with her peers. She had spent her entire time in the Lords, and Sellers had not seen her in the flesh.

Their lordships' House was the fiefdom of Black Rod, his opposite number, a retired admiral of impeccable aristocratic lineage. It was Black Rod, not himself, who greeted the Queen on her throne, Black Rod who marched in black stockings and silver-buckled shoes down the short corridor, across Central Lobby, past Churchill's and Lloyd George's statues to the entrance of the Commons. The lintel had been badly damaged during the war when the chamber had been destroyed; on Churchill's instruction the broken arch had been left intact, as a memorial and reminder. The shoe of the great man's bronze statue was shiny with the fingers of those who had touched it for luck, but Black Rod would not have been in their number. For then the carved wooden door was slammed in his face.

Every step was redolent of history. The whole charade commemorated an incident central to western democracy. Three hundred and fifty years before, the Queen's ancestor, Charles I, had reputedly ridden into the Commons chamber on a white horse and tried to arrest five MPs who had opposed him. Furious, he had turfed the Speaker out of his chair and demanded that the recalcitrants be identified and brought to him. Speaker Lenthall had knelt before the King. 'Sire, I have neither eyes to see, nor tongue to speak, except as this House doth command me.' The fugitives had been spirited away to the river. The King, no fool, remarked drily, 'I see my birds have flown,' turned on his heel and left the chamber. No monarch had ever been permitted to enter it since.

It might have been wise, Sellers reflected, had the King left it there. Instead armies were raised, cuirasses and helmets polished and Englishmen went to battle for the first and only time with each other. The outcome was commemorated in the brass plaque on the steps of Westminster Hall where the King stood after a show trial, condemned to death. And outside postured the grim statue of the victor, Oliver Cromwell: a tyrant to many, but to parliamentarians the Lord Protector of parliamentary rights against tyranny, and thus a hero on a day such as this.

For Black Rod, the Queen's Messenger, had the door closed to him, and had to bang hard on it three times, and wait as it was flung open. The Members inside would shuffle and titter and sit up straight. During tours by constituents they would tap the mark on the door where the battering was done, and recount the remarkable story to gum-chewing children and footsore pensioners. Black Rod, the ebony wand of office on his shoulder, would advance several paces. He would bow to the Speaker, who gathered up her robes. And in a stentorian voice, refined by a cultured accent, would intone, 'The Queen commands this Honourable House,' – he bowed once again to the Speaker, once left to the government benches, then right to the opposition, who would bow back, and try not to giggle – 'to attend upon Her Majesty in the House of Peers.' Then, like Charles I before him, the messenger would turn smartly and exit, but at a measured pace, his expression solemn, his mouth twitching, and be followed by a gaggle of frontbenchers falling in hurriedly, two by two, trying to catch the focus of the television cameras, and then by a horde of backbenchers anxious to do the same.

Once the Queen had made her speech outlining the government's forthcoming programme, had handed it back with a barely suppressed sniff to the Lord Great Chamberlain, and had processed out the way she had come, with her relatives at a respectful distance, a sense of anticlimax prevailed. Peers and peeresses in scarlet robes

tipped with ermine strolled aimlessly in their end of the
Palace and queued for taxis to go to lunch. Backbenchers
collected spouses, or trotted off to the television studios to
analyse the speech, denouncing or praising its contents
with fervour. And those who had left it a bit late to get
tickets for the afternoon's debate would hasten to the
Serjeant's office and badger him mercilessly, as if the
gallery's capacity could be trebled at a snap of his fingers.

The young man before him exuded an intensity the
Major-General had observed before in raw recruits who
had not seen blood or savoured the realities of a battlefield.
Yet he was no teenager, but wore a smart suit and had a
decent haircut. There was something familiar about the
eyes, but in the rush Sellers was unable to pinpoint it.
Was he supposed to recognise this man? Was he a relative
of a Member? Sellers shook his head and indicated his
list. 'Ms Clark hasn't arranged any tickets, I'm afraid.
Perhaps she intended to, but she isn't the best organised
lady.'

The man cleared his throat nervously. 'I'm sure Diane
wouldn't forget.'

'You'd be surprised.' The Serjeant-at-Arms adjusted
his spectacles. 'You a constituent?'

'No. I've come to work in her office.'

'Ah, have you indeed? Lucky chap.' Sellers gave him a
swift glance. Ms Clark's tastes had not altered with her
accession to office. Lamb to the slaughter.

Another Member burst in, envelope in hand. 'Can't

stop. Taking my mother to lunch in the Members' Dining Room,' he announced, to nobody in particular. 'But she wants to catch the three o'clock back to Scunthorpe so I've a spare ticket. Anyone want it?'

The Serjeant smiled, letting his teeth show, and whipped the cream envelope out of the man's fingers. Then he peered once more over his spectacles at the anxious young supplicant. 'Tell Ms Clark that next time I won't be so indulgent. I do have a waiting list, you know. Enjoy the show.'

The hat had become a liability, Hazel decided, but she was unsure whether it would be safe left in the scruffy cupboard in the Family Room. What a dusty, horrid place that was, with its nasty chintz and worn carpet and indescribable pictures. A few Russell Flints of half-naked ladies would do the place a world of good. And they ought to go shopping in Ikea like everyone else. So, the hat: two hundred and fifty quid's worth of silk and tulle, the most expensive single accessory she had ever bought. A ridiculous extravagance, but what else would Frank spend his salary on if not her? And, if the flashing cameras outside were any guide, it had been worth every penny. The afternoon editions had featured it and it would take pride of place on tomorrow's front pages. The front pages, no less, as if the new Mrs Bridges were the standard-setter for the whole government. Whatever Frank might say, he was partial to seeing his wife trumpeted by the tabloids as a style icon. Better than that old frump he had discarded.

Though one unfortunate effect might be that Gail would be stung into another slanging match. Why couldn't she see that the game was over? The stupid cow had *lost*. Lost him, lost her position in the world, lost every vestige of respect. Why couldn't she simply retire from the scene and go to sleep on a bench somewhere? Or volunteer for a charity, maybe, if she wanted to shine in the public eye. Anything rather than be a nuisance.

The bloody woman simply wouldn't give up. It was so unreasonable. She'd been in the press again last week, claiming that Frank was sending her hate mail. Of course he wouldn't do any such thing: he wasn't the type and, anyway, he had far weightier matters to attend to. He wasn't so petty-minded, though daft Gail must be if she suspected him. But the police weren't fooled. They said they were investigating, but so far no action had been taken other than to monitor Mrs Bridges' mail and alert the local sorting office. Much good that would do.

The former Mrs Bridges: Gail should stop using the name. It was Hazel's now, and nobody else's. Gail should revert to her maiden name and stop trying to make capital out of who she once was. The ex-wife. Poor Frank. Fancy being saddled all those years with such a misery. It was no wonder that he had wandered.

Now it was her role to keep him content. In her arms and nobody else's. It would be easier if he weren't so busy, and if he enjoyed going on holiday, but he didn't. He protested mildly that he hated hot places or anywhere with mosquitoes, but where were the glamorous spots without them? His response was unenthusiastic to the main locations she suggested: Kenya on safari, the Indian Ocean, Florida. Hazel had a nasty feeling that if she booked something he would find urgent business to detain him in London at the last minute. That was what had felled the former Mrs Bridges, right in the airport. She must make sure it didn't happen again.

He'd said she could come with him on official trips, but Euro-summits on transport were not the most enticing prospect. While he was embroiled in wearisome discussions that had him sitting up half the night shuffling the paperwork, she'd be stuck with the fat wife of the German ambassador or inarticulate and non-English speaking Poles and Romanians. Helsinki and Tallinn, the next two conferences in line, were not exactly throbbing suntraps replete with bronzed bodies. To her grumbles, Frank had said it wasn't always so awful. If he was still in the same post next autumn they might get a lively weekend in Rome. Lord, what an existence.

Hazel found a corner in the cupboard, dusted it with her handkerchief and placed the hat carefully where it would not easily be seen by a casual observer. She suppressed a yawn.

'God! Did you find it boring too?' came a pleasant voice behind her.

Hazel did not recognise the younger woman, who was smartly dressed in a peach wool outfit perfect for the cool autumn day. She was also removing a hat, a matching velour beret with a diamond pin, and patting her hair into order.

'No – not boring, exactly, but it was a bit tricky to follow didn't you find? All that "Honourable this" and "Right Honourable that" and bowing and scraping and everyone jumping up and down like jack-in-the-boxes.'

'They're trying to catch the Speaker's eye.' The girl laughed easily. 'Waste of time today, when it's been decided in advance.'

'It would have been nice to hear my husband speak, though.' Hazel allowed herself to sound duly wistful and laid some emphasis on the word *husband*.

The newcomer indicated that she was aware of Hazel's identity and introduced herself. 'I'm Fiona. I'm with Andrew Marquand.' They shook hands.

Another woman came into the room, removing another hat. Christine Ashworth had opted for pale blue. All three had chosen British designer outfits bought from off-the-peg collections, and for much the same reasons: they were easy for the fashion writers to identify, were neither outlandish nor frumpish, and didn't cost too much. Only Hazel's magnificent hat had quite deliberately broken the basic rule of modesty.

Christine sashayed smoothly into the conversation. 'You're the girl at the Mirabelle, aren't you? Fiona Sutton, isn't it? Delightful pictures. He seemed quite besotted.'

'Yes, well.' Fiona fiddled with her handbag. 'You shouldn't read too much into that. It was a bit too arranged for my taste.'

'I don't suppose you should be telling us.' Christine laughed conspiratorially. 'Most of what they print is a set-up, and we learn to live with it.' She gazed fixedly at Fiona's bare left hand. 'No ring? If the press were right, he was on the brink of popping the question.'

'Nonsense. As you say, we shouldn't believe everything that's in the newspapers.' Fiona's eyes were cold.

'Of course. So you're not moving into Number Eleven Downing Street yet? I'd have thought you'd find that most convenient. You'd get far more privacy behind closed doors.'

'No. I have a business to run. My relationship with Andrew isn't so involved.'

'Just good friends, eh?' Hazel nudged her. 'That's what we used to say too, me and my Frank. We got caught almost the same way. Not in a restaurant, out in the street. Same difference.' She held out her own left hand and wiggled the laden ring finger.

'Yes,' Christine drawled. 'Both Mrs Bridges here – it is Mrs Bridges, isn't it? – and I are recently married, so you should be careful, Fiona. It might be catching.'

Fiona bit her lip. 'Not at the moment, I'm afraid,' she answered crisply. 'Just good friends it is. Now if you'll excuse me . . .'

Long after the front benches had departed, Edward

continued to sit alone in the public gallery. He was riveted by every detail. The place was magic: every inch breathed history. He barely noticed as his joints became stiff, with his knees jammed awkwardly against the balustrade. The Victorians had not provided for modern elongated bodies.

He had to crane forward to see, and even then could observe the Members directly below only by half-lifting himself out of his seat, in some danger of tumbling down on to them. The acoustics also left much to be desired. A grille embedded in the back of the padded bench emitted indecipherable burbles. The jerky movements of the unmanned cameras were a distraction; from watching the broadcast in Diane's office he knew that the dull black eyes followed only whoever held the floor, and were not permitted to transmit flickers of impatience or boredom on the faces of those nearby. It was a skill universally admired to attract the cameras' attention mischievously while someone else was in full flow, by rising to make a point of order, for example. Far more entertaining for the audience was the Member seated behind an orator caught absent-mindedly scratching his crotch.

There was no real value in staying, not after the main speeches. By tradition, two backbenchers, one distinguished, the other up-and-coming, had opened the debate with what they hoped were sparkling *bons mots*. Now they were probably on the Terrace congratulating themselves over champagne. Their predecessors included Steve Norris and Neil Hamilton, jokers all, men whose debating skills perhaps exceeded their moral fibre but who were universally regarded as 'good House of Commons chaps'. It was the protagonists who counted. The Prime Minister had been magisterial, the Leader of the Opposition had tried to wound but failed, and Benedict Ashworth, with wit and good sense, had been paid the utmost compliment of having a virtually full House to listen and murmur approval.

Now the chamber was almost deserted, except for the handful of diehards dragooned by the whips to keep the debate going, or those with untamed egos whose remarks might achieve half a paragraph in their local newspaper in the middle of next week.

Edward wrestled with himself. He, too, should have found better use for the remainder of the afternoon. Diane might be searching for him, a chunk of work to be done (he was not yet important enough to be issued with a pager, and in any case would have had to turn it off in the chamber). Yet once he became busy on her behalf the chance to sit in the gallery would not present itself often and he was reluctant to curtail it.

Did this mean he really wanted to be an MP? The question, for anybody employed in the Palace of Westminster, was an obvious one, but still it was uncomfortable. Those men and women down there, notes clutched in hand, were not overpaid or much respected. Their potential for achievement was low, given that decisions were taken elsewhere. The hours they slogged for so little outcome were barmy, yet the House showed scant interest in reform. Their recognition factor in the street was far less than the average television weather girl's, unless they became embroiled in scandal. If they were remembered at all after their years in the Commons it would be in a short obituary in *The Times*. The life was a hiding to nothing for anyone with a genuine taste for getting things done. To Edward, the conclusion was that it made far more sense to be a backroom boy: with marginally less salary and exposure perhaps, but also with far less hassle, and potentially with fun and satisfaction in spades.

He had not seen much of Diane. Not yet. The moment would come. She had airily invited him to dinner in the Members' Dining Room, a privilege not afforded to every staffer or indeed to most, but usually reserved for constituency chairmen and visiting dignitaries. As the Serjeant-at-Arms had implied, he was lucky to be in her employ. Diane made a point of treating her staff well, he had been told. The remark had been accompanied by a wink he had been unable to fathom.

Let them criticise. It was merely an advanced form of envy. If that was his lot in carrying her name on his Commons pass, so be it. He was immensely thrilled to be here, and intended to savour every minute.

# CHAPTER NINE

O ne by one they filed in. The public would have recognised Andrew Marquand, his dark curly hair untossed by the wind – he had strolled the few yards down a corridor from his own residence next door. The stocky figure of the Environment Secretary with his undiluted Scouse twang would also have drawn approving comment, as would the breezy entrance of Diane Clark, the government's most popular member in every opinion poll. The voters would have been hard-put, however, to match names to the other faces. The fate of incoming ministers is to be derided as nobodies. The fate of most former office holders is to be forgotten. The perpetual misery of many serving ministers is that nobody knows who they are.

To begin with they collected in fidgety groups, with red folders under their arms, leaned on the ivory walls or propped themselves up on the leather chairs, hands tucked with apparent nonchalance in trouser pockets. They had passed the busts of Pitt and Disraeli outside the door but inside there were no images. Frank Bridges' index finger ran idly over the gold-embossed coat-of-arms on his chairback. He did not dare sit. No one smoked; there were no ashtrays.

Diane had chosen sky blue for her outfit and made a conscious decision to be smarter than she had been in Opposition. The three other women present were con-spicuous by their cream or red jackets and over-lacquered hair, for all had been through the efficient hands of Ms Barbara Follett, when the latter had been in favour. These ladies, respectively the Leader of the Commons, Leader of the Lords and Chief Whip, yearned to serve in splendour as Foreign Secretary or Chancellor, when, or if, the PM had the courage to appoint the first woman to these ele-vated posts. They made the effort not to congregate or talk exclusively to each other but to mix as equals with the men. Yet they were clearly not equals.

Behind the nervous clusters of politicians bustled advisers with clipboards and spin doctors in shirt-sleeves. One only was permitted to stay. Alistair McDonald was not strictly present, but without him no one would be sure afterwards which line to take.

Bringing up the rear, and about to enter together, were two tall, tidy men with flat bellies, trim haircuts and simi-lar well-cut grey suits. One was the Prime Minister, the other the Cabinet Secretary and head of the Civil Service. They moved like brothers as if from the same stock. Both tried to mask public-school accents, but their easy manner, their polite deference to each other, were unmissable.

A hush descended. Every eye turned to the Boss as they waited for their cue. He was grinning even more broadly than usual. He waved them to their places round the table, ranked in order of precedence.

The Prime Minister let them take their seats. His was in the centre of one side of the ovoid table with the fireplace behind and was the only one equipped with arms. 'Not had a lot of sleep, as you'd expect, but mother and baby are doing fine,' he enthused gaily. He slapped his palms on the table as if to reassure himself that the polished old wood and leather were real. A ripple of applause broke out around the room with calls of congratulations.

'How's fatherhood – again?' came a call.

'Terrific. Terrific.' The Prime Minister seemed unable to stop smiling and nodding. 'Not sure I'd recommend five. It doesn't get any easier, I can assure you.' He poked a jovial finger in Frank Bridges' direction. 'You'd better be careful, Frank, with that smashing young wife of yours.'

A discreet snigger was hidden behind many hands. Frank tried to smile enigmatically, wondered whether to make a crack about taking precautions and thought better of it. It might be wiser to change the subject. 'Now you've got the nursery set up, you can settle in for the duration,' he responded. 'With the majority we've got, you'll be in that chair for a decade.'

'Only a decade?' The Prime Minister grinned at him. If that smile got any wider it'd meet round the back of his head. 'So you don't believe we'll beat Margaret Thatcher's record, then?'

Frank was flustered. 'Of course we will. I didn't mean to imply—'

The Prime Minister could afford to be gracious. 'We must take nothing for granted. Our ever-present enemy is complacency.'

The group nearest to him exchanged indulgent smirks. Most had seen their majorities double or even treble at the last election. After years in the wilderness, a prolonged period of complacency was precisely what they felt entitled to enjoy.

'No, I'm serious,' the Prime Minister continued. 'Never mind the polls. They're great for us this year but they can turn sour overnight. Look, let me tell you. My constituency used to be part of George Brown's. He sat over there, as deputy PM to Harold Wilson. He was so certain of his seat that in the 1970 campaign he didn't go near it, but traipsed round the country making speeches for everybody else. Over two hundred of them, according to his memoirs.'

'Aye, he came to mine,' the Scottish Secretary reminisced. 'I was only a young lad delivering leaflets but he still spoke to me. A fine man, George, when he wasn't in his cups.' He made as if to expand on the event, but caught the PM's eye and fell silent.

'He finally deigned to appear in his own patch,' the Prime Minister continued severely, 'on the evening before polling day itself. Off he went to canvass the mining villages. A chap walked up and tapped him on the shoulder. "Great to see you here, Mr Brown. Won't you step into my house for a drop of refreshment?"'

A chuckle went round the Cabinet Room. 'An invitation George would never refuse,' said Frank.

'Quite,' the Prime Minister agreed. 'But his local knowledge had gone rusty, and nobody warned him. What he didn't realise was that the chap was a newly elected Tory councillor.'

'Oooh! Dirty tricks!' came a call from the far end. 'Rotten sods. I wouldn't put it past them, would you?'

'Tricks we wouldn't dream of perpetrating ourselves, naturally.' The PM giggled. 'So in he went, and enjoyed a cup of tea, then something stronger, and another and another. Till it was much too late to go out canvassing any more. He was struck by how knowledgeable his hosts were, and how interested in politics. And as they helped him down the steps into his car – few drink-driving laws in those days – he was heard to shout to all and sundry, "Don't worry about tomorrow! It'll be okay! We'll see the buggers off, won't we?"'

There was a respectful silence. The PM leaned forward and wagged an admonitory finger. 'So they stuck their heads in through the window and said to him, "Yes, Mr Brown, we know. *Because we are the buggers.*" '

'And the next day, he lost his seat, and the Tories were back in power,' Frank finished.

'Exactly.' The Prime Minister sat back, firmly in command.

Behind him came a discreet cough from the Cabinet Secretary. 'The officials are on hand now if you need them, Prime Minister.'

Immediately the demeanour changed. 'Right! Let's get on with it. Everybody ready? Chancellor, can we have the latest on the economy?'

Maddie Ashworth sat back in appreciation. 'I do like the Savoy,' she said. 'They do these teas so nicely, don't they?'

Her eyes roamed around the thickly carpeted lobby, which stretched virtually from the front of the hotel on the busy taxi-laden Strand to the back, overlooking the river. What a haven this was. Outside it was dusk, with trees blown bare and a touch of winter in the cold air. Inside were warmth and colour under brilliant chandeliers, the discreet hum of conversation masked by a tinkling selection from a grand piano painted white. Maddie's gaze roved over the impeccable damask linen, the tiered plates filled with cream cakes and scones, the fluted china, the enormous gleaming teapot almost too heavy to lift, and she bounced in delight.

As if on cue an elderly waiter with a bony face

appeared, grasped the teapot, placed the silver strainer in Maddie's cup and poured. 'Thank you,' she said, a mite too loudly. He murmured and glided away.

'Cake, Mother?' Christine nudged the plate.

'I shouldn't.' Maddie dimpled with pleasure. She selected an overfilled chocolate éclair on the grounds that she would have no trouble in naming it when describing the occasion to her friends. There was a correct title for that sumptuous puff-pastry scroll filled with strawberries and whipped cream, but it had escaped her. Nor could she guess what might be inside the delicate little pie with its tempting shortcrust dusted with icing sugar. The éclair was also the largest on offer, but that was irrelevant.

She turned over the cake-fork. 'Everything's silver. Hall-marked. But that's what you'd expect, isn't it?' Her eyes moved from the fork to her handbag: a small souvenir would surely not be missed. She coughed regretfully and put the fork back in its place.

A disturbance from the stairs closest to the street entrance caught their attention. A middle-aged female, a former Rank starlet and the doyenne of a dynastic television series, had arrived and was making her entrance. She was sweeping down the wide steps in a white wool suit tightly belted at the waist to show off her hourglass figure. At each step she would pause like a Ziegfeld girl and turn out her ankles. A black hat with jaunty feathers framed a heart-shaped face with perfect skin and high cheekbones, the lips glossy red, the eyes violet and mischievous.

*Diamanté* and pearl earrings dangled, bold and unmissable. If under the pearl necklace the skin was a little
crêpey, if crows' feet lurked near the exquisite eyes, those
imperfections only emphasised the magnificence of the
creation. About her scurried two dowdy women laden
with Harrods bags. Behind swaggered a tanned young
man with neat hips in denim. A hush fell.

'Oooh, that's—' Maddie began, but Christine placed a
finger on her lips.

'Don't, Mother, there are loads of famous people in here.'

Maddie's eyes followed the star greedily. 'Smashing
legs, hasn't she? And get that figure. I bet she works out.
Can you imagine it?'

Christine smiled. 'She's not bad for her age, yes.'

Maddie cocked her head on one side. 'How old is she,
d'you reckon?'

'It's forty years since she was at Rank. Before I was
born, anyway. She must be around sixty-eight, surely.'

'You're kidding!' Maddie wriggled. 'So she's older than
me. Exceptionally well preserved, then.' She continued to
stare openly. 'D'you think she's had a face lift?'

'I haven't the foggiest, Mother. It isn't a subject on
which I'm an expert.'

As the star swept into a side corridor with her scurry-
ing entourage the buzz rose again. Maddie sighed
wistfully. 'You're young, and pretty in your own right. You
won't have to worry about problems like that for years
yet. So, tell me, how's married life treating you?'

'Splendidly, thank you, Mother.'

Maddie paused. 'No babies yet?'

Christine stiffened. 'It's early days. I've only just set up my own company. I have clients to take care of. For some time to come.'

'I always say,' Maddie waved her fork to emphasise her words and scattered crumbs unheeded on the carpet, 'that the most important *client* a married woman can have is her own husband. You youngsters, you have no idea. It's all to do with loyalty and – what's that word the agony aunts use? Commitment. That's it, commitment.' She sat back, satisfied with her speech, her jaws still moving.

Her daughter-in-law flushed. Maddie took another breath. 'You won't see thirty again, dear, and neither will my Benedict. If you two leave it too late you might find you're too old to enjoy the children when they're growing up. That's what happens. Or, God forbid, that you can't have children in the end. This infertility, it's not an acci-dent. It has its roots in foolish decisions to postpone having babies for too long, you know. I've read about it. In my opinion it's the result of silly ambitious girls putting their business careers before their wifely duties. Why, in my day if you weren't expecting your first child at the age of twenty-five you were regarded as a bit past it.'

It must have dawned on the older Mrs Ashworth that she was having some effect, for she stopped suddenly and peered closely at Christine. 'Have I upset you, dear? If so, I didn't mean to. I wouldn't hurt a fly. I'm such a tactless person, everyone says so. Anyway, you're my Benedict's chosen and I wouldn't hurt you for worlds.'

Christine's head drooped. Maddie Ashworth folded her napkin and drew her chair closer. 'Christine, dear, everything is all right, isn't it?'

With an immense effort Christine assented.

Maddie Ashworth relaxed, though a frown creased her brows. 'Good. You're the perfect wife for him, dear. Your wedding was the best day in my life, apart from Benedict's graduation.'

Christine lifted her head. 'His graduation?'

'Marvellous, that was. The sun shone, even in Scotland. And guess what, his tutor said Benedict was the finest student he'd had in years. The finest! My Benedict. His tutor. That's Mr Marquand. He came to the wedding too. You remember who I mean?'


'At lunchtime,' Diane was explaining grandly, 'we swap the dining rooms around. The Members' is then used by people who want to bring in guests. The Strangers' is for Members only. In the evening, like now, they go back to their origins.'

'Why?' Edward saw it was obligatory to ask. They were standing in the entrance of the Strangers', a modestly sized but ornate room with the Commons' green embossed-leather seats and patterned green carpet. The waiters wore green jackets. The green was overpowering. The effect was of an amateur operatic production of

*Falstaff* in which it was held to be artistically important that everything in the Forest of Arden should match.

''Cause it's bigger,' Diane said. 'We like having outsiders in for lunch, but since when we're waiting for a vote the only thing to do is eat or drink, we keep that bigger room for ourselves at night. That also explains why there are so many bars and restaurants in the Palace of Westminster: twenty-six at the last count. And as they don't need a licence they're open as long as Members are here. At standing committees upstairs and the like. Some last through the night, especially on the Finance Bill.'

Outside it was already dark, and the lights of St Thomas's Hospital on the opposite bank blazed yellow across the wallowing blackness of the Thames. The waiter showed them to a table in the window and cast an appraising glance over Edward, calling him 'sir' with some obsequiousness. For some reason he could not fathom, Edward found the man's manner unnerving. The Serjeant-at-Arms had behaved similarly. Were they all admirers of Diane, or all critics? He found the open examination hard to read. He laughed nervously as he unfolded the white linen napkin and picked up the menu. 'So many arcane rules, aren't there? I suppose one simply gets used to it. For instance, it must be handy not needing to be licensed.'

'That's nothing to do with this being the Mother of Parliaments, but because it's a royal palace,' Diane explained. 'We're here by grace and favour of the Queen.

So it's Crown property: the law doesn't apply. More to the point, health-and-safety legislation doesn't apply here either. The kitchens have recently been brought up to scratch but when I was a new MP the staff went on strike one hot summer, and quite understandably too, because of the conditions. They were expected to cook in the bowels of this dump in a temperature of over a hundred degrees.'

'I don't think it's a dump—' Edward began.

'As a place to work, the Commons is appalling,' Diane said bluntly. 'Better for MPs, I grant you, with the new Portcullis block over the road. That has to be one of the most hideous buildings in London, yet someone called Michael Hopkins is actually proud to be its architect. And its cost – over a million quid per office. But I don't know about such niceties, I'm a Philistine. Value for money it ain't.'

Edward laughed.

Diane was in full flow: 'When I wanted my tiny office redecorated because it was filthy – the previous occupant used to chuck cups of coffee over the walls at random, some kind of budding performance artist he was – the Serjeant told me it was impossible. So I offered to do it myself, with the press taking photos. The *Globe* was quite keen. It was painted that weekend like a shot, and the curtains cleaned. Bingo. Nowhere else would you have to put up with such nonsense.'

The menu was contained in a gold-tasselled green folder with a sketch of Big Ben, complete with the ubiquitous portcullis. Simple fare, but very British, Edward noted: celery soup, roast pork with apple compôte followed by apricot slice or crème brûlée, though also available for the less carnivorous was an organic vine-ripened tomato and basil omelette or crisp-baked 'moneybag' of spicy spinach and dried fruits. Diane grinned. 'Moneybag indeed. There was a fuss some years ago about putting the entire menu into English, but they got their knickers in a twist. I mean, what's the English for tagliatelli? And who'd eat "burnt cream" if it was offered? So that's a compromise. You'll get better food in restaurants like Greens or Rules, but this is far cheaper. Subsidised by the taxpayer. Eat and enjoy.'

Edward selected the braised beef olives with cabbage, Diane the grilled chicken with black bean and mango salsa; they settled on a glass of house wine each rather than a bottle.

'You mentioned the *Globe*,' Edward ventured as the starters arrived. 'Didn't I hear you were suing them? How are you getting on?'

'Don't talk to me about the *Globe*,' Diane growled, then ignored her own advice and continued, 'There are rags. And there are *rags*. The *Globe* is the worst. They're not interested in reporting facts or intelligent commentary, and they wouldn't recognise "investigative journalism" if it slapped them in the face. Though given that we're the government now, that's probably in our favour. It'd be us they were investigating, if they could be bothered, not the other lot.'

She tucked into her soup with gusto and evident appetite as Edward passed the salt and listened politely. He had already guessed that when Diane was in such a mood all she needed was to be prompted occasionally. He was happy to oblige; it gave him a chance to look at her, and to reflect to his own surprise on her clear skin and bright eyes whose expression and animation were fascinating.

'A newspaper like that,' Diane said, 'is therefore incapable of contributing to our free society. Instead they target figures in the public eye in an attempt to increase sales. Which is a hiding to nothing, as shown by their falling circulation. The printed press are on the way out: most punters get their information from the broadcast media who are much fairer. But for the *Globe*, facts don't matter – indeed, are hostile to their cause. We're not talking Fleet Street at its finest here, only innuendo and nastiness. Unfortunately, they set the agenda in a way the TV news doesn't. Once you're slagged off, it's hard to retrieve a damaged reputation. Mud sticks.'

Her companion murmured agreement. Diane thumped the table and made the plates jump. Apparently she did not need alcohol to get excited. 'I get called "controversial and colourful" whenever I open my mouth. It grates, especially when on another page the leader column is whingeing on about how faceless and bland today's politicians are. Anybody with any sense these days'd run a mile before embarking on a political career. All that scrutiny, of our finances, our friends, our secrets, even where we spend our holidays and who with; we never, *ever* get the benefit of the doubt. Behaviour that in the outside world would be regarded as perfectly normal, like forgetting to pay your bills or getting drunk with your mates, is condemned as inherently evil. Evil? What rubbish. But trash is easier to report than in-depth stuff. The day after the Queen's Speech there was no coverage of its contents, but loads on the bloody hats. Drives me mental.'

'You could ignore the papers. They haven't said anything about you that any of your friends would believe,' Edward protested mildly. The main courses arrived. He was on his second glass of wine and he felt slightly light-headed. 'Are you going ahead with the libel case? Those comments you quoted, if I may say so as a former lawyer, are clearly defamatory.'

'What hurt most was the hint that I slept around and that somehow this disqualified me from high office.' Diane had dropped her voice. 'If that were so then centuries of statesmen from Palmerston to Lloyd George would have been condemned. Plus half of every Cabinet since the Second World War. But they're blokes, so they're openly admired as dirty dogs. It does them no harm whatsoever. When it comes to a woman, double standards rule.'

Edward felt a little out of his depth. Diane had not denied the 'facts'. It seemed to be the implications she resented. 'I'm not sure that would be the best line of attack in court,' he said diplomatically.

'True.' Diane dissected her chicken with energy. 'But I resent having to tailor my life to their demands. It's not as if the journos themselves are such saints. That Jim Betts is a slob. Some years ago it was rumoured he was an inch away from a rape case involving some kid who worked here. His boss Pansy's an active campaigner for the legalisation of dope. They hype up every dolly bird who's got a bit-part in a soap, then berate politicians for being dull and lifeless. But what we do is vital if sometimes mundane, and we don't need to be a dizzy blonde and size ten to do it.'

The waiters were in a corner, whispering, one eyeing Edward with unfeigned curiosity. He was uncomfortable again, his attention diverted from Diane's tirade. She noted his distraction, glanced at the waiters with an amused snort and wiped her mouth with a napkin. 'You should watch it, Edward. Next thing, they'll be accusing you of shagging me.'

'Oh, I don't think that's very likely,' Edward stuttered.

'You don't?' Diane teased playfully. 'My staff often get that kind of once-over, and in the past there's been every reason.'

Edward wondered, with a sense of panic, if she was flirting with him. Against that impish flicker of a naughty child, that vivacious, raunchy expression that had been caught on the BBC's *Question Time*, he found himself without defences.

Diane relented. 'Well, maybe you're right. I have taken

a personal vow of abstinence. No more hanky-panky, not while I'm in the public eye. Unfair as it may be, I can't go round suing the *Globe* and still having it off with every handsome young man who crosses my path. Not when a *Globe* photographer might be lurking behind the bushes.'

The wine glasses were empty; a waiter hovered hopefully. Diane paused. 'I've had enough,' she said. 'Got two boxes still to do tonight. Coffee?'

'I can help you if you'd like,' Edward offered. 'I wasn't planning to dash off.'

'Yeah, why not?' Diane called for the bill. Suddenly she leaned forward. Her cheeks were a little flushed, her eyes wide. 'What you should accept, since you work for me, is that I really do care passionately about the causes I take up. I hope you do too. That's why you seemed like the right guy at the interview. They're not optional, and often when I got started they were unpopular or sneered at. Teenagers needing abortions, women who get knocked about by violent partners, or raped, and nobody takes any action: what men are likely to pursue issues like that? A few brave ones back me up, but they wouldn't dream of striding out in front. Foxes and wildlife have more supporters than desperate inner-city women in trouble, believe me. And most of my detractors are men, not women.'

The thought occurred to Edward that life was seldom that simple; perhaps Diane did others a disservice by painting everything in black and white. But perhaps it was also an inner certainty that drove her on. 'What cannot be denied,' he said out loud, conscious that he sounded a tad pompous, 'is that you have serious achievements to point to. Your detractors have nothing.'

'Thank you for that.' Diane seemed pleased. 'I admire you, Edward. You're going to be a valuable member of the team. Tell you what, let's go back to my flat to finish off this paperwork. My coffee's not bad. I promise I won't lay a finger on you – meant what I said about that self-denying ordinance. Come on.'

# Chapter Ten

It was a minute before midnight. The tall man hung up his mackintosh, adjusted his half-moon spectacles to the accustomed point on his nose and nodded at the young woman on the phone. She acknowledged his presence silently but her attention was focused on her conversation; or, rather, she was listening intently, making occasional notes on a pad and murmuring in an encouraging tone.

The man slid the log book from under her arm and glanced at it. Nobody familiar had called that evening so far, but it had not been a quiet night. As the days shortened and Christmas loomed, for many troubled people the fears and loneliness multiplied. The switchboard would get busier. That was why he chose the shift after midnight before his own rostered day off work. In those grim hours he would be totally occupied.

He made mugs of instant coffee for himself and the girl, then settled at the next desk. He turned the page of the log book, ruled vertical lines and wrote the date and his code name. Then he waited for the phone to ring.

'Hello. Samaritans.'

For several seconds all he could hear was an almost inaudible sniffle at the other end of the line. That was nothing unusual. He noted the time and that it was a woman. She seemed to be talking rapidly to herself. As he said, in a neutral tone, 'Take as long as you need. No hurry,' he guessed at her age. Forties, maybe. This would not be a brief conversation. Women talked more than men and accounted for far more than their proportionate share of calls. They were more likely to carry out their threats and attempt suicide. On the other hand, men were more determined, and far more likely to succeed. Young men especially.

The woman's sniffs abated and he could hear her blowing her nose. 'Oh, God, I'm so sorry,' she muttered. Even on the phone to a complete stranger, the man reflected, callers could be theatrical. Perhaps that was the point: they could be demonstrative in a dialogue with someone unseen, non-existent almost, but were utterly tongue-tied or in denial when it came to unburdening themselves to a friend or relative. It stood to reason: if they had someone they loved to pour it all out to, why would anyone ring?

'I'm here,' he said patiently. 'Do you feel able to talk now?'

The woman gulped then was silent. That, too, was not unusual. Many calls were entirely silent. Though it was tricky to establish or confirm anything, it was believed that those who rang but could not bring themselves to speak were mainly first-timers. People sometimes needed simply to be reassured that a kindly listener was on tap. Only later, when the painful step of finding the number, dialling and hearing another voice had become less strange, even a habit, might words be coaxed out of them. Though it was not his job to persuade anyone to do anything. Nor to dissuade them, come to that.

'I'm so unhappy,' she started. 'It's my own fault, I realise that. I feel like my head's bursting. And, worst of all, I'm such a fool.'

She was trying to sound middle class but a northern accent intruded quite strongly as her voice rose at the tail-end of sentences. He could hear her gulping and hiccuping. He waited. From the corner of his eye he could see his young co-worker finish her call, enter a few scribbled remarks in her log book then sign off with a flourish. She pulled on her coat with a weary shrug and tiptoed out of the door.

The caller was settling into a steady stream of self-loathing. Like most of their clients her self-esteem was virtually non-existent. With some individuals who had committed crimes or damaged those who loved them, the flagellation was justified. Others had no cause to be unhappy with themselves. It made no difference. The clinically depressed did not have to be in pain to feel pain. This woman, however, appeared pretty normal, almost chatty now. Her listener found himself doodling on an envelope and with an effort made himself concentrate.

'They say I'm such an idiot. They're right. I am.'

'Why should you think that?' the man murmured. If she wanted to get it off her chest, he was here for her.

'Oh, loads of reasons. Because I let him go, mainly. It was my fault: he wanted babies and I couldn't have them. Oh, he said not to worry but you could sense he reckoned I wasn't a proper wife. He used to get cross at my dolls. Said those were for little girls, not grown women. But it was hard.'

She was calmer now. 'I should have gone to college. If I'd had an education I would have made something of myself. Been a teacher, perhaps. I could have been a head-mistress with my own primary school somewhere out in the country. I certainly wouldn't have married him. My mum never thought he was good enough.' She stopped, as if mulling over old memories.

He prompted, 'You didn't agree?'

'No. He was special. A policeman, looked smashing in his uniform, I can see it now. Pity he didn't stay in the force. He'd have been a better man.'

The Samaritan went through a mental checklist. Her speech wasn't slurred and she had not alluded to any form of self-harm. Nor any other violence. Though even if he feared she had taken tablets, he could not call the police or an ambulance. That was not allowed. He could try to persuade her to do so, but he could not do it for her. He was there to listen, not to interfere.

The woman's voice had become fiercer. 'What really gets me,' she was saying, 'is that they're spot on when they laugh at me. I am a pathetic creature, at the moment. And I've never been like this before. I wonder if I'm having some sort of breakdown. Beyond my control. The moment anyone talks to me, I fall to pieces. If they're trying to be kind I want to get hysterical and throw things. The flat's a pigsty – and I used to be so house-proud. A chap came to the place not long ago, a senior inspector, and you could see his nose wrinkling at the state of it. What am I to do?'

Her listener conquered the urge to suggest she clean up. That was not in the rule book. On the other hand, her awareness of the problem was the best means of conquering it. Instead he asked gently whether she had anyone else she could speak to.

'I used to have lots of friends,' the woman whispered. 'That was when I was the wife of a big man, a VIP. Most of the sods vanished, pronto. I think he's persuaded them to send me to Coventry. I get hate mail from him, awful stuff. I'm sure it's from him, who else could it be? So now no one comes near me, except that lovely Mr Maxwell. Well, at least he'll speak to me on the phone. God, I'm a mess. And I'm so ashamed.'

'Maybe there's nothing much to be ashamed of,' he offered. This seemed to give her pause for thought. A big sigh came down the phone.

'Yes, you could have a point,' she answered. 'I never used to be that stupid. I couldn't have coped with him and the life we led, always in the public eye and that, if I'd been such a terrible failure. I must have done something right all those years. I just wish I didn't feel so useless. And it's so bloody difficult to pull yourself together, you know? I need to take the first step. Easier said than done.'

There was another pause but he could hear her breathing regularly and more calmly. The first step was to ring Samaritans, in many cases, and she had done that.

'My name's Gail,' she said suddenly. He moved to stop her. 'We don't need to know.' He wondered, as he often did, whether he might be acquainted with his caller. From the information given, it was a distinct possibility. Maybe this was how she wanted it. He reflected that Gail, if that was indeed her name, was a good woman at heart.

She confirmed his opinion by asking shyly what his name was. 'Peter,' he answered, giving his code. 'Peter,' she repeated slowly. 'That's nice. Thank you for letting me talk to you. I hope I wasn't a nuisance.' Without any hurry, as he guessed she would, she ended the call. And he knew that she would not need to call again.

He removed his spectacles and pinched the bony part of his nose. Before he could replace them the phone rang again.

'Hello. Samaritans.'

'Hello?' It was a man's voice, young and hesitant.

'Hello. Samaritans. Can I help you?'

Silence, then a clearing of the throat. 'Is that Peter? Can I speak to Peter?'

The tall man considered. It was not unknown for a caller to refuse to speak unless it was to a familiar voice. On the other hand, personal contact and friendship was abjured; anonymity was at the heart of the matter, and of the organisation's success over the decades. The young man might deliberately have called at this hour, assuming Peter had a preference for the dark of the night. As indeed he had.

It could do no harm. 'Yes, this is Peter.'

The young man laughed. The tone was educated, the jollity a little forced. 'Oh, splendid. I've spoken to you before, ages ago. When I was suicidal. I'm not any more, I should hasten to add. In fact, I've put those terrible days behind me. Changed my job, got a terrific new position that suits me perfectly. In the House of Commons.'

Peter stiffened. He was uncomfortably aware that if he dared he would recognise the voice, though it was not that easy to place: not a prominent person, anyway, or someone with whom he had spent a great deal of time. The question would irritate him until he had figured it out, although that was totally against his training. He ought to terminate the call at once. But the young man was prattling on apparently quite happily so that it was difficult to interrupt.

'It's wonderful. I don't understand why I didn't get a grip earlier. Now my days are crammed, full of purpose. There's a reason for getting up in the morning, getting shaved and dressed and going out. Do you understand what I'm saying?'

'I do,' the Samaritan said calmly. 'I am glad to hear everything's going so well.'

'You see,' the young man continued more soberly, 'I wanted to thank you. When I was working as a lawyer, that was the last couple of times I phoned, Peter, I suspected I might be going mad. Stark raving crazy. Well, I was. I landed in hospital more than once. Sectioned under the Mental Health Acts. Not that I was going to hurt anybody else, but for my own safety. But you and your colleagues helped me through it, and persuaded me there was a reason to go on living and that I should persevere.'

His listener was quite sure that he had attempted no such thing, but if it pleased the caller to believe the fiction then he would not contradict. Many depressions cured themselves, if only temporarily. Without treatment or immense self-discipline they could recur. There was a pause. To get the young man talking again, and trying to ignore the extent to which he was overstepping the mark, Peter said gravely, 'The new job. It interests you more than the previous one, I take it?'

'Oh, it does.' The enthusiasm was infectious and unfeigned. 'I'm working for a wonderful woman, a senior MP. She has the most marvellous attitude to politics and she has taken me under her wing. Sorry if I sound a bit silly about her, but I've had a few drinks tonight. I needed to – to summon up the courage to ring to say thank you. I expected you'd be on duty about now.'

We change the rotas from time to time, his listener thought drily, but refrained from comment. With so many callers it was often impossible to remember the details of one in particular; without pulling out the old logs Peter could not be sure whether he had spoken with this man before. At least, not on the helpline phone. Face to face? Maybe. 'It's nice to leave the bad experiences behind,' he murmured.

'It is, it is.' The young man sighed. 'But I dunno, when I enthuse about her to other people, they don't quite share my view. They say she's aggressive, and belligerent, and the media can be ghastly about her. It's so unfair. Females in politics, they have to put up with such a horrible press. Double standards. Far worse than men.'

Peter made a sympathetic noise. The caller's identity was still unclear but the Samaritan was now fairly certain who the starry employer might be. Given the dearth of top women in the Commons, that bit was easy. He resolved to finish the call as tactfully and adroitly as possible.

He could hear a gurgle; the young man had fortified himself already with alcohol and he was evidently repeating the exercise. 'And was there anything in particular that you wanted to mention tonight? If not . . .' Peter said hopefully.

'No, nothing much. Only to tell you that I am *so* happy. Life has taken a miraculous turn for the better. I keep pinching myself. Diane is *so* wonderful – I think about her the whole time. She keeps popping up in my dreams, night and morning, would you believe? My saviour. I don't show it in the office, of course. There, I'm the soul of discretion. Behave beautifully.'

'Absolutely . . .' Peter murmured, and held the handset away from his ear. But he could not fail to catch the next few excited words.

'Wait, don't go. I simply have to say it to someone. She's twenty years older than I am but it's as if there's no age gap. The other way round. She makes me feel mature and valuable and important. I even flirt with her a bit and she laughs, she likes it. What a woman! There's nothing in it, can't be. But I swear I may be falling in love with her.'

'Nah,' said Betts. 'I don't go in for that sort of thing.'

Melvyn passed him the bottle. They had retired to the deputy press officer's flat in Victoria after a West End first night, once it was obvious that few of the promised starlets had turned up, and that those who had were already paired. The bottle of House of Commons whisky was already half empty though neither had bothered to find a glass.

'Wise up! Get a life! It's harmless,' Melvyn urged. 'And you get some crazy birds on the line. I'll put the speaker-phone on, then you can hear. And join in, if you like.'

'Your phone bill,' Betts muttered, 'must be bloody astronomical.'

Melvyn shrugged with a grin. 'What the hell? I don't pay it, do I?'

The journalist cast a sly glance at his host. 'Even so, these chat lines charge a pound a minute or more. Don't your superiors check?'

'Gotta be joking,' Melvyn said. 'Too much else to do, honestly. They're supposed to be running the country. They're not bothered how much of a bill I run up at home. 'S long as it's within reason.'

'What does that mean?'

'That it's not the biggest, of course,' Melvyn answered, as if it were self-evident. Betts's disbelieving snort drove him to further elaboration. 'Look,' he said, 'they'll check out my entertainments, my lunch expenses and the like. Line by fucking line, if they're in the mood. And woe betide me if I claim petrol to bleedin' Northumberland or wherever when I'm supposed to be in London, or when it's my weekend off. Got my fingers burned more than once. But the phone bill? Nah. That's a necessary tool of the trade. Can't manage without it. Plus the mobile, which costs loads more.'

'Lucky bugger,' Betts muttered. 'Our lines in the office are monitored automatically. And our e-mails, every single one. If I tried calling a premium number, even a lonely-hearts ad out of curiosity, I'd be hauled over the coals by close of business unless I could prove I'm writing an article about them.'

Melvyn brightened. 'You could say you're researching a piece about sex lines,' he offered. 'Then next time we can do it at your place, and you could claim it back.'

'I'm a fucking political reporter, not the social services correspondent,' said Betts sourly. 'As for doing it again, it depends on whether I get any fun out of doing it this time. What's the point of wittering on to a complete stranger? It isn't proper sex.'

'You can say what you want, see.' Melvyn was punching the numbers with a podgy finger. 'Anything. You won't get your face slapped. Here we are.' He pressed the speaker-phone button.

A bored female voice filled the room with pure Estuary. 'Lucinda 'ere. Hello. Who'm I talking to?'

She sounded as if she was chewing gum as well. 'Melvyn,' said Melvyn eagerly. Betts's eyes widened and he shook his head, but too late. 'An' me best mate Jim. Two gorgeous beefy boys needing a cuddle. You a blonde or a brunette?'

'I'm twenny-four years old, vital statistics forty-eight, twenny-two, forty-six, and I'm a part-time model. And blonde.'

'Great. Whatcha wearing, Lucinda?'

'Oooh. You naughty boys. We've got a right pair of jokers 'ere.' The woman tried a throaty giggle and coughed. 'Lemme see. I'm taking a proper dekko at meself, just for you boys. Where d'you want me to start? The top or the toes?'

'The toes,' Melvyn yelped. 'You got bare feet? I love bare toes, I love to suck them,' and he made slurping noises with his mouth. The hand that was not holding the phone had slid between his trouser legs.

'Now, boys. I'm wearing black stockings wiv seams up the back, sheer and silky, and shiny black leather shoes wiv four-inch heels. When we get together I will lay you out on your back, Melvyn, an' take your shirt off, right off, an' I will grind them heels into your bare chest. D'you reckon you could stand it?'

Betts began to chortle and mimed falling backwards in his chair clutching his heart. 'Yeah, well,' said Melvyn, apparently disappointed, 'I still prefer your feet naked. And the rest of you.'

'Not yet, naughty boy. Don't be in such a hurry,' the voice purred. 'First you have to take off my clothes. One by one.'

Betts, who had his mouth at the neck of the bottle as she spoke, spluttered the whisky over the carpet. Melvyn squared his shoulders as if the talker were in the room with them. 'Yeah, I could buy that,' he conceded shakily, 'but only if you tell me that those baby toes of yours, when we get them pesky stockings off, have dinky little painted toenails.'

'What colour would you like them painted?' Lucinda asked.

'Scarlet. I like a scarlet woman,' Melvyn answered briskly.

'You're in luck,' came the immediate reply. 'Me favourite nail polish. On me fingernails too. They're like talons, my fingernails. I like to scrape them down my lover's back and leave brilliant red scars in his skin. Makes him scream for more. Now then. Do you know what you have to do next?'

'Yeah!' both men chirped.

'Well, Melvyn, first you have to talk dirty. And while you do that, I'll be running my hand up my thighs, to my stocking tops, until my fingers reach the suspenders. Black they are, black as midnight. You there, Melvyn? Jim? I can't hear you.'

Melvyn's arm was pressed tightly between his own thighs and his face was turning puce. 'Oh, yes, go for it, oooh, lovely Lucinda, I can see you now, big curvy thighs and a currant bush at the top. You're not wearing any knickers, you naughty girl, your cunt is all wet, I can see your fingernails now, oh, God, oh, God . . .'

He began to jerk about as the voice from the phone spoke loudly and with more authority. 'That's it, keep moving, I've undone the suspenders and I'm rolling the stockings down my legs and *off* my feet, and now I'm wriggling those toes – and, yes, Melvyn, you're right, I'm not wearing any knickers, only a thong, black lace, I'm opening my legs, you can put your fingers there . . .'

Melvyn made a noise like a strangled chicken, fled for the bathroom and slammed the door. Betts, his eyes popping, sat mesmerised by the phone whence the woman's

voice was still issuing in steady accented rhythm punctu-
ated by 'Oooh! Oooh! Oooh!'

'Oh, piss off, you silly cow,' Betts said, and pressed the
stop button.

A few moments later Melvyn emerged from the bathroom to the sound of a flushing toilet, wiping his hands on
a towel. He gazed bewildered at the silent phone, then at
Betts, examining his companion for signs of disturbance.
'Not your cup of tea?' he asked sadly. 'Or maybe you
simply weren't legless enough. Too respectable by half,
you are. Let's finish off the bottle and then we can try
again. Or we can get a takeaway if you prefer.'

She flung back the covers. The bedroom was too hot. That
damn thermostat – the place was either freezing or roast-
ing, there seemed to be no satisfactory average. But it was
probably foolish to expect better from this cheap walk-up
flat near Morpeth Terrace. It was within walking distance
of the House, and had been the best she could afford in
backbench days. The elderly couple overhead were the
only neighbours she ever saw. Since her elevation there
had been scant opportunity to find anything better, not
least because of the intense demands of the job. Only those
more senior in the Cabinet pecking order were offered
stylish grace-and-favour residences in Admiralty Arch and
the like. Lucky devils. They probably had air-conditioning
and ideal temperature control in all seasons, courtesy of
the long-suffering taxpayer.

A sliver of steel-grey light slid in under the blind. Diane gritted her teeth. She needed to talk to somebody. Dammit. She did not like sleeping alone. With her dressing gown half on half off, she trudged to the bathroom then returned and sat on the edge of the bed cradling the phone in her lap.

There was someone she would love to be able to phone. Someone whose current name she did not have, whose address and personal details were a mystery. She did not even know if he was still alive, or in which country he might be located. He might have died ages ago, or been injured in an accident, or suffered from a life-threatening disease, and she would not know; nobody would tell her. Not now, not ever. Even her mother did not have access to the information, and she herself, despite her significant position, had no means of obtaining it. The hole it left in her heart was as big as the universe, not least because it could never be acknowledged or filled by any action of hers.

But she knew how he had looked in the first few days, before he had been handed over. For his own good and, she had believed, for hers. The anguish had been so great that she swore to herself that never again would she risk such misery. *Never*. Yet in the dread dead of night what she had done would return to haunt her, and she would never be free.

It had been a tiring session. Peter rubbed his eyes and

prayed that he might be lucky and have no more clients. The young man with the clipped accent and the employer in the House of Commons had unsettled him, and made him wonder whether he ought to take a break. Lots of Samaritans continued for years, but perhaps they were the most sanguine, or realistic. Try as he might, he often felt he wanted to get involved. The realisation that he could quite easily establish the identity of the young staffer – and that, moreover, something in him wanted to – undermined his sense of duty to the charity and his respect for its long-established methods. He would have to stop himself, he muttered sternly. He could not allow himself to show, even by a flicker of an eyelid, that he suspected a particular individual had had the misfortune to be hospitalised for mental illness, nor that the same young person was in danger of going over the top in his admiration for his boss. Given who the boss was, this was a danger not to be lightly dismissed.

He yawned and stretched, then folded his arms behind his head. His finger joints ached and he cracked them one by one, wincing at the advancing arthritis. He would go home, kiss his wife as she stirred in bed, have a shower then climb in beside her and sleep all morning. Later, since she had adjusted her working days to coincide with his, they would go to the supermarket and relish the simple ordinariness of their domestic lives. This was his bedrock, especially in comparison with the disorder and misery of those who felt driven to lift the phone—

It rang again, shrilly. He picked it up and gave the usual greeting.

The voice was male, soft, barely audible. 'Hello? Can I talk to you for a few minutes?'

'Of course, that's what we're here for.'

'I have done something really terrible. Cruel and wicked. And I am being punished for it, God in heaven.'

'Do you want to tell me about it?' Peter made a note of the call, the time, the opening statement. Even though no details could normally be passed on to the police, if a crime was about to be described he might discuss the issue with his organiser. Decisions like that were taken over his head.

'I got married. To a beautiful, lovely woman. God help me.'

'Ah. And why is that a problem?'

The man at the other end began to groan softly, as if unwilling to disturb someone who might be in earshot. He did not answer, but his faint whimpers were like those of a mortally wounded animal. Then he went quiet.

'If it helps to explain, I'm listening. Take your time.' There were myriad reasons why marriage to a beautiful woman might not bring the equanimity and love his own home conferred. It was not for him to make any suggestions or drop any hints.

It came at last, after an agonised silence. 'Because I wonder if I'm gay. And if so then what I've done is truly unforgivable. And I've no idea how to cope with it. I thought I could manage, but I can't cover it up any more and it's driving me crazy. I suspect she's guessed, too, which makes it worse. I'm fine during the day, but at night – oh, God . . .'

Suddenly there was a rustle, as if the phone had been brushed against a body or garment. Peter heard a female voice speaking in alarm: 'Darling, it's five-thirty in the morning. Who are you talking to? Benedict – are you okay?' And then the phone went dead.

The tall man removed his spectacles and placed them carefully in their case. He rubbed his eyes then examined the fingers, as if the wisdom of the world had been stored in their swollen joints. He would be desperately glad to get home. He would not return to this desk for at least six months. Enough of charitable service. It was his turn for a break.

And Major-General Sellers, Serjeant-at-Arms at the House of Commons, rose, put on his mackintosh, belted it thoughtfully and went out into the cold bleak dawn.

# Chapter Eleven

Gail stood helplessly on the pavement and gazed at her car. The blue Vauxhall Astra was hardly a magnificent motor. At the date of the divorce it had been sitting neglected in the garage for months, the battery flat, and would not start when she had tried to drive it away. This car, unlike Frank's adored old Jaguar, had had no repairs or servicing for years; the main use to which Frank put it was for toddling round the constituency during election campaigns, the better to convince the punters that their Member was a man of the people. In fact, older voters preferred to see him in the bigger car, which advertised his authority; they would wave and flag him down, peer inside the back and touch the cream leather interior, full of curiosity. They felt included in, not excluded from, his fame and shared his taste for the trappings of success.

Those youngsters who sneered and showed two fingers as the Jag swept majestically past were unlikely to vote anyway, for anyone.

So the Astra's paintwork was dull, its rust and blemishes a testimony to lack of funds and care. But with some effort Gail had got it moving, and had laid claim to it beyond the final settlement. Frank had seemed puzzled that the insignificant vehicle could mean so much to her and had been quick to give in. Not that she needed a car daily, when she was spending most of the time indoors and was not employed, but a car was a status symbol. And it was precious: something she had demanded and won from her husband, in the darkest days after her world fell apart.

It was no surprise therefore that he should have tried to destroy it. The car, her scruffy little runaround, was the symbol of her independence. Frank resented that. He had treated her like dirt. He had wanted her to turn a blind eye to his infidelities, wanted her to accept his betrayal with That Woman. She had risen above such humiliation. She had divorced him and won a settlement. She had demanded and got the car. And now look what the monster had done to it.

The nearside tyres had been slashed, crudely, with a large knife. That would have been the work of a moment; the knife could have been hidden inside a sleeve and then, maybe with shreds of black rubber trailing, concealed again as the perpetrator walked on. He would whistle, under his breath maybe. This was a crime of revenge, and would make the criminal feel wonderful.

For once she did not feel like crying. The hysteria seemed to have abated. Instead rage welled up inside her and she kicked at the driver's door, which made no impression on the metalwork: whoever had put that dent in the offside wing must have done it with far greater force. A man, obviously. Perhaps Frank himself had stopped here during the night and vented his frustration on her by wrecking the tyres, then, finding that act insufficiently satisfying, had booted the wing as well. She hoped the brute had hurt his foot. He deserved to.

The scratches down the side . . . She bent close, then straightened up. It was possible that those were not fresh; a film of rust surrounded the widest. Perhaps they should be omitted from her official complaint. Of course, leaving a car in any public car park, but especially in the grimmest holes in the constituency, was an invitation to hooligans. Whatever they could not have for themselves they were wont to destroy. That was exactly Frank's own approach to their life together.

It stood to reason that he was responsible. Who else would want to trash the car? Hers, in particular, and none of the others in the street. Why on earth would anybody do such a thing?

A passer-by stopped. He was elderly and tidily dressed, a pensioner on his morning constitutional. At his inquiry Gail growled wordlessly, giving herself the luxury of sounding like a lioness at bay. Her own desire to return to a normal life, as expressed to the Samaritans, was again under threat. That must be Frank's intention.

'The pig,' she addressed the passer-by. 'The pig. I'll get him for this, just see if I won't.'

The pensioner hesitated. He made a noncommittal noise.

'I'll get him,' Gail assured him. 'Frank Bridges. He'll rue the day, he will.'

The question to be resolved was, how? Nice Mr Clifford Maxwell? Or the press, direct? The police? The memory of her two interviews with Inspector Stevens came flooding back. As the elderly man trotted off into the distance, she pondered. The police would have to be informed, but it was also a matter for the media. If the boys in blue chose to protect one of their own, it was her duty to expose him, and them.

Inspector Michael Stevens ran his fingers distractedly through his hair. Strands of dark brown came away interspersed with grey. He rubbed his moustache and wondered, not for the first time, if that trademark of the Met had not outlived its appeal; in the new century the chap most likely to be sporting a luxuriant lip growth was not one of Her Majesty's boys in blue but a gay man, a Freddie Mercury type, advertising his testosterone. That was not the message he wanted to give.

He wished he had a wife to consult. There had been a

Mrs Stevens, but she had left in a flurry of recrimination years before, taking their sons with her. He was too wrapped up in his work, she alleged, too engrossed in the details of street crime and burglary, too ambitious for promotion, to notice her unhappiness. Indignation at the unfairness of her accusation had swelled in him. A policeman's job was never going to be nine-to-five with every weekend off: she must have realised that when she married him. But it had been an honourable profession in those days, its success central to the fabric of society, and should have secured her admiration.

His protests fell on deaf ears. She went, and he had found solace in the lonely times afterwards by concentrating on the tasks in hand. It was not till some time later when a casual girlfriend made exactly the same parting remark that it occurred to him these women might have a point. By then it was too late. He enjoyed his work, and relished being carried away body and soul into an investigation or inquiry. He loved the camaraderie, the sense of a team together with a single objective, the joshing good humour and the inbuilt satisfaction from an essential job well done. Perhaps he had a mildly obsessive nature, but police work was often like that.

The years had sapped his ambition even as his sons had grown up and distant from him. On days like this he wondered whether he had sacrificed too much, with too little to show for it except a scattering of Commissioner's commendations and a golf handicap that did not bear boasting about.

'I'm beginning to associate Mrs Gail Bridges with a bad day,' he admitted ruefully to the sergeant. 'I do wish I could be more sympathetic. What's she on about now?'

'Car's been vandalised.' The sergeant was brisk. 'Says the tyres have been slashed and the bodywork dented. She's brought some Polaroid photos to show us.' He placed the collection on the desk and fanned them out.

Stevens frowned. 'Bit calculating, that. Odd how she happened to have a Polaroid camera, plus some film, when she just happened to need them.'

'It's an insurance job, really,' the sergeant said, in a neutral tone, 'but of course she's got to report it to us first.'

'I do wish people wouldn't do that. We're not a validating authority. It makes the crime figures look terrible and wrecks the progress we've made towards our targets.' Stevens allowed himself to sound testy.

'"Failure to reach targets may result in the service being penalised in subsequent years,"' the sergeant intoned. Both men knew the Home Office documents virtually by heart. It infuriated them that the forces which recorded crime with less assiduity than their own scored more highly in national league tables. And received both praise and extra funds that, by rights, were not their due. A crime that was not recorded did not exist; by definition all were unsolved, and subsequently unpursued. Nor were their snippets of information available, on record, to help in other inquiries. Her Majesty's Chief Inspector of Constabulary had railed against the practice, had demanded accurate record-keeping, even if it was apparently to the detriment of a particular establishment; but had succeeded merely in drawing the problem to the thoughtful attention of senior managers in forces that had resisted the idea up till now.

'Damn.' Stevens struck his fist on the desk. The model Porsche leaped an inch or two and he grabbed it before it could fall off and suffer more damage. 'Do you know, I quite liked her. She's been badly treated, there's no doubt about that. That visit I paid to her flat, it was depressing, but apart from her completely unrealistic pursuit of her husband, underneath she seemed to be a nice woman.'

'Ex-police officer's wife,' the sergeant said diplomatically.

'What?' Stevens was preoccupied, fiddling with the Polaroids, and did not notice the slight smirk on the sergeant's face. At last he pushed away the pictures. 'Well, let's have a report on the details, especially the time, place, that sort of thing. I don't suppose there'd be any witnesses. Send a uniformed constable round to check. See if she requires advice with the insurance. I'm conscious that she might be stuck without the car. We can give her the name of a good garage. Oh, and one more thing.'

'Yes?' The sergeant's face had returned to gruff inscrutability.

'Ask her if she's managed to get her drains fixed. When I was there she was having problems. Everything getting on top of her a bit, I reckoned.'

'Her drains?'

Stevens waved a hand helplessly. 'If she can get her life sorted out, Ron, she might put herself back together. Then we might hear no more of this nonsense. Understand?'

'Bloody 'ell.' Frank Bridges spread out the midday newspaper on his desk and smoothed it flat with the palm of his hand. He hissed through his teeth.

'The latest MORI poll merely confirms our own private polls, Secretary of State, and the trends shown in the NOP in the last couple of months.' The young staffer hovered nervously. His name was Norman; his cheeks were smooth and shiny, his eyes prominent. He had a doctorate from the prestigious South Bank University and a pronounced 'sarf Lunnun' twang.

'But our lead's been halved,' Frank said indignantly. 'And see the headline: "GOVERNMENT LEAD SLIDES. CRISIS MEETING IN DOWNING STREET".' He reached for the daily diary. 'Are we having a meeting? What time?'

'No, sir, not you,' said Norman. 'That's for the inner Cabinet and press officers only.' His cheeks had turned pink.

'It is, is it?' Frank shoved away the diary. 'So now we know who runs the country, don't we? But not for much longer, if these polls are accurate.'

'It's not quite so bad,' said Norman nervously. 'True, our lead was twenty-nine points at its peak and is down to fifteen. But it's worth remembering that every government benefits from post-election euphoria. We expected a surge up, and now we've got a surge back down.'

'But we were bloody invincible!' Frank roared, and slapped the newspaper with the back of his fingers. 'The Boss laid down the law. The Great Project means we have to be in office for a decade. If we start slipping in the polls, it'll vanish. Melt like snow in our hands. Ashes to ashes. Then there'll be no more meetings in Ten Downing Street for any of us. We'll be out for a generation.'

The young staffer, who at some stage in his education had been taught by a lover of good English, winced at the plethora of mixed metaphors. 'It isn't so bad, honestly,' he said hesitantly. 'We have forty-eight per cent support. If you remember, we won the election on forty-five, so we're still way ahead. The official opposition haven't budged much above thirty per cent in any recent survey. We're not going to lose. Barring a miracle.'

'Miracle? For who? Barring a miracle, we could see these figures continue to crash, and back to the opposition benches we'll go.' Frank refused to be other than gloomy. 'Opposition. Years in the wilderness. I tell you, Norman, I couldn't face that again at my time of life. Ghastly, with those buggers sniggering at us with their pinstripe suits and self-satisfied smirks. And tell me, clever clogs, if we're losing out, and the other lot are static, where are the votes going?'

'Mainly to the don't-knows.'

'Oh, terrific. The great unwashed army of the don't-knows, don't-cares and don't-bloody-votes. The can't-be-bothereds of this world. If that tribe begins to grow seriously, it can be God's own job to budge them. Specially in constituencies like mine. In last year's local elections, in the heartlands, we had turnouts of ten per cent. Horrible. And undemocratic. Too damned easy to let the other lot in, if they get keen.'

'Or extremists,' Norman murmured. His doctoral thesis had been on Militant, the left-wing conspiracy that had almost destroyed the Labour Party in the 1980s. The South Bank University, situated in Lambeth, had a mountain of authentic material. 'People who merely use our banner to cloak their real intentions.'

'Or one of the other lot,' Frank ruminated. 'If you take out the don't-knows, is there anyone else with reason to smile?'

'Oh, yes, the New Democrats. They're doing fine, compared with the election. But even there the level's slipped. When Benedict Ashworth got married he could do no wrong. That's worn off too.'

'Tiny span of attention, the punters, haven't they?' said Frank, in despair. He folded the newspaper angrily. 'I blame Margaret Thatcher. She ruined this country, and now the chickens are coming home to roost.'

The staffer was about to comment soothingly that the
antics of Mrs Thatcher had eventually resulted in her
demise, and in the destruction of the electoral hopes of
her party. Frank Bridges and his cronies had been the
beneficiaries. But the Iron Lady was not a subject guaranteed to raise his master's spirits. He thought better of it
and changed tack. 'I guess it's action they want now, not
words. Enough of targets and promises. They're looking
for results. That's how we'll be judged.'

'God help us,' said Frank again, and threw the newspaper to the far side of the room.

The polls were being perused avidly and with varying
degrees of delight and misery throughout the square mile
of crowded streets in SW1 that is the political marrow of
the nation. To Diane Clark they were not news. Her safe
seat was crammed with voters dependent on public services, men and women whose inarticulacy and lack of funds
relegated them to the end of every queue. The new government had awoken in them a latent yearning for
inspirational leadership and had been the object of much
awe and admiration, mostly overdone. Their hopes for
rapid growth in those public services were soon dashed,
for improvement required changes that would be resisted,
inevitably, by recalcitrants within those organisations who
stood to lose out. Rationing, queues, delays and waiting
lists suited a surprising number of operators. The complaints of the disadvantaged were outweighed, for a long

time, by the interests of the unions, boardroom and share-holders while the government stood aside.

It should have been no surprise. The most senior members of government do not use trains. They do not send their children to the nearest council school. They pay their dentist for porcelain veneers and purchase the smartest spectacles. They do not, by and large, live in the more desperate parts of the capital, but in the centre in serviced flats or in the leafier suburbs where the shops stock Brie, chorizo and fresh pasta. Their advisers own shares. Their closest friends are wealthy men. They holiday in private villas for which they do not have to pay. They move in congenial company, and are bewildered when they are accused of losing touch.

Their most devoted supporters could express their disapproval in one way: they might exercise their limited choice by staying at home on polling day. For the most burdened sector of society, doing nothing was always an effective option.

Diane and Edward were eating a sandwich lunch in her office before she was due in the Commons for Question Time.

'You see,' she explained in a low voice, glancing at the door, 'the Prime Minister and I will take opposing views over this. He'll faff around worrying about presentation and PR. He's probably closeted right now with Alistair and Melvyn and the whole gamut of pollsters and focus-group pundits. They'll be asking how they

can improve tomorrow's headlines and wondering
which key journalist to grant an exclusive interview to.
The strategic centre of government. They're mad. I hate
the lot of them.'

Edward blinked. He had not expected to hear a senior
Cabinet minister express such a stark opinion of her
leader. He ate his turkey sandwich slowly.

'It's no wonder everyone gets cross with us,' she continued. 'Never mind the Dome – that's a fiasco engraved
on every heart – we spend ten million quid a year running
Ten Downing Street alone. Just the Prime Minister's
office. The bill's risen three times over since the last lot
were in. Dozens and dozens of "special advisers," all useless, all at taxpayers' expense. That kind of money every
year would improve a clutch of schools in my constituency. I can't bear to think what we might be doing
with it. And it's counterproductive, a complete fucking
waste.'

'But we have to be on top of the media. They'll do us
no favours,' Edward protested mildly.

'That's crap. We should take no notice.' Diane's eyes
burned, her mouth twisted in anger. 'The press are there
to torment us. That's their job. And if we continually make
obeisance to what the papers say the public say they want,
we'll go round and round in circles for ever. Till the voters
get fed up and turf us out. And they'd be quite right to do
so.'

Edward nearly choked. The sandwich had come from

the departmental canteen and was not of the highest quality. He pulled a piece of gristle from his mouth. 'So what *is* the answer?'

'Bloody obvious.' Diane almost shrugged. 'As old Mrs T found. Ignore the polls, get on with your manifesto, push it through, whatever the howls and squeals. They'll hate you, but they sense the integrity, I guess. Then, on election day, you stand back and say sweetly, "See? We've done it. You said it couldn't be done, but here's the evidence. Now vote for us." And they do.'

'Mrs T wasn't such a runaway success,' Edward argued gently. 'She never had a majority in the country. More people opposed her than supported her, in every single election she fought.'

'Sure. Undeniable. But we were split down the middle. We couldn't agree on how to fight that kind of aggression. Whether to be more extreme, or to take on board the bits that were popular, however evil. In the end we had to accept that she'd changed the political face of the country, and pretend we could do the same only better. *Awful.* But she succeeded by driving home her agenda, and we should do the same.'

'Takes a lot of courage,' Edward murmured.

'Yeah.' Diane pushed away the remains of her sandwich. 'Courage. And belief. You have to believe in what you're doing in the first place. That's the trouble with some of my colleagues.' She halted, as if discovering an unpleasant truth.

Edward prompted her. 'Go on.'

Diane sighed, sadly. 'They don't have any beliefs, any convictions. Nothing. No bedrock of philosophy as to how society ought to be run, only a vague feeling that it should be "better", whatever that means. So they ask the public, and monitor their progress through the opinion polls. But the poor geezer in the bus shelter or the single mum hanging out her washing from a tenth-floor flat hasn't the foggiest. That's why they put us up here, in power: we're supposed to know without endlessly consulting them. Otherwise we're just chasing our own tails. And meanwhile nothing gets done.'

There was an unhappy silence. Diane twiddled the limp salad garnish on her plate.

'Diane,' Edward said slowly, 'the most popular figure in the polls is you. Has been for ages. You mentioned integrity, and you've got it, in spades. You would make a great Leader of the party. Have you ever thought about it?'

'Balls,' said Diane bluntly. 'I don't have the Oxbridge education, I don't have the talent, I'm not slippery enough. And I've made too many enemies in my time.' She grinned. 'You forget you're talking to the vilest lady in the country, if the venerable *Globe* is to be believed.'

'Just for the sake of argument, then. If you were in charge – it could happen some day – what do you think? What would *you* do?'

Diane roused herself. 'That's easy, Edward. Shoot the

spin doctors and buy a handbag. Come on, let's go, we'll be late.'

Gail waited in the wings, fidgeting nervously with her sleeve. On the set another interview was under way, with the author of a book on babies. The monitor to the left showed the soundless pictures, the gesticulations, the author intense, the presenter attentive but vapid. No live babies who might squall or otherwise misbehave were within a mile of the studio, only colour stills. The presentation was all.

It was her turn next: instead of watching television alone in the weary empty afternoons, she would soon be on it. Behind her, the handsome grey-haired man with the watchful eyes and the professional smile took a step, careful to avoid the cameras, and whispered to her. Gail listened attentively and nodded. She was ready.

Dear Mr Clifford Maxwell. He was described in the press as a 'PR adviser', but he was so much more. He was so kind. He had been the most helpful person imaginable. The decision to consult him, back in the darkest days of the marriage break-up, had been the wisest she could have made. He was a genuinely nice man who cared about injustice. He had never asked her for money, never pressed on her the sordid business of contracts and legal documents. His anger was directed at the people who misused their power to crush those they regarded as beneath them. He understood how dreadfully hurt a woman must feel, and had been the soul of discretion as she had poured out her heart to him. He could be trusted absolutely. It was only a pity that others were not as considerate.

If Frank had once phoned to ask how she was . . . Maybe she was wrong. Was it possible that she had jumped to the wrong conclusions, that it wasn't Frank who had been attacking her? The police thought secretly that she was doing it herself and took her for a hysteric, an attention-seeker. Their indifference was outrageous, but somehow she had failed to convince them. Perhaps she had not tried hard enough; her manner had not been conducive in recent months to convincing anybody about anything. If they mounted a surveillance operation they would see, but even as the image of a policeman outside her flat formed in her mind, Gail recognised it as improbable. The police simply did not have the resources. They had no problems providing Frank and his VIP pals with Special Branch officers armed to the teeth, but the needs of lesser mortals were way down their list of priorities.

She was an ordinary person now. That hurt. She had been the adjunct of an important politician for so long. Although that meant she was living her life in another's shade and was seldom appreciated for herself, it had suited her. She did not have to strive or work the crazy hours, or put up with the endless criticism and intrusive scrutiny that were Frank's lot. Her position had had its attractions:

a police officer was indeed in evidence at the entrance to their London home whenever Frank was in the news, or at election time. Gail was unsure whether that applied to every prominent public figure, but it was certainly routine by the time Frank was a frontbencher and a leading protagonist on television. And the police had been deferential and friendly to her. To Frank they had been comradely. Once a policeman, always a policeman. That stood to reason.

Sooner or later she would have to give up being Frank Bridges' wronged ex-wife. She was feeling better, more secure and less frightened; or at least, that would be true if it weren't for the attacks on her person and property. Those would terrify anybody. Gail reminded herself that her reaction was reasonable: to be a target for a deranged maniac whose sole objective is to scare you is very scary. It undermined her efforts to help herself. She wanted the man caught. Stopped. Arrested, charged, imprisoned. Whoever it was. But, somehow, there had to be a connection to Frank. If she made enough fuss, if she embarrassed Frank enough, he would have to accept that publicly. And then he'd have to insist that his pals in the force took action to protect her, even if the trail led straight back to himself.

The floor manager touched her arm. The previous guest was whisked out clutching her coffee-table book of baby pictures. The presenter was mouthing words at the camera. Gail heard Frank's name, and then her own. A

burst of applause came from the studio audience. She was
on.

'What d'you reckon, then?' Pansy and Betts were standing
by the television monitor, smoking companionably.
Behind their backs a young sub-editor irritably waved
away the smoke of the Gauloise and scowled. Pansy
pointed, cigarette in hand. 'Is she telling the truth?'

'The first Mrs Bridges. Great scenario, isn't it?' Betts
was noncommittal. He was unlikely to jump till he saw
which way his editor's mind was leaning.

'Someone is making her life a nightmare. It's because
she refused to back down. That much is entirely plausible.
The question is, who?'

'If it is Frank it's a hell of a story.'

'How well do you know him? Is he the type who could
order revenge attacks on his ex-wife?'

'Blimey. That's a question. We could ask our tame psychiatrist for an opinion.'

'Better broaden it a bit. "What kind of mentality would
do such a thing?" Plenty of other examples to quote. Hell
hath no fury, *et cetera*.'

'Yeah, but she's no posh bint. Remember that city wife
who cut her husband's Savile Row suits to ribbons and dis-
tributed his wine cellar among the neighbours when he said
he was going off with his floozy? Mrs Bridges is a forlorn
little dope. If we're after examples of men who decide to
shut their wives or ex-wives up, intimidation is the key here.'

'Great story, as you say, Jim, if there's a grain of truth in it. Me, I wouldn't put it past our Frank. You get cynical in this profession: anyone could do *anything*. He may be the salt of the earth, these days, but he's got a history as a bruiser. Gotta watch the libel, though.'

Betts stubbed out the cigarette in an empty coffee cup. 'You don't usually worry about that, Pansy.'

'Yeah, well.' Pansy moved away from the desk and motioned Betts to join her. 'The proprietor's getting twitchy. Doesn't want any more rows with the government. Genuine press freedom's one thing, he says, we can criticise, publish the polls as we like. But getting embroiled in court cases and defamation is another matter and he'd much rather we didn't. Been made clear.'

'I thought he gave us a free hand – no editorial control?' Betts raised his eyebrows. He might not be working for ever for the *Globe*; who could tell to which commercial rivals life might lead him? Such titbits were to be inscribed in the little black book at the furthest recesses of his mind.

'He wants to be ennobled,' Pansy said, emphasising each syllable. 'He's miffed that everybody under the sun in the media has been except him. His mates. Some of whom, you can bet, swore at leftie dinner parties they would *never* accept a peerage. The moment the vellum envelope arrives with the embossed crest, they're jelly. So he wants his. He's forked out plenty to party headquarters in the past and wants it recognised. And we're to lay off the guys who are in command.'

'Does that include Diane Clark?'

Pansy grunted. 'Probably. It goes against the grain, believe me, Jim. She's a tart and a whore. Abuses the boys who slave for her and corrupts their lives. A wicked woman. I stand by everything you wrote about her. But we may have to make a fulsome apology. With a bit of luck, she won't press for damages.'

Betts did not miss the emphasis. It told him everything about possible blame.

'Anyway, that's inside information.' Pansy spoke more loudly. 'As far as Mrs Bridges is concerned I suggest a sycophantic interview. Could you manage that, Jim?'

The man with the strong Scouse accent was fretful. His mouth moved, his tongue flickering over brown, cracked teeth. Slashing the tyres had achieved an objective, but it had revived in him the old edgy sensation. It was one thing to set up a master plan and work his way steadily through it. Normal people would get great satisfaction from simply following it, step by step. Normal people would not allow their vision to become distorted by dreams of blood and torn flesh. But he was not normal.

He cracked his knuckles. In the smoky pub, nobody took any notice. But no one approached him, either. His demeanour was too threatening, as if he were wrestling with private devils.

The prison psychiatrist had said he was not stupid. He had cunning, self-discipline, a clear sense of direction. There had been women, but his heroes were exclusively male. He loved Frank, almost longed to be him: for both their entire lives, as their accents diverged, he had dreamed of being under his friend's skin, of being him, and had awoken to a wistful feeling that it had nearly been possible, once.

He tore at a hangnail until it bled. Frank, too, had been hurt. Damaged. By that cow of a wife. She had to be stopped. And it would take more than a knife in rubber to do it.

Christine listened once more to the message on the flat's answerphone. It had been recorded several hours earlier. The caller's number was withheld, but from the traffic noise it probably came from a callbox. What on earth could it mean? 'Message for Christine, personal. Darling, sorry. I've not been feeling too brilliant recently. I've gone away for a few days to think things through. Don't worry about me, please. I'll be all right.'

Gone away? Where to? Why?

Benedict was not given to pouring out his innermost emotions at the best of times, and it had to be admitted that the last few weeks had hardly been that. He had been preoccupied and silent, brusque with her. He had seemed calm only when he was engaged on political work, writing a speech or researching for a media appearance. He was then still capable of making jokes, but they had acquired a harder edge, had taken on a tinge of cruelty. As such, the jibes were far more effective and widely repeated, with a concomitant gain in his poll ratings. Christine had sensed, however, that Benedict was uneasy at the blacker direction he was tending to take. But if it was successful, he had little room for manoeuvre.

She had put his increased moodiness down to the gruelling hours during the session. Their private life could have nothing to do with it, surely: Benedict was a political animal first and foremost. He had had no sex before he met and married her, and had been content with celibacy, or so he had insisted. Its lack now should have made only a marginal impact on his well-being. The individual who had expected too much and got little was herself. She was the one to feel sorry for. Benedict had everything going for him.

But now this. It was a puzzle.

She went into the bedroom and started pulling out drawers. Most were undisturbed. A couple of leisure shirts had gone, a pair of jeans, two sweaters. His favourite black leather jacket, which he never wore in town, was not on its hanger. Some bits of underwear, nothing much. And his passport was missing.

Christine sat on the edge of the bed and let it sink in. Her heart like ice, she picked up the phone. If he had left her, then a press statement would have to be agreed. After several attempts she located Lawrence, his cousin, best man and closest friend. 'I don't want to sound like an over-anxious wife, but I'm wondering what's going on.'

The voice at the other end was soft, measured. 'What do you mean?'

'Thinking the worst. I suspect Benedict's gone and done a bunk.'

'Ah.' There was a drawn-out sigh.

Even as she heard the faint hiss on the line, it came to Christine that another possibility had entered Lawrence's head. 'God in heaven,' she said suddenly. 'We'd better call the police.'

# Chapter Twelve

Benedict lay still and kept his eyes shut. If he breathed very slowly so that his heartbeat slowed and his need for oxygen became almost irrelevant, he could make himself float, an inch or two, above the bed. His body became weightless, his limbs lost their connections, tendons and sinews no longer constrained his joints. All he had to do was slide away from conscious thought, put a temporary hold on existence. It was not difficult, but it needed a strange kind of imploded concentration he had avoided for ages. The result was almost a trance, too pleasant to be scary, and too welcome to avoid.

This wasn't a state of sleep, or even drowsiness: his mind was sluggish but watchful. The masters of those mysterious techniques of transcendental meditation would have been proud of him. Instead his physical being felt as if it had simply disintegrated and become insubstantial. The sensation was wonderful, as when in childhood summer days he would sometimes take a boat and row out into the bay, then ship the oars, lie down full length and doze. Above him the restless seagulls would flutter and squeal, but he would dismiss them and let the waves rock him gently into oblivion.

If he remembered those moments now, he felt no regret, no desire to return to those places, for they would not be as isolated, or as coolly windswept, as free of interference from other children and their parents as in the days of his youth. But memory could play tricks. Perhaps twenty years earlier it had been busier, when his neighbours mainly spent holidays on their home beaches and licked ice-cream cones and rode donkeys into the foam. He never recalled the jagged edges of their intrusion, only the calm and peace of the lolling boat, as the clouds parted and a shaft of sunlight made him turn away his face.

As an adolescent he would walk those dunes for miles, especially in the chillier periods of the year when taking out a boat would have provoked questions or produced from his mother an insistence that he take a mackintosh or lifejacket, or – to defeat the object entirely – someone else with him. He had considered taking up golf but the cost defeated him. Any ridicule from schoolfriends would not have been a bother: he was used to their judgement that he was odd. Not odd but unusual, he might have claimed, though to evade bullying he would simply smile as if he had not quite heard. He did not want what they wanted. He was not excited by talk of teenage fumblings with girls. Their competitiveness was closer to his taste, but he did not share its direction: sport, the best team, the biggest goal-scorers, or the latest pop group, did not grab his attention. If they were not inspired by poetry and the Romantics, that was their loss. But Benedict was not in the thrall of writers or singers. His self-indulgence was his own company.

On some days, risking the wrath of his mother, he would choose a spot out of the wind, spread his jacket on the dunes and lie down, with his face towards the grey thrashing sea. The sand would slip through his fingers, grain by grain, slightly damp, leaving his skin smelling of seaweed. How inappropriate that this sand should be used in hourglasses to mark the passage of time when it was so anonymous, so indistinguishable mote from mote; yet anyone who used a timer, as his mother did for his morning egg, had a specific purpose for that moment, and an identity that separated them from everyone else.

He liked being alone. He liked lying silent, not thinking, barely moving. The traffic-jam of ideas inside his head would slow down, their jangle would quieten, as if they had run out of energy. But sometimes they slipped instead into fantasies, when a half-awake brain would conjure up a hazy but familiar image. Often it was a face, unremarkably similar to his own but without the imperfections, the spots, the small scar, the quizzical expression that

protected him from the world. This *alter ego* face was free
of physical marks. Its presence was an immense comfort.
It enveloped him, shut out the cold, and cosseted him
without alteration or limit. Most of all, it sensed how he
felt about everything.

You could never really get inside the mind of any other
person. You could only guess at what was in somebody
else's soul, just as they had only the faintest inkling of the
depths and predilections of yours. If you tried to connect
you took a chance not only of misunderstanding but of
wasting a great deal of time that could be put to much
better use. Trying to connect was, however, an activity
that marked us out as human. We had to try. We had to
risk being rebuffed. We had to risk hurting someone else's
feelings, but in one sense that didn't matter. The only pain
you had no choice about was your own. You had to suffer
that. Other people's you could ignore, even though con-
vention dictated that sympathy be expressed about it. But
you didn't *feel* another person's distress. Only your own.
In the last analysis, we are alone.

The reverie always came to this juncture, and Benedict
was never sure whether it was satisfactory or deeply dis-
turbing. Perhaps there was something fundamentally
wrong with him, that he lived so much inside his own
head and was cut off from the rest of mankind. When he
had gathered the courage to mention it at university, in a
one-to-one tutorial, Andrew had laughed, but not cruelly.
'You have a finer brain than most,' he had said. 'That's

why you get impatient with other's stupidities. Ah, yes, I
have seen you.' Andrew had advised him to treat people
with more consideration: seeing inside their minds was a
matter of practice, not intuition. And for the most part,
other people were worth it. Benedict would discover that,
when he fell in love.

From the prone figure on the bed came a low groan. If
love was the answer, he was more alone than ever.


Maddie and Christine sat at the unadorned wooden table
in the Devon farmhouse kitchen, their backs resolutely to
the door. The blinds were drawn against the light. Above
their heads, shiny copper-bottomed pans, bunches of
herbs and dried lavender hung from the beams. A tea-
towel pinned to the wall carried a recipe for meat pasties.
Before them stood a sturdy china teapot, almost empty,
and a plate of bought-in scones with jam and yellow clot-
ted cream, almost untouched.

Outside a gaggle of press and curiosity-mongers were
kept at bay by the police. From time to time a burst of
laughter could be heard and once a window was rattled,
but a curt, official voice intervened and the intruder was
removed.

'You say the police found him?' Christine glanced over
her shoulder, as if the sleeping Benedict, upstairs in his
old room, or the crowd outside might hear them.

Maddie picked at a scone. 'He wandered into the service station near Bridgwater. Scruffy and dirty. Lost his

jacket. Called them himself. That's been hushed up, of course.'

'Why didn't he simply catch a train if he wanted to come down here?'

'Search me.' Maddie's eyes were down. 'He must have hitched a ride. That's the only thing I can think of. When he was a little boy I used to warn him not to, it's too dangerous. But he took no notice. Once he got as far as Reading. I was frantic. You don't like to imagine what might have happened, do you? He was only ten.'

'Spirit of adventure.'

'No. I don't think so. Defiance, more like.'

Christine smiled despite herself. She could understand Benedict needing to defy his mother. On the other hand, 'Defiance is not an emotion I've tended to associate with Benedict. He's quite the conformist.'

'That's what I used to drum into him. But I often wondered. Water off a duck's back, a lot of it. He would go his own way.' Maddie picked the currants out of her scone. 'Perhaps I should have warned you. You can't tell what's going on inside his head. Defiance you call it, though heaven knows if that's what got into him this time. When he was a kid he was very independent. This time he was running away.'

Her daughter-in-law gave her a sharp look. 'Running away? From me? From our life in London? He's not the sort to shirk responsibility. All he told me was that he was off for a few days. He took some kit with him. But running back to you? With respect, Maddie, I'm sure it's more complicated than that.'

If she expected Maddie Ashworth to bridle she was disappointed. Benedict's mother had been as worried about her son's welfare as anyone. The crisis of his two-day disappearance had not set the women at odds, but as both recognised, it had the potential to bring them together.

'What, then?' Maddie asked wearily.

Faced with the challenge Christine was taken aback. 'Oh, I – I don't know,' she stammered.

'Something in bed, was it?'

'Oh, Maddie, you can't ask questions like that.' Christine's mask began to crumble.

'I'm his mother. I did wonder. It was you, my dear, when we were chatting at the Savoy. You should have had the bloom of a young bride about you and it was missing. You should have been blushing and giggling, maybe even asking me about his personal habits – like, did he always leave the top off the toothpaste tube? Instead it was as if you two were living in separate households. You simply didn't give the impression of being a happily married pair.'

The remarks would have been hurtful had they been delivered in a cutting tone. But Maddie spoke almost mournfully, as if lamenting the loss for her son and his wife. As she finished, her shoulders, usually so proud, sagged a little.

'You may have seen what I couldn't.' Christine's voice faltered, then she sat up. It was time to stop fencing. 'Maddie, this may seem harsh, but did anything, when Benedict was a young man, give you cause for concern? That he might have, ah, difficulties . . . ?'

'I used to tease him about his lack of girlfriends, if that's what you mean. But he was smart. Immediately after I'd mentioned it he'd appear with some lass on his arm, simpering and pretty, as suitable as any mother could want. She'd be dotty about him, you could take that for granted. Then it'd fade, and we'd see her no more. No explanation, but you got the message that he wasn't interested.' Maddie chuckled grimly. 'He'd only dated her to shut me up.'

'He did the right thing to keep people happy. Or off his back,' said Christine slowly. 'I'm beginning to wonder. Was I a necessary convenience? Like washing-powder or loo rolls? Can't manage without 'em in a civilised society. A man must have a wife. "Christine, are you available? Are you keen?" "Delighted, Benedict, honoured to be asked." And here I am.' She fingered her wedding band as if testing whether it would come off without a tug.

'He does love you,' Maddie said. 'I'm sure he's not lying over that.'

'You believe him?'

'Stands to reason. If he didn't, if you didn't matter to him, he'd carry on regardless, wouldn't he? Lots of men find that dead easy. He'd be charming and . . . what's the word? Punctilious. But he wouldn't *care*. I know – I was married to a man like that. Benedict's father.'

Christine gazed at her in surprise, but Maddie waved a dismissive hand. 'A story for another day. What I drilled into Benedict was the importance of good manners, but it was obvious he grasped that better than anyone. Got it from his father, I suppose. But what I admired about the boy was that he did care. He felt things deeply, and he'd think till his head ached. So I reckoned he'd never hurt anybody, wouldn't ever tread a path that'd cause grief. Sounds like I was wrong.'

They did not need to spell out what had taken place. In such a family, between such women, oblique references were sufficient. Christine's throat was dry. When she spoke she felt suddenly old. 'He did try, you're right. He would get upset, but I never thought . . .'

'Mothers can tell.' Maddie poked a finger into the remains of her scone. 'Somehow you suddenly see you're not going to get grandchildren. Better, maybe, than littering the streets with the pups, like some young men do these days. And I won't say anything against him. I won't say I wish he hadn't been born. I won't grieve. He's my son, and I love him.'

'So do I.'

Christine and Maddie clasped hands, the older woman with bowed head, her hair framing her worn face untidily, Christine with a stony expression.

They were sitting silent as the back door creaked open

then shut. A camera bulb flashed, the electric motor whirring aggressively. The noise of rushing feet could be heard, then the gruff official voice once more, ushering the nosy-parkers away.

A tall figure had entered the kitchen.

'Aunt Maddie? Are you there? Christine?'

They withdrew their hands as if they had been discovered in some guilty embrace. Maddie brushed her hair back into place and sat up, reaching automatically for the teapot. 'Lawrence! You've come all this distance? Come in. The tea's gone cold, I'm afraid. I'll make some more.'

'Thank you. It's nasty out there.' Lawrence pulled off his gloves, unfastened his coat and flung it carelessly over a chairback. Neither of the women rushed to hang it up. He jerked a thumb. 'And we have company.'

His hands seemed unsure what to do: they lifted, and flapped, and fell back awkwardly. He was given a mug of tea and curled his fingers around the handle. 'Don't blame me, I voted Tory,' was the slogan round its edge. He read it out with a hollow laugh.

'Benedict's still asleep,' Maddie announced, in a brittle tone. 'He was in a bit of a state when the police brought him – at a guess, he hadn't had a wink in days. But I gave him a hot toddy and tucked him up. We haven't had a peep out of him since.'

'Good, good. That's probably what's best.' Lawrence was trying to sound businesslike.

Christine struggled to smile at him. 'What are the press saying?' she asked quietly.

Lawrence considered. 'I've got the London editions in the car,' he answered, 'but they've nothing much to go on. Benedict Ashworth cancelled engagements and disappeared from view for a couple of days. It isn't a great news story – it hasn't legs. No crime has been committed and the police have kept schtum, thank heaven. I've told them he had a dose of flu and came down to Devon to recuperate. If we don't feed them any more information, it'll die. Provided . . .'

The women waited. Lawrence sighed. There was a strong element of whistling in the dark about this approach, but it was their best hope: if nobody elaborated on the episode, it would slide quickly from a headline to a footnote. 'Provided, of course, that he gets back to work promptly and doesn't hint at another version. Have we any inkling yet what he wants to do?'

Maddie shook her head, her eyes on her daughter-in-law. Lawrence drank his tea, his eyes darting about the kitchen. 'And can I take it nothing's seriously wrong?'

The silence that greeted this query was an eloquent response. He sat down at Christine's side and touched her arm. 'Do you want to tell me? Did you have a row, was that it? We are all family. Whatever happens, we're in this together.'

The word touched a raw nerve. Christine sat up in anger. 'Family! Family? It sounds as if everybody in this family knew perfectly well that Benedict had problems, yet nobody bothered to tell *me*. I'm just the wife.'

They stared at her. It had to be said: 'I'm the one that has to put up with the tears and the groans night after night. I'm the one who has to try with him, and encourage him, and soothe him when he fails. You have no idea. Family! My God, you should be ashamed of yourselves. You especially, Lawrence. I bet you knew. Didn't you? *Didn't you?*' Her voice had risen with a tinge of hysteria. She squeezed his arm tightly till he winced and tried to free himself. She continued, 'He can't help it, and he does his best. But if you were aware of this all along – and you, Maddie, suspected – then why the hell did you push him into getting married? He could have survived happily enough as a bachelor. I didn't push him, that's for sure. A gay bachelor is okay, especially if he refuses to apologise or explain. A gay husband, darlings, isn't. What you've done is create upstairs a very unhappy man.'

'He's not—' Lawrence began, but a glare from Christine quelled him. He took a breath and started again. 'I have no evidence that he's gay. I'm not sure I believe it.'

'What you mean is you've never slept with him,' said Christine rudely. 'Well, I have, and I can give you chapter and verse. Whatever Benedict's sterling personal qualities, he's not into women. Literally. Oh!' She began to weep, her head bent over the table.

'Don't, Christine. It shouldn't matter,' said Lawrence

stubbornly. 'There are gay Cabinet ministers now. The world has become more tolerant.'

'It hasn't,' said Christine, through her tears. 'Not in this country. Not yet. Not on our side of the political fence. And not as long as you politicians try to win votes by bleating on about *family values*. It makes me sick.'

'Enough.' Maddie busied herself putting plates and cups into the sink. 'We're making so much racket we'll wake him. Or those pests outside will hear us. Don't forget, Christine, that he was a grown man, a fully responsible being. And he was very taken with you. That was not a deception. He wanted to get married. He wanted to be like everybody else. He wanted kids, I'll bet.'

'Maybe. Maybe not.' Christine scrabbled under the table for her handbag and found a tissue. She blew her nose. 'The fact is, he's totally wrapped up in his politics. His speeches are his babies. He takes a huge pride in each one, spends hours crafting them. He lives and breathes politics. If we did have children it would humanise him – he'd be a fine father – but the instant he was back on the job they'd be tucked into the furthest recesses of his psyche. Nobody would suffer: he's too good and thoughtful for that. His manners, as you say, are impeccable. But emotionally, we would never be his priority.'

'It's probably too easy to forget that *you* are suffering, Christine.' Lawrence tried to be emollient, which seemed effective. He refrained from commenting that Christine had been equally determined to marry, to such an extent that her own ambition had been remarked upon; she must share any guilt they might have at fitting Benedict into an unsuitable mould. But if Christine stayed loyal, she would take the brunt of the anguish. Only if she broke ranks and began publicly to blame his mother or his friends might she avoid that; and it might be a path she would choose if the misery became too great to bear.

'Lawrence, I was going to ask. Is there any evidence that Benedict was, shall we say, corrupted? Introduced to homosexual practices? When he was a student?'

Lawrence's eyes flickered. 'He was in Scotland, I was at Oxford, so it's hard to say,' he said, then caught Christine's grim expression. 'It sounds as if you might have some evidence, as you put it. What have you found? Some letters, or a diary?'

'God, no. I hope to heaven no such stuff exists.' Christine paused. 'But I did find a photograph. It obviously meant a lot to him, because it was tucked away behind another that was on the wall. It must have been at university. I recognised one of the other people in it. One of the other *men* in it,' she corrected herself.

'Who?'

She had their full attention. 'Does it matter? He's a prominent public figure. He's in this business as well.'

Lawrence was nonplussed, but it was Maddie, busy at the sink, who twisted around and waved a dishcloth in admonishment. 'Watch your mouth, Christine. What are

we talking about? Ruining another life if we chatter about
who it might be? What purpose would that serve?'

The other two blinked at her, astonished. She scrubbed
vigorously at a plate with her dishcloth. 'Whoever it is,
and I can guess who, he's another woman's son. Mothers
can tell, you're right to be critical about that, but admitting it to yourself, or God forbid to anybody else, can be
impossible, honestly. If I must, then I apologise. *There*.
But it keeps coming back to the same point. Benedict is a
grown man. He knows his own nature. He made a free
choice and I'm certain he'll honour it. And he loves you,
Christine.'

'*That's right*.'

The haggard figure in the doorway, hollow cheeks
unshaven, appeared to have aged ten years since his wife
and cousin had last seen him. In a brown dressing gown
tied loosely round the middle with a frayed cord, Benedict
seemed to have lost two stone. His eyes were dull and
puffy. He ran fingers through his thinning hair and
brushed fallen strands from his palm. 'Is that tea you're
offering, Mother? Thank you. I could drink a whole pot by
myself.'

He sat down at the table, picked up a scone and broke it
in half without using a plate. He put a few dry crumbs into
his mouth, then thirstily drank the tea placed before him,
averting his eyes from the three watchers. At last he
seemed ready to speak and motioned his mother to leave
her chores and sit down.

'First, I owe everyone an apology. To you, Mother, for arriving just like that and dragging the rat-pack of the press to your door. And to the neighbours – it can't be fun for them either. And to Lawrence. You've been such a steadfast friend. I've let you down so badly.'

He turned to his wife, met her eyes briefly, then with a twitch of pain looked away. 'Mostly you, Christine. I don't know how to say it – and I'm so slick with words usually, always find the phrase for the moment. But this isn't politics, it's real life. And I ache to the very bottom of my soul for what I've done to you. Because I worship you, and you don't deserve this.'

'Oh, Benedict,' was all Christine could manage. Her fingers crept along the table top till they touched his sleeve, but he moved his arm away.

'Forgive me, I overheard part of your conversation. You understand me rather better than I understand myself. But I've sensed for ages that I was probably gay, perhaps without openly saying it to myself or accepting it. I lived in shadows. I hoped there was an alternative. In those circumstances, taking a wife was unforgivable.'

He seemed about to start on a long narrative. Christine could not stop herself interrupting. 'So why did you?'

'Oh, that's simple. How many people would vote for an openly gay man as a party leader? How many of our activists would say, "Go ahead, chum, it doesn't matter a jot?" A handful. Look at the fuss over Michael Portillo in the Tory Party, the vicious attacks on him by his own side.

And the fact is, equality in law only came when it was forced through against the bitter opposition of their lordships. Sure, we've had bachelors in the past who have been great leaders, but they've survived by keeping it quiet. If they want to get on, they have to conform. Or appear to. They have precious little choice.'

'But there are plenty of those sort in public life. In the arts and theatre, especially,' Maddie said. 'The TV's full of them . . .' She gestured at the shuttered living room.

'They get away with it. In other fields that's impossible. Why? Because most people in this country think homosexuality is a perversion. They find the whole business disgusting. They equate one perversion with another – they think being gay means you're automatically a child molester. How could such a person be entrusted with upholding the law? Such terrible untruths are uttered as if they were gospel. *Gays spread disease. Gays corrupt the young. Gays destroy the fabric of society*. If we were to make gay relationships equal in law to heterosexual ones, we're destroying the family. As if straight men and women haven't done a cracking good job of that already.'

'I have never heard you speak this way before,' Lawrence murmured. 'You sound like a campaigner. But you stayed out of the debate in the House. You are not exactly associated, Benedict, with the equal-rights lobby.'

'Maybe I should've been. I'd have been less of a hypocrite.' There was bitterness in Benedict's voice. 'If what's being said is nonsense, and cruel nonsense to boot, then it's criminal to stay quiet. Especially when people are suffering.'

'Whatever.' His mother narrowed her eyes. 'You were under no obligation to align yourself with such people. Martyrdom gets you nowhere. And there were excellent reasons for that.'

'Yes, and that's because men like me are cowards,' Benedict said angrily. 'We accept society's verdict instead of trying to change it. We let prejudice and bigotry become respectable instead of seeking an intelligent and well-informed debate. We go along with it, we keep our heads down, we're too busy on the day of the vote. What did Burke say? All that is required for evil to triumph is that good men do nothing. When the "good men" are among those who stand to benefit most from change, it's compounding the evil to stay silent.'

He stood up and paced agitatedly around the room. 'That makes it harder for those brave souls who are willing to stand up and be counted. And, anyway, what kind of society are we trying to create? One in which everybody's the same? Heaven help us! We refuse to speak up for diversity, and we conform ourselves, in our own lives. Or try to.' He glanced at Christine, who sat silent, staring at him. 'In the end, it's a lack of leadership. I don't deserve to be where I am. I shall resign at once.'

There was a chorus of 'No, no' from his listeners.

'You're going too fast, Benedict,' said Lawrence, entering a note of caution. 'Tell us what triggered this off.'

Benedict sagged. 'It simply got too much, I suppose. Everyone hinting, asking, "When's Christine going to get pregnant?" Watching our body language when we're out together – are we like any other young couple? Are we touchy-feely? But it was a pretence, and suddenly I couldn't stand it any more. The moment I started to analyse what I'd done, how irresponsible and mad I'd been, I needed some time to sort it out, in my own head at least.'

'If it isn't an entirely stupid question,' said Christine, 'why did you decide on the rock-solid commitment of marriage? We could have been platonic friends, and you would have avoided a lot of this trouble.'

'That wouldn't have worked,' Benedict said. 'I suppose part of the problem lay in my upbringing. I'm not blaming you, Mother, but it's a fact. I was brought up to believe that family life was the best thing going, and I still passionately believe that. In the shadows was the unspoken assumption that a man who preferred men was letting the whole side down and, moreover, that he could never find happiness. It becomes a self-fulfilling prophecy. Tell some poor bloke that he should be disgusted with himself, and he will be. The urges won't go away, but he'll do his damnedest to eradicate them by trying something else.'

'Like finding a supportive woman,' Christine finished for him.

Benedict nodded. 'I've thought about it till my head nearly burst. It's no wonder so many gay men drift around and are promiscuous – they can't stick with a relationship beyond almost anonymous sex. One-night stands are so much simpler. And I'm not like that. I do strongly believe in that commitment you referred to.'

'You always were a serious child,' his mother said comfortingly, but she was sidelined. Benedict was speaking solely to his wife.

'When I said in the past that I regarded myself as a lucky man that you accepted my proposal, it was no more than the truth,' he continued. 'You are a marvellous, lovely, desirable lady. If anybody could have helped me to overcome my, ah, natural tendencies, it was you. And I desperately wanted to eliminate them. To be normal. I needed your help to do it, and I was thrilled when you agreed.'

'That's what you said before we got engaged. You are right: I went into it with my eyes open,' said Christine wryly. She saw Maddie's raised eyebrow. 'Yes, I tried to blame you earlier, Mother. But we make these decisions in a vacuum. I was convinced I knew what I was doing.'

'Well, you didn't. And nor did I. It was an experiment I could never have pulled off. Had I mixed more with gays, read it up, I'd have realised that our plans were a hiding to nothing. Perhaps if you'd had lots of gay friends, darling, you'd have taken me by the hand and told me not to be so foolish. Fact is, you can as easily persuade a gay man to screw a woman as you can persuade a straight man to screw a man. It can't be done.'

'Hold on there,' Lawrence protested. 'What about

Oscar Wilde? He had kids. He was heartbroken when he lost them.'

Benedict pulled his earlobe. 'Maybe he was better at it than I was – the pretence, I mean. But it defeated him in the end, too.'

Christine touched his sleeve. 'When I promised to love, honour and obey, darling, I did it with my eyes open. You were frightened and appalled by what had gone before and I was willing to support you. It never occurred to me, to be frank, that we wouldn't succeed.'

The four sat at the table, avoiding each other's eyes. In the hallway the letter-box rattled. They could hear a high female voice inquiring after Benedict and whether the occupants could confirm he was present.

'We will need to consider carefully,' said Lawrence slowly, 'what we are going to do now. No sudden resignations, if you please, Benedict, for all our sakes. This can't be done in a hurry, not with the howls of that ghastly mob outside. So I suggest we issue a short statement saying you have been unwell, and you expect to be here in Devon for at least a week. That should give us some breathing space. Is that agreed?'

A faint sigh of relief came from the others. Someone had taken charge. Lawrence took the silence as concurrence and left the table.

Benedict rolled over and opened one eye. It was seven o'clock; outside the rain splattered angrily against the window. He would have to rise soon, shave, bathe and dress. This was the day he would return to London, recovered from flu, or a mild dose of pleurisy or whatever it was they had settled on as the cause of his flight.

He trailed a hand over the floor and picked at the carpet, trying to remember the sensation of grains of sand. But it no longer worked: the rough wool tufts did not soothe him.

Back to London, back to the flat, back to the sham marriage. Lavender marriages, they were called, in which a gay man hid by pretending to be straight, with a woman content to act as his accomplice. The options had been stark. He could have left Christine, announced to the world his true nature, offered to resign his post. A divorce would probably have followed, tinged inevitably with recrimination. The world would have sniggered. His credibility would have been damaged beyond repair, whatever tolerance the party might have exhibited. After hours of discussion he had come to accept that this was the most selfish of all the choices. It would hurt his family, his colleagues and his political prospects, none of which he had any right to damage. Perhaps if he had fallen in love with a man, the drive to leave the closet would have been overwhelming. But he hadn't. So it could be resisted.

It was a big help that at least he had spoken openly to his wife, and that she understood, as far as she could. They had talked privately, and they no longer shared a room. Her desire to see him at the top was as strong as ever. She had cited other prominent wives who supported secretly gay husbands. She referred to harder cases, like Hillary Clinton, who had stood by her man even as he interfered with vulnerable young women in the Oval Office; or those who had waited faithfully while a husband served a prison sentence. Benedict had done nothing illegal or even remotely distasteful. His chances of success were undiminished, even by this episode. She would remain loyally with him and urge him on. They would continue to pretend that they lived in conjugal bliss. At some future point they might even try sex again, before Christine was too old to bear children. They both liked children, or claimed to. But success at the hustings would fill any gaps.

This was an equally selfish outcome, Benedict was aware. But it was the one that required the least alteration in their lives, the fewest explanations to outsiders. And it seemed to suit his wife, though Benedict could not fathom why. Maybe she was as ambitious as he was. If so, and if she wanted, she could stand for election herself in due course – and, he suddenly saw, probably would.

The frustrations had to be dealt with, or he would risk breaking down again. It was resolved, with Lawrence's help, to modify the work pattern to leave time to relax. In particular, he would try again to do half an hour's meditation each morning, when his resolve to behave like a model husband – apart from the sex, of course – could be repeated to himself until it became habitual. On top of that he would have set periods for regular exercise. The Commons gym was too public, running did not appeal, while most other sports took too much organisation. He would, however, join the House of Commons rifle club, in the basement, and enjoy taking mental pot-shots at his enemies one evening a week. Lawrence's student interest in martial arts, which he had not practised for ten years, had also surfaced during one brainstorming session. Benedict was intrigued; the idea of a physically demanding hour or two attracted him. Exhaustion was the answer. And it sounded suitably manly.

It was agreed that the two cousins would tackle the ancient art of tae kwon do. Lawrence would find a tutor, and a location. Benedict rubbed his shoulder, naked under the pyjama jacket. He felt slightly more serene. This Oriental sport might prove to be the answer to his prayers.

# CHAPTER THIRTEEN

Diane Clark stared at herself in the full-length mirror. The loose black silk trousers were her own, the fitted jacket in a lurid shade of green still had its price ticket hanging from the collar. On a nearby chair waited several other vivid outfits in plastic covers.

'It's ghastly,' she announced. 'What are you up to? You're trying to make me into something I'm not. You'll have me wearing pearl earrings next. Why can't you pesky people leave me alone?'

'No, no, Secretary of State, it's superb. It shows off your figure to a T. It gives you authority and style. It makes a powerful statement about you.'

The small skinny woman in the black and white suit and teetering high-heeled shoes stepped back and almost tripped over the ministerial red box that had been left carelessly, its lid open, on the floor. Diane grunted crossly, marched over, pushed the woman to one side and slammed the lid. The woman jumped sideways like the scrawny magpie she resembled, as if caught in the act of pilfering official papers.

'Effing boxes. We're supposed to guard them with our lives,' Diane said. 'The other day I was on the train heading to my constituency and I had to go to the loo. Off I went, and I bought a coffee on the way back. When I returned to my seat there's some fat bastard in pinstripes saying, "Well, *Mzzz* Clark, I don't think much of your security." He reported unguarded secret papers to the police, would you believe? Back in London Monday morning there was hell to pay. The Boss issued a solemn warning to the entire Cabinet: watch your boxes, there may be spies about. Huh!'

The colour consultant retreated as if the accusation of spying had been directed at her personally. Then she drew herself up to her full diminutive height. Her head bobbed back and forth above the frills of the crisp white blouse. Diane felt the urge to feed her peanuts. 'With respect, Secretary of State, you are changing the subject. We don't have long. I am tasked with assisting you to select three new outfits which will trademark your unique image and enhance the government's standing in the eyes of the public. As a committed supporter of the Prime Minister I can't leave till that is completed.' She stood her ground stubbornly, her mouth set.

'As it says here, does it?' Diane's finger traced an invisible line on an imaginary memo. She grinned. 'Sorry. I'm being a pain, as usual. It's just that I don't feel comfortable in this fancy get-up, hand-stitched seams and padded shoulders. I thought they went out with the ark, no? If I had my way, we'd have Fridays every single day.'

'Fridays?' The woman was mystified.

'When companies tell their employers that on a Friday they don't have to come to work in formal gear. They can wear jeans or whatever. Helps them feel more relaxed. It's a great idea.'

The woman shuddered.

Diane tugged the emerald cloth over her bosom and twisted to look over her shoulder. 'The trouble with green,' she said, as she unfastened the oversized buttons, 'is that it vanishes into the green leather of the Commons benches. You get a disembodied head floating above a hazy body. But orange or red, the colours we're supposed to wear, are so bloody reminiscent of the Thatcher era that I can't bear them. This malarkey serves no purpose anyway since nobody's watching our ancient and ceremonial duties in the House. Not any more. We're mouthing inanities, merely going through the motions. So why can't we wear decently sludgy colours and a pair of old trainers, as if clothes didn't really matter, which they don't?'

The woman flushed and opened her mouth again, but Diane pretended to read the invisible memo to silence her. 'Yeah, I know. Orders have gone out. But I hate the whole business.'

'We have that one in ecru,' the woman said doggedly. 'Not your best shade since you have such strong features, but it would perform quite well in the Commons and under lights in the TV studio. Ecru makes a woman appear both dignified and feminine.'

Diane bared her teeth and hissed, then laughed at the woman's affronted reaction. 'I give up. I'm summoned to see the Boss tomorrow. Could you bring one round tonight? Then I can make an impression.'

The woman reached for her notepad. 'Certainly. And, if I may say so, you have made an excellent selection. Would you like it in royal blue as well?'

In the *Globe* conference room it was business as usual. James Betts lit a cigarette and moved away from the smoke detector. The campaign to name and shame paedophiles had been a tremendous success. Circulation figures had soared and appeared to have stabilised some thirty thousand higher than in the previous quarter. The proprietor would be delighted. The fact that two unfortunates had committed suicide and several convicted child abusers had been driven from their homes by vigilante groups had also been front-page news. It was the right thing for good, honest citizens to do. It helped protect their children from the evils of society, especially those wide-eyed infants who accompanied their parents as they screamed abuse and hurled bricks through windows. The newspaper could afford to ignore the notion peddled by hand-wringing liberals that the vast majority of abused children were victims of their own relatives. That established fact was not the press's currency, for how could you accuse such citizens of being as wicked as their neighbours? Particularly when they bought and read the paper.

Betts chuckled to himself. Pansy Illingworth, the editor, was still poring over the figures with the circulation manager. Circulation was all. Every aspect of the paper was measured by it. If the public wanted dumbing down, then dumbing down they would get. Screaming headlines certainly helped a lot. The *Globe*'s role was to identify any current unease in society, translate it into prurient adjectives and print it in full colour across seven pages. A balanced view would have diluted the impact so was banned. It was emphatically not their job to postulate solutions, only to keep scratching the wounds until either the government came up with a convincing remedy, which was unlikely, or some more attractive campaign surfaced. The public were not only easily aroused, they were easily bored. You had to move on or they would – to a rival newspaper with another scandal to plaster over the billboards.

'It's a rat-race out there. And I'm a rat,' Betts murmured to himself with satisfaction.

Pansy completed her discussion and approached him.

'Sorry to nag, Jim, but I was wondering how you were getting on with the abandoned wife.'

He blinked. 'I haven't got a wife . . .' he began, then saw he was being teased. 'You mean Mrs Frank Bridges,' he continued huffily. 'You sure you want an in-depth interview with her? She's barmy. And he might sue.'

'So? It's a terrific story. We don't have to check her allegations, merely report them. Keep the juicy bits in quotes, Jim. And on tape. Then she's the target if he wants to go to law, not us. You know the rules.'

Betts was aware that this was not strictly true, but he was unstinted in his admiration for the slipperiness of the paper's lawyers, the sole exemplars of the legal profession entitled in his view to be regarded as members of the human race.

'By the way, the proprietor and the PM met at a fundraising dinner in Downing Street Tuesday.' Pansy dropped her voice. 'You were mentioned as one of the finest investigative journalists of the decade. No, don't go modest on me, you've won awards.'

Betts sucked pensively at his cigarette and stayed silent.

'The proprietor is a fan of yours, says he reads your main piece first – after the sports pages and the leaders, of course – so he pointed out to the PM that it's not great if we and they are in dispute.'

Betts reflected privately that, in another era, an investigative journalist like himself would have regarded the government of the day as prime targets, not as allies. He kept the thought to himself, along with others more agreeable about the low-cut sweater Pansy was wearing, and grunted.

'What I'm getting at, Jim,' Pansy glanced about, her voice a low hiss, 'is that we're about to get some movement on that article you wrote about Diane Clark. Remember?'

'Oh, yes. How she was the vilest lady in the country, and a disgrace to politics?'

'That's the one. You may have to swallow your pride a little, but we'll make it worth your while. Anyway, you don't care either way about her, do you?'

'I don't care,' said Betts, holding his cigarette between his teeth and blowing smoke nonchalantly as he spoke, 'about any of them. Not a scrap.'


Diane twitched the new jacket about her shoulders. Ecru? Muddy beige, more like, but at least that was closest to the shade she would have picked for herself. The cut was a disaster; it was tight under the arms and pulled across her back. The image consultant had insisted that the fitted shape showed off her firm bosom, but that probably meant the garment was too small.

'Just run that past me again. You want me to drop my action against the *Globe*?'

'Yes. I feel it's in the best interests of the government.'

Diane tried to read the Prime Minister's expression, but the bland friendliness of his half-smile was belied by cold blue eyes. 'So it doesn't matter that they call us liars and cheats, and imply that women like me shouldn't be in public office?'

The PM smiled more broadly. 'I'm not sure it is always wise to challenge such comments in court, unpleasant and offensive though they may be,' he said smoothly. 'I remember my early legal training. Our head of chambers took his lead from one or two notable libel lawyers. "It is within the law to accuse politicians of lying, since they do so daily." Prominent individuals have even admitted it at the despatch box or in select committee. Dissembling is the kinder word.'

'Being economical with the truth.'

'That was a civil servant, Sir Robert Armstrong. The wittier version was "being economical with the *actualité*".'

'Alan Clark. Yuk. He was a horrible man. Thank heaven he was no relation.' Diane sniffed, as if an unnatural smell had entered the room. 'He pretended to love women but that was for one purpose. Bed. In reality he hated them. Or, at least, intellectual women, those who could match his brains and resist his sexual charms. *He* didn't think women had a place at the top table.'

'He adored Margaret Thatcher.'

'He was crackers. That proves it.' The two politicians laughed self-indulgently at one opinion they could share. The PM shifted in his seat so that he could catch sight of the clock on the far wall. The movement was not lost on Diane. 'So what happens next?' she asked.

'You'll be made an offer. Haggle by all means, but don't

let it go on too long. You should come out fairly well. You'll get an apology in open court, which will feel as if you've won. From the government's point of view, it's one less dispute, one less forest fire to fight. We will be profoundly grateful to you.'

Diane sighed. 'I suppose I can still make something of it, talk as if it's a victory?'

The PM smiled that broad, toothy grin, the one the cartoonists had exaggerated with such glee. Along with his prominent ears it gave him the appearance of a jack-rabbit: fussily in charge, but emphatically not in control. 'Say whatever you wish. Downright whoppers are entirely acceptable. But don't get us into any more trouble, please.'

Five items lay in the post-box: three slim white ones redirected from her old home, one brown oblong from the Inland Revenue – nothing that looked as if it might contain hate mail. And one large scruffy Jiffy-bag, re-used, stuffed with envelopes addressed to her care of the magazine, which had already been opened.

Gail carried the mail into the flat and spread the contents on the kitchen table. An invitation to a charity lunch at the Dorchester detained her briefly until the accompanying application form told her that the tickets were seventy-five pounds apiece. An appeal from another charity to support its work in Rwanda, a relic of days when she had impulsively phoned donations to emergency

numbers. A reminder, not particularly tactful in its wording, that her credit card was about to be withdrawn. And
a reassessment from the taxman that still overestimated
her income: she would have to write to them again.
Nothing was personal. No note from a friend or family, no
acknowledgement that she existed, except on official mailing lists, rather out of date.

And the letters from *Today's Woman*, inquiries from
readers, the personal issues that they thought she might
like to handle as their new agony aunt. Another money
earner handled by dear Mr Clifford Maxwell on her
behalf.

It would be, he had assured her, well within the capa-
bility of a mature, intelligent person like herself. Anything
specific would have been weeded out already, to be dealt
with by their specialists: how to remove ballpoint from
suede, how to dye navy blue curtains pale pink, the difference between pesto and basil sauce, how to serve lumpfish
roe. Most of these questions, Gail felt, she would have
enjoyed having a crack at. She would have told the curtain
lady not to be so silly, to get herself some pink fabric and
make new curtains – or buy them from John Lewis, it
would be quicker. The pesto puzzler would have been
advised to stick to Heinz tomato ketchup: it was still the
best. And the lumpfish roe? Gail vaguely recalled that it
was like caviar. Like caviar, then, on tiny water biscuits.
The Russians washed it down with vodka; she had helped
Frank entertain delegates at a TUC conference and been

staggered at the alcohol they had put away while remaining upright. What a load of rubbish.

The postmarks suggested that somebody in the office had been hanging on to the readers' inquiries for weeks. Even if she responded to every one today and caught the afternoon post it would be two months before the next edition appeared with her advice. No individual replies were possible. So whatever good she might do by offering sensible comments, it would probably be too late. She hoped no one was depressed or threatening self-harm. If so, they might well have jumped off Westminster Bridge by now.

The envelopes were accompanied by a typed note from a girl named Tina, whom Gail did not know. It asked for fifty words per reply in Word on a disk or by e-mail. Gail sniffed. Tina could go whistle for that; the most she could manage on the battered computer was to compose and print out. Just about. If the machine was playing up, longhand on lined paper would have to do. The note continued,

Sorry this is such a thin collection. We asked round the office and came up with some more you might like to try; just do your replies and we'll fluff out the details.
1. My fellah says we should be more adventurous. He wants to tie me to the bedposts when we make love. Should I let him?

2. I've fallen in love with my boss. She's gorgeous. Am I a lesbian?
3. My mother has seduced my boyfriend and now he wants to live with us both. She's a great cook and I'm hopeless. Should I say yes?
4. I'm fifty and my husband says I'm sagging everywhere. Time for the gym, for a facelift or for a new husband?

Gail sighed. They were so obviously synthetic, not least because of the underlying assumption that the inquirer had a free choice and some degree of influence over the outcome. Real life was not like that. In any case they did not lend themselves to discursive answers. 'No', 'Yes', 'You must be joking' and 'Tell him to be thankful for what he's got' were probably not what Tina had in mind.

She fetched a notepad and pen and opened the first genuine envelope. The letter had a sour smell and brown stains on the back as if it had been written in a patch of spilt coffee.

I have been living with my boyfriend for six years and we have three adorable little girls. I also have a teenage son from a previous relationship and my boyfriend has twin sons who stay with us at weekends. He spent a week away at a sales conference and it has badly unsettled him. When he came home he said he couldn't stand the mess,

the nappies and the smell of sick and poo, and that
he had fallen in love with the receptionist. He's
packing his bags as I write. I still love him and
want him to stay. Is he selfish, or should I try to
tidy up and fight to keep him? What have I done
wrong?

'Shown appalling taste in men,' Gail muttered. 'But
that's not a crime. Lord, what a pickle. Selfish bastard. At
least I didn't have children to worry about. Maybe the
best answer would be to see a solicitor and screw some
money out of him. Though that would have been easier if
you'd been married to begin with.' She chewed the end of
her biro. Such remarks would sound callous on the
printed page. The column had to make a favourable
impression; she could hardly ask for public sympathy if
she showed none herself. The next one was typed, more or
less neatly, on blue notepaper.

I'm thirty-one and have a two-year-old son with
my boyfriend, who I've been with eight years. But
recently I slept with a workmate. It wasn't a real
affair, more of a fling after we'd had a row at home
about something trivial. It felt great to be wanted,
but now I feel awful. I want to tell my boyfriend,
but I know that's simply to ease my conscience and
test his love. I'm terrified I'll lose him. What
should I do?

'Keep your big mouth shut, ducky,' Gail said aloud. Honestly, what fools these women were. They seemed to have precious little idea of loyalty, or of guile. Keeping a marriage going needed both in substantial quantities. Not that this girl was married. In fact none of them seemed to be married. Had it gone out of fashion completely?

Nobody seemed to understand commitment any more. These stupid women who were so upset and muddled that they felt compelled to write to a stranger for advice: did they seriously expect simple answers? Marriage was hard. She could tell them that. But worthwhile, mostly. Except that they hadn't even taken the step of getting married. Odd, how they could spawn children and yet find it so hard to lead a man to the altar. For her, it had been the exact opposite. Yet the outcome had been no happier.

Why didn't any of the letters say, 'My husband abandoned me after twenty-five years' of marriage and now seems to regard me as a nuisance. He's been trying to get rid of me, and if I were to be entirely honest, I'm not only lonely and miserable, I'm scared. It'd suit him if I disappeared off the face of the earth, never to be seen again'? And that, as far as erstwhile friends and family were concerned, was precisely what had occurred.

Suddenly Gail felt a great sense of hopelessness. She was in no position to give anyone else advice on emotional matters, not even half in jest for the manufactured items in Tina's note. She put down her pen and tried to avoid revisiting the slashed tyres, the hate mail. But on the table, under the envelopes, lurked the demand from the credit-card company. Their nastiness could be defeated with a cheque, but she had to earn the money.

It was as she was sitting there, nibbling the pen and her thumbnail alternately and turning over the letters, that the phone rang. The sound made her jump.

'Mrs Bridges?' A man's voice, polite and emollient.

'Who wants her?'

'James Betts of the *Globe*. I'm so sorry to bother you like this. I was recommended to you by your PR adviser. He said you might be ready to give an interview. Could I come round so we can discuss it?'

Gail racked her brains. Which newspapers, which columnists, had nice Mr Clifford Maxwell suggested to her? She could not remember. He had not wanted to put too much on paper. He had told her to call him if she had any problems.

'Mrs Bridges, my editor wants me to write a piece that is entirely sympathetic. Otherwise it won't be printed. You can see it before it goes in, if you prefer, to check. Would that help?'

Editorial control, that was called. Mr Clifford Maxwell had said that was rare. 'Can you guarantee that?' Gail asked.

'Of course, Mrs Bridges. Whatever you want.'

Gail hesitated. Another opportunity to have her say, to get it off her chest, would be welcome. But the *Globe* did not have the cleanest reputation. Her eyes strayed to the table where the demand from the credit card company seemed to have grown larger, the letters for the agony column smaller but more numerous and less comprehensible. The voice came again, wheedling and hopeful. 'And, naturally, we can ensure that there will be a substantial fee.'

What choice was there? Refusal, and a nasty tussle with the bank which she could not win. Acceptance, and her monetary worries would be kept at bay for some while longer. It was hardly a Faustian pact: she wasn't selling her soul, provided she told the truth. But still she felt uneasy. A vestige remained of the old, shy Gail, who had avoided publicity like the plague, who had deplored the humiliation to which public men and women were exposed: that Gail had found the whole business utterly distasteful.

'Two thousand, Mrs Bridges. In cash if you want it,' came the voice.

Twenty minutes later the street bell rang and the same tones floated through the intercom. Gail pressed the entry button. In a few moments James Betts was in the room, removing his mackintosh and accepting a cup of instant coffee.

The écru jacket lay neglected and crumpled on the floor of the inner office. Diane glared across the table. 'Edward, it's no good looking at me like that. You may be ecstatic. I am not.'

Edward leaned forward, his brow puckered, his

expression that of an earnest and loyal sheepdog. 'It is a victory. You should definitely treat it that way.'

'Huh. You're the second person who's tried to placate me with that today. The other was the Boss, and he didn't make a much better fist of it than you're doing.'

Edward tapped the fax. 'They're going to withdraw the article, every word. They will apologise to you in the newspaper, on the main comment page. They will pay you substantial damages and every penny of your costs. If you went to court and won, you wouldn't get that, only a proportion of what you'd spent. So what more could you ask?'

'Stop being a bloody lawyer! I want my day in court. I want them to grovel for what they said about me. It wasn't merely the horrible remarks, deplorable though they were. It was the sheer hatred of women they revealed. Our sex is not capable, in the author's view, of holding high office. If they're normal, in a settled partnership with kids or whatever, they should be at home serving their husbands like nice women do. And if they don't have such distractions, they aren't normal and couldn't possibly be trusted with a top job. Misogyny rules, okay? Even in this new century. Makes me sick.'

Edward pondered whether to humour her, but realised suddenly that Diane was not fighting but seeking an honourable way out. She was under instructions.

'You could still have your day in court,' he suggested. 'Ask for the apology to be made by counsel before a judge. It'd be at the Royal Courts of Justice in the Strand.

Everything said is agreed in advance. You'd still have them grovelling in print too. You wouldn't have to pay for the QC, they would. They have to agree the wording in any eventuality. That's what this fax is about.'

'Bloody lawyers. Bloodsuckers and creeps.' Diane let herself pull faces as she had done as a child when thwarted. Then she smiled sweetly, showing her teeth. 'Oh, sorry, Edward, darling, you're one of them. I'd forgotten.'

'I hadn't.' Edward's courage was growing. 'We'll tip off the media and they'll be there in force. You can be present too. Then every one of the following day's papers, not only the *Globe*, will have your delighted face on the front page. And you'd be on TV too. The winner! It won't simply feel like a victory, it'll *be* one.'

The ministerial clock ticked quietly as Diane reread the ten-page fax. 'It'd give me a reason to wear my new outfit, I suppose. What do I say about damages, Edward?'

He was noncommittal. 'You will be asked what you're planning to do with them. You should decide the line now.'

'Can't say I need the money. I've no chance to spend any. The most precious commodity in this game is time. An extra day a week would be bliss, but that's not on offer. So d'you recommend I take the cash and give it to charity?'

'By all means.' Edward recognised in his use of the phrase everything about oily legal practitioners he had most despised. He smiled. 'Damages are tax-free. Take the money, put it in a separate account, then give it to some worthy causes as they occur to you. That should cover any impertinence.'

'But not quite the lot,' Diane responded, with a laugh. 'We'll use some to have a party. For everyone who helped put me where I am. And for those who are assisting in keeping me there, a much harder task given my total unsuitability and crassness and dreadful taste in clothes. And that includes you, dear, sweet, adorable Edward. Will you come?'

'Oh, no. He was a decent husband. I wouldn't say he was a rogue, not really. If he'd been a rogue, I would never have married him. Or stayed as long as I did.'

Gail was tired. Over an hour had passed and the ferrety journalist from the *Globe*, whose name she could not now remember, was still firing questions at her relentlessly. They had long passed over the state of her car, the unpleasant threat in the mail, which she could not show him as the police had it in their files, and the unhappy circumstances in which she was forced to live. Her penury had been touched on several times. It was taking a considerable amount of effort to concentrate, word for word, on both his inquiries and her responses. The problem was that the questions, of course, were never quite what they seemed.

For example: if asked whether Frank had been a bad husband by anyone else, she would have retorted, 'Yes.

Why do you think he was playing around? Isn't that the definition of a bad husband?' But to say it to the press would elicit the headline, 'Frank Bridges: Rogue and Serial Philanderer,' with hints that it was her unsympathetic behaviour (worse, frigidity) that had set him off. In this man's world of double standards, the woman would be landed with the blame, it stood to reason. And this journalist was a man.

He did not seem interested in her fears about her own safety, or the reluctance of the police to interrogate or arrest her husband. It had been on the tip of her tongue to say tartly that they'd have jumped to it had Frank insisted, but of course Frank as instigator could not do that. Gail was sufficiently experienced in dealing with the press from the days when she had protected Frank (or pushed him forward) to note that Betts's eyes lit up only when she referred to their earlier life. What he was after was her version of it, with details as shocking and intimate as possible.

'But would you have him back?' Betts composed his expression into one of unctuous empathy.

'No, I wouldn't,' Gail answered guardedly. 'Anyway, that's daft. We're divorced and he's got a new wife. Crossed that bridge a long time ago.'

Betts bent his head and wrote a short phrase. Upside down, Gail could not decipher it. She hoped it would not translate as 'Bitter ex-wife shows she still loves erring husband. "I would have him back if I could, but he has abandoned me for ever," she sobbed.' Gail had read enough reams of human interest stories in papers like the *Globe* to guess precisely how such a statement of the obvious could be twisted.

It occurred to her that such queasy tittle-tattle masquerading as serious reporting frequently appeared in the women's section of the paper. That was a puzzle. Surely women readers would admire and empathise with others who had been through the mill, so why did the slant seem so negative and hostile?

Her own adverse reactions to the agony column letters flooded back to her. She, too, had been critical of other people's misfortune, not least – in fact, rather more – since they were also women. Perhaps the same was true with the *Globe*'s lady readers. Snug in their cosy homes, they turned over the pages on the kitchen table among the remains of the morning's breakfast, drinking tea, discarding the business section and getting marmalade on the cartoons. They believed, if they considered it for a moment, that anybody in the mess she was in must be the architect of their own fate: that they had merited it in some way.

'I don't deserve this,' Gail said. 'It's not fair.'

'Oh, absolutely,' said Betts. 'So tell me, Mrs Bridges, these days Frank has quite a reputation on the sexual front. A philanderer. It appears he was forever chasing women. Several have contacted the paper and are keen to sell us their stories.'

Gail's hand flew to her mouth. 'Several? How many? Will you be interviewing them as well?'

'Ah. We don't indulge in chequebook journalism. The proprietor does not allow it.' This, like many other assertions Betts had made in the course of the afternoon, was not quite correct. It would have been truer to say that the proprietor made speeches expressing his abhorrence of chequebook journalism, then let his editor go her own way. 'They won't talk unless paid. And the evidence that one or two have ever met your husband, let alone indulged in three-in-a-bed sessions with him, is a bit iffy.'

'Three in a bed? Frank? Good Lord. One in a bed was enough for him, and then he'd be snoring the whole night.' It was out before she could stop it: Gail could have bitten off her tongue. Faust had been caught by his own duplicity and had gone to hell, willy-nilly. Betts shrugged and said nothing.

In the pause her curiosity surfaced. 'These girls who make allegations about my Frank that aren't true, why would they do that?'

'For the very worst reasons, Mrs Bridges. It must be awkward for a respectable person like yourself to understand.' Betts let his eyes water as if in grief.

'For money? But what about the damage to their own reputations, let alone my Frank's?'

Betts's eyebrows lowered. Gail answered her own question. 'What reputation, eh? I'm being naïve.'

'No, no. But my editor would appreciate it if you could fill in the background. What sort of chap was he, when you were together? Was he romantic? Very active in bed, keen? Would you call him the passionate type? In other words, Mrs Bridges, was your Frank a great lover, and should we be fearful for the health of his new marriage? Or does she have nothing much to worry about?'

# CHAPTER FOURTEEN

The basement of the block of flats was reached by taking the lift to the lower ground floor, ignoring the sign to the underground car park, and opening an unmarked steel door. Its rivets were almost buried under layers of grimy white paint, bringing to mind, Benedict thought, an old crone's warts under makeup. It was noisy and hot. From a nearby chamber came the rumble of central-heating boilers; steam gurgled overhead through fat pipes encrusted in yellow and rusty dribbles. Spiders scuttled and curled up under blackened cobwebs like so many twitching asterisks. In a cupboard the lift mechanism sighed and hissed incessantly.

A set of fire extinguishers and a hydrant, its red paint dirty, barred their way. The door was four inches thick, and heavy. Benedict grunted as he broke a nail on it. 'Not much used, this place?' he inquired.

Lawrence propped the door open with a fire extinguisher. A whiff of cooler air stirred the cobwebs. 'Not recently. Lord Smart persuaded the landlord to do it up for his personal use, though since he was jailed nobody much has come here. There isn't any movable equipment; the noble lord's wife whisked it away the moment he was in financial difficulties. But the basic services should be operational and I tipped the caretaker to give it a thorough scrub. This time of the day, he said, nobody'd want it. Privacy guaranteed. Here we are.'

He switched on the lights. A handsome low room of over thirty metres square was revealed, its pale wood flooring swept with a dull gleam. Although the skylights were obscured by grime, the neon strip-lights gave an almost too brilliant illumination. At one end a brick climbing wall had been installed with ropes as thick as a man's fist; full-size mirrors at the other reflected the two men's images brazenly back at them.

The atmosphere was airless and dusty. 'There must be some form of ventilation.' Benedict put down their bags. 'And showers, maybe. If we can get everything working it won't be too awful.'

Lawrence frowned as he paced along the inner wall. 'Let's explore. Our teacher arrives in ten minutes and I'd like to impress him.'

At the far corner he located a beech-veneered door. He

opened it and they were greeted by the faint smell of bleach and a blue-tiled suite of modern showers and toilets. They draped their towels on the heated rail and switched it on. They tried the gold-trimmed taps: everything appeared functional. As the water flowed warm over their fingers and the ventilators hummed into action their spirits rose.

'You did well to find this,' Benedict said, sensing that he had appeared ungracious. 'Feel like the Nibelungs down here. Hammers, anvil and rings optional.'

He stood hesitantly as Lawrence laid out his kit on a wooden bench and kicked off his loafers. Lawrence stopped. 'Come on. You can't do martial arts in your ordinary clothes. Not unless you're attacked in the street, that is.'

'Doesn't it need special jackets and trousers?'

'I brought some for you.'

Benedict smoothed the simple garments. They felt clean and crisp, like hospital sheets, like the linen at his prep school on Fridays, the day the beds were changed. Clinical, fresh, puritan. He stripped off to his shorts and hung each item, including his tie, carefully on a hanger. Keeping his back to Lawrence he picked up the sportswear and put it on, tying the belt loose.

A new voice greeted them. A small shaven-headed man with a squat muscular body, pecs and biceps bulging through a blue tracksuit, filled the doorway. His face was square and hairless, his ancestry European with a hint of

Chinese, the skin tanned and taut. He introduced himself as the instructor Lawrence had arranged. In a few moments he too was ready in white, loose-fitting garments with a prominent black belt.

Out in the gym their bare soles made contact with the floor. Benedict curled his toes. 'Our feet'll get filthy,' he remarked. The tutor scowled and shook his head as if such levity was inappropriate.

Lawrence punched Benedict playfully. 'Do this right and we'll be black and blue in no time,' he said. 'Just forget what you look like. Nobody's watching. We're entirely private and no one else will be allowed in here during our sessions. It's a different world. One in which, to say the least, you can get rid of all those tensions that have been causing you grief.' Lawrence ignored the warning glance in the tutor's direction; the man himself remained impassive. 'I mean it, Benedict. Thump the hell out of me if it helps. That's the whole idea.'

'Let me check,' Benedict pressed, with a grin, as the tutor waited. 'You won't sue me for common assault if I wallop you from here to high water?'

'Don't be an idiot. Of course not.'

The tutor faced them and bowed. 'Now, gentlemen, if you please. Let me explain the essential philosophy.'

For the next hour the men were pupils and teacher of the ancient art of tae kwon do. The first lesson was the honour ceremony. Hands clasped over their heads the cousins faced the master. With solemn expressions they stumbled through the chant of salutation. Benedict started to giggle, until chided by a gruff command from Lawrence. Their sport was a commitment to themselves, to their opponent and to the gods that made them, the teacher explained. It was important not to skip this bit but to take it seriously. A contact sport undertaken in a selfish frame of mind was more likely to lead to bad practice that would result in injuries. This was not tennis.

He took them through stretching exercises till their tendons ached, then demonstrated the principles of attack and defence. There were so many misconceptions in the West. It was a gross oversimplification of such arts to assert that one fighter simply used his opponent's weight against him; the fundamentals were vastly more complex. The action involved understanding the opponent's tactics and favourite moves, anticipating and inviting their repetition. And figuring out, in advance, how to use those predictabilities against him. An experienced fighter who had done his homework would react instinctively at a lunge or sidestep, guessing where it might lead; when the thrust came, split seconds later, the target had vanished. The attempt would be abortive, the attacker thwarted, pinioned in his turn, and the point won.

'It sounds exactly like politics,' Benedict grunted, as he hit the ground for the third time. He knelt, winded. 'But it's a little difficult when you've never done it before.'

'But this shows why it's perfectly satisfactory for two people to fight together regularly, as you two intend.' The tutor lifted him to his feet. 'As in chess. You've got to burrow into your opponent's mind. It'll vary depending on his mood, the weather, what his boss said to him in the office and so on. No two sessions will be alike. This is quite a cerebral sport. It always surprises those who come to it fresh.'

He motioned the novices to take a breather, then to try a few feints with each other while he barked comments. In a moment a red-faced Benedict, though he struggled to use his weight as instructed, was again flat on his back, though on this occasion he had managed to remain upright for longer. Lawrence and the tutor applauded. 'You're getting there, well done,' said Lawrence, and hauled his cousin up.

As he spoke he reached out, as he might for a child, to rescue Benedict's belt, which had come loose. The jacket had swung open to reveal a thin chest, the flesh livid with red bruising. They were standing close. Each could feel the other's quick breath on his cheek, the glow of his hot panting body, sense the air flowing between them. A sheen of sweat covered Benedict's forehead, and he brushed it away with his bare forearm, then pulled the jacket to hide himself.

Lawrence tied the belt nonchalantly and patted his shoulder. His cousin flinched. Their eyes met, and Benedict stepped away awkwardly. The tutor pretended not to have noticed, as if present at an intimate act.

A few yards over their heads on the ground floor, the

caretaker, who preferred to be called a concierge, was interrupted as a tenant made an inquiry about a lost key. Alone once more he reverted to observing the basement room through the security camera high in its ceiling.

On arrival, the tutor had passed the time of day amiably enough and mentioned he was booked for five lessons only. The concierge checked the reservations folder. Then he searched for and found a number in the phone book. And, after watching Benedict, Lawrence and the shaven-headed teacher intently for a further twenty minutes, he reached for the phone.

Melvyn O'Connor tossed his jacket on to an armchair, selected a CD from an anonymous pile and began to warble tunelessly.

Betts put his hands over his ears. 'I wouldn't mind so much if you could actually sing,' he muttered. 'Silence would be preferable. Where's that bourbon?'

Melvyn was dancing round his room whirling his arms like a windmill. His tubby belly wobbled, lank hair fell over a greasy forehead, his eyes bulged wetly. Life at the top was clearly taking its toll.

'Here.' He plonked the Jack Daniel's, two glasses and an ice bucket on the table and sat down heavily. '"Spinning Wheel". My favourite. Blood Sweat and Tears. Do you remember them? I don't honestly myself, I was too young, but you're about the right age.'

'Your signature tune, you might say. Spinners of the world, unite: you have nothing to lose but your House of Commons pass.' Betts poured a treble over the ice and ignored the remark about his age. 'Thanks, I need this. At a guess, you've been at it already.'

'Had a couple with Alistair before I left. He's cock-a-hoop. Brags that Diane Clark and our lot have scored over you and the *Globe*, Jim. I said he shouldn't be so sure.'

'I was banned from the High Court,' Betts said gloomily. 'Told very firmly to be nowhere near the Strand. To get lost. The *Globe* would do as it had pledged, put a full apology on the comment page in the same spot where we told the truth about the Secretary of State for Whatever She Is ages ago. Pardon me.' He burped loudly. 'Libelled her viciously. I forgot. Stupid cow. There won't be any more column inches in my newspaper about the case, however much others may hype it up. But it goes against the grain, I tell you.'

'She was prancing around in the street tearing up copies of the *Globe*, whooping like a banshee,' Melvyn reported helpfully. 'Claimed the settlement vindicated women. And she invited everybody to a party. I imagine she's smashed as hell right now.'

'Which is what I'd like to be.' Betts poured another drink for himself and Melvyn. 'Nobody from our place wanted to help me drown my sorrows. Skirted me the whole day as if I'd been in the wrong, not her. Course, they'll have forgotten about it by next week. I've just inputted a snappy piece on the long-running saga of Frank Bridges, with quite a nice twist if I say so myself; and then it'll be "Done it again, lad," and "Great stuff, Jim." But for tonight I'm a bloody leper.'

'It was fifty grand she got, wasn't it?' One of Melvyn's motives in inviting Betts to his flat for a drink instead of attending Diane's party was not only their rather fragile friendship but curiosity and a desire to fill the gaps. On his home computer in the bedroom the file was poised for the diary he planned to complete before the night was out, if he was sober enough. The diary would not, could not, see the light of day until after Melvyn had left the government's service. Inevitably, given the insecure nature of his profession, that day would come. When it did, publishing his account would keep him afloat. Rainy day money. By comparison, a bottle of bourbon dispensed in the cause was as nothing.

Betts nodded. 'More or less. The amount's confidential. Who does she think she is? What I wrote was too close to the bone. She sets herself up as a champion of women, yet she's a million miles from most of them. She's never had kids but she pontificates about how to bring 'em up. And about child care and child support, creating mayhem and misery for perfectly respectable blokes who'd rather forget about the grotty first wife and her brats, thank you very much. She pretends to be ordinary, and to speak for ordinary mortals, but she's been a full-time politician since her teens. Never lived the everyday life on which she claims to be a friggin' expert.'

'That's not a crime,' Melvyn remarked mildly. 'It's true for most politicians. They aren't normal people and they've never lived normal lives. Look at the Boss, I ask you – five kids at their age. In any other family that'd be taken for fecklessness. As for the rest of them, they blather on endlessly about family values yet the last thing that comes into their heads when there's a spat on is the kids' tea party or taking Grandma shopping. I'm exactly the same. Truth is, for most of us almost anything is more exciting than going home.'

'"Home is a place to go to when there's no more work to be done,"' Betts quoted.

'Margaret Thatcher,' Melvyn supplied promptly. 'Bloody woman. Fancy a pizza?'

'Yeah. Double meat feast with extra topping.' Betts fumbled in his wallet and handed over a ten-pound note. He laughed wryly. 'I can afford it. To keep me quiet they put a sweetener into my bank account. Bonus, they called it. So I'm not moaning.'

As he called the pizza parlour, Melvyn kept an eye on his guest. The odds were that on the day Melvyn did leave the government's service, Betts would write a witty character exposé on Melvyn's traits. It would be great, but unlikely, if Melvyn emerged from such a review smelling of roses. Perhaps nights like this when Betts needed a friend would redress the balance. Host and parasite: each feasted on the other.

'Simply the best!'

The Tina Turner CD was on full blast. The Red Lion in Whitehall had seen many celebrations and wakes over the decades but this one was proving memorable. The old pub downstairs was packed with regulars and tourists, the type who will find the action most evenings in any capital city. The door leading upstairs was hung with a chalked board announcing a private event. In the room on the upper floor, tables had been pushed to one side and the carpet rolled up. Music from a disco blasted out at top volume. In the centre of a group three deep the Right Honourable Diane Clark was swaying, feet apart, hips pumping, an empty Grolsch bottle serving as a mock microphone in her hand, doing a fair imitation of her favourite rock singer.

'Better than all the rest!'

Her audience sang or shouted along with her, stamping their feet until the floor heaved. Behind the bar, away from the music, the manager smiled, shrugged and pulled another six pints of draught beer, lining them up on the counter. He noted who was present and who was not. Not the PM, though it was rumoured he might show his face; his wife had appeared briefly, accepted a glass of wine, sipped it, left it, graciously answered inane questions about the new baby, waved and was gone. The

Chancellor, Andrew Marquand, was busy burning the midnight oil for the Budget. The rest of the Cabinet likewise had more important engagements, including the pasty-faced Secretary of State for Culture and the Arts who was dining out with the Architects' Association and hearing from them why bridges built across the Thames were bound to wobble. His junior minister was rumoured to be writing the definitive inside history of the Dome, as a lesson for posterity. The Foreign Secretary was in Islington, endeavouring to explain to Amnesty International, of which he had been a contributing supporter for thirty years, why it served the cause of human rights and world peace to sell fighter planes to the Indonesians. The Home Secretary was in prison, sampling supper as cooked by prisoners while being followed everywhere by a television crew filming a sympathetic documentary. His youngest son, unbeknown to everyone present, was heading for another barred cell later that evening after a bender with his friends, but such inoffensive indulgence was now smiled upon as proving the genuine humanity of the parents. And the Minister for Agriculture was raising his cholesterol level, as Ministers of Agriculture must, with red meat and drink offered by the National Farmers Union, chewing the fat with them with every sign of sincere enjoyment.

Frank Bridges had turned up with a senior trade-union official, though not with his pretty new wife who was the object of such fervid and understandable curiosity. Any mature man who managed to land an attractive young female was the envy of his peers. The older ones wondered wistfully how he had done it, and whether he could keep up with her. The younger ones were peevish, resentful of a man their father's age stealing what was rightfully theirs. But Frank was solidly present, full of bonhomie and comradeship, slapping money on the counter, even though Diane would be picking up the tab, and shouting manfully above the hubbub.

The bartender reached for empty glasses as Frank gave Diane a bear-hug. 'Good on yer, girl. Great day. You deserve it, every penny.'

'Great day? If I'd had my way I'd have taken a mint off them.' Diane's green eyes flashed, then she subsided. She panted in her silk trouser suit and flapped a hand. 'God, I'm hot. Friggin' hell, Frank, I was forced to settle. Those bastards have got off lightly.'

'Yeah, well, best not to be in dispute with the press. Not the mass-market papers, anyway. They're our natural allies.' Frank handed a pint to the trade-unionist, grabbed one for himself and downed half in one gulp.

Diane spluttered. 'Those sods'll support us at election time if it suits their purposes, and not otherwise. Any idea that we can expect some kind of *entente cordiale* is crap.' Her attention was caught by an eager youth calling her to the other side of the room and she moved away.

'She may have a point.' Frank's eyes roved around the

pulsating room and he addressed himself to the union man, a laconic veteran of many political battles. Tucked in a corner they could have what approached a conversation. 'Tremendous crowd here. Don't recognise many. Who are they?'

The veteran laughed. 'Search me. They're a tad juvenile, aren't they? Still got eggshell behind their ears. The economics experts from my own office don't seem old enough to have started secondary school yet. Kids! Babes in arms.'

'The next generation, Dave, don't knock 'em. They'll be paying our pensions, so let's hope they're competent. They'll be after our jobs next.'

'Already are. I've been requested, er, *told*, to get ready to pack my bags.'

'You, Dave? But you're a youngster. Relatively. Why should they want to do that?'

'They need the post. For my deputy, who's been hanging on for it five years. Then they can fill his space with somebody superannuated from the Commons. Mike Todd, I gather it is. And that'll release a safe seat for some teenage whippersnapper, one of the PM's favourite advisers who's set for the front bench after the next election.'

'Blimey. News to me. Why don't they just offer old Todd a seat in the Lords?'

''Cause they're getting immune to that. Boring as hell it is there. And no salary or perks. The constituencies won't deselect 'em because they adore anybody that'll stand up to the Boss. But what's on offer at our place? Fifty thousand a year, a chauffeur-driven saloon and a free flat in Hammersmith. For that the bugger will budge. The other unions are being pressed to do likewise.'

'For that I might retire early too. But not yet,' Frank mused.

The trade-unionist backtracked. 'Mightn't be fifty thou' when he actually arrives. Depends on budgets. But it'll be enough for a bloke whose original pay packet in the Post Office was four quid a week.'

'Funny old world, to coin a phrase,' Frank said. Their attention returned to their hostess. 'I'm pleased for Diane. She's the same vintage as me, but she doesn't act it. Hey, will you take a butcher's at that!'

Diane had been wearing a flowing silk trouser suit with a long tunic top. A line of sweat had marked it from the back of her neck to her waist and under her breasts and arms, yet the effect was to underline her joyous animality. To the yelps of the crowd she lifted up the tunic to waist level, stuck her fingers in the trouser belt, wriggled out of the trousers and kicked them away. Underneath were black tights: the tunic had become an alluring mini-dress. To the renewed music she flung her head back, legs splayed, hips grinding to the rhythm, roaring to the chorus and waving a beer bottle like a trophy.

'She's totally pissed,' remarked the union man.

'Yeah. But she needed to let off steam, Dave. I love her dearly, we all do, but sometimes she struggles with the proprieties.'

The union man downed his pint grudgingly and reached for another. 'Can't help admiring her. Look at her go!'

The pizza was taking its time but Melvyn did not mind. He had arrived at what felt like a profound revelation. Host and parasite. *Symbiosis*, that was it. He voiced the observation aloud: that the relationship between the media and their targets was symbiotic.

'What?' Betts settled back in the armchair. 'How do you work that out?'

'Stands to reason,' Melvyn said. 'You need people like me to fill in the background. I know what's going on, see. We like it reported in a certain way. And the mention of my name in passing, as one devoted to his task, doesn't go amiss. It'll help me get to the top.'

'And that'll come when they recognise your unique talents, I imagine?' Betts teased coldly. 'Sounds more like incest to me.'

'I am overdue for promotion.' Melvyn waggled a finger. 'Put that in your gossip column and smoke it. I've been in this post longer than most. It's not fair. There are seventy-five of us on the Whitehall press and public relations listing. Every Tom, Dick and Harry on the front benches has got to have his own press officer these days, even those idiots in the Lords. Devalues our currency, I grant you. When Margaret Thatcher was in office they made do with less than twenty. She expected ministers to deal with the media themselves without any spin – except herself, of course.'

Betts considered. 'We were probably less well informed about what was going on,' he conceded. 'But we'd still get to hear the bones crunch as every knife went in. Like when Michael Heseltine resigned. And this stuff about the Cabinet members spinning against each other – nothing new in that either.'

Melvyn concurred. They reminisced about spectacular betrayals, many of which seemed to involve one or two particularly arrogant ministers. Strange, how poorly such men covered their tracks. They acted as if they were invulnerable, yet memoirs appeared earlier than used to be the case and were more vindictive and charmless. The truth, however, often became more elusive the more versions emerged.

Then Betts became impatient. 'So let's get down to business, Melvyn. Who is the blessed Diane sleeping with these days?'

'Her? Nobody, if you can believe that. She made a vow of celibacy on entering the government. Alistair read her the Riot Act and she took it to heart. Allegedly.'

'You have to be kidding. She's only ever man-free in between men.'

The doorbell rang and Melvyn fetched the pizzas,

slapping the open cardboard box straight on to the table with a toilet roll to serve as napkins. 'Help yourself.'

'So Mark Squires, the boyfriend who got elected, that's over?'

Melvyn nodded emphatically. 'Absolutely. She sent him packing, back to his wife and baby. He's a model of spotless behaviour, these days. But there's a new face on her team. Edward Porter. He's keen. Just out of interest I tried to pick an argument with him and he leaped to her defence. I'd keep an eye on him.'

'They're probably having it off right now,' Betts growled. 'Very clever at concealing their tracks, these people are. Leopards don't change their spots.'

'There are such things as reformed characters,' Melvyn protested, but his mouth was full of pizza. A string of sticky mozzarella trailed from his lips.

'There aren't,' Betts assured him. 'We don't blacken their reputations, they do it for themselves. I bet you a tenner, if Miss Diane Clark isn't in bed with some lover half her age right now, she soon will be.'

'No bets.' Melvyn wiped his chin. They ate greedily for several minutes. 'Okay, so what have you written on Frank Bridges?'

'The usual. That he's been rotten to his wife. The first one. Cheating on her and so on. With the gentle implication that he's been doing it for years, and if he's done it once, he'll do it again. Once a philanderer, always a philanderer – leopards, see? We contrive to feel sorry for the new Mrs

Bridges, Hazel, the cat who thinks she got the cream. The original Mrs Bridges gave us reams of useful quotes. I had to leave out her accusations that her husband's trying to maim her, though. The lawyers wouldn't wear that.'

'What's your guess? Anything in her claims?'

'Nah. Not a scrap. She needs psychiatric treatment, that one.'

A useful tit-bit for the diary. 'But tell me, you yourself, Jim, what's your personal opinion of people like Frank and Diane?'

Betts paused in mid-chew. 'My personal opinion?'

'Yeah.'

'I'm not paid to have personal opinions. If you mean, are they nice kind souls at heart, I haven't a clue. And, frankly, I couldn't give a damn either.'

Melvyn poured out the remainder of the bourbon, crammed the empty pizza box into the overflowing waste-bin and licked his fingers. 'I like Frank Bridges. There's a lot of snobbery about him in the press, because of his accent and his rough manner. But in our party that's a plus. He came from the gutter. Made it without benefit of a posh education or fancy relatives. Rather like your own proprietor. We'd be grateful if your lot would treat him with more respect.'

'Oh, you would, would you?' At the mention of the *Globe*'s owner, Betts reached for his drink. He eyed the empty bottle regretfully. 'Would your lot prefer us to lay into Mr Benedict Ashworth instead?'

'He's worth an in-depth investigation,' Melvyn agreed eagerly.

'Been peaky since his so-called disappearance, but his staff say it's business as usual.'

'Where did he go? Who saw him? What was the mystery illness he says he was suffering from? It's all to do with that odd marriage, I'll be bound. I've never met anybody so cold-blooded. Can't picture him having sex with a fish, let alone with a ripe lady like Christine.'

'The cold one could be the wife. I hear he's taken up contact sports,' Betts said mysteriously. 'Kung fu, or something like that.'

'Wow.' Melvyn's eyes widened. 'That's fantastic. What's he up to?'

'Flinging a bloke who works for him down on the floor three times a week. Getting rid of naked aggression, maybe.'

'Blimey. I hadn't heard that.' The diary entry was growing by the minute. Melvyn resolved to drink no more that night.

'Supposed to be a big secret. A pal of mine has seen them at it. We may try and get pictures.'

Melvyn digested the information. 'So it'd do no harm if the occasional reference to kick-boxing or other Oriental specialities featured in the Boss's replies to his questions in the House?'

Betts snickered. 'Oriental specialities? Couldn't be better,' he replied. 'That'll put the wind up him. Now, if

we've assassinated enough public characters, I'll mosey
on home to my tragically empty bed. Thanks for the drink
and nosh. Cheers.'

As Frank, Dave and the barman craned their necks to
watch, Diane was gyrating round the serious-looking
young man who had called her from the bar, the centre
of a chanting circle. The noise and heat were overpowering. The man had removed his jacket and tie and was
dancing vigorously, though without much skill, trying
to match her hip thrusts as onlookers squealed and
applauded.

The tune changed to a Caribbean rhythm and the
volume increased. A limbo-dance contest was suggested
and the idea taken up immediately. A pole was found from
behind the bar, two guests were designated to hold it. A
double file formed, a tight squeeze in the confined space,
with couples attempting to get under the bar and being
disqualified if they touched it and sprawled on the floor.
Diane stood to one side and clapped, until she herself was
urged to join in. She grabbed the hand of the gyrating
young man and led him into the centre.

Hands held high, the two danced, both light on their
feet, Edward sweating and pink-faced. They arched their
bodies back, feet edging forward, laughing wildly. The
pole was lowered a few inches. Their torsos were underneath, twitching with the effort. Then Diane was through
and, still holding Edward's hand, pulled his head round

and under, until he, too, was upright, eyes bulging, and being congratulated on his success.

The game continued for several more raucous minutes until the hostess and her partner, and a black couple, more athletic than Diane and Edward, were the only ones left. The atmosphere was electric, vibrant with sexual energy and defiance. The pole was no more than two feet off the ground. To get under it required either consummate skill or an undignified scramble. When Edward tried the latter he knocked the bar down and lay on the floor, squirming and laughing uncontrollably. Diane fell upon him, held his face in her hands and kissed him. The black couple were declared the winners.

It was Diane who helped Edward to his feet and brushed down his shirt, streaked with sweat and dirt from the floorboards. They stood together, close, arms entwined, as heads swivelled to identify Diane's new flame. Edward, uneasy, was the first to begin to sober up and mutter that it was time to quit: enough, he hinted, was a feast. For a moment Diane argued, then madness prevailed. In the next sentence she had offered him a lift in her car: it was not far, but driving would be safer than walking. And Edward responded diffidently, quietly so that only she could hear, that coffee would be welcome, might prevent a hangover in the morning.

Thus as Frank and Dave settled blearily into a further pint and recalled days when they could drink all night without ill-effect, Diane led Edward down the stairs and out into the night, pushing him into the leather back seat of the Rover and instructing the driver where to go next.

# CHAPTER FIFTEEN

'She did what?'

'Went off in the arms of a young man. It's been God's own job to keep them out of the papers. As if I haven't enough to do.' Alistair McDonald was huffy.

The Prime Minister sighed and ran his fingers through his hair. 'I made her promise not to do that again. We had enough trouble with young Mark Squires' wife when she found out. Diane was a dubious influence, she said.'

'Why can't that woman keep her hands to herself?' The Chancellor was equally irritable. 'We have the greatest opportunity a socialist government has ever had in modern times, the trust of the people and a fat majority, and she goes round threatening to unravel all our good work. She's still supposed to be a socialist, isn't she?'

In the rivalry between the Prime Minister and Andrew

Marquand, his Chancellor, it often suited the former to assert his dominance by changing tack. Andrew could be a clumsy political performer whereas the Boss was noted for his adroitness.

'Socialist? Perhaps. As much as any of us. She's loyal, Andrew. And a great performer on television. She'll see off David Frost or Jeremy Paxman any day and have them eating out of her hand. The public adore her too. We don't want everybody in the government to be a bland identikit little chap, do we? A dose of humanity is no bad thing.'

The tactic worked. Andrew spluttered. 'But family values! Aren't they the bedrock of our programme these days?'

The Prime Minister smiled at him pointedly. 'Thank you for that reminder. So when are you going to get married, then, Chancellor?'

Diane rolled over and cast a lazy eye over the body slumbering beside her. Edward's breathing had slowed and barely stirred the duvet. His face was almost buried in the tumbled pillows but she could see one eyebrow, raised like a circumflex. His upper body was uncovered and revealed a fine, dense down over each shoulder blade. Diane leaned carefully over him and smiled, then relaxed on her elbow.

She wondered if his photo would be in the newspapers, snapped last night as they emerged from the Red Lion, or earlier in the day at the High Court when he had hovered nearby with her briefcase. The image would find its way into archives to resurface some day, his face highlighted, when he himself was famous. Time enough to check the front pages when she got to the office. For now, she wanted to savour his presence and make the enjoyment of it last as long as possible.

He had been restless during the night. At first, ecstatic from their lovemaking, he had buried his head in her breasts and dozed. But then his body was racked with shivers; even while he was evidently subconscious, a limb would shoot out with such violence that it seemed he must wake up. She had laid him down and covered him with her arms but still he shook. A moan would come from his lips, which he would wet with a parched tongue. Yet his eyes remained tight shut the whole time. Diane suspected that if challenged about these nocturnal physical jerks he would deny all knowledge: she would be unable to convince him that he had apparently been climbing Everest in his sleep.

Her gentle reaction amused her. Usually, with a fidgety lover she would become impatient, the odds against the relationship's survival. Life was too short to lose sleep when other more comfortable companions were to hand. But with Edward she felt remarkably protective.

It was nearly seven, too early to get up. In the grey light of a Friday morning she examined him more closely. The upper body and shoulders were neatly but not heavily muscled; whatever he did to keep fit was not undertaken excessively, but neither was he a couch potato.

He shifted; stubble showed, heavier on the upper lip. The hair under one arm was dark and silky. She bent her head to it; it smelt good to her. Her lovers were either alarmed or amused when she did that, but to her it was quite normal to fix a man's scent in her brain. Edward's was warm, wholesome, natural, as if she had already known it a long time.

He muttered, spasmodically, in his sleep. The scattered phrases had woken her more than once. Inquisitive, she had tried to decipher them: was there a girl's name, perhaps, that she could use to tease him? For a while nothing made sense. Then, as the jerking subsided, one low moan resolved itself into a simple question, over and over again. It startled her, and made her wonder what it meant, and what the correct answer might be. If the moment presented itself, she would ask.

On the hour the radio alarm clicked. A mellifluent female voice read the news headlines. Edward stirred and opened his eyes. At the sight of Diane naked above him, a bewildered rictus crossed his features, as if he could not grasp why the voice was not coming from her.

'The government is launching an initiative later today to combat the threat to black and Asian girls who are forced into marriages against their will,' the voice intoned.

'About bloody time,' Diane said.

'What?' Edward answered automatically.

'The Cabinet Women's Unit has been sitting on those proposals for ages,' Diane said. 'As if we might insult the

Pakistani or Yemeni community if we stopped their most
backward tribesmen selling their daughters.'

'Difficult.' Edward's face was in the pillow, his voice
muffled. He still seemed puzzled, or amazed, at where he
found himself.

'Not difficult.' Diane pulled the duvet over herself; the
heating had come on but the flat was chilly. Edward muttered something into his chest that might, or might not,
have been intelligible had Diane been able to hear it. 'If
you are saying,' she added sternly, 'that this is a form of
social imperialism, as Benedict Ashworth alleged the other
day, I will put this pillow over your head and suffocate
you right now. We are here to govern according to our
mores, and not those of greedy fathers of young girls who
expect to be paid a dowry, not have to find one.'

The newsreader had moved on to another topic.
Edward sat up. He shook his head as if to clear his eyes,
making him resemble a sleepy puppy. 'Where am I?'

Diane chuckled. 'In my bed, sweetie. And very nice it
was too.'

Edward turned his head from side to side, taking in the
trail of clothes, his and hers, leading together from the
doorway to the bed. He seemed bewildered. He shifted his
weight, glanced down at himself and touched his genitals
briefly, as if hoping to find a history written there. 'We
made love?' he asked.

Diane gave a throaty laugh. 'My God, have you forgotten so soon? We did, sweetie. Twice, if you want to know.'

Edward rubbed his eyes, but whether that meant he did not remember or just could not believe it Diane could only guess. At this juncture most of the young men she had slept with would be in fits of giggles, or wondering aloud what their mothers or current girlfriends would say, which would kindle the light of triumphant conquest in Diane's eyes.

'Shower's over there. Clean towels in the cupboard. You'll find a new razor in the bathroom cabinet – a disposable one, but it'll do the necessary. I'll go first if you don't mind. Busy day ahead.'

With that, Diane slid from the bed and padded to the bathroom. When she emerged with one towel tied in a turban round her wet hair and the other twisted over her breasts, Edward had not budged, but was sitting bolt upright in the bed.

She plugged in a hairdryer and began to speak over its hum. 'You'd better get a move on, unless you plan to stay here all day. You okay?'

Edward raised his eyes. 'Not sure. Was this a good idea?'

'Oh, yes, brilliant. We're made for each other, you and I.' Her voice was matter-of-fact, but with mischief in it.

'I mean, you're my employer.'

'So what? You like me, don't you?'

'I adore you.' Suddenly Edward sounded bitter. 'Wasn't it obvious last night? I worship you, Diane. I think you're the most magical person. I just wonder whether . . .' His voice trailed off.

'Oh, pish to that. Don't worry, I won't demand of you

anything you can't give.' For Diane this was a standard
line, but it did not appear to make Edward any happier.
She relented, abandoned the hairdryer and sat beside him.
One hand stroked his thigh. 'If something's bothering
you, sweetie, you can always unburden yourself with me.
You were having a helluva conversation with yourself in
your sleep, d'you know that?'

'What was I saying?' His glance was wary.

'Most of it I couldn't make out. I didn't want to pry.
But then you started to ask, "Who am I?" over and over. Is
that a problem?'

Edward quietly slid out from under her caressing hand
and rose from the bed. 'Sort of,' he said. 'I have bad
patches. Had some depression, but nothing too serious.
Part of it, it's been suggested, comes from having been
adopted. So I haven't the foggiest idea who I really am. A
more secure person wouldn't worry about it, I suppose.
Most of the time I fill the gap with work. But, as you
heard, it's never very far from the surface.'

Diane had begun to dress. 'Have you ever tried to trace
your birth parents?'

He rubbed his chin, as if surprised to find stubble. 'Too
scared. Suppose they were dreadful? Or they didn't want
to see me?'

'Do you know who registered your birth?' Diane had
unconsciously become the MP, the giver of advice. 'It
might have been only your mother. You're about thirty,
aren't you? Very common in those days.'

Edward was silent. It seemed that this intelligent, articulate man did not have the vocabulary to cope with emotional turmoil.

Diane brushed her almost dry hair and flicked it back. Then, with a grimace, she complied with the instructions of the style guru and began to apply makeup. 'You should take into account,' she said, as she fiddled with the mascara wand, 'that your mother may have been desperately miserable when she had to give you up, and that she longs to hear from you. But the law says that only you, the child, have the right to make contact. Not her.'

Edward picked up his clothes listlessly and began to pull them on. Diane raised an eyebrow. 'I'll go home to shower and change,' he said, by way of explanation. 'Be in a bit later. I'll say I have a hangover.'

'Most of the office will have hangovers.' Diane laughed. It was eight fifteen; the car would arrive soon. The radio programme had moved to a heated interview with the Home Secretary about his son, whom he had had to bail from a central police station in the early hours of the morning. 'And one or two others. If that lad had come to my party I'd have made sure he got home safely.'

She held open the door as Edward, shambling and awkward, made his way out. Her hand on his shoulder stopped him. 'Edward. First, you were wonderful – you *are* wonderful. I should like this relationship to continue, if you would. If not, I won't pester you and it'll never be alluded to again. And second, though it's none of my business, if it matters so much to you, you should decide to find out more about yourself. The worst outcome would be that your birth mother doesn't want to know. But she might be somebody splendid whom you could love, and I'm certain she'd be very proud of you. So take the first step. Get your birth certificate. I'll give you as much support as you need, both as employer – and, I hope, as your friend.'

The little speech appeared to inspire the young man, who stood on the threshold lost in reflection. Then he smiled. 'God, I'm a mess,' he murmured. His crisp manner returned. 'I'll get cracking. And, Diane, thank you. From the bottom of my heart.'

Unwilling to tamper with the elegantly made-up face a few inches from his own he hesitated, then pulled her towards him and kissed her mouth, a lingering, sweetly loving kiss. She laughed again and ran a finger over his lips. 'Russet brown suits you,' she said. 'I hope everything else on offer does too.'

Frank folded the newspaper with an oath and threw it theatrically across the kitchen. The corner of one page caught the marmalade pot, which flew through the air close to Hazel's ear and smashed spectacularly on the tiled floor, scattering gobbets of orange jelly and glass fragments in sticky rivulets.

'Bugger,' Frank growled. 'Sorry. Didn't mean to do that. Gimme a dishcloth and I'll clean it up.'

'Aaah!' Hazel's eyes were wide with shock. She clutched her pink dressing gown. 'What did you do that for?'

'I didn't mean to,' Frank repeated testily. 'It was an accident. I've said I'm sorry. What more do you want?'

'Frank! That was special marmalade. With Grand Marnier. I went to Justin de Blank's shop in Mayfair to get it. Cost over a fiver.'

'Bugger,' said Frank again, but he made no move to clear the mess. He glanced at the television set perched high on a cupboard; fighter planes whizzed over the screen, library footage illustrating the Foreign Secretary's tussle with Amnesty over the Indonesian order. The sound was down to a background mumble. He reached for another newspaper from the pile delivered by his driver, opened it and, breathing heavily, tried to concentrate. 'You might have asked,' he said levelly, to the comment column in front of his nose, 'why I was so bloody furious with the *Globe*.'

Hazel was still rigid, a teaspoon of boiled egg half-way between the egg-cup and her mouth. 'Was it because they're being nice to Diane Clark? She won her case yesterday.'

'Of course she won yesterday,' Frank growled. 'That's headline news in every other newspaper. Bloody good thing too. But in the *Globe* it's a different matter.'

Since he refused to enlighten her, Hazel was obliged to step over the gooey disaster on the floor to collect the offending pages. When she did so she screamed with rage. 'Gail! She's at it again. Oh, this is unforgivable.' Her eyes scanned the page, then she yelled again. 'My God, did you read this bit? About how I trapped you? She reckons if I hadn't come along and by pure chance we had that fuss at Heathrow just after the election, you'd have stayed with her for ever. What rubbish.'

Since it was not entirely rubbish, Frank kept his own counsel and merely shrugged. Gail had never raised objections to his occasional forays beyond his marriage. She appeared to believe it was her wifely duty to ignore them. What neither of them could have sidestepped, however, was the press deciding to make a song and dance about one particular adventure. Which admittedly had been closer to home (or rather the office) than some of the others, had lasted far longer, and involved a more sexually attractive and determined creature than he had ever tangled with before. Plus, nobody was getting any younger, Gail in particular.

Hazel resumed her seat. The egg-laden spoon was lifted again. 'She says she's still in love with you. That you've been led up the garden path, or words to that effect. That she'd be glad if our marriage foundered; she won't be happy till you've seen the error of your ways.'

'I bet she didn't say that,' Frank interspersed. At Hazel's raised eyebrows, he continued, 'Not the sort of phrases she'd use. I bet it was words put into her mouth by that journalist. They'll say, "Would you agree that the marriage will founder?" And she'd have said no, or yes, or maybe, it wouldn't have mattered. That sort of thing,' he finished lamely.

Hazel glared, but for the sake of harmony, Frank guessed, left unsaid her usual riposte that his first wife was capable of anything. In another minute, however, she was spluttering once more and the egg-spoon had fallen into her tea. 'They call you a philanderer. You! And say you'll never change. And that I should watch you like a hawk.'

Frank grunted. His beautiful wife's face was so contorted with fury, her lips drawn back, eyes blazing, fingers claw-like on the newsprint, that a raptor was exactly what she resembled.

'And that they feel sorry for me! Me, Hazel Bridges! Wife of the Secretary of State!'

'Now that, I agree, is outrageous,' Frank murmured. He brightened. 'But have you noticed that they don't mention any of her accusations against me: all that palaver about hate mail and trashing her car? They've left it out.'

'They don't believe her,' Hazel muttered. 'Pity they didn't take the same attitude to everything else she says about you. And about me. Oh, this is ridiculous. You should sue. Take them to court. You could win thousands, like Diane Clark.'

'I doubt it.' Frank began to explain the hazards of court action, then noticed that his wife was not listening. Her expression had become dreamier, which probably meant she had begun to spend the money. On the television screen he could glimpse film of a gleeful Diane outside the High Court with yesterday's edition of the *Globe*. 'Don't get your hopes up. If they haven't mentioned Gail's insistence that I'm a common criminal it's because the lawyers won't let them. That really *is* libellous. So it means the rest probably isn't. Or not to such an extent that we can make a case.'

'What about the Press Complaints Commission?'

'Now you *must* be joking,' said her husband scornfully. 'A body designed to keep the privacy laws at bay? Toothless, slow, useless. The members *are* the press, editors, mostly, smarmy buggers laughing behind their hands. No, that's not the way to deal with that article. Best to forget it.'

'I can't forget this,' Hazel announced loftily. 'I'm humiliated and hurt. If you can't muzzle the media, Frank, you absolutely must do something about her. We can't go on being the butt of her allegations and nastiness.'

'She's not a nasty woman,' her husband protested. 'It'll die down. They'll pursue somebody else in time, some other poor prat caught with his pants down. Someone who's flavour of the month today, who'll be mincemeat next week. Could be Diane, could be the Boss, could be the new baby. Tomorrow morning it'll be the Home Secretary and his miscreant son. They don't care.'

'Well, I care,' said Hazel grimly. She stood up and drew herself to her full height. 'And there are moments, Frank

Bridges, when I wonder whether you care as much for me as you should. You're not half as upset on my behalf as you should be. I'm your wife, not her. And your cruelty is making me very unhappy!'

Her voice had risen to a squeak. Frank covered his eyes with one hand. Hazel stepped away from the table and immediately put her slippered foot into the marmalade. When she slithered and almost fell, Frank had to move his hand over his mouth to avoid laughing. It felt as if she had received her comeuppance.

He gave in. 'Okay, but I don't know what else I can do. Please, Hazel, understand. Go and get dressed and mind the glass. Do you still want me to clear up?'

Diane was humming 'Simply The Best' as she drove up the motorway. A busy day, she had said to Edward; it would have been terrific to have had him by her side, lover and staffer and helpmeet. Had it been merely a visit to the constituency, a standard Friday afternoon, with the prospect of drinks at the working-men's club and a turn calling the bingo numbers at the community centre, or even a fund-raising dinner in a local hotel with the mayor in his gold chain, she would have suggested it to him and tried to persuade him to come.

She wondered what he would think about her home in the patch, a modest bungalow set away from the road with a pretty if limited garden full of laurel and roses tended by a devoted pensioner. She had bought it cheaply during the housing recession some years before, furnished it simply, ensured it was warm in winter. It gave privacy to a surprising extent, though with one significant hazard. At the instigation of Special Branch the alarm system was connected to the local police headquarters: if set off by mistake it produced car-loads of unwanted police officers. All visitors had to be warned, especially anyone who, impatient of waiting for her arrival, might be tempted to climb in through a window. Once four student staffers had spent the train journey from London holed up in the bar; then, having found the correct address, had decided to force the back door. She had had to rush to the police station where she found them crestfallen and somewhat the worse for wear; the humourless sergeant, who had eventually released them into her custody, held her responsible for the incident since she was their boss and had made it clear he would not be voting for her next time.

It could be infuriatingly hard, Diane reflected as she hummed, to live a normal easy-going life while being famous. The more Bohemian one's tastes, the harder it got. Especially when the profession was politics. For a start, much of the nation, the other side, was automatically against her. They would try to make matters tough. That bloody sergeant had probably never voted for her party in his life. It wouldn't have hurt had he said so, politely if formally. He might have had the grace not to mention politics at all. But no, they had to rub it in whenever there was trouble, even over something minor like her shambolic friends.

She slowed down. For anyone else a speeding ticket was a nuisance. For her, it was a hostile headline. An argument with a neighbour about an uncut hedge or rubbish bags left out untidily gave her a sleepless night; the tabloids would seize it greedily. None of the deference shown to politicians in other countries came into play. The press were foul. Diane had no illusions: the headlines she had gloated over that morning in the office could be overturned in a trice. In the *Globe* the target had already moved on. Poor Frank Bridges or, rather, poor Hazel: though Diane did not have much sympathy for a woman she regarded as a gold-digger, or at least someone not sincerely motivated by the party's cause, she recognised that the wife would be more immediately wounded by the comments than the hard-bitten husband. Diane, Frank and their colleagues had had to become inured to it. If they couldn't stand it, they got out. Their families suffered more, and without defence.

She would have to warn Edward. Dalliance with Diane Clark, if he wished to continue, meant he must put himself on guard. He was wise beyond his years, which had attracted her to him, but she felt a twinge of guilt. Common sense dictated that she should not have seduced him, or invited him in, or tried to make him coffee, which had still been in the pot, cold, when they left. She should not have offered him a lift after the party: that had been risky – many witnesses had seen them get into the back of the official car together, both rather drunk, and noted with glee that they had clutched each other with every sign of affection.

A promise had been broken. The Prime Minister would get to hear of it, no doubt, and would not be impressed. He would be irritated not merely that she had taken a new lover, but that she had agreed not to and proved unable to keep her word. But in certain aspects, the Prime Minister was wrong: his elevated position did not give him the right to dictate to independent souls like herself. Nor was her behaviour quite as reprehensible as he implied. She resented his assertion that her friendships had an element of exploitation about them, that her employees and volunteers were not free to choose to resist her. That was offensive nonsense. All those she came close to were perfectly capable of standing up to her, otherwise they were not the sort she would want to employ. Sycophants had nothing going for them.

In any case, none of this had come from the Prime Minister's own mouth. The request, or command, that she desist and let Mark go his own way and, by implication, not replace him had been conveyed by Alistair McDonald, not by the Boss himself in direct conversation. Alistair, an employee, a minion, had never stood for election, had no idea of the hard slog to get to high office, and how grimly one would hang on to it. He had been a journalist prior to his appointment, one of the lowest of the low, a smirk permanently on his face. Now he imagined himself vital to the welfare of the country simply because he was the Prime Minister's official spokesman. But that was supposed to be for dealings with the media, not for intimate conversations with close colleagues. She resented that. If the PM had wanted her to promise, he should have asked her face to face. He didn't. He hadn't. He should have.

Diane switched on the radio for the news, but was obscurely disappointed that her name was not mentioned. Yesterday's story was no longer headlines. She would be featured for sure that evening on *Have I Got News For You*, or the radio *News Quiz*, and perhaps her snappier remarks might surface in *Quote Unquote* or some other upmarket quiz show. So would the antics of the Home Secretary's son, who would never live down his public collapse: fifty years from now in his obituary in *The Times*, or its future equivalent, the inglorious incident would surface. It made her glad she didn't have children. It was enough of a struggle to keep herself in order, let alone be responsible for a brood of recalcitrant infants.

If she had had children, would they have been chips off the old block? Would they have been feisty, energetic, sexual creatures as she was? Passionate about politics, or about something else as fascinating and thankless? She hoped they would not have been simply interested in money. A son of hers making fistfuls in the City, a derivatives dealer, a capitalist with no consideration for his fellow human beings: such progeny she could disown, with few regrets.

What proportion of a person's personality was due to genes? Probably more than the educationalists liked to admit. For them nature took second place to nurture. Instinctively, however, Diane believed that people followed their parents in tastes, proclivities, attitudes; though she tried her damnedest not to be like her own mother, she shared her stubbornness and self-centredness. Unlike her mother, though, Diane had striven to put these qualities to use in the service of others. If a child of hers had adored the world of politics and seen it as an opportunity to serve, their meeting of minds would have been complete.

Mother. Drat Mother. Diane pressed buttons to flip to a CD and went on singing along to Tina Turner. The miles disappeared beneath the old Volkswagen's tyres. It was a long journey up to Tyneside to see her mother, whom she did not love, had never liked much, and visited only out of a nagging conscience. If the older woman had become curmudgeonly with the years, that could be put down to frustration, a lack of any satisfying occupation, or to a limited education that had left her bereft of enjoyable escape through books. For her mother was often ill, and dismal with it, which hardly made her the most pleasurable companion.

Diane had loved her father and missed his impulsive kindness. It was, of course, unlikely that a child would have all the characteristics of one parent and none of the other. If one was kind, the other selfish, what would be the outcome for the offspring? A mixture, maybe, a conflict, an erratic person. Much like herself. If one was cheery and the other prone to depression, what then? Diane shivered a little, remembering Edward's remarks. His reflections troubled her. Mental illness carried such a fiendish, destructive stigma. People from every level of society pretended it wasn't happening, or claimed that an episode had been caused solely by external events. A psychiatrist on TV had said that it was not necessary for a chronic depressive to suffer pain in order to feel pain. The mechanism for suffering was already in his mind.

If Edward had children would they be prone to depression? Did it suggest he had inherited it from one or other of his unknown parents? Might it be in his interest to find out?

What strange reflections, Diane chided herself. Her conscience seemed to be in a turbulent state, perhaps because of the new relationship, perhaps because she would soon be seeing her mother. Edward was splendid and would, with sensitive handling, make a fine long-term lover. His ardour last night, his puzzlement in the dawn light, his fear about his position and willingness to accept her assurances, most of all the quality of his intellect and his commitment to the job intrigued her. She would take more care than usual with his feelings. Their affair was to be a source of delight and joy for them both, not anxiety. She would take a maternal interest in him, look after him to the best of her ability.

The slip-road to her mother's village was signposted. With a sigh Diane switched off the music and coasted to the roundabout. She hoped that her mother would be happy for once about the reporting of her daughter's activities.

Frank was more than a little startled by the phone-call – at home, too, which was unusual since his number was ex-directory, and when Hazel was out. It was as if the caller had been aware of this, for his opening words were, 'You alone, Frank?'

The accent gave it away. One of the Admiral Benbow gang. Sounded like Vic the villain. He appeared to be speaking from a call-box: every few moments his voice was drowned by a big vehicle, a lorry or bus, driving alongside.

'Yeah. Doing my boxes. My first quiet evening in for a month. Hazel's gone to the Dorchester for a charity do, posh frock, the lot. How's everyone at your end?'

'Ain't seen you for a while, Frank. The boys and me were wondering how you're getting on.' There was a gruff snicker, as if the caller felt Frank was under an obligation or would grasp some underlying meaning.

'Not too bad. Got a knocking in the papers today from the old lady, though. Did you see it?'

'Yeah. That's why we thought, the boys and me, that we'd better touch base with you, see if we can help.'

'If Hazel had her way, you'd be tying Gail to the stake

right now and lighting the blue touch-paper.' Frank laughed hollowly. 'My lady wife – the new one, that is – was not thrilled to read the personal reflections of her predecessor in the nation's gutter press.'

'It were odd, though, Frank,' Vic continued, with what passed for him as a thoughtful tone, 'no mention from Gail of the pressure she's been under. How she swears you've been getting at her.'

'Lawyers,' said Frank bluntly.

'Do you think she might be persuaded to back off?'

Frank realised that Vic had misunderstood. 'I'm not keen to get lawyers involved, injunctions and the like. Not if I can help it. Costs a fortune, and even more bad publicity. But if there was any other way to persuade her to lay off . . .' He breathed a heavy sigh and wondered what had prompted the call.

'Put her out of action.' It sounded like a statement, not a query. A hint, just a hint, of excitement.

Suddenly Frank wanted to end the call. It had a sinister ring that was totally out of place with his elevated position in the Cabinet. This sort of joshing, wishing someone ill, had never been his cup of tea even in the bad old days of his police service, and he was uneasy with it now. The records of some of his former acquaintances, Vic in particular, made him shiver. He made his voice good-natured. 'All we'd like, both Hazel and me, is an end to her whinges. I feel sorry for her but there's nowt I can do. Silly cow must realise that. If anyone could dissuade her,

Vic, I'd be eternally in their debt but I doubt it'll happen.'

'Do me best, guv'nor,' said Vic, and suddenly the line went dead.


Diane filled the kettle, plugged it in, found an opened packet of chocolate biscuits and put them neatly on a plate with a doily, laid the tray with an embroidered teacloth, cups, saucers, sugar bowl and milk jug the way her mother insisted, and carried the tray into the living room.

Mrs Clark lived in sheltered housing. She was a tiny woman almost hidden in an ancient armchair. Her hands were restless on the rug wrapped around her knees: thin, pale hands, the skin so translucent that the blue veins showed through. But the eyes were sharp as they swept over the tray. 'What about spoons? Can't stir our tea without spoons.'

'Right, Mum. Sorry.' Diane returned to the kitchen and corrected her mistake, wishing her mother had at least uttered a word of thanks.

'Got yourself in the paper again.' The old lady pointed to the folded newspaper down the side of her armchair. 'Bit more complimentary than usual. They tried to get a quote from me, but I'm too wise. I wasn't talking.' She cackled.

'Fine, Mum. But you could have said you're proud of me, or something to that effect.' Diane poured the tea.

'Why should I do that? Only give you a big head. No, better to say nothing. Then they can't get at me.'

The logic was unassailable, but an ally instead of an onlooker would have been nice. Diane recalled how Frank Bridges, despite himself being targeted, had turned up at her celebration party to give her support, and felt grateful.

'Still,' Mrs Clark conceded, 'the article you sued was not pleasant reading. My next-door neighbour showed it to me – she was quite upset. It said you didn't know what it was to be a normal woman. I couldn't answer that.'

'You could have said,' Diane supplied gently, 'that it's true your daughter doesn't lead an ordinary life, but if everyone did we'd never get anybody into Parliament. That doesn't mean I don't understand the needs of mothers and children.'

'But you've never been normal,' her mother replied sharply. 'Even before you got so obsessed with politics. You could have been, of course.' She folded her hands firmly over the rug.

'Oh, Mum, don't start.' Diane glanced wearily out of the window, but the day, which had dawned happy, was fading into bleak dusk.

'It was your own fault. And your own decision. You could have been normal. You could have been a mother like anyone else. But no! You wanted a career, didn't you? Now see where it's got you.'

It was an ancient refrain and Diane had heard every twist and turn many times before. She busied herself with the tea tray and broke a biscuit in half. How much easier it would have been had she not done her duty and come here, if she had contrived to ignore the miserable old woman who could not make her welcome. Her mother had never loved her. Or perhaps she had wanted for her daughter, or through her, what Diane could not give. It helped explain why it was so much easier to find love in bed. And if that love faded, to move on to another with some haste. But a parent could not be exchanged for a new model. If they had faults, if they lived in a selfish cocoon, that was too bad. Duty had brought her here, and would keep her until the verbal abuse, a ritual to establish superiority, was completed. Then they might get on to other topics: the antics of the other residents, the forth-coming outing, the failings of the local council, the iniquities of the pensioners' Christmas bonus.

Diane roused herself. 'I had no choice, Mum.'

'You did. You could have gone in a different direction.'

'I *couldn't*,' Diane heard herself almost shout. 'Give it a rest, Mum, I've had enough of this.'

'You'll live with what happened till the day you die,' said the old woman smugly. 'God will punish you.' She reached out a shaky hand and lifted her cup, slopping tea into the saucer, but victory was in her eyes.

Diane sighed and clamped her mouth shut. Once more, her mother had won.

# Chapter Sixteen

'I was watching you last night,' Diane said, as she brushed her hair. Early mornings had acquired a kind of magic, even though the days were drawing in so that the radio alarm often woke them in the dark. She smiled. 'Want some coffee?'

'I'll make it.' Edward pulled on a blue towelling robe he had brought to the flat with a small collection of his clothes. 'Was I talking in my sleep again?'

'A little,' Diane said. 'You're not nearly as disturbed as you were. The kicking particularly seems to have diminished. It has to be confessed that you weren't the easiest person to have around, that first couple of weeks.'

'Apologies. You were very patient with me.'

'I had faith that once you settled down, and got used to the notion that we are special friends, you might feel more comfortable. Your subconscious might like what it found. And give you some peace.'

Edward stood in the modest kitchen, measuring ground coffee into the filter. He switched on the machine and they savoured the aroma with pleasure, noses in the air. Diane was already showered and dressed, though without tights or shoes. She dug her naked toes into the living room carpet. 'I admit to being fascinated, Edward. You're not the only man I've heard burbling his life story in his sleep, but I wondered whether you'd decided to find out about yourself. It might help.'

'There's a downside,' Edward answered slowly. 'My adoptive parents are wonderful. They gave me everything, and I've always thought of them as my mother and father. They might be terribly hurt if I started this investigation.'

'But why?'

'That's obvious. To my mother especially, it'll feel like a rejection. It's as if they didn't give me enough, that I'm not satisfied with them.'

'You could solve that problem by not mentioning it just yet. Or discuss it only when you've discovered something, and invite their support.'

'Maybe. But you got me thinking hard about my identity. Why on earth should it bother me that I've never met my natural parents? They didn't bring me up. Whoever they are, they abandoned me. I have quite negative feelings about them. Anyway, who I am doesn't depend on who or what I was born. I believe that very strongly.'

Diane poured coffee and filled bowls with cereal. She had not regularly eaten breakfast before Edward, but now relished the few private moments with him at the start of each day he was with her. 'Go on, I'm listening.'

'Well, we must all have traits we inherited from our parents. Plus what we've been brought up to value or believe in. But we should judge people on what they do. The theologians called it free will, the gift of God to Adam. Our lives are not merely determined for us but to a large extent are under our own control. So what matters in evaluating people is how they deploy the talents they've got, what effort they put in, what they set out to achieve and why; and how far, with a fair wind, they can get.'

'Not on what they say?' Diane teased.

'Only up to a point. Our world at Westminster is one of speeches, statements, questions in the House, interviews, soundbites on TV and radio. Books and articles, memoirs, autobiography. Margaret Thatcher's total runs to fourteen million words and is available on CD-Rom. She can't deny anything she ever said, such as being in favour of Europe or voting for flogging – yes, she did. People such as her or yourself, Diane, are endlessly hoist by the petard of what they've committed themselves to, what they've said. Of course that's true. But more importantly, as the polls show, ministers are getting judged on what is actually done. Talking alone isn't enough.'

'I couldn't agree more. But what has this to do with your search for your identity?'

Edward's brow furrowed. 'I haven't achieved much – haven't had much chance, yet. But I would hope to. Maybe as an MP myself, though for the time being I'm content as a backroom boy. I love working with you, Diane, as much as I enjoy being . . . here with you, as we are now.' He blushed. 'So I lack a clear sense of my own worth, and that's got little to do with what my real name is and whether my real grandma died aged fifty or lived to be ninety-four.'

Diane pondered. 'But it completes the picture. Knowing oneself involves putting together a jigsaw puzzle. There are gaps to be filled. Other people can provide a perspective. You may be too introverted, or too preoccupied by the daily grind, to see the overall picture.' She prodded him playfully. 'At least you haven't been depressed lately. I seem to be having a beneficial effect on you.'

'Absolutely. I feel safe with you. Daft, isn't it? Given, shall we say, that I must be one of many?'

'You are totally, utterly special. Do you have to take tablets? You can leave a supply here.'

'Not at the moment. I haven't had a bout of Black Dog since I decided to get out of commercial law and follow my instincts here.'

'I knew someone similar to you once.' Diane collected their dishes and rinsed them quickly under the tap. 'Ages ago. Bill, his name was. He was taller and thinner than you; knocked himself about a bit with drugs, but then we all did in those days. I lived in a commune for a while – my mini rebellion, to escape the stifling atmosphere of home. He had pale eyes that seemed to glow in the dark, or maybe that was just the grass we smoked. But black moods would come on him that he simply couldn't shake off. I never found out what happened to him.'

Edward had taken his clothes and disappeared into the shower. As she waited Diane finished dressing then leaned against the bathroom door and reminisced. 'It was marvellous then. It gets labelled the Permissive Society, but that's exactly what we were aiming at: permission to be whatever you wanted, to achieve your potential. We believed we'd find our identities through enlightenment, but really all we were doing was getting high and screwing around. I had sex with five men in one night for a bet. Including Bill, now that I remember.'

Edward's head came round the shower door. Foam flecked his body. 'Am I supposed to judge you by *your* actions? Is that what you're trying to tell me?' His tone was jocular.

She handed him a towel. 'Course not. But you could infer that I'm a reformed character. More or less.' She told him about the Prime Minister's injunction. 'You're not supposed to exist, sweetie, but what a drab world it'd be without you.'

Edward stood before her, rubbing his wet hair. Diane reached out and stroked his damp belly, then his penis. He jumped as if he had received an electric shock. She ran her fingers lightly over the purple skin, over the scrotum, let her fingernail pause on the glans, all the while smiling at him. An erection was beginning. 'No, not now,' he said, and firmly pushed her hand away.

'Why not?' She pouted.

'Because we have work to go to. Duties, obligations. We may not be a married couple but we should aim at a degree of respectability. Or, at least, reliability. That means, not letting sex take over. Doesn't it?' He suddenly looked anxious as if he had overstepped a mark. The erection had subsided. He pulled on his shorts quickly and moved away from her.

'Suppose so. But if we were a married couple, would that mean you'd make love to me more often, sweetheart?'

'Probably. Is that what you have in mind?' He was fastening buttons and his belt, putting on socks and shoes, his face turned away from her.

Diane sighed. 'Impossible, for the moment, while I'm so prominent. What an extraordinary discussion, to have marriage enter the frame so soon, if ever. I'm amazed at myself. But I've never thought this way before. Something about you, Edward, makes you terribly precious to me. I don't feel any age gap. I'm falling in love. If you mind, you'd better warn me. My old style was exploitative, I see that now, not least because with you I feel totally protective. The critics were not entirely wrong.'

Edward was now fully dressed and checking the contents of his pockets: wallet, handkerchief, keys, spectacles,

Filofax, mobile phone. He kept his eyes averted so that Diane could not easily read his reaction to her remarks. 'If I were to get married I would probably need my original birth certificate,' he commented gruffly.

'Not necessarily. When were you born?'

'The family always celebrated the day I arrived, which was two or three weeks after the actual date of my birth. My mother says I was an April Fool's Day joke, but that as a baby I made them laugh every day of the year.'

'She sounds lovely, your mother.' Diane was wistful.

'She is. She's a fan of yours. I should love you to meet her.'

But it was time to leave. That day they were heading in different directions. On the doorstep, out of sight of the street, they kissed. Diane marched towards the official car parked nearby. After a few minutes more, Edward glanced up and down to ensure that he was not under observation, locked the front door and walked resolutely away.

Andrew Marquand was seated at the Chancellor's big leather-topped desk in the oak-panelled room in the Treasury, his boxes opened wide in front of him. Behind on the mantelpiece sat a marble bust of Disraeli. Andrew would have preferred one of William Pitt the Younger, inventor of income tax: a man who had left his country in a better financial state at the end of office than he had found it on entering, a result Andrew profoundly hoped to repeat in due course.

To reach his office he had taken a back route from his rooftop flat in Number Ten Downing Street. The official residence of chancellors was Number Eleven next door, with the Chief Whip a few yards further on at Twelve, the shabbiest and darkest of the properties. Andrew had swapped for the comfort and convenience of the Prime Minister's wife, older children and new baby, and felt no rancour about it. If that's what the Boss wanted from him, he was happy to oblige. One per cent inflation and a viable exchange rate, however, were proving tougher to deliver.

Apart from their location, the properties were not ideal for their purposes. Money had been spent on the two main residences under all three of the last prime ministers, not least Margaret Thatcher who had appointed herself guardian of their eighteenth-century heritage. Until her time it had been possible for the public to walk up the narrow cul-de-sac to within a few yards of the doorways, and indeed to be photographed without hindrance standing on the steps of the famous house, as Harold Wilson had been as a boy. But fear of terrorists, whether from Northern Ireland, Libya or further afield, had compelled governments to adopt security measures. Massive wrought-iron gates were erected at the entrance to Whitehall with barriers and police boxes. Behind them ministers could come and go under cover without any need to smile and wave at onlookers. Andrew reflected, none the less, that it was typical of the woman and her blinkered outlook that she had not thought to create a television studio in the cellar. When press reaction was required, he and other ministers could find themselves out in the cold, their backs to the police boxes, pontificating into a wobbly microphone and struggling to keep their hair in place against the wind. It was thoroughly unprofessional, but even this media-savvy Prime Minister had failed to put it right.

The terrace was a rabbit warren of interlocking corridors and staircases. It pleased him to become acquainted with the more unusual corners. His favourite loo, for example, was situated in a nook near the White Room in Number Ten. It was done up in gold foil from top to bottom in the most hideous style. Not real gold, but gilded aluminium cladding, which presumably could be removed by plumbers. He had been unable to discover who was responsible: if it had been Mrs Thatcher, her taste was more ghastly and provincial than he had previously assumed. But he wouldn't have put it past her.

Andrew had dismissed his officials and had been working quietly for an hour. There came a tap at the door. It was Melvyn.

'Order some tea and sandwiches,' the Chancellor said. 'One or two things I have to clear up with you.'

The refreshments came as they were discussing Andrew's Mansion House speech, due to be delivered the following Tuesday. Melvyn was less anxious about the content, over which he had little influence, than about the inevitable human–interest questions the press would be asking. He made notes.

'Will you be refusing to wear white tie, as usual?'

'Of course.' Andrew glowered.

'And what shall I say is the reason this year?'

'Same as last. It's a load of tomfoolery. It creates and foments class distinctions. It is part of the Establishment's effort to keep the working class in their place.'

Melvyn wrote dutifully. It occurred to him that, if he were in playful mood, he could add a few other explanations: that the Chancellor was too mean to invest in a set of expensive garments he would wear but seldom. That the Chancellor was a vain man who realised that his spreading girth did not look its best in formal attire. Melvyn sucked in his own belly, experimentally, and felt his face turn red. That the Chancellor would feel a fool, for no good reason, and that the Chancellor did not enjoy feeling a fool. Or that the Chancellor liked to strut his radical stuff while maintaining one of the most conservative fiscal programmes in memory: the best Tory chancellor for decades, one wag had called him. But his refusal created an incident every year, and made him sound silly. It gave the impression he was being prickly and dogmatic for the sake of it, which made his negotiations with City authorities on bigger issues more fraught than they might otherwise have been. Conformity had its benefits.

'Another point that'll come up. Will you be taking Fiona?'

'For heaven's sake, that's none of their business. I shall be making a keynote speech about preparations for the euro. What does it matter whether I have a woman with me or not?'

'I'm afraid that is what the media will want to know,' said Melvyn meekly.

'Then we had better keep them guessing. The truth is I haven't decided. I may, or I may not. Which would produce the effect I want?'

Melvyn was mystified. 'What effect?'

Andrew thumped the table with his fist. 'That they take some notice of what I'm actually saying, you idiot.'

'Ah. I see. I'm not sure. I'll cast around and let you know. Is there anything else?'

The Chancellor sat back and put the tips of his fingers together. 'There is,' he said solemnly. A pause ensued as Melvyn tried to guess what was in his master's mind. He settled on a bland expression. Then Andrew leaned forward and locked his gaze on Melvyn's face, until the pudgy young press aide began to squirm. 'Have you been spinning against any colleagues in the government, Melvyn?'

'What? Me? No. Not at all. Not my style.'

'Oh, I think it is. We had a discussion about this over dinner last night. Too many unpleasant comments are appearing in the tabloids, and in the gossip columns. Some obviously from internal sources. One or two had your fingerprints on them.'

'Such as?' Melvyn challenged fiercely.

'Well, the *Globe* is not the friendliest of rags. Nor overly scrupulous, despite being forced to apologise to Diane Clark. But I keep seeing feeble bits of malice in there that run her down, that imply she is less than competent. That she is more interested in her love life, for example, than in doing her job properly. That she has defied the PM on more than one occasion including his efforts to make government policy more family friendly. That she is a loose cannon, and not to be trusted.' He raised an inquiring eyebrow.

'But those are exactly your views,' Melvyn protested.

'Are they, indeed? It doesn't follow that I want them divulged, especially not by you. Not least because it is a matter of public record who you work for, so it will be assumed it comes from me.'

'But it does!' Melvyn exclaimed.

'Which I would deny. Diane is a splendid woman whom we all adore and admire. Honest, outspoken, innovative, brave. The fact that she'd do better if she kept her trap shut and her legs crossed is neither here nor there. And not to be broadcast, either as my views or yours. Do I make myself plain?'

Melvyn was gasping, his mouth opening and closing like a fish's. Yet he wondered fleetingly if that twitch around Andrew's mouth was a smirk or a smile. How seriously was he supposed to take the ticking-off? Was it, perhaps, an oblique briefing session – the opposite of what it appeared to be? His mind racing, Melvyn tried to work out the nuances. Maybe Andrew had twigged that he kept a diary. Maybe Andrew kept a diary. An interlocution of this kind, recorded verbatim, might be designed to cover his back. Andrew's, that was, not his own.

'One more thing. The reason the fingers are pointed at you, Melvyn, as far as the *Globe* is concerned, is that your own name seems to surface remarkably frequently, and in complimentary terms. On the Titbits page and the Insider column. Four times last week, I understand. If I had a suspicious mind, I would wonder if you weren't a mite too pally with somebody on the paper. One of its reporters, a pretty girl, perhaps, who feeds you pasta and Chianti in her flat and wheedles from you opinions you should be keeping to yourself.'

'I wish,' Melvyn muttered. He gave a deep sigh. 'Okay, message received and understood. I shall be more circumspect. The silence of the grave it is. But it isn't me who's spinning against Diane, or any of the others. To coin a phrase, the press don't give them their bad reputations, they do it all by themselves.'

As the Chancellor glared humourlessly, Melvyn backed out of the room, still gabbling: 'And that, Andrew, explains why everyone thinks so highly of you. But if you'll listen to a word of advice, you'll take Fiona to that do—'

He dodged the book that was thrown at him and scurried out, but not before he thought he heard the sound of muffled laughter, as Andrew turned away.

*

Inspector Stevens pulled off his leather gloves and rubbed his eyes with the knuckles of one hand. Then he picked his way slowly round the room, stepping cautiously over broken picture frames, vases, coats, cosmetics, the stuffing of cushions. There was a sickly smell, which he suspected was urine. The walls had been daubed with paint and crayons. A mirror hung crazily lopsided. Dolls were strewn over the mess, many missing limbs or heads, their faded garments torn and scattered. One window was broken, letting in the gloomy drizzle. Someone had been on the rampage in the flat, with a vengeance.

At his side Gail was shocked and rigid. 'I can't believe he's done this.'

Stevens paused to give instructions to the fingerprint and photographic teams who were picking their way through the obstacles on the floor to reach the inner doors. He took Gail by the arm. 'Come and sit in the car. They'll be ages yet.'

They dodged the weather to reach it. He let her into the passenger seat, motioned his driver to go elsewhere to have a cigarette and sat in his place. 'So tell me once more. You got home. Had the door been forced?'

Gail shook her head. 'It was ajar a few inches. That was strange – I'd left it locked.'

'Deadlock? Or just on the latch?'

'On the latch. I meant to get a Chubb fitted but haven't had a chance. To be honest, I didn't have the money.'

'You will now. This is an insurance job. Have you notified them?'

Gail nodded dumbly. Her face was chalky white. 'They'll send an assessor tomorrow.'

The atmosphere between them was different. Gail could sense that the inspector no longer saw her as perpetrator, nuisance or crank, but as a victim. They were on the same side now. That did not, however, solve all the problems.

Stevens considered. 'You'll need somewhere to stay tonight.'

Gail shrugged. Then, 'It must have been him. Or somebody acting for him. He hated my dolls but knew I loved them. Why should anybody destroy a few dolls unless it was deliberately to upset me? They haven't touched the TV or video, or the computer, or pinched anything as far as I could tell.'

'But they have made a mess,' Stevens continued for her. 'And left messages.'

'"Next time you, bitch." In letters three inches tall. The whole place will have to be redecorated. But why, oh, why? Is Frank so mad at me? Why can't he leave me alone?'

Stevens almost, but not quite, replied that it might help if she left Frank alone. The two-page character assassination under Jim Betts's by-line in the *Globe* had created quite a stir, with snippets repeated in the Sundays and in digests of the week. The broadsheets had ignored it, altogether too preoccupied with the teenage son of the Home Secretary and waxing indignant that magistrates chose to condone such youngsters' bad behaviour. An information blackout had irritated the hacks even more: the terms 'censorship' and 'a free country' had appeared in the same sentence in more than one portentous leader. Stevens was glad he had not been the constable obliged to arrest the youngster or call his parents, but felt that the force had conducted themselves reasonably well and emerged smelling of roses. Which is more than could be said of the private flat occupied by Mrs Gail Bridges.

'Right. Several points, Mrs Bridges.' He resumed his official manner. 'First, if you will please take my advice, don't go whistling off to the media about this. You could have been burgled by practically anybody: there were forty-five forced entries in this area last week alone.'

'It wasn't a forced entry,' Gail muttered. 'I couldn't see any marks on the door. He had a key.'

'If you have to allude to it, forced entry's the best way to describe it. Your security was less than perfect – master keys for those locks are ten a penny. But I beg you, as I have before, if you want us to pursue this matter properly, it would help if our inquiries were not hampered by intrusive press interest.'

'You're telling me to keep quiet. Is that an instruction?'

Stevens took a breath. 'As far as it is in my power to instruct you, Mrs Bridges.' Both sat staring out of the windscreen. The rain pattered down, street lights making

yellow and green patterns on the curved glass. Then
Stevens stirred himself. 'You need to feel safe, and you
can't stay there tonight, not if the insurance assessors are
coming tomorrow. You mustn't touch anything. Can we
arrange a hotel for you?'

'Hardly private, is it? They'll want to know why I'm
there.' Gail sounded weary, as if ready to abandon the
fight. Stevens fought an urge to put an arm round her.
Seated next to him she was a small beaten creature. The
rain patterns reflecting on her cheeks made it seem as
though she was weeping. Yet her profile had an appealing
nobility: as she stared ahead he could understand what
Frank, his former fellow police officer, had seen in her, for
all her peevishness and insecurity. If any man could bring
himself to break through those barriers and reach her, she
might blossom again into an attractive woman.

The silence stretched into several minutes. Then a
solution suggested itself, though its nature startled
Stevens. 'There's room at my house in Pinner,' he said
suddenly. 'Spare room with its own bathroom. You'd be
welcome.'

'What would your wife say?' Gail turned to look at him
in surprise.

'Mrs Stevens is living elsewhere,' he said gruffly. 'I am
divorced. Oh, don't back off. I'm not offering you anything other than sanctuary. If you can find something in
the fridge or freezer to cook, then make yourself at home.
There's lager and white wine in the garage. The TV is

cable, so watch whatever you want. The washing machine and dryer are at your disposal. Stay a few days till you get yourself together.'

'I couldn't possibly.'

'Why not?' The inspector warmed to his theme. 'You'd be safe there. And private, absolutely.'

'I'll have to pack a bag,' Gail said doubtfully. She seemed to be holding herself a little straighter than before.

'And I still need to get a statement from you, but there's no hurry. I have to radio in my report and retrieve my driver from the pub where he has taken shelter. Shall I expect you back here in half an hour?'

# Chapter Seventeen

**B**enedict had arrived early and in a positive mood. He nodded amiably at the middle-aged concierge whose surly demeanour was so off-putting. Perhaps the man behaved better towards the block's regular residents who presumably gave him bottles of whisky and tips at Christmas. The concierge studiously avoided his eyes. Well, if the fellow did not want to engage him in conversation that was a relief. These days, with the government slipping down the polls, everyone wanted to buttonhole recognisable politicians. Some wanted to discuss the prospects of the next election, so that when the moment came they could say, 'I told you so.' Others whose support for the Prime Minister was still extant, if shaky, needed to explain their anxieties to someone – anyone – in the hope that the message would get home. Of these, Benedict reflected wryly, a good few assumed he was a minister himself; it took an aficionado to distinguish between those public faces who did, or did not, hold the reins of power. Especially when those who did had been so cavalier about their supporters.

How could the government have slithered so quickly into the wilderness? They had started with such fabulous results at the hustings, gaining a bunch of new MPs so huge it dwarfed minor parties like his own. The New Democrats' dreams of holding the balance of power in a hung Parliament had been dashed two hours after the polls closed as the whopping majorities came through. The record swing had swept the old regime into oblivion for a generation, or so it had seemed. Benedict recalled the nation's euphoria that night as the haggard faces of former Cabinet ministers were broadcast first in puzzled denial, then wiped clean of that arrogant assumption of perpetual office that had so destroyed them. Johnson alone, their star young performer, had looked faintly smug, secure in the knowledge that a leadership contest was inevitable and that his main rival had lost his seat.

This government had promised to do better than its predecessor. It had promised as if promises had recently been invented: pledges, targets and guarantees had poured from Downing Street, couched in the simple language designed to speak directly to the aspirations of the people. 'The people', indeed, had become the logo slapped on every initiative: the people's government, the people's budget, the people's health care. Ownership and organisation of the vital services, however, had not changed. It had turned out as difficult to recruit effective managers within the private sector as under any other system, which the railways showed. The decision-making processes had continued as ramshackle, short-sighted and underfunded as before.

The vision touted in the heady days of the new era, the glory of 'national renewal, of a country with drive, purpose and energy', to quote the Prime Minister, had lost none of its enormous appeal. The trouble was, Benedict reflected, it had had precious little substance. When challenged to show what progress had been made, the government's spokesmen were stumped. The translation of hope into action had proved beyond them. Energy and drive had waned, purpose had become enfeebled by compromise and bickering. Within a remarkably short space of time nobody in the administration seemed able to articulate what they intended to do or how, precisely, they planned to carry it out. Instead, squabbling among frontbenchers, who were back-stabbing each other as if in rehearsal for an amateur production of *Julius Caesar*, and intense media scrutiny had taken their toll. Their ratings in opinion polls had plummeted overnight, a collapse that most of the 'people' regarded as richly deserved.

It seemed an age since the election. Several prominent names had already resigned or been relegated to minor roles. The first to choose to spend more time with their families had issued their press statements, with more expected as careers disintegrated or slowly came to a halt. Others were openly at risk: Diane Clark, Frank Bridges, two of the most genuine and honourable frontbench veterans, who rated highly in the popularity stakes especially among their own activists. Such stars should be fêted by their peers, cosseted as the electoral assets they undoubtedly were. The fact that the Prime Minister saw them as expendable said much for his own integrity and loyalty, and for the ambition of those who conspired to replace them.

Slowly Benedict descended the stairs to the basement, lost in thought. It was not in him to decry ambition: he suffered from it too deeply himself and had been surrounded by sufferers his entire adult life. He felt sympathy for a man like poor Johnson, Leader of the official Opposition, who had been taunted with the nickname 'Pig' when he had joined a right-wing party at the age of sixteen. Why not? Why not join up and get involved, if the passion of politics had already entered the soul, if a spirit of destiny had whispered that he, too, might influence the course of history? That was ambition, and it led men and women to display both the finest and worst of human qualities. Johnson, like himself, had striven to enter university, had immersed himself there in the most rigorous political education the state could provide. Both had revelled in the intense discussion, had taken full part at every opportunity to debate and defend their views, had researched and analysed and written up the latest findings supporting their interpretation of events and their forecasts for the future. It took ambition to do all that, and altruism: a heady mixture of self and selflessness that few outsiders could ever comprehend or appreciate.

Benedict tugged open the heavy door. To his surprise the lights were already switched on. The airless room was stifling. He fiddled with the ventilator controls but they moved only a fraction then stuck. It would be a sweaty session. He hung up his coat then sat down to wait for Lawrence.

The election was still some way off. Strong governments, like Margaret Thatcher's, tended to go to the country early, impatient for a renewal of their mandate. Weaker administrations like Jim Callaghan's or John Major's, doubting their ability to brazen out their critics, tended to wait till the last minute or, at least, to delay. That could be fatal: they risked losing the initiative and created an impression of hesitancy and peevishness that was often all too accurate. They lost the plot, in other words, and tended to do poorly at the ballot whenever it came.

It remained to be seen how this government would react. There was time for them to recover their nerve and regain lost ground. Or they could cut and run: a snap poll was possible. The other contestants would have to be on their toes. But if that narrow gap began to widen between the main parties, caution would probably prevail. It might be a couple of years yet before the chance came. The odds were, it had to be admitted, that the Cabinet would see sense, smarten up its act, drop those pledges impossible to keep, apologise for mistakes and grovel for forgiveness. Benedict would not be surprised to arrive at the close of poll with an outcome much the same as before.

Idly, he began to lay out his kit and take off his clothes, hanging up the suit and shirt with care and tucking his socks inside the shoes, aligned side by side. As he sat in his shorts the mild air felt warm on his skin, welcoming instead of too hot. In hot countries everyone stripped off; unclothed torsos were everywhere. He picked up the padded box and strapped it on over his shorts, but that was not comfortable. He frowned. Then he dropped his shorts and put the box on by itself, adjusting the elasticated straps round his buttocks until they lay tidily. He caught sight of himself over his shoulder in a wall mirror and laughed. The Ashworth corpus was in better shape than it had been for some years: the exercise had clearly had an effect. His abdomen was tighter, his hips less fleshy, his thigh muscles leaner and better defined. Only the chest was still a little narrow. Perhaps he should buy some weights to use at home in the flat: an extra few centimetres on the pectorals and deltoids would do no harm, and increasing his upper body strength might mean he could start winning more points in his sessions against the experienced Lawrence.

'Very nice,' came a murmur. Benedict was startled. He

had not heard Lawrence enter. He went to reach for a towel, then saw the amusement in his cousin's face.

'Don't be so damn silly. You don't have to cover up for me. Anyway, why shouldn't you admire yourself? You're not too bad these days, considering that you still spend far too much time on your backside, like most sedentary people. Let me see.' Lawrence put a hand on Benedict's shoulder and half turned him round, then patted his shoulder playfully. 'Your arse is okay. There's a splendid tight curve to your lower back. Just keep up those shadow-boxing patterns the master taught us. Use the straddle stance to practise the punches. That'll keep your bum in trim.' He took off his jacket. 'I wrote to thank him. We may not need him any more, but he set us off on the right track. Whew! Hot in here, isn't it? Aren't the ventilators on?'

'They are, but I can't get them any higher. Maybe somebody was in here yesterday and left everything going full blast. The temperature must be over eighty. Bit of a pest.' Benedict felt himself flush and stood uncertainly, towel in hand.

Lawrence shrugged. 'Doesn't matter. We're supposed to get steamed up. Nobody's watching, anyway.' He smoothed his trousers over his arm, his eyes seeking a hanger. 'The one essential item of clothing is what you've got on. Everything else is for decency's sake. The Greeks wore nothing – must have been painful on occasion. But I'm happy to follow your lead and forget the rest. How about it?'

And so it was agreed, and Lawrence, too, was soon
attired only in the stiffened convex box. In the heat it felt
more than sensible: it felt great, as if an undefined freedom had been rediscovered. Whoever had left the heaters
on had done them a service. They went out into the gym-
nasium, faced each other and bowed in the correct
manner.

It struck Benedict, seeing his cousin virtually naked
for the first time, that Lawrence was more of a presence
than a physical object: Benedict was aware of him completely, not simply visually. He could not have said if
Lawrence's shape resembled his own, only that the other
man was slightly taller, had darker hair and nipples, and
seemed to breathe in all the air round him, as if leaving
none for his opponent. Lawrence held himself well, his
legs apart, his centre of gravity low down in his pelvis,
whereas Benedict felt light and intangible. Last time he
had had this sensation he had been at his mother's cottage,
ill and soul-sick, when he had fantasised about lying on a
beach or floating on the waves. But this was real: the hot
sweet air had been in contact with another man inches
away. He could lean over and touch whenever he liked.

Benedict shook himself. He adopted the tough,
forward-facing straddle stance, elbows dug into his sides,
forearms at right angles in front, fists held out palm up,
thumbs horizontal and inwards closed tightly over his fingers. It made the long thigh muscles bulge with power.
But in another moment Lawrence had swung him over his

knee and held him head downwards, toes dangling off the ground. And Lawrence was laughing.

'Blast!' Benedict grunted, as he sprang to his feet. 'I wasn't concentrating. Bloody Japanese trick to catch a man off guard.' He took up a more defensive stance.

'Tae kwon do's not Japanese, it's Korean,' Lawrence said, rubbing his hands in glee. 'And you forgot to bow. I won that point. Ready.'

The two men began to struggle together in earnest. Benedict became more aware of Lawrence's physicality: his cousin seemed to have a rich, frictional kind of strength, rather mechanical perhaps, but technically superior. Their bodies crashed together, feinted, slid away, crunched once more, ribcage to hip, heel-bone to upright palm. Lawrence flushed red where he was hit and soon had weals and marks on his body whereas Benedict remained white and tense, managing better to stay out of reach. Their skin was turning shiny with sweat, becoming slippery. They halted, discussed methods, practised grips and throws. They were becoming accustomed to each other's rhythm, much as in their usual clothed sessions, when within twenty minutes they would achieve a mutual bodily understanding; but this time their attention was far more focused, conferring an astonishing intensity and potency on their every move.

'Enough!' Benedict backed off, conceded a point, bowed awkwardly. 'I'm desperately thirsty. Where's the water bottle?'

The two stood close together, drinking straight from the plastic bottle and panting hard. Lawrence flicked hair out of his eyes and towelled his face and arms. 'Your blocking is brilliant today,' he started to say, but Benedict had reached out and gently prodded an angry red mark that had erupted over his cousin's ribs. 'I kicked you a bit hard there. Sorry. Does it hurt?'

'That? No, it looks ugly, but it'll fade. If we were really going for it, you'd have broken a couple of my ribs with that kick of yours. The master told me that in competitions that happens even when everyone's wearing full body armour. Contact sports are not for the squeamish. Anyway, there's nobody at home to complain: you're the one we have to cosset, in case Christine gets upset or thinks you've been beaten up. Let's crack on.'

So they wrestled again, swiftly, rapturously, intent and focused, each pitching his weight, balance and wits against the other. Benedict forced his intelligence into play, trying to anticipate Lawrence's feints and kicks, feeling the edge of the blows on his defending forearms. His awareness of Lawrence as a fuller, physical presence grew by the minute. Now and again came a sharp gasp of breath as a blow went home, or a tackle was broken, then a thud on the floor, or the strange sound of flesh slapping into and escaping flesh. Frequently, in the whole interlaced knot of the violent, threshing being that swayed and tumbled, there was no head to be seen, only the intertwined limbs, the solid curved backs, like monstrous Siamese twins fused into a single writhing shape. Then the gleaming damp head of one or the other would reappear, Lawrence's face always with teeth parted in a grin, Benedict with eyes he knew were wide and fearful yet exultant.

They should have stopped for another breather, but each time they broke away, one or the other would take up a stance, free fighting, or forward, or sideways, one leg bent like a crane, offering a more limited target to a full frontal onslaught. Lawrence jumped to the advance, spinning and lungeing, his extra weight beginning to tell, but Benedict danced away, attempted a kick, tried a punch to the jaw, missed, then leaped to one side. The fight flowed mindless and rapid, neither man conscious of the clock, till suddenly a blow landed, or two, simultaneously: and they both collapsed lengthwise to the floor.

Lawrence rolled over on to his back, his breast rising in a great heave of panting, while Benedict raised himself and knelt over him, half-conscious, exhausted. The room began to tilt and sway, his eyes saw only blood red, and darkness threatened to come over his mind. The earth was whirling, they were in danger of sliding off the edge of the world, they must cling together or they would be lost. He sank down prostrate on Lawrence's body, and they lay together, flank clinging to flank, the weals livid on Lawrence's skin, the sweat like a dusting of diamonds on Benedict's back.

His heart hurt, his lungs hurt. A knee twisted under him screamed in pain as he moved. He put out his hand to steady himself. It touched Lawrence's lying out on the floor. And suddenly the two hands closed together as if of their own volition, the one clasped tightly over the other.

They lay inert together for what might have been a long time, till their breathing subsided and their heart-beats returned to something like normal. Dazed, Benedict dragged himself to his knees and helped Lawrence into a sitting position. They tried to avoid each other's eyes, but then sat, as Benedict stroked his cousin's face.

'Blimey,' Lawrence whispered. 'I didn't hurt you, did I?'

'No. I'll be stiff in the morning.'

'You sure you're okay?'

'Never felt better.' Benedict bent and kissed his cousin, gently, on the lips. He put a finger quickly on the same spot. 'Hush. Don't say a word. Nothing happened. Nothing will happen.' In the hot air the only sound was their breathing. Then Benedict began to rise. 'But thank you.'

In silence they headed for the showers. When they emerged they were laughing and joking but their jollity had a brittle tinge. With exaggerated nonchalance they switched off the lights and climbed the stairs. Kitbags on their shoulders, the two men disappeared unchallenged into the chill autumn night.

And the concierge, who had watched every minute and who had double-checked beforehand that the ventilators were jammed and that the strategically placed video and

still cameras were operational, leaned back with a con-
tented smile. And pondered whether to spend the
proceeds on a beautiful villa in Spain.

## CHAPTER EIGHTEEN

Gail wondered whether to laugh or cry. It was all very well that nice Mr Maxwell arranging a fat contract for her to tell her own story. It would be published in book form, he had promised, to coincide with the next party conference, to guarantee maximum coverage. Serialisation was arranged in a national Sunday paper. If she aimed merely to tell her version of the story she would obtain the undiluted attention she deserved. If she wanted revenge it would come in spades. Sales of the order of twenty thousand hardback copies were likely. Every public library, every college and university would feel obliged to have one, or more than one. The House of Commons librarian would request a signed copy, given its subject matter. There would be a high-profile signing session in Harrods. Ladies in charge of charity committees would beg

autographed first editions for their tombolas. And a year
or so later it would re-emerge in paperback, perhaps with
an additional chapter bringing it up to date. At that
moment she would have made her mark on history.

The payments lured her on, though of course she
wasn't writing for the money. But she had resisted the
temptation to announce donations from the royalties to
charity; no particular charity sprang to mind that was
more important than paying the rent and keeping the bank
manager at bay every month. So the initial cheque,
received when she had agreed to do it, had kept her out of
overdraft until quite recently. The next was not due until
she delivered a text 'ready for press', whatever that might
mean, and the remainder would come on the date of pub-
lication. Aware that she had begun mentally to spend the
sums long before they had been received, the impending
date of delivery had tipped her into a state of panic.

To be paid to say exactly what she wanted was a wholly
attractive scenario. The lawyers would get at it, she had
been warned, but she was determined to stick to her guns.
The publishers had been enthusiastic and supportive.
They had suggested a ghost writer, a notion she had indignantly rejected. Did they think she was stupid? So instead,
making soothing noises, they had offered an editor, which
Mr Maxwell assured her was no longer common practice
in the publishing world: she was being treated with kid
gloves. The editor, an earnest young man, had provided
her with a list of tentative headings and various questions

that the reading public would expect to be answered. He had explained that this was merely to assist her with a logical structure. Now all she had to do was get on with it.

There were serious problems none the less. The biggest was that getting on with it was easier said than done. Revenge no longer seemed so sweet – even though wise heads said it was a dish best eaten cold. Whenever she began at chapter one, 'The Early Years', the picture of Frank that came to mind was so much the man she had married that she would dissolve into tears. It didn't matter that that person no longer existed. The burly young police officer, chest bursting out of the uniform he wore with such pride, had disappeared into the mists of time; the fresh face in the passing-out photograph was irreconcilable with the blotchy jowls of Frank in middle age, so familiar to the tabloid-reading public. But as she doodled he came back to life, and sat at her side urging her not to betray what they had once held so precious: their young love together.

One nagging difficulty was that her anger seemed to have cooled. Those quiet few days at the home of Inspector Stevens had had their effect. He had been gentle, and kind, and respectful. Despite the long hours he worked he had left a small tray with breakfast, a newspaper and a mug of sweet tea outside her room each morning. That had been such a pleasant surprise that she had cried the first time she had seen it, even as the front door closed without him saying goodbye. Each evening he prepared a simple supper and talked as they ate it about the events of the day, before disappearing into his study (the downstairs dining room in a normal house) to finish off his paperwork. He had not minded that she spent hours watching television; she had reciprocated his courtesy by keeping it turned down so low she could hardly hear it. Her sense of uselessness was assuaged by clearing up the kitchen, washing the few dishes and pans, leaving the damp tea towel hung out tidily, in a fashion she had not had the heart to do for ages in her own place.

Inspector Stevens had said little about his own life, about the wife who had left. If he, too, had been badly hurt he did not share it. There was a sadness about him, an incompleteness: he was a man who needed a wife, but who would not demean himself with efforts to find one. Not for him a casual dalliance with a secretary or with a colleague's spouse or girlfriend. He was not the sort to answer contact advertisements even in respectable newspapers; it was unimaginable that he would place one. He gave the impression of a man of discipline and dignity who accepted that solitude and loneliness were to be his due, and instead sublimated his wasted emotional energy in his job. Yet Gail knew enough to assume that he must be nearing compulsory retirement age, and a senior police officer would have a reasonable pension. But what would he do to fill his days if he had no close companion?

She exclaimed in disgust with herself. She was supposed to be thinking about her life with Frank, the way he had betrayed her, and writing about it for money that was desperately needed, not dawdling about pondering the possible needs of Inspector Stevens. This was ridiculous. The publishers were right: she was stupid and too easily distracted. She must get on, open up the neglected computer, concentrate, find that list of the editor's suggestions and start inputting text. There was no time to waste. And yet the values exhibited by the gentle inspector seemed to have touched her soul. It was nigh impossible to summon up the raw edge of bitterness when she had been cosseted with such discreet kindness.

The flat was clean and orderly once more, the graffiti wiped from the walls, the clothes hung in the wardrobe, the dishes replaced in the kitchen cupboards. The dolls were piled once more on the sofa and window-ledges, though a couple had been too damaged to save. The inspector had arranged it, he said, after the Scenes-of-Crime Officers had taken the evidence they required. He had treated her with some deference after he had received their report. She was certain that he believed her at last. Whether it was something the SOCOs had found, or whether her manner had convinced him that, however upset she might be about Frank, she was not capable of wrecking her own home to spite him, she did not discover. But the policeman had switched from the role of cynical observer to friend. The man was now on her side.

They were not, however, any nearer to knowing who the criminal, or criminals, might be. The sole explanation that made sense was that somebody wanted to intimidate Gail, and the only person with a strong reason to want her silent was her husband. Or possibly his political friends, though they were so inept at running the government that the idea they could successfully arrange to scare off an enemy was laughable. It might have been some of his murkier pals from the bad old days before he entered politics, but they would not have budged without Frank tipping them the wink. It all came back to *him*.

Gail sighed. The inspector had asked her gravely if she would manage alone in the flat. It had been clear to them both, though unspoken, that she could not continue to stay at his house for longer than it took for the police inquiry to be concluded; anything else would be inappropriate and might invite comment. She had not wanted to come home. This was not home, anyway, and never would be: it was a place of temporary respite, a transitional pad, with nothing to show off or take pains over. But his concern for her welfare surfaced in a phone call each evening, not at a fixed time, when he would ask her to relate how she had spent her day, whether she had eaten, whether there was anything he could do to assist. He was checking up on her, as a concerned friend might. Gail had the feeling that if she responded as calmly as possible, the moment might come when his reserve would be breached. He might ask her to dinner. And she would accept.

Meanwhile she had to pay her way. A contract had been

signed, the publisher was waiting, a tad impatiently, nice Mr Clifford Maxwell was pressing her. The computer would not write a word of text by itself. Gail made a cup of coffee, gathered up the file with her notes, fetched a cushion for the chair, and switched on.

The counsellor adjusted her spectacles and examined the nervous young man seated before her. He was well dressed, in a dark suit, white shirt and an unremarkable silk tie. He had told her that he worked in government, though he had given no further details. A civil servant would have said so or named his department, a local government officer would have offered a complicated job title that confused rather than illuminated, but this young man, Mr Edward Porter, had the distinctive combination of sheen and innocence which revealed incontrovertibly that he was a supporter of the new government. Cynicism had not yet set in. Experience had not yet undermined the veneer of self-confidence. The counsellor, who had once harboured political yearnings of her own, wished she did not feel so disappointed.

As a client, however, Mr Porter was a standard case. He had been adopted and after much heart-searching wanted to trace his natural parents.

'Do you understand the process?' the counsellor asked. 'Since you are over eighteen you are entitled to ask for your original birth certificate. Your birth mother and father cannot approach you, but in law you are allowed to approach them. In practice we recommend that you do it through us.'

'I don't quite see why,' Edward began. He squared his shoulders. 'I'm a lawyer by trade.'

He was not the first to attempt to pull rank in this way, and he would not be the last. The counsellor put on a practised frown. 'Then you will know, Mr Porter, that this process of counselling is written into the law. It is compulsory. Making use of our agency's services to help you trace your birth parents is not. But decades of experience suggest that the moment when you meet, if it is to happen, should not be one of confrontation. That can be too fraught for everyone. It needs preparation. We can do that for you.'

She waited. The client was full of an intense energy, though it was under control. He was the type who, once convinced of a course of action, would stick to it stubbornly, perhaps beyond the point of withdrawal; a desirable quality, but also a nuisance. He was not going to admit it, but he was finding the interview extremely awkward.

'I have given careful consideration,' he said, as if to recover her approval, 'to the effect that my search might have on my parents. The ones who adopted me. I have known only them; they love me and it is mutual. I asked their view and they have been encouraging. So has my employer.'

'That might be useful if you have to travel to find your birth parent and take time off work,' the counsellor said drily.

'I don't think that will be an obstacle,' Edward said.

The rigid intensity showed in a slight tremor of his right hand, the counsellor noted. Some applicants wept; others laughed with hysteria; most did not listen or take in what was said to them, had to have it repeated, were given written leaflets that spelled out every bit of legislation and advice, yet still they often took no notice.

'And you must discuss it with those others near to you.' The woman consulted her notes. 'You're not married – but a partner? Or any children?'

Edward shook his head. 'Nobody else is involved,' he said gravely. 'The woman I love takes the same line as my parents, that I should go ahead.'

*The woman I love, but not a partner.* The counsellor swiftly decided that it was not her business to pry. 'Do you understand why we recommend that you do the tracing through us, Mr Porter? Believe me, we are not seeking work.'

The young man appeared to quell his fidgets. 'Tell me,' he commanded politely. 'Take me through it.'

The counsellor took a breath. Having dealt with so many cases it seemed obvious to her, but she was obliged to recognise that each applicant came fresh to the issues and could be uncertain or incredulous. Bank managers and estate agents, let alone lawyers, must face identical problems with ill-informed clients. 'Your birth parent may be as delighted as you to be found. She – or he, or both – may have given you for adoption in the most trying circumstances, and may have been hoping ever since that you would turn up. On the other hand, that isn't always the result. Your appearance may reawaken painful memories long since deeply buried. She may have denied your existence to all and sundry, including a new family: it is thirty years since these events, in your case. She may not want to see you. To refuse is her right. And it's better that we are able to find out before you do.'

'How can a parent not want to see a son?' Edward swallowed hard. 'It's not as if adoption is anything to be ashamed of.'

'Oh, but it is. There you are wrong. Pregnancy and illegitimacy carried a great stigma then. In many communities they still do – Muslims, for example. And we have no idea how the conception occurred. You might have been a love child, Mr Porter, but you might not.'

The young man sat brooding. 'I feel so sure that I won't have this difficulty,' he said at last. 'And I have my lawyer's training: I could persuade somebody to see me, even if I wasn't entirely open about why.'

'You mean you'd check up on them first? That is not a sound way to proceed, Mr Porter.' The counsellor closed the file. 'The best outcomes are often where parent and child find they have a lot in common, that is true. If you discovered that your mother is a professional person, much like yourself, I'm sure you'd hit it off. We can establish such facts for you.'

'If my mother turned out to be a raving lunatic, a drunk

and a drug addict, I should still feel some sense of responsibility for her,' Edward retorted.

'Yes, but she mightn't feel the same in return. Or if she did, she might prefer that you did not become entangled with her life. Mother-love is a strange and unpredictable commodity, Mr Porter. You must understand that she has the right to say no, and not to be troubled by you further.'

A silence followed. The counsellor waited. Edward seemed to relent.

'So the first step is what?'

'We can get you your birth certificate.'

'Can you just send it to me, without further discussion? Then I can make my mind up what to do next.'

'The names might mean nothing to you. Looking at the certificate will tell you very little, Mr Porter. But certainly, if that's what you want, that is what will happen. It will take about a month. Then it will come by registered post. The original adoption papers can be retrieved at the same time on your written request. And then I hope you will make another appointment with me and we will discuss how to go from there.'

The two rose, shook hands formally and a trifle coldly. The counsellor handed over an information pack, which she feared would remain unread. Edward muttered gruff thanks and left the office.

Pansy Illingworth had had a struggle on her arrival in the editor's office of the *Globe* to convince the hard-bitten hacks of the newspaper that she, whose most noteworthy task to date had been editing a woman's glossy magazine, had what it took to run a national daily tabloid. Rumours abounded as to how she had landed the position, with the most reputable journalists willing themselves to believe that it had involved some version of the casting couch with the proprietor. The lady pandered to these suspicions with her low-cut jerseys, black leather trousers and the cloud of frizzy hair that never seemed to be under control. Such men would have resisted in public the calumny that their doubts were entirely due to misogyny, while proclaiming in the pub after a few whiskies that this was not a suitable job for a woman. But as her reign stretched from months into years, story coups mounted and circulation steadied, their disapproval turned slowly into acceptance and then into grudging admiration.

One rumour that had proved true was that Pansy chose to defy the smoke-free ordinance of the building's landlords in her own office, though for safety's sake she felt obliged to enforce it elsewhere. It was said that she had arranged for the battery in the smoke detector above her desk to be removed, or for the instrument to be disabled in some way. That alone granted her the loyalty of most sub-editors and hacks. As far as they were concerned the militant non-smokers could go and work elsewhere, and several did.

Conferences on Pansy's territory were therefore a powerful mixture of Gauloise, Silk Cut and stale air, enlivened by the editor pacing about, tossing her mane and poking a scarlet fingernail at whatever was on the table. Occasionally she would shriek with laughter, or raise objections in a low purr. She was proud to be called tactile; she had been known to stroke a man's cheek or ruffle his hair, though she was careful not to touch a woman. Her behaviour was both sassy and unpredictable, for Pansy loved keeping her listeners guessing.

Seated at the table were Jim Betts and a thick-set man in his early fifties. The caretaker of a block of flats occupied by some of the most famous names in London had an upright, officious bearing with a distinctly obsequious manner as if accustomed to the presence of VIPs but wary of them. Pansy guessed that in a previous life he had been a batman in the army or a steward on a luxury liner.

In the background hovered the paper's house lawyer, an anxious older man who preferred the security of a monthly pay packet to the rough and tumble of the courts. It had surprised the *Globe* that the caretaker, who insisted on being called a concierge, had decided not to bring a legal adviser or agent; that suggested arrogance on his part and some foolishness. The man seemed satisfied with repeated assertions that he was being offered a standard contract. His name was on the paper's list as an occasional tipster about his residents' more nefarious activities. Perhaps the prospect of substantial remuneration and a signed agreement seemed to him such a good deal that he felt it unnecessary to share the proceeds with some greedy lawyer. The *Globe* was not about to argue.

The contract ran to seventeen pages. As a courtesy and a precaution the house lawyer had read out every line in his well-modulated voice, asking the concierge if he understood. The man answered with a gruff Estuary affirmative: his irritation was obviously being kept in check. Not until all the pages had been initialled, the final page signed and witnessed and hands shaken could he count on his money.

Pansy picked up the brown envelope that was the subject of debate and tipped out its contents. The incriminating video was still in the machine. They had watched it from start to finish as a preliminary to the contractual discussion; its vivid fleshy images stayed in the mind. The concierge had been advised that if he wanted to negotiate international rights to the grainy excerpts, that was up to him, but the newspaper would buy the photographs outright. That was why he was being offered such a handsome sum. The only outstanding matters were in which country and which currency he wanted it paid, and whether in cash or by other means. Nobody was worried when he demanded cash in used notes and at once.

It would be a day or two before articles using the photographs and out-takes from the videos would appear, accompanied by pieces written by Jim Betts with his pen at its most vitriolic. The exclusive would probably run on a Monday, with snippets shared with the Sunday press to ensure plenty of free coverage. Sunday-evening television advertising was cheap and might be justified if the story could be blown up into a corruption-and-perversion-at-the-highest-levels-in-our-land campaign. The proprietor would be relaxed, provided nobody currently in government was attacked. The newspaper's job was to report on other people's peccadilloes these days, now that disputes with such as Diane Clark had been settled. While that restricted the size of the zoo they were paid to observe, nobody in the paper's employ was much troubled by it; with another election in the offing the rules could change at any time.

At last the formalities were concluded. Betts and the house lawyer signed with a flourish as witnesses, and Pansy offered the man another cigarette. 'So what do you plan to do with the money?' she asked casually. The man's name would never appear in the paper: he had asked for a confidentiality clause, but it was more than likely that other papers would track him down and do a hatchet job on him. If he had any sense he would charge them, too, for the privilege.

'Go abroad,' the man said, with a grin. 'Gotta brother-in-law in Marbella. Says I can go in wiv him.'

'Your employers at the block of flats, will they cause you or your family any grief?' Pansy tried to sound anxious.

'They'll go ape-shit. Don't matter. We're packed, out on the first plane from Luton t'morrer.'

This fellow has more of a head on his shoulders than I thought, Pansy reflected. 'You've been planning this for a while?'

'Yeah, well,' the concierge conceded, 'stands to reason. Lots of dodgy goings-on in our block. In and out of each other's bedrooms they are. All you need are sharp eyes. That basement, those lads tossing each other around. Butt-naked, mostly. Something seriously interesting here, I told meself. So I checks out the names. I dunno who anybody is, I ain't interested in politics. Never vote. Then I rang Mr Betts here. We go back years, Mr Betts and me.'

'I don't suppose you actually saw them . . . having it off, did you?' Pansy asked hopefully.

The man considered. 'I don't fink they was having it off, to be truthful,' he answered. 'They was chucking each other abaht like they wanted to 'ave it off but didn't dare. A swanky pair, those two. Never said, "Good afternoon," or left a tip, even though I had to clean the place up special.' He sniffed. 'They'll get what they deserve. I don't care tuppence.'

Betts nodded agreement, but suddenly everyone in the room wanted the meeting to end. The cash would be fetched from the bank; the recipient was asked to return in a hour. Betts was motioned to remove him to the pub for a celebratory drink.

In the street outside they lit up ostentatiously to express solidarity with those members of staff too junior for Pansy's office who were banished to the pavement for a smoke. Betts felt cautious. The newspaper could still be sued if they had made a horrible mistake: pictures don't lie, but insinuations can be wide of the mark. 'If you're asked, though,' he said, 'ever, I mean, by anybody else, you reckon they were having it off, don't you? That they're a pair of poofters? Even though Ashworth's married?'

The concierge considered. Betts repeated the question: 'Do you think, deep down, from what you've seen and the way they behaved, that they're poofters?'

'I don't approve of shirt-lifters,' the man said firmly, avoiding a direct answer. 'People like that deserve to be put in jail like they used to be, not paraded as examples to the rest of us. It's not natural, is it? Especially when they're pretending to be somefink else. That's what gets my goat. Now, where are we goin' for this drink?'

Gail was not sure when it happened. Not when she turned the machine on, that was clear in her memory. The menu page had appeared, more slowly than usual. It had been distorted, purple lines running through it diagonally, zizzing about with a strange crackling noise coming from the speakers. She had stared at the screen for a moment, pressed buttons, felt alarmed and frustrated. Perhaps the unit had been knocked about when the burglars were in, or the SOCOs had interfered with it during their investigations. Either way, something was wrong.

With a curse she switched it off and sat brooding as the purple faded. Just as she had psyched herself up to start work on the book: how infuriating and depressing to hit a malfunction.

She must resist the temptation to feel outgunned by an inert piece of equipment. It was merely a collection of wires, metal and silicon chips. It would do what she told it to do, if only she could get it right. She took a breath and switched on the machine again.

Gail heard the bang almost before she felt it: she was blinded for an instant as the glass screen shattered in her face, but until she was lifted off the seat and blown with the force of the blast over to the far side of the room, she felt nothing but amazement. Computers were not supposed to explode. This could not be happening. She did not understand: what was going on?

Above her the ceiling caved in with a crack; the electric light sparked, flashed and fused. The desk sagged in a cloud of smoke, bent and slowly collapsed, tipping the equipment forward, printer, monitor, paper, notes and hard-disk drive, to the carpet with a deafening crash of broken glass and metal. A doll mascot was the last to fall. The monitor with its empty black face looked agonised as if it had been personally responsible for the attack. The smell of singeing rose from a file cover. Above her head, torn scraps of paper, some with typing still visible, fluttered like snowflakes. The printer broke open and whirred for a minute, then with a shudder lay still.

'Aah!' Gail tried to stir, but she could barely see. She lifted a hand to her face; the palm came away covered in sticky blood. She was bleeding heavily from a deep gash above her eye. She tried to lift the other arm and found she could not: it hung useless at her side. Still there was no real pain, only bewilderment and confusion.

A banging came at the door. 'Hello! What on earth was that? Are you all right?'

'Don't know,' mumbled Gail. 'Can't get up . . .' And with that she slumped senseless to the floor.

# CHAPTER NINETEEN

Frank was uncomfortable. It was an age, he realised, since he had last visited anyone personally in hospital. An auntie came to mind, an elderly lady he had hardly known, suffering from a chest infection that had proved terminal; the duty visit was undertaken solely because she had been his mother's favourite sister, though he did not recognise the wizened creature with the yellowed skin and glassy eyes when at last he had traced her to the geriatric unit. Her open mouth with its purple toothless gums had scared him with reflections that he, too, might one day be like that, collapsed and empty.

That had been long before the election, when he was a mere shadow spokesman and not entitled to red carpet treatment. He had been in a hurry, and irritated at being twice misdirected, as if they had lost a paper parcel. He had introduced himself to staff and attempted to engage in banter, determined to glean something from the hour spent away from the campaign trail; but they had been too busy, or not interested. He had been glad to get out of there.

There had been happier official visits, of course. The opening of a new ward block at the infirmary in his constituency by a minor royal had been an occasion of some ceremony. Frank had been impatient again, but for different reasons: he would have preferred Nelson Mandela, or failing him the Prime Minister, but both had expressed regret that their timetables were too crowded. The local mayor had hinted that such delusions of grandeur were not really welcome. They had toyed with the idea of inviting a distinguished black trade unionist, or a leading nurse, or a local comedian to unveil the official plaque. But, as the mayor tartly pointed out, the first might not be quite as welcome as Frank would like in a constituency where black skin was uncommon, the second might excite jealousy from medical colleagues and the third had a tendency to appear in public drunk and ill-mannered. In the end the minor royal, who occupied a grace-and-favour mansion not far from the unit and who had been treated there following a polo accident, had expressed keenness to help. Before Frank could protest, hospital managers had accepted. The event had passed off without incident; Frank had been obliged to admit that the monarchy had its uses.

Today, however, he had insisted that his presence was private. The bodyguard had remained with the official Jaguar two streets away, parked as inconspicuously as was possible with such a vehicle; he would call on his mobile when it was required. In one hand he held, somewhat sheepishly, a paper-wrapped bunch of flowers bought from a shop in the lobby. The blooms were not at their freshest: the petals drooped and fell behind him like a coloured paper trail. Dank water dripped on his trousers.

He paused to check his destination. Two wheelchairs propelled by hefty porters bore down like tanks on a military exercise and he was obliged to press himself against the wall. A trolley with a patient on the way to theatre rattled past, the woman clutching her X-rays envelope to her chest with a pale, frightened expression. The very walls smelt of fear. An ache surged in Frank's chest.

Then he was at the correct ward. He pushed open the double doors. Nobody greeted him. The narrow entrance was grubby and dismal. His nose wrinkled at the prevailing smell of urine; his eyes scanned the scrappy signs in felt-tip pen: 'No rubbish bags here!' and 'Would all visitors PLEASE vacate the premises by 9 p.m.' A green poster, scribbled on illegibly, invited staff to a union meeting. The toilet for female patients was out of order, he noted. A bucket and mop stood in the corridor, the mop-head like grey rats'-tails. The place was a disgrace – no wonder patients often went home with infections. That old tyrant Florence Nightingale would have turned in her grave.

A male nurse sidled past, head down; Frank detained him with a question and managed to catch the mumbled reply. He wondered what should play on his features and settled for concern and sadness, neither of which was his dominant emotion but this was no time for anger. He walked hesitantly towards the room where Gail lay.

He could not fathom what to think about Gail's accident. All he knew was that his former wife had been hurt in an incident of some kind at home. The message had been relayed to him by his Private Secretary William, with the hint that, should he want to see her, the hospital authorities could accommodate him and would ensure that no press were around. William seemed to assume that he would wish to pay his respects in this manner, had indicated a gap of half an hour in the day's diary and murmured that the itinerary would bring him conveniently close to the back entrance. Refusal would have been churlish and would have lowered him in the eyes of his officials. Frank was pretty sure that it would also have led to a story detrimental to his reputation appearing in a gossip column, probably in the *Globe*.

Gail was in a side ward, one with two beds: the other must be empty, for only one label – 'Mrs G. Bridges' – was on the door. He felt a surge of resentment at the name. It wasn't hers any more, it was his. Would she never let go? Would she never find her own identity, and resume a life from which he was absent? Was she going to cause him grief for ever?

He squared his shoulders. Such thoughts were unworthy, not least from a man who publicly professed to care deeply about the welfare of others and who was an important player in an elected government whose priorities were the poor and the sick. Gail was his former wife and had occupied a place of honour at his side. They had been happy together, once. Moreover Gail, whatever her faults, was a human being. She deserved as much consideration, even warmth, from him as did the most insignificant constituent. He sighed, hitched the flowers from one hand to the other, wiped his palm on the back of his trousers, and went in.

Gail was watching television. The hospital bed was too firm but she could drift in and out of sleep at will. The television set was small and at a slightly awkward angle, high up, controlled by the remote control under her bandaged hand. The sound came through headphones adjusted over her stitches. The flickering images were oddly pleasing, a reminder of normality outside.

The lunchtime news was on. Diane Clark had been filmed making an announcement at a conference, the details of which passed Gail by. What held her attention was Diane herself. Old revolutionary Marxist Diane with the slapdash body language had vanished. In her place was a modern, bold, larger-than-life figure. She looked handsome and assured, far more so than Gail remembered. Smartly dressed – at least for Diane, who had

always made a virtue of disordered scruffiness. That cream
jacket with tailored lines fitted her rather well. Her hair
was fashionably cut, bobbed, and must have been tinted;
Gail was under no illusions as to Diane's age. And earrings, big stud pearls, their presence a revolution in
themselves, glinted under the hairdo. But it was the minister's demeanour that fascinated Gail. Whatever was
going on in Diane's soul, she was enjoying every minute.
Even on a television screen, as her body moved before the
camera, the glow was unmistakable. She was radiant: that
was it. Lucky woman.

Slowly Gail became conscious of the embarrassed man
at her bedside, the bunch of flowers held before him like a
medieval shield. With an effort she continued watching
the screen and pointed. 'Looks great, doesn't she?' The
words came out indistinctly through the swollen features.

'Yeah.' Frank drew up a chair and sat down. 'Got herself a new boyfriend. Quite a decent sort of lad. Young, as
usual. Works in her office, by all accounts.'

'Not a reformed character, then?' Gail attempted to
smile.

'God, no. Our Diane? Spectacularly chaotic, her love-
life – that was her own description. This time she's
besotted. And he's nuts about her.'

Silence fell. Frank thrust the bouquet on to the bed.
Gail acknowledged the gift with a touch of her fingers to
the battered petals, then gestured towards a vase near the
sink. He did as she bade and set the filled vase near the

bed. Apart from a scattering of cards and an unopened box of Quality Street, there were no other flowers or gifts. The ache in his chest returned: anger, undeniably, and shame.

'And what about you? How are you?' he asked, in a forced jocular tone.

Gail turned her head. He recoiled, shocked. Her face was livid and blotchy, with curls of stitches caked with blood on her cheek and forehead. The skin round the eyes was puffy, one eye so thickened it was almost shut. Her upper body was covered with the sheet but there must have been wounds there too for a plastic drip line emerged from one shoulder. Both hands were bandaged, the fingertips peeping out like baby mice from a nest.

'My God, you're a mess,' he exclaimed.

Gail turned away. Seeing his mistake, Frank struggled for something positive to say. 'You should contact the Criminal Injuries Board. You'll get compensation for that.'

He strained to hear her answer: 'No thanks to you.'

'What?'

He saw the lips set harder. 'I said, no thanks to you. You must have realised, Frank, when you started your campaign.'

'What campaign? What are you talking about?'

'You know. Your campaign of intimidation.' She had the greatest difficulty with the word and had to repeat it. 'In–tim–i–dation.'

Frank sat back. 'Me intimidate you? You must be mad. Why would I do that?'

'To shut me up. And you've succeeded.' A grim laugh came from Gail's throat.

'Now see here,' Frank felt his blood pressure rise, 'you've been making these allegations for months. Over a year now. They're complete nonsense.'

Gail turned again. Her gaze was so ghastly that Frank swallowed hard. His heart was thumping. This was moral blackmail. However sorry he felt for Gail, whatever obligations he owed her for the many years of their marriage, he must not let his better judgement be overridden. Experience suggested that what was best with Gail, and women like her, was to be firm.

'I can't imagine from what depths of your mind you've dredged up this idea,' he continued. 'You must be off your rocker to suggest any such thing. Heavens, Gail, you could have made something of yourself. You were upset at the split but you could have used it as an opportunity. For freedom, whatever. Instead you focus on me, and tell all and sundry I'm out to get you. Nothing could be further from the truth.'

'The police believe me,' said Gail, with weary triumph.

'They do?' Frank became alarmed. Public figures never had the benefit of the doubt. Even if he was absolutely innocent a case could be made against him and, worse, might acquire the patina of credibility.

'It's being investigated properly now.' Gail tried to nod.

'Then I'll be exonerated.' Frank nodded back, aggressively.

The injured woman in the hospital bed shifted. Frank realised how cruel his words would sound if repeated to the press. 'I'm so sorry this has happened,' he continued, more gently. 'Every bit of it – the hate mail, the attacks on your car. To be honest, Gail, to begin with I believed you were doing some of it yourself.' She gave a little cry and he continued quickly, 'No, that's got to be wrong. Of course I see that now. But the police are bound to realise it's got nothing to do with me.'

'It has. Somehow. If it isn't you, Frank, then it's somebody on your behalf.'

Frank drew himself up. 'You forget you're talking to a Cabinet minister, and former police officer. I'd never countenance such a thing.'

The two glared at each other frostily, then relented. Frank felt disturbed, some remnant of the suspicious mind-set from his days in the force coming to the fore. He cursed inwardly that he was so busy: with the Cabinet job, the slide in the polls, Hazel's petulant demands, he seldom had a spare moment to think. It had been easier to dismiss Gail's problems in the hope that they would simply go away. He spoke slowly and more softly: 'Bugger me. If it's not you, and it's not me, then who the hell is it?'

The male nurse hated visitors. The agency had sent him to fill a gap, when what the hospital needed was fully operational nursing staff in its permanent employ. Plus a couple of clericals, those underrated necessities. The paperwork

always had to be in last month, with consultants screaming for beds that were simply not available. Let them
squeal about patients stuck on trolleys for ten hours. Or
more. The fact was, if the staff were not in, then an empty
bed did not exist. It might be visible in a side ward, its
blankets folded neatly, the charge sheet empty and waiting.
But that did not count without a bedder to make the bed,
a cleaner to sweep under it and a couple of RGNs to
administer the necessary medication to the occupant. As
long as the government insisted on paying nurses less than
a junior teacher and the management demanded that they
come in all God's hours and spend their time cleaning up
vomit and refused to provide even the most basic facilities
like a crèche, they would go elsewhere. He personally
knew of three experienced nurses contentedly working in
Sainsbury's four mornings a week, glad to do so while
their children were small. It was time the NHS got wise,
or there'd be no NHS.

The hospital had fared badly in the published league
tables. No one associated with it was surprised. There
were no doctor vacancies, but a patient in Poland or
Hungary would have seen more doctors. The waiting lists
for surgery were within national guidelines, but a patient
in France or Germany would have been seen at once, their
cancer excised, their bypass operation performed the next
week. Lab technicians, physiotherapists, radiographers all
struggled with scrappy facilities and headed for the nearest teaching hospital whenever advertisements appeared.

The budget for basic services had been cut so the cleaning company cut down too; three wards with thirty-six patients in each had to be done in four man-hours, a task so herculean that it regularly laid the operatives off sick themselves. The managers, to give them credit, filled in the forms with some accuracy and answered complaints with fulsome apologies, but then faced up to the difficulties by remaining in their offices half a mile away. He would not recognise one in a corridor, and neither would anybody else.

Mrs Bridges was proving popular today. Mrs Bridges had been injured in some sort of accident; the police were discreetly involved. The nurse felt vaguely excited. If this was self-harm, he could be called as a witness in a prosecution for wasting police time. Given the self-pity she showed whenever she was bathed or turned, self-harm could not be ruled out; the nature and extent of her injuries, however, suggested it was unlikely, unless it had been a stunt gone wrong. At least that meant she was not dangerous to others. Saturday night was the worst when the fights and knifings came in. However weak they might initially appear with shock or loss of blood, it was wisest to stitch them up, men and girls, and send them home pronto. If they sobered up on a ward they were liable to smash the place about, plus anyone foolish enough to get in their way.

Once, the man reflected, as he peered at the shadowy movements behind the frosted glass of Mrs Bridges' room, this job had brought both satisfaction and status. TV programmes like *Casualty* had educated the public. When he had said he was a male nurse he would be called 'Charlie' after the popular character in the series. Governments, however, of every colour had persisted in taking the organisation for granted, had squeezed budgets to trumpet their prudence instead of increasing them to demonstrate their humanity. Now even Cabinet ministers were discomforted on visits. He had seen the wrinkled nose on the face of Mr Frank Bridges, the unconcealed rictus of distaste. It was as nothing compared to the contempt in which such people were held by those in the caring services for which they were responsible.

Inspector Stevens removed his leather gloves and halted by the side ward. He could hear low voices inside, and recognised the bulky shadow of the Cabinet minister. He stepped back, took off his cap, walked a few steps, found a battered plastic chair and sat on it.

In a few moments Frank emerged. Stevens stood up. 'Good afternoon, sir.'

'What?' Frank looked puzzled.

It came to Stevens that perhaps he thought he was about to be arrested. 'Michael Stevens, Metropolitan Police. I'm the officer on Mrs Bridges' case.'

Frank grabbed his arm and pulled him into an alcove. 'What the fuck's going on? I thought she was going off her head, sending herself that hate mail and such. She was often a bit close to the edge, was Gail, what with those stupid dolls and not having enough to occupy herself. But now . . .' His voice trailed away.

'This is genuine.'

Frank began to bluster. 'She thinks I organised it somehow. Complete rubbish. The product of a disordered mind, even if she didn't actually do it herself.'

Stevens felt confused. If Frank Bridges were ever to face charges, in itself unlikely, a far more senior officer than himself would handle it. But his new friendship with Gail might continue, and that was increasingly important to him. He adopted an emollient tone. 'It may be that somebody's trying to get at you, sir, and targeting her instead. I am in contact with your protection officers, and with CID. I wish now that I had handed it over sooner.'

The two men glanced briefly into each other's eyes. Frank understood that Stevens was making a remarkably candid admission: it was not normal practice for an officer to volunteer that he had made a mistake, and certainly not to an outsider. He sighed. 'I feel sorry for her. Guilty, to some degree. But she's got to see there's no going back.'

Stevens remained detached. 'I shall need to interview you formally and take a statement. Meanwhile it would help if you could draw up a list of contacts, constituents maybe, individuals who feel aggrieved, who might take it into their heads to do this sort of thing.'

'Old cons I put away?'

'God knows. This is needle-in-haystack territory.'

Frank nodded, his head lowered. Stevens did not need to elaborate.

The lean man with the Scouse accent settled into the sleek grey carriage of the Eurostar train. As it pulled silently out of Waterloo he smiled.

Job well done. This time. The computer had gone up with a fair bang, but the pinhead of Semtex had been insufficient to kill. The intention had been to maim, and it had done that effectively. The lady would have the scars for ever. On her face, where she would see them whenever she caught a glimpse of herself in a mirror. Every time she combed her hair or put on lipstick. It was a satisfying sensation.

But it was not enough. Enough for Frank, maybe, whose purpose had been to have her scared off. When Frank had said he wanted her off his back, six feet under ground was not what he had had in mind. Frank was not the killing sort. Indeed, deep down Frank was appallingly squeamish, which is why he had ended up going straight.

When they were kids, and the gang had delighted in capturing a cat and torturing it, Frank was the one who would thump each of them and try to rescue it. He was a strong lad, and nobody much liked to argue with him, but inside he was soft as butter. He didn't enjoy the final cut, did not relish the shudders of the mangled animal as it gave up its last. Causing pain held no pleasure for him, death did not thrill him. He would never have made a serious criminal: a burglar, maybe, or a fraudster, but not someone who was prepared to hurt or finish off anyone who wanted to play the hero.

The traveller laughed to himself. One parole report years ago from Walton jail had labelled him a psychopath, a continued threat to the public who should never be released. Prisons bursting at the seams had put paid to that. But he trod carefully, these days. He preferred not to be caught. In prison you could get up to little; outside, opportunities presented themselves unexpectedly. A homeless teenager here, a drunk under a railway bridge there. They called it mindless violence but that was inaccurate: the mind was engaged at every single second, as the bones crunched, as the brain matter spurted out. He loved to feel under his hands those surges of desperate energy. But he also enjoyed contemplating the more distant murders, those he could not himself witness. Like sorting out Mrs Bridges. And, whether Frank liked it or not, this time the task would be completed. Frank would not be told. There would be no contact. Vic the Villain did not need thanks.

The oil from her car was still on his fingers. Odd that nobody had been guarding it. The police should have been, but were nowhere in sight. Another staff shortage, no doubt. Next time somebody switched on the ignition, the result would be spectacular. If anyone lived through that, it would be a miracle.

# CHAPTER TWENTY

The afternoons were special. They didn't happen very often and were too soon over; more than one in a fortnight or so would have been spotted and was too risky. But when an evening engagement required smart dress, a long frock or a top with glitter or sequins, Diane had a credible excuse to leave the office early and return to her flat to change. And Edward would be waiting, the coffee made, the curtains drawn, the bedclothes pulled back invitingly.

Those afternoons, grabbed by both whenever possible, were ring-fenced for love. And for love alone. No papers came home. The ministerial boxes were still on officials' desks, half filled with drafts and briefs and lines-to-take. 'Close of business' would be around six-thirty. After that the boxes would be locked and delivered wherever the minister had ordered: to the office in the Commons if a vote was expected, or home or elsewhere. Government drivers knew where ministers slept and whether they were with official or unofficial partners. But in the afternoons, no boxes got in the way.

For Diane these snatched interludes had become increasingly precious. Edward stayed most nights, of course, but she was often weary then, or struggling with a mind still focused, anxious to be prepared for the following day before she dropped off to sleep. Edward would be earnestly supportive: if she was preoccupied he would tactfully produce some worthy volume from his briefcase and read silently. He was never fretful, never complained. But papers strewn over the bedclothes were not conducive to laughter or lovemaking. It was no wonder that political marriages fell apart when sex was supposed to take precedence over parliamentary reports. Those spouses were being naïve. They should have realised what they were letting themselves in for, when they took up with a politician.

Diane pulled her sweater over her head, her arms up, lifting her big breasts closer to where they used to be when she was young. She felt Edward's eyes linger on her body. 'Not bad, huh?' she teased, as she reached behind to unhook her bra.

'Let me do that,' Edward said, and rose to join her. He was wearing jockey shorts in a muted tartan. Not for the first time Diane saw with a pang how young he looked.

Unlike hers, his body was naturally firm; the skin clung neatly to the muscles and joints whereas her own sometimes felt slack. Lack of exercise was making her belly sag; a clear line had appeared under her navel. He stood behind her, unfastened the bra and slipped his hands over her breasts as he kissed her shoulders. His fingers found the dark nipples and pinched, gently, till Diane shivered with delight. Then he turned her till she faced him and kissed her full and hard on the mouth. She pretended to resist, then hugged him to her as if fearful that it might all be a dream.

She adored him to take charge. It surprised her a bit, her willingness to be submissive; she had allowed it with only one or two others, when her lover's own vulnerability had softened her innate objections and let her encourage him to dominate. It was compensation for the fact that she was the older one, far more famous, better paid, more experienced sexually and emotionally. It did not follow that she was the more mature or decisive of the two; not one jot. Indeed, at moments such as this, as Edward showed a sureness and confidence he had not had at the beginning, it seemed to Diane that they were closer to being true equals than at any time since the limbo-dance party, when he had come first to do her bidding.

Their lovemaking, as always in the afternoon, was languorous and satisfying. He took over with real energy, playing with her where he knew she would react, making her squeal and twist away from his exploring hands. For

fun, they would try new ideas: he had bought a humming
dildo from a catalogue, which tickled and purred. Both
had been convulsed with giggles but had decided they
preferred to play without toys. It was more than half an
hour before Edward entered her, and hazily, through the
convulsion of orgasm, she knew he was more in command
of her than ever.

And knew with absolute certainty that this was the one
lover she did not wish to treat as a chattel, as women had
been dealt with since time immemorial. That was how she
had tended to handle her men: casually, dismissively, especially the younger ones. But not Edward. Selfishness was
still predominant in her mind: Diane was aware that, in
her personal life at least, she had had no practice in putting somebody else's needs ahead of her own. Selfishly, she
did not want to lose him. But her feelings for him compared with those for previous lovers were far stronger and
more confused, unfamiliar, and yet as natural as if she had
been born to love him. For it was for his sake as well as her
own that she did not want to give him up. She could protect him, and care for him, and give him all the love any
man could want or hope for.

But what if . . . ?

She lay half under him, panting softly, and stroked his
damp hair. 'Edward. Do you want children?'

'Good Lord,' he said, and settled himself beside her. 'I
don't know. I don't think so – though I can't say I haven't
thought about it.'

'So tell me your thoughts.'

'The opportunity hasn't presented itself, but I probably wouldn't make a perfect father. And I have to think what I might be passing on.'

'How do you mean?'

'Genetics. I do get this depression. It's in abeyance right now, or seems to be, but on the days when I don't see you, Diane, I feel crazy with misery. Maybe it's inherited, in which case I wouldn't want any child of mine to suffer.'

'That's very altruistic of you,' Diane murmured, smil-ing. 'Most would-be parents don't start from that viewpoint.'

'I have to consider such matters.' There were times when Edward was impervious to teasing, when he refused to make light of the issues at hand. 'And I must have come from some sort of dysfunctional family, or why would I have been given away? It does worry me that maybe there's something seriously damaged in my background. So till I have more information, I'd rather not slip haphazardly into parenthood.' He paused and looked at her. 'Is that the answer you wanted?'

She nibbled a thumbnail. 'I guess so. It means I'm not depriving you of anything, since I can't give you half a dozen kids. A relief, I suppose. But in the long run you'd make a terrific daddy.'

'And you,' he nuzzled her neck, 'would have made a great mummy. It's a pity your genes were never passed on.'

Diane was silent, then sighed. 'Lots of things might have been different, ages ago,' she said, almost to herself. She glanced at him, her eyelids flickering, as if she might say more. Then she snuggled down, her face in the hollow between his shoulder and chest.

'So, if you're not bothered about kids, how about marriage?' she asked, keeping her voice light. 'Some pretty bird'll come along and I'll have lost you.'

'No.' His tone was sombre. 'I don't see myself as ever marrying. Odd, isn't it? I'm not anti-marriage but since you came into my life, Diane, it's been such a remote possibility that I've dismissed it.'

'Why?' Diane could hardly breathe.

'Because it'd have to be somebody exactly like you. Somebody remarkable, with your feistiness, and your honesty, and your passion. It'd have to be you, or nobody. I have come to realise that I love you, and I will love you for ever. And as there are no substitutes for the real thing, I'm resolved to enjoy what I have as long as I can, with no regrets.'

'It could be me.' Diane could feel her heart pounding so hard in the still room that she was certain Edward must be able to hear it.

'Why? Would you marry me?' Edward lifted his head so that he could stare straight into her eyes. 'You are kidding me, aren't you, darling? Don't, please, that would hurt.'

'Not kidding.' Diane's voice was muffled. 'Oh, not

now. Not while I'm so much in the firing line, it wouldn't be fair on you. The press'd make mincemeat of us both, not least because of the age gap, which we're sure is nonsense. But when this life is over, of course I'd marry you. Or whatever permanent arrangement you prefer. I love you to distraction, Edward. I can't treat you the same as any other, casting you off when I've done. I can't imagine ever being tired of you. If you share any of the same feelings towards me, then maybe we should start considering it. Properly.'

'God in heaven.' Edward kissed her hair, and held her, squeezing her tightly to himself as if fearful she might slip away. 'If that's a proposal, Diane, then I can't imagine ever leaving you either.'

'Nuff,' Diane said gruffly. 'Let's just think of staying together. When this mad time is done, we can make a home. Till then, it'll have to be our secret, won't it?'

Andrew Marquand stared out of the window. A red box lay open on a bookcase and from time to time the door would open, a civil servant from his private office would slide past noiselessly and deposit more folders in it. It was his intention as usual to devour the material before he finished for the evening, and leave the box, locked and dealt with, alongside any others on his desk.

He would have explained that he did not permit work to intrude on private time. To an alternatively worded question, he might have implied that in the political milieu it was virtually impossible to insulate home entirely from the job; that the role of a government minister was not quite the same as that of a dustman or bus driver. That was because, as he was ready to admit, the workload was heavy and far more than a normal timetable could accommodate. The boxes filled and emptied relentlessly as if by magic; they would have fitted into a Greek myth, a trial of Sisyphus that would have defeated any hero.

But the failure to separate home and profession had a more profound cause. An elected individual offered himself in his entirety, his personality, defects and all, to voters who were insatiable for tit-bits of personal information. Andrew might have been aware of sounding smug as he said this, as many people are who do not bother to hide their opinion that they are smarter than everyone else. In his case, though, such an opinion was justified.

He brooded quietly. What did a man have to do to win the top laurels? How far must he go before he was given the full credit he was due, with the accolades that went with that recognition?

He moved from the window and paid gloomy homage to Disraeli's bust. The sightless eyes in the white marble gazed beyond Andrew's ear at a distant horizon; the expression was solemn and earnest, as if the great politician's ghost was engaged in detailed exposition of the benefits of buying the Suez Canal to some audience of bored angels. But the hero of all chancellors was William Pitt. His achievements stood the test of centuries. 'Oh, my country! How I leave my country!' he said as he died, as if he were king rather than an elected lackey.

It was unusual for chancellors to succeed in becoming Prime Minister. Pitt, Gladstone and Lloyd George were the exceptions. It was said that parliamentarians listened so raptly to Gladstone's three-hour speeches less because they admired his intellect than because they were keen to know whether he could ever complete his interminably convoluted sentences: no doubt they had also run a sweepstake on the length. Most, like Stafford Cripps or Hugh Dalton or R.A.B. Butler, were but footnotes in historical archives. Churchill had also made it to the top rank, but only because of the crisis of 1940; his father was more typical. When, in a fit of histrionics, in 1886 Lord Randolph Churchill offered to resign, the Prime Minister of the day accepted, murmuring that he was 'not a man to prevent the suicide of a nuisance'. Roy Jenkins went off to found the SDP and so ensured the supremacy of Margaret Thatcher for a generation. Nigel Lawson ended up talking more about his diet than his economics. It was difficult to recall more recent chancellors than that: had they simply vanished into the ether, along with turgid statements on social security upratings and the odd tweak of inheritance tax? Was that to be his fate too?

In Andrew's breast burned the fire of unsatisfied ambition. The transition from Number Eleven to Number Ten Downing Street was not impossible. Macmillan had made it, and so had John Major. If John Major could, then anyone could. What hurt was the realisation – the simple *fact* – that the government's returning fortunes were entirely due to the buoyant economy; and that he, Andrew Marquand, Chancellor of the Exchequer, could claim that remarkable turnaround as entirely his doing. It was not the efforts of the Prime Minister, who was fine at making speeches and appearing serious and leader-like on television. It galled Andrew that, with his own lugubrious face, large jaw and pugnacious manner, the electorate found him forbidding when in private he could be witty and pleasant company. Who outside Westminster was aware of that? And why should one have to be witty and charming to win the necessary support in this fast-moving modern world where global business took decisions at the flick of a switch?

Surely ability to do the job well was vastly more important. The image-makers indulged in the superficial and pandered to tastes that were wholly inappropriate: an unremitting interest in the personal lives of ministers, when they should have been asking how they measured up in terms of competence and efficiency.

'If we were judged by results, I'd be the Boss already,' Andrew growled to the silent Disraeli. If men were judged by potential, he'd have been in the leader's shoes right from the start. That grated more than anything. The gap between where he stood and where he wanted to arrive was physically barely a hundred yards. In reality it could have been from here to Mars.

Other chancellors had been eaten by their own self-regard. If they didn't make the promotion leap they disappeared, often in a flurry of recrimination and bitterness. It might be enough to bide his time. The Prime Minister could not manage without his talents and no one else came close. Who could tell what might happen, if some day the PM stumbled over his toothy smile or decided to spend more time with his adoring family?

His own daily grind was much bleaker. The homework would expand to fill whatever void existed. Andrew did not like taking the boxes back to his grace-and-favour flat in Admiralty Arch because it was the loneliest place on earth. He did not care to be reminded that he was alone, and would be sleeping alone.

Alone. Oneness, solitude. Isolation. This was his own choice, but it felt a self-imposed penance. The lovely Fiona was always available if he wanted to dine out *à deux* or to go to the theatre or opera; but the opportunities, when there was no vote, were so few and unpredictable that one got out of the habit. The lovely Fiona, in any case, was an employee. She gave no hint that she actually enjoyed his company; her greatest concern, Andrew judged, was to do the job in hand superbly. No more.

He wished he had never embarked on the lark of a pretend girlfriend. Melvyn should have had more sense than to suggest it. There was something fundamentally unpleasant about the idea: it stuck in his craw. If he hadn't already gone down that route, he would have refused to co-operate. But in a moment of weakness, under pressure from a prime minister busy promoting family values, he had succumbed. And now it was accepted, if not totally believed, that he and Fiona were an item.

She had understood, of course. The consummate professional, she had not been inquisitive. She seemed to have sensed that the prospect of sleeping with her was abhorrent to him, and didn't seem to mind.

It wasn't her, of course. It was all women. Yet even as his eyes strayed to her photograph in its pretty silver frame on the desk, Andrew saw that Fiona would have taken the pretence the whole way, had he wanted. If he had courted her, asked her to wed, it was quite possible that she might have agreed, signed a premarital contract and gone through with it, though Heaven knew if such a fake of a marriage could last. Till death, maybe, if other couples' lavender marriages were any guide. There were dozens in the House of Commons, in every party. If the couple were genuinely fond of one another and shared the same ideals – especially in politics, where it was so useful to conform – then twenty years or more was not unknown. Long enough to see him into the House of Lords, anyway. But he could not bring himself to do it.

What galled him most was that others did, without any apparent strain on their consciences. Young men who had kept him amused back in his days as a university lecturer, who had lounged at his feet and not objected if he let his fingers stroke their bare arms as he spoke. It would be excessive to suggest that he had expected to find a new coterie on the green benches, to carry on as if there had been no break. That would have been grossly unfair, as well as unlikely. But was it unfair to have hoped that one or two former students who had also been lovers, however briefly, even initiates such as Benedict Ashworth, might have given him more?

One had to be discreet. Always. It went without saying. It was not in their manner or repertoire to flaunt their orientation. They were not campaigners: let others expose themselves to ridicule, to the whispers behind hands. Denial was the key. So no problem arose if a sexual partner preferred anonymity: the cloak of secrecy was firmly in place. Better to get on with what one wanted without demur or revelation. Then, in daylight, elusive and dignified, one could concentrate on one's career with no fear that it might disintegrate in a welter of accusation and tears.

Ashworth would have been perfect. He had been perfect in those endless, sensuous student days when the topics under discussion over wine were Proust or E.M. Forster rather than economics. It didn't matter one jot that he was in another political party now: discretion alone would hide names, places, identities. But one had to be supremely self-assured to set out on such an adventure when the stakes were so high, and skilled at securing its concealment. Both were talents that Andrew possessed abundantly.

But Benedict Ashworth had become embroiled in a

lavender marriage, just like so many others. It was dishonest in the extreme. It was an abrogation of one's true nature, a different form of denial: denying it to oneself. Surely Ashworth, and others who claimed not to be gay, could see that. They were on a roller-coaster to nowhere in their personal lives, even if their public images had been officially enhanced.

But these liaisons were wrong in a more fundamental way. If gay men pretended not to be gay, if men prominent in public life talked disparagingly about their 'youthful indiscretions' and implied that on reaching maturity all that was required was the will to conform, overnight the environment became friendlier for homophobes. It bolstered those narrow-minded bigots who wished to eradicate homosexuality from society entirely, to drive it underground, or to 'rescue' men who were 'sufferers' from what was seen as a curable disease.

But, if one were not where one wished to be. If image were everything, and if image were the only barrier, should one adapt one's image? The awful evening at the restaurant with Fiona returned unbidden. He felt nauseous. That kind of media massaging came easily to the Prime Minister and was one of the main contrasts between them. The question remained, however: how far should a man go, against his nature if necessary, to take his career onwards to the most fulfilling post of all?

He let himself dwell on the idea, but a more compelling picture troubled his mind. Benedict Ashworth, the day he got married. Beautiful Benedict, who had once been such a delight. It had not been mere ambition that had swept him to the altar; it had not been a simple marriage of convenience, although beyond doubt it was convenient. The boy's demeanour since, however, did not suggest that it had made him deliriously happy. Some spark had fled from him. Andrew, who had kissed that fair cheek in secret affection, did not care to ponder in detail what might have taken place. Suffice that Benedict had tried what was being urged on himself, and the outcome had been dismal.

Damn Benedict. Had it been too much to dream that he, of the whole gang, might have stayed loyal? It was not an entirely far-fetched idea. Benedict had been at the admiring centre of a group of acolytes for ages, then he had drifted away. Now he wore a wedding ring, but did not touch his wife.

Andrew grunted. He did not want to do the boxes in his flat at dead of night, the dun-coloured files spread out on the bedclothes where a lithe smooth body should be. Better to power one's way through the material in the gloom of the afternoon. Then he would eat dinner in the Commons and practise being gracious: slap a few backs, listen gravely to the odd complaint, before heading off into the darkness celibate, frustrated and alone.

Nemesis.

'But we didn't,' Benedict said angrily, into the phone. 'I

haven't the foggiest what you're talking about. Lawrence is my cousin and campaign manager. He was the best man at my wedding, for God's sake.'

At the other end of the line the voice of the veteran news-gatherer for the Press Association had begun to wheedle. 'Known you since your first contest. Always written kindly about you. Help you put your point of view.'

'I don't have a point of view,' Benedict spluttered. 'I didn't do anything of the sort, never have, and I'll sue anyone who says I did. You damned well put that into the headline news, you hear?' He slammed down the handset.

Nemesis: the sound of fluttering wings about their heads. It seemed to get darker though it was not yet six. Lawrence paced agitatedly up and down their Commons office on the Speaker's corridor, hands clasped tightly behind his back. The walls were covered in posters from old campaigns; above the fax machine were extracts from the previous week's opinion polls, with Benedict's high ratings outlined in green. On the desk lay several new sheets of fax paper. The lines were fuzzy, the pictures obscure, but the meaning was crystal clear. 'You can't sue, Benedict,' he said wearily. 'That's an empty threat.'

'I can,' said Benedict. 'And you can back me up. If they're claiming that the photos of you and me wrestling in that gym show we had a sexual relationship, nothing could be further from the truth.'

'Of course I'll back you up. Though if the pictures on

the inside pages are as incriminating and juicy as they claim, it wouldn't matter what we said.'

'What do you mean?'

'If it looks as if we were necking or embracing or whatever, then our denials aren't worth that.' Lawrence snapped his fingers. 'And we can explain till we're blue in the face that the gym was particularly hot that day and that we didn't normally wrestle in the nude, but they'll laugh us out of court.'

'But they must believe us. That is the whole, unvarnished truth. We would both uphold it on oath.'

'Oh, yeah? And the caretaker would no doubt declare that the temperature was normal, and that he'd seen us strip off together more than once. If they can find him.'

Benedict looked puzzled. 'That caretaker hasn't been on duty the last couple of dates we've been,' he said. 'You don't think he was behind this?'

'It doesn't matter what I think, or who was responsible,' Lawrence said savagely. 'And the truth, to which you are so addicted, is also a casualty. It's what appears to be the case that'll take over. And what people make of it.'

'I don't see why. Two men, close friends, do a bit of martial arts together. They're the latest craze. Even women are doing high kicks and blocking moves now. So what?'

'The photos,' Lawrence almost shouted, 'suggest we were doing a lot more than that. And they're – well, salacious would be an understatement. Pictures of naked men rolling about together still aren't common currency, despite the new century. Prudish Victorian attitudes still apply, especially among the tabloids.'

'Even if we were, which we weren't,' Benedict continued, in a troubled voice, 'there'd be plenty who would spring to our defence, surely?'

'Like who?' Lawrence grated. 'Your gay pals? You think they'd come forward? In a month of Sundays, sunshine. You've not exactly backed them, have you? Comes the invite for Gay Pride and we're too busy, as if we might catch an infection. Your blue-rinsed ladies? You joking? You got hitched to satisfy them, remember, and they cheer Christine to the echo at every party conference. They'd say, "Stick it out." What are you planning to tell them? That it was a sham?'

'No, no.' Benedict launched into what sounded like an oft-repeated speech to himself: 'It wasn't a sham. I loved Christine, really loved her. Still do, if she'd let me. Wanted to take control of myself. Join the mainstream. Fed up being a freak. Wanted to be normal. Nothing wrong with that, is there?'

'Oh, Benedict,' was his cousin's sad response. The two main-line phones rang insistently but were ignored. Whenever one stopped the jangle started on their mobiles, until both men switched them off brusquely and threw them on the desk as if on to a waste heap.

The heavy carved door was flung open. On the threshold, clutching a Sellotaped fax of the following day's front page of the *Globe*, stood Christine. Her face was white, her

hair dishevelled. She thrust the sheet at her husband.
'What have you done?' she hissed.

'Nothing, nothing,' Benedict burbled. 'Pictures are
misleading. We weren't doing anything—'

'You great prat.' Her eyes bulged. 'This is the second
time, and it's once too many. I could put up with your van-
ishing act when you reappeared like a dishevelled ape at
your mother's. Then, you promised to behave. Impeccably.
But now this.'

'I can explain.' Benedict spread his hands in a suppli-
catory gesture but it was lost on his wife.

'You steaming great idiot, Benedict. How could you let
yourself get caught so easily? And you!' She whirled round
and almost spat in Lawrence's face. 'You should have had
more sense. Wasn't this martial arts lark your idea? Why
didn't you do it at home, or somewhere you wouldn't ever
be spied on? Instead you chose a public place—'

'It wasn't,' Lawrence protested mildly. 'But you're
right to be annoyed, Christine—'

'Don't you try that smarmy blather on me,' she
retorted. 'You silly pair. Jesus, you've dropped yourselves
in the shit. And me. And your mother – Benedict, have
you any idea what this'll do to her? It doesn't matter so
much what you are: she's not stupid, she guessed years
ago, as she told us that horrible weekend in Devon. It's the
public revelations, the accusations that will wound her.
The humiliation. You should have considered that before
you unbuttoned your shirt.'

'We didn't do *anything*,' said Benedict furiously. 'That is not fair. We didn't know we were being watched. We took every precaution necessary to guarantee our privacy. My God, Christine, if I'd wanted to have it off with Lawrence, choosing somewhere more private is exactly what we'd have done. But that wasn't what was going on. It was completely innocent, you must see that.'

'I don't think I give a fuck,' said Christine, with crisp fury. 'You promised, and you broke that promise. It took a matter of months. So don't count on me sticking up for you any further. I've had it up to here.' She made a slashing sign at her throat.

The two men glanced away. In the small office their breathing was harsh and short. Christine folded her arms. 'The question is, what are you going to do now?'

It was a question to which, apparently, neither man had given much consideration. 'Deny it, I suppose,' said Benedict slowly. 'Our lawyer is on his way and we will issue a statement. I'll check whether we can get an injunction as the pictures were taken without permission. That must violate our human rights. Or something.'

'Now I'm certain you're off your head,' said Christine bitterly. 'That'd take months or years. Or loads of money that we don't have. Or both. No, Benedict. You're going to have to decide in the next half-hour. Resign from the party leadership, or not?'

'But why? I haven't done anything wrong.'

'Because you're a laughing-stock, that's why. Your

credibility is shot to hell. Or it will be tomorrow morning, when these photos are on every breakfast table in the country. *In flagrante delicto*, you stupid bugger. Don't you see?'

'What I can see,' said Benedict quietly, 'is that I don't appear to have your confidence, Christine. That is the least I would expect from my wife.'

'Really? Well, we can correct that right now.' With awkward, excessive movements Christine tugged off the wedding band and threw it on to the desk, where it rolled and came to rest against the mobile phones, rocking slightly. 'Stuff your sodding marriage. It was all a front, anyway. I wish you well for the future. You don't need me, never did. And I will surely be better off without you.'

'Christine!'

But she had slammed the door behind her and they could hear muffled sobbing retreating up the corridor. Benedict picked up the ring and slipped it on his little finger. 'She'll return to her senses, you'll see,' he said defiantly.

'Shouldn't count on that,' Lawrence muttered. 'But she's absolutely right on one thing, Benedict. Brazening it out is not an option. If you want to sue, you'll have to do it from the peace and calm of the backbenches. Sword of truth, shield of justice and so on. If you don't sue, you're tacitly admitting that the spirit if not the substance of these stories is correct. In which case you've been grossly misleading the public and the party for ages. So resignation is what's left.'

'I do not understand,' Benedict said slowly, woodenly. He had the air of a man at the barricades, wearily aware that the battle is lost but reluctant to abandon a defensive position. 'Why should I have to resign when I haven't done anything wrong, when I am one of the most popular figures in British politics, more so than the Prime Minister, when my record is exemplary and everyone speaks highly of me? Last week's poll confirmed it. The future is bright. I am an honourable man. I've always done my best.'

'An honourable man in an honourable place,' Lawrence mocked. 'Don't talk daft. It's all spin, all appearance. Precious little substance. Honour? What a barmy notion. Not in this House.' He gestured at the ornate ceiling, at the carved wood fascia, the posters, the green library lamp that cast a pool of inadequate light on the leather-covered desk.

'But why are you so convinced that I've got to go?'

'Because you're a fool,' said Lawrence. 'And this time you've been found out. Come on, I'll help you draft your statement. There is one consolation.'

'I don't get it.' Benedict had taken to rubbing his palms distractedly over his pate. His eyes had an empty glaze.

'Tomorrow, you'll be free of artificial obligations. You'll be able to do whatever you want, with whoever you want. Say whatever you truly feel or believe. Get laid every night if you like, with somebody who suits you. No more sleight-of-hand, Benedict. A free man. Not a bad start to the rest of your life, is it?'

# CHAPTER TWENTY-ONE

It was wonderful that the trains were running again. The last year had been a nightmare of broken rails, fatal accidents, go-slows, leaves on the line and cancelled services. It didn't help either that the stations were dilapidated, that the information booths provided no information, and that the train companies seemed keener to dispute fractiously with one another instead of working together.

Frank sipped a cup of quite respectable coffee and spread the newspapers on the table before him. The British Rail breakfast, as it was still known, had settled comfortably in his stomach; he burped gently and tasted once more the poached eggs, bacon, sausage and black pudding mixed with croissants, buttered toast and marmalade. Hazel did not approve of such high cholesterol fare and refused to provide it at home. A man had to seize his chances.

His eye was distracted by the countryside whizzing past. Fields and copses, not much altered, he guessed, in half a century; sheep here, horses, a few cows grazing contentedly. A picture of peace and natural beauty. He found it hard to understand why farmers were forever bemoaning their lot. His own constituency was urban but he did not envy those parliamentary colleagues who were dragged regularly through the metaphorical mire by their local National Farmers' Union. The farmers seemed convinced that somebody owed them a living. In any other business, a firm that made persistent losses would fold and its directors, albeit disgruntled, would find something else to do. Why couldn't people in agriculture?

Because of lingering sentimentality, he supposed. Because it was assumed that the pretty rural view flashing past the window would vanish and be replaced by houses if farming subsidies ceased. But it was farming subsidies that had ripped up the hedges, spread pesticides and excess fertiliser to pollute the watercourses and built the ugliest sheds and farm buildings, and it was further subsidies that had paid farmers to clean up and restore the landscape. There were times, Frank felt, when the world had gone crackers; and that unwittingly, whenever he failed to protest in Cabinet, he was adding to the madness.

His attention reverted to the headlines. Poor Benedict Ashworth. Pilloried and made a laughing-stock, but then, these photographs were priceless. Frank allowed himself a deliberate stare and a smirk; he peered closer at the one showing the writhing legs, the naked butts of – was it one or the other? Ashworth had a toned, fit body and looked superb, far better than Frank would in such a pose. The companion Frank knew vaguely, had been at Benedict's side in press conferences and the like. His cousin, the text said. Not that it mattered who he was. The relationship was close, that much was evident from the pictures; far too close, too intimate for it ever to be revealed in this fashion if the participants were to survive in politics.

Ashworth was on every front page including the broadsheets, standing with shocked face, statement in hand outside St Stephen's entrance to the Commons. *The Times* had three pages on him and his career. The television news had shown him emerging into a scrum of reporters and photographers, each vying to capture the most arrogant expression or body language; but Ashworth was distraught, as if it had not yet sunk in to him how relentlessly and absolutely he had been slaughtered.

It was a pity, Frank reckoned. Ashworth was a decent enough chap; had he been a member of Frank's party, he would probably have been promoted quickly to the front bench. He was pleasant, charming, attractive. He had a beautiful wife – *had* had, it appeared, since the ubiquitous Christine was notable by her absence. In these dire moments the spouse was supposed to stand shoulder to shoulder with her man, to declare her undying love and

faith in him. Support either existed or it didn't. Mrs
Ashworth's silence was as eloquent as any words she
might have uttered. Who was to say what had taken place
behind closed doors? Who could point the finger of
blame? The winner would be he, or she, who shouted
loudest. In all likelihood her reaction, whatever it was,
was currently being solicited by the *Mail* or the *Express*, or
even by the very newspaper that had shopped her husband, the *Globe*, with a great deal of money being offered.

Frank felt slightly sick. He knew exactly how it could
be: Gail had made his life a misery after their own scandal,
had deliberately sought additional publicity until he had
wondered if she was seriously trying to drive him crazy. It
was unclear, then as now, what precisely she hoped to gain.
If she was aiming to persuade him to abandon Hazel and
return to her, she was going about it in the worst possible
way. Had she wanted to attract a new man, anyone sensible would have wondered if she was slightly unhinged,
whether she could devote her attention to anything but
herself and her resentments. She must have been paid,
but Frank doubted that greed was her main motive. Gail
was no moneygrubber.

That Inspector Stevens had spoken of her in the hospital with warmth and kindness. Indeed, to such an extent
that Frank had begun to wonder. The police officer had
acted almost suspicious of Frank, ludicrous though that
was. It had taken a long chat to satisfy the man that Frank
had had nothing whatever to do with Gail's accident, or

with whatever had befallen her before. Fortunately the injuries had proved superficial and she had been allowed home as soon as the stitches were removed. The memory of her bandaged head made Frank close his eyes in despair. That shouldn't happen to anybody.

If, however, the official police reaction was to take Gail's accusations on board, Frank was put at a big disadvantage. He wished her no harm. He wished, in fact, that she would vanish from his life. She had destroyed his serenity, had set out on purpose to destabilise his new marriage and to some degree she had succeeded. But it was not in him to damage another person, nor to set anything in motion with that end.

Frank pursed his lips and tried to put himself under the skin of the investigators. If Gail hadn't done it herself – and she did not have the skill to wire up the computer, of that he was as convinced as Inspector Stevens – then who would? The most plausible theory was that someone was trying to get at Frank, through Gail, and had possibly misunderstood the relationship. It made sense: Frank was a prominent Cabinet minister. Anyone repeatedly in the news became a prime target for nutters. In that case the authorities were indeed searching for a needle in a haystack.

A more promising line of inquiry was his own previous career in law enforcement: somebody he had arrested, put away for a stretch, whose intention now was to seek revenge. But in that scenario, Frank reflected, he would have expected some claim of responsibility. There was no point in undertaking such a venture so obliquely without scaring the target, by issuing a threat via a news agency or radio programme, maybe, or at least writing a letter. Some rubbishy hate-mail had indeed been received at the department, but it was indistinguishable from the usual junk. It went straight into the 'funny folder' or, if it were especially evil or expressed racist sympathies, to the police unit who kept dippy people under surveillance. Experience showed that those who started by writing nasty sentiments heavily underlined in green ink to public figures occasionally progressed to attacking them in the street.

He was getting nowhere. He had promised to try to help and had come up with a few names, though he would have been amazed to discover that any of them had embarked on a sustained terror campaign. The only men he knew who were capable of that were his old mates from school, one or two of whom were, in police parlance, borderline psychopaths. By that Frank meant that they had resisted the civilising influence of home, school and society, and gone their own way oblivious of the needs and feelings of anyone else. Scouser and Vic the villain were the most blatant examples. Vic had a record of violence, much of it carefully planned and executed. He was not a nice man, in anyone's estimation.

Frank had said nothing about this to Stevens. The notion had only occurred to him after the interview, as he

racked his brains to come up with anything useful. As far
as Frank knew, Vic and his pals were still ensconced in
their Merseyside hideaways, too provincial to venture
beyond the land of the Liverpool accent, too lazy to bother
with any kind of hassle. It was hard to see a link between
Gail's miseries and that crowd of deadbeats. Other than
himself, of course. It was like one of those association
games in which spurious connections were made: horse,
book, page, queen. The idea was preposterous.

But this weekend he had kept a few hours clear. He
would go along to the Admiral Benbow down by the dockside and ask around. He would be doing his duty, no more
and no less. He hoped he would find nothing to report.


The pictures of Benedict Ashworth had found their way
on to more than one noticeboard. At Cannon Street police
station, relocated to the Embankment side of the new
Portcullis parliamentary building, they were pinned up
around two a.m. in the canteen, alongside the poster
urging membership of the Police Federation and the mug-
shots of known criminals believed to be operating in the
area. It was there that Inspector Stevens saw them later
that morning, as he stirred sugar into his tea.

'One more chap not to worry about,' a sergeant commented. 'Smashing pics, aren't they? You'd think they'd
learn.'

'One born every minute,' Stevens answered noncom-
mittally.

'They really believe they can get away with it,' the sergeant continued. 'Makes you wonder, when there's so much to lose, why these geezers still take such risks.'

'Feasting with panthers,' Stevens answered.

'Come again?'

'Feasting with panthers. That's what Oscar Wilde called it. Top people are risk-takers. They can't help it, that's their nature. When they've won everything and have everything to lose, that's when they take the worst risks. And get caught.'

The sergeant blinked. 'Oh, right. But most people'd be more careful, don't you reckon?'

Stevens shrugged. 'It's like gamblers. They win a packet, they see it all lost on the turn of the dice. They don't think they'll ever come a cropper. But the odds are exactly the same.'

This was proving a mite too intellectual for the sergeant. 'So what are you here for? This isn't your usual beat.'

Stevens drank his tea and checked his watch. 'Handing over a duty,' he said. He rose, tugged down his uniform jacket and headed for the door.

On the stairs he wished he had been more friendly with the sergeant. Or more accurate. Ashworth and his friend had not believed they were taking risks at all. Whatever might have been going on in their minds, Stevens accepted their version of events. But they should have recognised what would go on in other more cynical minds

the instant those coiled sweaty limbs were revealed to
public gaze.

'Ah, Stevens.' Assistant Commissioner Moore was
expansive in more ways than one. He had attended too
many force dinners, had eaten too many bread-and-butter
puddings, and it showed. He was fat – not grossly so, or
comments would have been made about his fitness for the
job. But as with the military, in a normal year more police
officers were disabled by heart-attacks than killed on duty.
The AC looked set to become such a statistic before too
long. Stevens sucked in his own stomach, shook hands
and took a seat.

'I understand you want to be taken off a case?'

'Yes, sir. The one involving Mrs Bridges. The wife –
former wife – of the Secretary of State.'

'Ah, yes.' The AC consulted a file. 'How is she? Better?'

'Not too bad. The trouble is that nobody had taken her
case on board, sir, not properly, until this last incident. But
it was clear she couldn't have done it herself. So I'm
inclined to accept her version right from the start.'

'In that case, why leave it?'

Stevens shuffled his feet. 'It should be CID now, sir –
it should have been from day one, and that's my bad
judgement. But the lady in question . . .' His voice trailed
off.

The AC waited. Stevens would not be the first officer to
quit a case because he had got involved with a witness; it
occurred frequently, not least because close proximity was

readily replaced by intimacy. Too often a relationship was kept secret, and emerged in court when a case collapsed in disarray. Male and female officers were only human, as open to temptation as anyone else, a fact too readily ignored by their myriad imperfect critics.

'I have become very fond of Mrs Bridges. She is a lonely and unhappy woman and it definitely is not her fault. I'm sure she has been treated very badly. I would like to be the person, or one of the people, to help her back on her feet. That means I face a conflict of interest. It is necessary for me either to bury my personal feelings, if I am to continue taking some responsibility for this file, or to stand aside. I choose to do the latter if I am permitted.'

'She's a lucky lady, Stevens. It's about time you started skirt-lifting again.' The AC chuckled, then halted as he saw the irritation on the inspector's face. The chap was too prone to take offence, but he was a sound if somewhat unimaginative officer. And close to retirement. If permission were refused he might quit in a huff. That would not assist the drive to improve the force's recruitment figures.

The AC made up his mind and rose with a broad smile. 'Now you've explained yourself, I don't see why not. Take a month off. You deserve a holiday.'

They shook hands on it; the AC found his bonhomie revived. Perhaps Stevens needed a word of manly advice. 'Take her with you. Abroad. Why not?'

More rapidly than he had expected Stevens found himself outside in the corridor. An oppressive burden had been lifted from his shoulders: not guilt, since he had committed no misdemeanour, but fear of dereliction of duty, or the danger of it. The sense of relief surprised him, till he reflected that he had become virtually demob happy. It would not be long now before he would be on holiday every day, drawing his pension. He could start at once, discard the inevitable pressure of work, learn to enjoy himself again.

He found himself smiling, then laughing, then punching the air. He almost ran down the stairs, knocking over the sergeant and tipping the mug of tea intended for the AC over the navy uniform. Without waiting to apologise, he sped into the street and began to hunt around for the nearest travel agent.

'Aha! The conquering 'ero returns.'

The greeting was delivered in a loud, mocking tone. Frank screwed up his eyes against the gloom and headed for the dimly lit bar. The Admiral Benbow was smaller, scruffier and smellier than he remembered it. How long had it been since his last visit, just after the election? Once it had been at the centre of his activities in this ward, the spot to which he resorted after any constituency engagement of such stupefying tedium that the memory had to be eradicated with a drink in convivial surroundings. But tonight the public bar was nearly empty, while the dusty room that passed for a lounge was devoid of activity altogether.

'Where is everybody?' Frank asked, as he lifted the pint glass to his lips. The beer tasted sour as if the pipes were not kept clean.

The barman shrugged. 'Mostly at Her Majesty's Pleasure,' he replied. 'Long stretches for that Post Office van job. Armed robbery, but the daft buggers got away with only a couple of thousand each. Not enough to afford a decent lawyer. They picked the wrong day. The van with the millions was the following Tuesday. They simply couldn't count.'

'They weren't capable of doing a bust for millions. Don't have me on,' Frank scoffed. 'Who arranged it? Not one of them has the brains.'

The barman's manner became wary. 'It was suggested it was a Chinese bloke, but nobody came forward with any names.'

Frank nodded. The barman knew more than he was admitting, and he would not be alone in that, especially if some scion of the local Chinese mafia was involved. But that was another story. They reminisced on about other acquaintances, petty criminals mostly. Frank recalled why he had instinctively given the pub a wider berth in recent years. He did not want to be associated with any old lags, particularly not those with whom he had consorted as a boy. While at the start of his career it might have worked in his favour that he had hauled himself up by his boot-straps, once he had been elevated a clean record was vital. Not merely clean, *pristine*. The self-same facts that had won him admiration and votes as a salt-of-the-earth type on the way up had the power to tarnish him permanently and drag him down now. There was always room at the top.

He drank his beer in large swallows and gazed around. One bent shape at the pool table appeared familiar. Frank took his glass and stood for a moment watching the play until the set was finished. He held out his hand. 'Mad Max. Well, well. Good to see you.'

'Yeah, Frank. Stranger. What are you doing here?'

'Bit of this, bit of that. I don't need a reason to rub shoulders with me old mates, do I?' Frank could hear his former accent returning, as it did whenever he was under pressure or tired. Hazel did not like it: she said it made him sound common. In her presence he made a conscious effort to speak more middle England, though he did not relish the lie that implied. He drew the man by the arm to a table in the corner, where they drank amiably for a while and gossiped.

'So, where is everybody?' Frank asked again, and was given more detail about the prosecutions and outcomes for each of his erstwhile friends. He counted them off on his fingers, then queried, 'Hang on. What about Vic the villain? The chap who used to be a boxer. Nasty piece of work – he knocked my front teeth out when we were kids. Did me a favour in a manner of speaking – saved me having to go to the dentist.' His laugh was a little nervous.

Max thought for a minute. 'Nah, that robbery wasn't

his scene. He likes a bit of pushing and shoving, does Vic. He's been around the pub here, and some other dives nearby. But then he buggered off recently, said he had a job in France to go to.'

'Beats me how blokes like that can make ends meet, let alone afford luxury holidays and foreign travel,' Frank said, his tone artificially jocular.

'He said he'd been doing a job for you, Frank.' Max drained his glass.

'He what?'

'Said he'd been doing you a favour or two. Said you'd see him right eventually. Quite proud of himself, he was.'

'What kind of job?'

'Dunno, he never said. Blimey, Frank, you must have been busy, if he's working for you and you don't remember.'

'Haven't a clue.' Frank was mystified. 'Did he say anything else about this, er, job?'

Mad Max studied the dregs in his glass. Frank got the message. He fetched two more pints, then repeated his question.

'Something about a person you wanted sorted. Taught a lesson to. A woman, maybe?'

Frank Bridges felt his heart stop. He grasped the handle of his mug as if for support. The frothy liquid slopped violently and spilled on to the table. He cursed. 'What sort of lesson?' he ground out.

His drinking companion took his time, as if seeking a

tactful reply. Then, 'You know him, Frank. Gotta be trouble of some kind. Somebody in pain. That's what makes his life complete, innit?'

Gail waited by the car as Michael Stevens lifted her suitcase and inserted it into the boot of her car next to his own. She wanted to pinch herself. It just couldn't be true.

It was true, though. The tickets fluttered in her hand and she checked them once more. Stansted to Tenerife, they said. Return. Outward journey today, in about four hours' time. In the envelope in her handbag was a voucher for the hotel: seven days half-board. He had said she needed a holiday, a pick-me-up to speed her recovery from the accident; she was not required to remain in the country. The police inquiries would take some while yet. And he was due some leave, and had announced shyly that he could imagine no one better to share it with him, if she would do him the honour . . . ?

Two rooms adjacent, he had been most insistent about that.

She ached to tell him that he needn't have wasted his money on modesty. Had he asked her in advance, she would have smiled and said that of course they could share a room. She was not some simpering girl. Maybe she would say so on the plane when they sat arm to arm. She would squeeze his hand and whisper it quickly before her courage failed her. If all went well the holiday would feel like a honeymoon.

He was a fine, handsome man, for all that his manner was a mite careworn and he needed more colour in his cheeks. He was tall and solidly built, though not heavy. He seemed larger in a sweater and slacks, but far less intimidating than in uniform. He was not paunchy like Frank, or red-faced and blowing with the mildest exertion, or full of endless complaints. She itched to glance around, to see if any lace curtains were twitching. She yearned to call out, 'Look at me, and look at him. Aren't I lucky? Isn't he a catch?' His hair was cut and his moustache had been trimmed, though Gail wondered how he'd look clean-shaven. Too many police officers had moustaches. He had been hinting at early retirement. A new face, a new appearance, might be timely.

Her thoughts jumbled around in her head like the lottery balls on television: each equally important, in no particular order, their very randomness delicious and exciting. She was the winner, of that she was certain. Quickly she pressed her lips together with the unaccustomed lipstick, ran her tongue over her teeth, hugged the new white handbag to her bosom. She had let herself go so badly since the divorce. She would acquire a suntan, and have her hair set in one of the island's boutiques, and choose some new dresses. With Michael's help. With Michael holding her bag, and with Michael commenting on the outfits, saying firmly if they suited her or not. He would laugh as she pirouetted about the shop for him, and she would be glad. It was her task, at least for the next week, to make him happy. If that worked, then maybe it would continue after the holiday's end. The future began to take shape, and it was rosy.

They had decided after some debate to take her car, but the inspector would drive. It gave her a great sense of confidence that she would be in the best hands. He helped her into the passenger seat and slid behind the wheel. She wanted to jump with joy; his presence made her feel feminine and no longer so alone.

'Ready, dear?' he asked, and put the key in the ignition.

'Ready? I'm so thrilled I could burst!' she exclaimed, then found herself giggling like a girl.

'Tickets, passport?' he checked gruffly.

'Yes, everything. Suntan lotion, makeup, clean knickers.' She giggled again.

Michael Stevens began to turn the key clockwise. It seemed to stick momentarily, then gave with a jerk and slid to make contact.

The explosion was heard three streets away. Parts of the car were flung high above the rooftops, along with the fluttering scorched tickets, Gail's handbag and her shoes, with the heels missing. The boot of the car broke open and spilled out its contents like the guts from a carcase: shirts, sandals, shampoo, boldly striped towels torn and singed. A dog started to yowl in a back yard. The acrid smell of burning was in the air as a flash fire started under the bonnet. Alarm bells rang shrilly in nearby cars and houses. At the bus-stop a woman uttered a thin high scream.

Then came the sound of people running, and a siren in the distance, then another.

Three hundred miles distant, Frank Bridges was frantically yelling a name into the phone, with a description, and wondering desperately what Vic the Villain might have got up to this time.

# CHAPTER TWENTY-TWO

'Conference, everybody.'

Pansy Illingworth clapped her hands and walked briskly past the main news monitors. As she entered her office and reached for the packet of cigarettes on the desk, she was gratified to note the members of staff who had anticipated the call: her newly promoted deputy Jim Betts, the features editor, the Saturday-magazine editor and those in charge of travel, sport, the business pages and the women's section.

The rest filed in. Pansy frowned. Only the senior fashion writer was missing, at the Milan catwalk shows – allegedly, for the contact sheets of outlandish garments and poses came from agencies and the accompanying copy could have been dictated from an armchair in front of the TV. The hotel and travel slips could easily have been altered from last year's; fiddling expenses in this business had grown to a fine art. Pansy resolved that for the Paris shows she would attend alongside, and reward herself by graciously accepting a lorryload of free garments.

'Right! We have an excess of news today,' Pansy announced. She flicked through the latest morning edition. Photographs of the mangled car, smoke rising from its bonnet, dominated the front page along with potted biographies of the victims. Much speculation accompanied the terse police information. Had Mrs Bridges been in the driving seat she would certainly have died. It was her good fortune that her male companion was almost twice her size and took the brunt of the explosion. Though seriously injured both would survive. And nobody had claimed responsibility, though both the Real IRA and Arab terrorists, said the paper, were in the frame.

Page two featured Frank's anguished face as he returned to London, his second wife Hazel on his arm, all solicitude. He had rushed to the hospital without making a statement, so the political correspondent had made it up for him: 'Frank Bridges will be devastated . . . has cancelled his engagements to be at the bedside . . . will be wondering now if he made the right choice in the VIP lounge at Heathrow when he abandoned his wife of twenty-five years . . . The Prime Minister is reported to be upset . . .'

On the inside pages there were views of the official residences in London and Buckinghamshire that Gail had not shared with her husband, the Secretary of State, with estimates as to their value and descriptions of their contents, juxtaposed with a snap of the plain apartment block where she had more recently resided. Elsewhere there was a poor mug-shot of Inspector Stevens and somewhat prurient speculation as to what he and Gail were doing in the car; a rumour that they had been planning to elope together was discounted, though it had been confirmed that he had taken a month's leave and had spoken of a new woman in his life.

'We got the ex-wife,' said Jim Betts, unable to keep the glee out of his voice.

'I thought she was the ex-wife? Gail, I mean?' Pansy asked, nonplussed.

'Nah. The other ex-wife. His. The former Mrs Stevens. The police officer's missus.'

Pansy's eyes lit up. 'I'm listening.'

'Turns out she cleared off five years or so ago, couldn't stand him any longer. He was so engrossed in his career she never saw him. Bit of a cold stick, she says.'

'Did he have girlfriends? Boyfriends? Dodgy habits?'

'Unfortunately, no.'

'Hmm. What's she like, this ex-wife? Presentable? Would she make a decent photo-spread?'

The pictures editor shook his head. 'Middle-aged, grey-haired, shapeless,' he announced.

'Darn. This is not proving fruitful,' Pansy grunted. 'Okay, then, we need a small piece from her, as much colour as you can manage. No payments, mind.' The men nodded. She switched back to Betts. 'But Mrs Bridges herself. The original ex-wife, the classic model. We have a lot on her, don't we?'

He sniggered. 'As you would expect, we have had her PR adviser Mr Clifford Maxwell on the phone with a proposition.'

Eyes were rolled to the ceiling and muttered oaths were heard. Pansy berated them: 'Hush, children. This is our bread and butter. Go on, Jim.'

'The saga of Mrs B's dispute with her former husband can be resurrected. It has gone quiet in recent months. But there's a chance that a three-thousand-word extract from her forthcoming book on the subject could be published in our weekend edition.'

Pansy punched the air in delight. Betts continued, 'Don't celebrate just yet. Mr Clifford Maxwell regards that as a distinct possibility, provided he can lay hands on the unfinished manuscript.'

Groans came all round. 'He says it'll be safe, inside the flat. Assuming it exists, of course, though he does insist there was a contract signed and sealed with one of our top publishing houses. He says Gail swore she'd written quite a chunk.'

Pansy became decisive. 'If it isn't ready for press, the *Globe* will provide a ghost writer immediately, tell him. Plus a reporter to take down any additional information from the patient as she lies in her bed. We have sent her a bouquet, I hope?' Betts grinned. Pansy pushed on: 'Exclusivity would have to be guaranteed, naturally, but money is no object. Savvy? I want that piece, and I want it *yesterday*.'

The news editor coughed gently. 'We still have some mileage in the Ashworth story, if you're interested.'

'Shoot.'

'The caretaker has been in contact from his hideaway in Spain. Says he was wrong last time and that he did see some naughty goings-on. The tapes have long since been wiped, so he's the sole person with any evidence. Not that it's a crime, these days.'

Pansy considered. 'Bit thin?'

The news editor shrugged. 'We can make something of it. He's asking for ten grand before he'll sing.'

'And presumably if we say no thanks he'll go else-where?'

'I imagine so. He hasn't made any threats, but he wasn't the sweetest guy we've dealt with. Probably spent every penny already.'

'Offer him five. He took a packet from us and we have full rights to those pictures till kingdom come. Can't keep feeding him. This newspaper is not a milch-cow.' The news editor seemed about to argue, then thought better of it.

Pansy lit another cigarette. 'What I would like, chaps,' she said, 'is an in-depth interview with the Ashworth ladies. Either or both, preferably. How does the hard-nosed

Christine react to the revelation that her husband's been having a gay affair throughout her marriage? Does she feel deceived? Is she furious, or does she still love him? And that harridan of a mother. What did she know about her precious son's amorous tendencies, and did she cover them up? Will she stand by him? What will her friends at the Women's Institute think? Pictures at home, lace curtains, doilies on the plate, that sort of thing.'

'Crap,' came a murmur from the back of the room. Pansy ignored the remark.

The foreign editor held up a tentative hand. 'I have some excellent material on the intergovernmental conference in Stockholm,' he ventured. 'Big stuff about our veto.'

'Can we do a headline: PM Sells Us Down The River?'

'Sure. Whatever you want. That'll get a rise from Downing Street.'

Pansy considered. 'Okay, that'll do for page ten. And a leader piece, please, a hundred words or so. No more. This is a popular newspaper, not the bloody *Herald Tribune*. Got it?'


'Gail. Gail, can you hear me?'

Frank spoke quietly, but with an edge of authority. It had its effect: the limp, pale figure shifted slightly and the eyes half opened. It was hot in the IC unit; his palms were clammy. The equipment above her bleeped rhythmically. He touched her knuckles, careful not to disturb the

cannula of the drip. 'Gail, I'm sorry. For all this, for everything I've done to you. I wish from the bottom of my
heart that none of it had ever happened.'

The eyes closed, as if in acknowledgement. Frank
leaned closer, choosing his words with care. 'We think we
know who did it. He's gone abroad. He thought I told
him to.'

The eyes opened again, wider this time. The breathing
seemed to quicken and a flush spread over the features.
The bleep became faster. Hurriedly, Frank continued, 'I
didn't – I didn't – I wouldn't hurt a fly, you know me. But
it was somebody from my past. He believed he was doing
me a favour. God, I could rip my tongue out!'

He felt a slight squeeze under his fingers. 'Oh, Gail, I
can't ask you to forgive me. I did a terrible thing to you.
You'll have to live with the consequences for the rest of
your life, and so will I. But when this is over . . .'

He lifted the hand to his lips and kissed it gently, the
tears streaming down his face. 'You've got a new man, and
he'll survive. He'll give you a better future than I ever
could. But I hope some day we can be friends, you and I.
I hope so.'

Gail closed her eyes and her hand slipped away from
his. The bleep slowed. He sat for several minutes, his back
to the exit, then found a crumpled handkerchief and
dabbed at his cheeks. He rose abruptly. ''Bye.'

Outside he breathed deeply, then approached the uniformed officer who was seated on a creaking chair in the

corridor, helmet in hand. Since the suspect had not yet been located and had a record of finishing off a job, a police guard had been deemed essential. The two men spoke briefly, then Frank was startled to see a more senior man down the hall, a heavy, thick-set figure in uniform with a great deal of silver braid on his shoulder flaps and round the edge of the cap held in leather-gloved hands.

'Mr Bridges? I'm Assistant Commissioner Moore. Can we have a word? Quite informally, you understand.'

They found an empty office and perched in the cramped space between filing cabinets and a laden desk. Staff scurried past, too busy to pay them any attention. A crackling came from the assistant commissioner's radio, bursts of staccato, until he turned down the volume.

'We're on the trail of the gentleman in question, Mr Bridges. That much is reassuring. As far as we're aware he isn't back in the UK yet, but he's a clever bastard so we aren't taking any chances. Your own protection has been augmented, and obviously you should be cautious about who you open the door to, and so on.'

Frank assented, then waited.

'Mr Bridges, this is an informal conversation. But you do realise you could be charged with conspiracy to murder, don't you?'

Frank fell back and clutched at the cabinet behind him. 'What? But I didn't conspire with anyone.'

'You don't have to agree to a conspiracy to be in one,' the AC said gnomically. 'If we charge our villain with

GBH and attempted murder, we'll put him away for eight years or so and he'll be out in four. But he'd go down for a lot longer on conspiracy. That's a life sentence, and given his peculiar tendencies he might never get out. To do that, however, we'd probably need to charge you both.' He registered Frank's stricken face without a flicker on his own. 'Of course, it isn't my decision. The Crown Prosecution Service take it on board. They can, as you know, be rather unpredictable.'

'But I'm innocent!' Frank shouted.

'That might just be for a jury to decide,' the AC said, his head up. 'My advice to you, sir, is to get yourself the best lawyer you can afford. Pronto.'

At the Cabinet meeting the mood was subdued. Many of those present knew Gail well. Though they liked Frank and were automatically on his side (whatever that might mean), there was room enough in every heart for them to be appalled at the tragedy. Several had also been through divorce; for each of them it had been painful and had involved much soul-searching. They were glad that in most cases their marital disputes had not had to be conducted quite as vividly and publicly as Gail and Frank's. If pressed, the older ones might have said they preferred the original Mrs Bridges to her replacement, and that Frank would have been better off had he stayed faithful. Then, perhaps, none of these ghastly incidents would have taken place.

Another factor played on every mind. While anybody

could be the target of a lunatic, this attack had not been
random. It had happened precisely because of who they
were. The inspector was particularly unfortunate, for he
was a friend, a mere bystander. Next week, next month,
somebody might step out of a crowd and hurl a tomato, a
bag of flour, a knife or a bomb, to make a point, to splatter,
mutilate or destroy. Here was a constant worry never mentioned in polite company yet hovering, endlessly present,
like a sulphurous grey fog: the downside of being famous,
the price paid by those who sought public office.

The mixed sense of collective guilt and fear was voiced
by the Prime Minister as he explained Frank's absence; a
junior minister would give the reports of that department.
But he was not expecting any changes in government as a
result. Flowers had been sent and a message on their
behalf. It was time to move on.

Diane Clark found it difficult to concentrate. Her
department had items on the agenda, but nothing so controversial that she was anticipating problems. In some
ways she felt marginalised. The important matters of state,
the economic issues, the Home Office and education, were
settled at inner Cabinet meetings earlier in the week. That
was efficient and acknowledged as such, but it did mean
that she and colleagues from other parts of government
were at a disadvantage if they tried to put their oar in. A
powerful triumvirate ruled apart from the Prime Minister:
the Chancellor, the Home Secretary and the Education
Secretary. Strictly speaking, it wasn't a triumvirate, it was

four men. She glanced at the Prime Minister, so adept at uttering the right words, so troubled and anxious. He had aged since the election. Despite his young family, the impression he gave was not one of confident experience but of weariness. Secretly he was regarded as under the thumb of his most powerful ministers. Perhaps a triumvirate was accurate: decisions were taken by the three strong men, particularly Andrew Marquand the Chancellor, and the PM had been reduced to a grey-haired figurehead.

If that were so, it was a depressing prospect. It raised in her mind exactly what her own position might be. For years now she had done all that had been asked of her. She had worked hard and enthusiastically at the department and had been proud of its achievements. The civil servants treated her with respect, she had more invitations to speak both at home and abroad than she could possibly manage, her life peerage in the House of Lords, should she want it, was guaranteed. She could earn a fine living from the backbenches as a consultant; many of those speeches for which she was famed would have payments attached and could be quite lucrative, others would be for charities but with expenses paid. The lecture circuit in the USA beckoned. She could write her memoirs: plenty of meaty stuff there. Later, when her nest-egg was secure, she could opt out, help run a worthy organisation, make her expertise and prowess available to those in need. Her obituary in *The Times* would be effusive. Even her mother might come grudgingly to admire what she had become.

There was another life. And it was one in which she could do what she liked, create her own agenda. Sleep with whoever took her fancy and do it openly. Better still, get married. It could be done, and Edward had said he would. It was out of the question while she still sat in this room, but might become a reality if she quit.

The Prime Minister had moved on to the foreign situation. The intergovernmental conference bored her; rich men in rich countries putting their heads together to plot how to keep their wealth for themselves. Only the *Financial Times* would report it properly, to their own readership of rich men. The *Guardian* would burble on, print laboured letters from its more extreme readers, but fail to suggest what other form of world order could maintain the peace and prosperity of nations such as her own.

As she doodled on the blotter Diane realised that her mind was made up. She was in her fifties; she could expect a place in the next Cabinet, but not for anything much higher than her current position. Agriculture, maybe, or Leader of the House. The most elevated offices of state would go to younger people, probably men. Misogyny still ruled at Westminster, especially as the women MPs had not formed themselves into anything resembling an effective voting block. Had she been able to command the support of a hundred females as well as most of the left-wingers, then her position would have been secured; indeed, she would have entered the Cabinet far higher in the pecking order. But the left wing was not as significant

as it had been in former years. As the working-class vote
had shrunk so the Prime Minister had positioned the
party more solidly in the middle ground. It was understandable and had been highly beneficial electorally. But it
meant that Diane and her beliefs were no longer the cor-
nerstone of the party.

It was time for her to give serious consideration to resignation. Not from the Commons – the appellation 'MP'
was still invaluable – but from the government. She would
have to choose her moment with some discretion. Better
to get out while one's health and reputation were intact;
better than waiting until, as Enoch Powell had cogently
warned, it all ended in tears.

Later that afternoon Diane was restless. It had gone chilly.
The wind moaned through the trees lining Whitehall and
it threatened to turn dark earlier than usual. Nothing
pressed her to stay in the office. She debated with herself
whether to stroll over to the Commons and spend the
evening being convivial, but decided that it might be
worth popping home to get a warmer coat.

Maybe Edward would be available for an hour or two.
She had had to leave early that morning to prepare for
Cabinet; he had said cheerfully that he would wait for the
post. She buzzed her private office at the Commons but
got no reply. Maybe he was in the library doing some
research, in which case he might not like to be summoned.
He would be at the flat at the usual hour later tonight.

For once she decided to take the bus. It was such an unusual act for a Cabinet minister that she felt quite secure. It would be her chosen mode of transport soon enough when the hundred thousand salary and the chauffeur-driven car had gone. She bought a copy of the *Evening Standard* and carried it upstairs to the top deck, where she opted, as she had when a child, to sit in the front row. The bus was not full and she was left to her own devices.

The paper was crammed with stories and pictures of the Bridges saga. How horrible it was, for everyone involved. The police were sure it was an attempt on Mrs Bridges' life. How much better it might be if, as in many other countries, the personal activities of public figures attracted no interest: though of course, since this was a bomb explosion in a public street, it would have been impossible to ignore. And in other countries, even those with privacy laws, politicians and magistrates and police chiefs were just as liable to be blown to smithereens, whether by locally grown activists or madmen from overseas. The media were not to blame for every outrage.

Diane allowed herself to sink into reverie. How different her own career might have been. Suppose in those early heady days she had been more responsible: might she have married a good man, as Gail had, and settled into some form of domestic bliss? In that case, might she still have gone on to stand for Parliament, with the obligations that entailed? Absolute commitment was required.

A politician was most fortunate if their family supported them completely. It was far more likely to occur for a man than for a woman. Wives were more willing to accept a subordinate role than their husbands. Most of the men she had consorted with in her twenties were not reliable types and hardly fans of equality. At least, not in practice, whatever they might have declared.

She had been ruthless, in those days. Carefree, and determined to be carefree. Nothing was permitted to stand in her path. She recognised in herself now, with some sadness, those narrow, selfish qualities she so derided in others. There would have been no room in her diary for a husband or for children. They would have got in the way.

One had almost got in the way. And she had not allowed it. The baby . . . oh, the baby . . .

Her stop had arrived. Snuffling a little and feeling unaccustomedly sorry for herself, Diane stepped quickly off the bus and pulled her jacket around her.

It was quiet in the small apartment block. At this time of day most of the inhabitants would be out; even the retired couple from the top floor would have taken advantage of the better weather earlier and were probably shopping. The lights in the stairwell would come on automatically as it became dusk. The area behind the stairs leading down to the basement was already dark.

Diane trudged upwards. There was nothing much to

hurry for; the reflections at Cabinet, unanticipated, had left her with a sense of her own vulnerability, even of her age. Gather ye rosebuds while ye may, old time is still a–flying. I will love you for ever. How long is for ever? Twenty years, fifty? Not the latter, for sure, not any more. If she and Edward got married the odds were against a golden wedding. But a silver might come if their love matured and strengthened, as there was every chance it might.

The door to the flat was open. Ajar, not wide. Diane stood back in surprise. Then she recovered herself. Maybe Edward was home and had gone to take a rubbish bag to the bin. But in that case she might have heard him, or met him on the stairs.

An intruder? But a thief would shut the door behind him for fear of being discovered. Diane stepped silently into the doorway and listened, but could hear only the ticking of the clock and the fridge's purr. It sounded comfortable, normal for this hour of the day. There was not the slightest noise of anything untoward. None the less she felt alarmed. Her heart began to thump.

On tiptoe she entered the hall and searched around for a possible defence weapon. An umbrella stood against the wall. With it in her left hand, she pushed open the door into the living room.

It was empty, with no sign of disturbance. The clock seemed to tick louder. The fridge shut itself off with a faint gurgle. On the table was the usual detritus: folders, letters, some opened, a bunch of keys, a handful of coins.

On the mantelpiece the presentation pieces, some of silver, had not been moved. If the place had been burgled it had been left remarkably tidy, and by a very idle burglar.

Yet it was strange. Those were Edward's keys. His briefcase was standing by the leg of the desk in its usual place, open, as if he had been interrupted while getting ready for work. Was he here already? If so, where was he? She peered inside the briefcase and was puzzled to see the reports he had dealt with last night. Something was definitely wrong.

Gingerly she turned over the post. Most had been opened, but not everything. He must have halted half-way through. One large envelope had a Special Delivery sticker on it; Edward must have had to sign for it. It was addressed to him, not to her. It was empty but had not been discarded.

Then she saw what must have been inside, the covering letter from the adoption agency: crisp, efficient, with no individuality. Attached was an old pink birth certificate with the spidery handwriting common in the 1960s. Edward's birth certificate, the original. And somehow it looked horribly, desperately familiar.

The umbrella clattered unheeded to the floor as she forced herself to examine the scrawl. For though the name of the boy child was not Edward's, it was a name she had chosen herself. And the name in the column marked 'Mother' shrieked out at her as if thirty lost years had vanished at a stroke.

It was her own.

Diane did not know where to find him, but find him she must. A sound rose in her throat, a wordless cry of agony. How could this have happened? She knew the birth date, had it engraved on her soul. How could she not have realised that Edward's must be the same? But she had not read his CV with any attention to that sort of detail. She had scrutinised the photograph, as was her stupid wont, searching shamelessly for a handsome young man, one with brains but also with physical appeal. Stupid, stupid, stupid. The habit was so ingrained that even when she had resolved to stop doing it, that was the automatic approach her eye took. So she had registered only that this was an attractive male candidate with excellent quali- fications.

Hadn't he said he kept a different date for his birthday? That occurred often enough with adopted children; some parents preferred to celebrate the date they took delivery. Only the original birth certificate would tell the truth, not the revised papers issued to adoptees to enable them to obtain a passport or driving licence. Edward could not have known without going through the agency. But now he had, and the truth was dreadful.

Diane paced distractedly about the flat, turning papers over, the pink certificate scrunched up in her hand, talking to herself in broken phrases. She had not wished to give up the baby. A little boy, perfect in every way. Tiny fingers and toes, fat dimpled knees. But she had been so young, and in the middle of her university course. To keep the child would have meant leaving her studies and her plans for a future away from her overweening parents, especially her mother. It was different then, such a stigma for pregnant girls, for illegitimate babies. To keep the child would have implied that her background had won: that motherhood and domesticity had claimed her as it had so many of the others at school, burdened with nappies and wet washing and unloved husbands while they were still barely out of childhood themselves. It had been such a struggle to win the college place and the state scholarship that went with it. To abandon it would have meant that her mother had been right. That was not going to happen.

Termination of the pregnancy had been an option, just. The law had been changed only a year or so before. There were doctors who would do it. But then abortion had not been generally available on the National Health Service and she had had no money for private treatment. Besides, something in her was revolted at the idea. Better to have the baby and give it away. Then some other woman, denied the chance of children, might be made happy. That was how it had worked for thousands: it was not the unkindest solution.

But once she had held the soft, warm infant, she had wept, and had known as night followed day that she would love the baby for always. For ever . . . A life sentence, to be pushed down into the deepest recesses of her soul, to be denied as if he had never existed. When asked in adult years she would say she was childless, and imply that that was not by choice but because of an infection. The truth was simpler. She did not want to experience that level of pain again. If she were to concentrate on a political career and make the best of it, then bearing and loving her own children would involve an unwarranted conflict. So her barrenness was confirmed. Nothing interfered. She had ended up in the Cabinet, had had loads of friends, had had a wonderful time with lovers galore. And she had slept with her own son.

It was as if the gods were laughing.

From downstairs came a commotion and a shout. Leaving the door ajar, just as she had found it, Diane left the flat and headed woodenly down the stairs.

The lights had been switched on. A draught came from the open street door. The elderly neighbours were present, the woman wringing her hands and crying. The stairs extended beyond the hallway, down to the right into an ancient cellar. A turn in the balustrade concealed a darker area where bikes and boxes were stored. Diane began to descend the steps, her hand over her mouth, fearful of what she might find.

And hanging from the banister, a cord tied tightly round its neck, swinging gently in the chill air from the street, was a body.

# CHAPTER TWENTY-THREE

It seemed strange, Major-General Sellers reflected, to be watching the State Opening of Parliament not from the Palace of Westminster but on the monitors of Sky TV in the international departure lounge of Heathrow airport, waiting to go on holiday with his wife without a care in the world. Five years he had held the post of Serjeant-at-Arms. Five splendid, complex, infuriating years. A snip, he had been told, after commanding troops on the windswept hills of the Falklands or in the dank streets of Armagh. A wonderful retirement job. Mixing with the great, the good and the *hoi polloi*. Responsible for Members' security, in full consultation, of course, with the police and Special Branch. Attired in eighteenth-century court dress at the Members' insistence, as if they preferred their staff to strut like marionettes. The daftest, most extraordinary role he had ever taken on. And yet, ten weeks after leaving and retiring for the second time, he missed it dreadfully.

His replacement was acting distinctly nervous, as well she might. The lady Minister for Women's Affairs, a formidable six-foot dame in the House of Lords, had put her size tens down: the post would no longer go by recommendation to a 'gentleman who had borne arms', but would be advertised, with a clear preference for a woman to succeed. Mandy Williams had risen as far as assistant chief constable in her native Lancashire. Her Bolton accent, it was said, had dazzled the lay members of the appointments board, while the others saw at once that not appointing her would cause a frightful fuss. She got it, naturally, on merit. It would not do to think otherwise.

Ms Williams was too short to bring grace to the uniform, now a mixture of ancient and modern: neither fish nor fowl, with a short ill-fitting skirt over Ms Williams's haunches and the ruff so stiff at her throat it threatened to choke her. She had disdained to wear the sword. Sellers's eyes twinkled; he did not blame her for that. The pesky thing entwined itself around one's legs and made turning sharply an impossibility. But then a gentleman, especially a military type, would probably have had some practice.

At Buckingham Palace, the Queen was climbing into the State Coach. Not the glittering gold contraption of the Coronation Coach that had turned her, almost fifty years before, into the world's favourite fairy-tale monarch. That monstrosity, which Her Majesty complained privately was so draughty, was in for repairs and renovation to be ready for the Golden Jubilee. The fabulous vehicle was popular with the tourists and public, but Sellers hated it; somehow it, and her evening dress, crown and white fur wrap inside it, confirmed her realm's status as a clapped-out museum piece incapable of gazing into the future with any confidence.

Tradition. That was all. That was everything: the Commons and Lords seemed unable to adapt to the new century, clinging as they did to the trappings of a more flamboyant age when Britannia really did rule the waves and a quarter of the globe flew the Union Jack. But the Mother of Parliaments remained determined to resist the march of events. Its occupants refused to recognise the advance of other nations to greater world pre-eminence. They failed to note the prosperity and success of their continental cousins, deriding 'Europe' as if it were full of hostile foreigners bent on subjugation instead of crammed with wealthy customers. No wonder the chaps in Paris and Berlin got so exasperated. If Britain wanted to be in the leading rank once more, it had only to learn how to play the power game in Brussels. But that would involve admitting that the United Kingdom was merely one among equals, and that would not happen in his lifetime.

Sellers screwed up his eyes and concentrated. His successor was not the sole new face in the Commons. The winners of the two by-elections, sworn in promptly the

week before, were identifiable by their delighted smiles
and the many handshakes with which they were greeted.
The New Democrats had held Benedict Ashworth's seat
with a much reduced majority; their Member was a
dumpy woman in a plain blue suit with a pudding-bowl
haircut. She had a frown line between her brows and had
come across at the hustings as rather fierce and hot on
family values. Sellers hoped she would not prove to be
another Ann Widdecombe: one was *quite* enough.

Ashworth himself had bowed out of politics. That had
not been absolutely necessary. Despite the strident condemnation from both the homophobes (Lord Tebbit:
'Time to eradicate this evil from British society') and the
homosexual lobby ('His claim that he is not gay is an insult
to us all'), his intelligence and charm might have allowed
him to continue on the backbenches and maybe rise again
to prominence, after many years as chairman of obscure
committees, as Deputy Assistant Speaker. By their service
shall ye forgive them. As far as was known he was abroad,
seeking his Nirvana. The divorce had been speedy, as one
might have expected, and the former Mrs Ashworth was
now seen on the arm of a distinguished banker from the
City.

Frank Bridges was in attendance, his expression defiant. He was not the first prominent figure to be arraigned
for conspiracy to murder: the name of the unfortunate
Jeremy Thorpe came to mind. The latter had been acquit-
ted, as probably Bridges would be. Men of their ilk might

utter oaths, as Henry II did about Thomas Becket, implying that they longed to be rid of a thorn in their side. But
they didn't mean it, and were as horrified as anyone when
the remark was taken seriously. His current spouse Hazel
was not entitled to be with him as the Commons rushed
into the Lords to hear Her Majesty, but no doubt she
would be visible later in the corridor near the Strangers'
Dining Room, clinging to the poor bloke as if they were
joined at the hip. She had a sour look about her, as if the
new marriage had failed to satisfy her, yet they were both
stuck with it for the duration. Frank Bridges would escape
jail, but Sellers suspected that that marriage must make
him feel like a condemned man.

Gail Bridges had remarried. The event had been caught
on camera for *OK!* magazine, with shyly radiant smiles
from the bride and a gruff solemnity from the newly
clean-shaven groom, and then she and her ex-police officer husband had disappeared from view. It was to be
hoped that, despite her dreadful suffering, she would now
find happiness with a man who truly loved her and put her
interests first.

The other by-election victor hove into view: a portly
young man with a pompous bearing whom Sellers instinctively disliked. Why, when a Member had suffered a great
tragedy as Ms Clark had, did the constituency react by
choosing somebody as opposite as possible? This man had
no opinions of his own and appeared, if his public pro-
nouncements were any guide, to have left his brain at

home. If he had one. Even now Sellers could see him pat his pager for reassurance. He was the type of wimp who, invited to talk on a late-night phone-in programme, would put the pager on the table by his microphone and check it for the correct 'on-line' message, even at one o'clock in the morning.

What fools these people were, the lobby fodder, the so-called 'PM's Patsies'. They believed that if they stayed loyal and obsequious, promotion would be automatic. Sellers's observations over the years, however, told him that it was the awkward squad, provided they talked sense, who were more likely to be pulled in by the whips and emasculated with the seals of office. The surgery didn't always work: just occasionally a light would shine, an original thinker would be given a platform. This ghastly young man was likely to move in obscurity all his parliamentary life.

He so regretted the resignation of Diane Clark. Her absence had left a gaping hole, not merely among the depleted ranks of women members, but among those memorable enough to have won public affection and respect. That applied to so few MPs these days and to hardly any ministers. Too full of their own importance most of them, mouthing the same empty platitudes in the unconvincing, mellifluent tones they'd been taught by the image consultants. They bored the electorate to distraction: the UK was heading the same way as America, where even a fiercely contested national election meant that half the voters didn't bother to turn out.

The spin doctors were absent this day. When ceremony took precedence, they went out to lunch. Last night the most senior of them would have attended at Ten Downing Street as the Prime Minister read out the pages of the Queen's Speech; but then, they knew its contents by heart, for they had written it. Or most of it. With sheaves of private opinion polls on one side and reams of qualitative focus-group notes on the other, they would attempt to devise memorable phrases that would please the electorate. Soundbite politics, it was called. It might have been more useful, Sellers considered, if their talents had been directed to asking what kind of nation they might be governing in ten or twenty years' time, and what policies might be set in train to secure its long-term well-being. But short-termism ruled; prejudice, set in aspic, replaced independent research. They might claim they functioned with a deep-seated commitment to running the country in the interests of the populace as a whole, but they didn't do it. No wonder when anything went belly-up the policy makers were so astonished.

Diane's bowing out had been inevitable once the inquest had taken place. The sense of horror at what she had done, how she had so casually ruined a young life simply to satisfy her own excesses, had stunned her friends. The condemnation had been near total: *Woman's Hour* alone had tried to express sympathy for a mother who both found and lost her son in a single day. It was generally agreed that had Diane been more open from the start about her adopted child, none of this could possibly have happened, not least because the young man would have made the connection, or at least mused about the chances of the coincidence. Sellers, with his Samaritan hat on, could see that it was no coincidence. The unfortunate son had as much of a taste for politics as his mother, and the same energetic, passionate approach: the genes kicked in even when one didn't know about them. And while opposites attract, so do similarities, more dangerously. When lovers gaze into each other's eyes, they may seek features that are comfortable or even familiar. That can lead to great love, but to utter destruction as well.

The inquest had been heartbreaking. No one had known what to say. No suicide note had been left but, with the birth certificate so clear, one would have been redundant. Edward must have committed the fatal act quite soon after opening the mail, or perhaps he had waited till he heard the old couple go out. He had been dead at least an hour when they found him. He had made sure of that. No other verdict was possible.

So Diane had had a breakdown, and was a voluntary patient somewhere in the north of England. When she emerged it was to be hoped that she could continue to function with that bright spark that had gained so much public affection. Or maybe she would be on medication for the rest of her life, and regularly need to seek asylum in the hands of the doctors. Those whom the gods wish to punish they first make mad.

Someone in the lounge was shouting at an airline official. A woman, fashionably thin with skinny black trousers and a mass of uncontrollable hair. A fuss about wanting an automatic upgrade to first class. Sellers blinked: he recognised Pansy Illingworth, newly unemployed since her newspaper's takeover by a porn king. Her post as editor had been handed to her deputy, Jim Betts, whose lugubrious face now graced the paper's masthead. Sales, however, had begun to fall once again.

The flight was being called. Mrs Sellers, the dear lady, was checking the tickets and passports for the umpteenth time. Sellers rose and gave the screen a final wistful glance. The carriages and limousines drove into view. In one Andrew Marquand rode with his 'fiancée' at his side; she looked bored. That relationship was going nowhere, which given the Ashworth scandal was probably the best outcome, or maybe Marquand had more sense. And at last the prime ministerial vehicle, with the new infant cradled on its mother's lap. The proud parents smiled and waved as if they were royalty, as well they might. Their position in the polls was secure. Several rivals had been seen off. The opposition was riven with strife over Europe, sex, money and just about everything else. The election would probably return much the same result as before.

Business as usual. Sellers picked up his hand baggage and coat, took his place at his wife's side, and headed for the plane.